Jon Thurley is a Lit
and lives in a large
his wife and assorte
British public schoo
Cambridge.

Household Gods is based upon his childhood memories
of India during the last years of the Raj. His father was a
schoolmaster in the Punjab, and the family experienced
the horrors of Partition at first hand. When the rioting
and looting became intolerable, they decided to go to
relatives in Bangalore – only to find themselves travelling
on one of the infamous 'Trains of Death'.

Despite the memories of Partition, he remembers India
with affection and nostalgia. *Household Gods* deals with
a way of life which has now become part of history.

By the same author

The Burning Lake

JON THURLEY

Household Gods

GRAFTON BOOKS

A Division of the Collins Publishing Group

LONDON GLASGOW
TORONTO SYDNEY AUCKLAND

Grafton Books
A Division of the Collins Publishing Group
8 Grafton Street, London W1X 3LA

Published by Grafton Books 1989

First published in Great Britain by
Hamish Hamilton Ltd 1987

Copyright © Jon Thurley 1987

ISBN 0-586-20410-5

Printed and bound in Great Britain by
Collins, Glasgow

Set in Times

For my father

'Regard the waves, my friend. Each one that batters away its life upon this inhospitable shore varies only infinitesimally to our eyes from the one before. Think of them as the passing generations. Then think, if you will, of Marcus who has put aside Herodias and taken to himself a new wife. Have we not all commented at one time or another that both Livia and Herodias bear a more than passing resemblance in everything to Marcus' mother, Drusilla? And look at this child mending nets. No doubt he uses the same knots that his father did, without thought. And if, with thought, he changes those knots it will be to recognize the pattern and in response to the pattern and thus affected by the pattern. For the pattern, which has its own waxing and waning, is stronger than most men.'

REFLECTIONS OF PRAETOR JUNIUS MARCUS TERTIAN AT TIBERIUS' COURT IN EXILE IN CAPRI.

'It is a fiction to say that people are consistent. Most people are capable of simultaneous feelings of love and hate for a single object. Indeed, such is the perversity of human nature that men often desire that they most fear . . .'

ATTRIBUTED TO SOCRATES. DISCOURSES: PLATO

There is a legend of a mountain-girt valley somewhere on the Khorasian border in Central Asia which is strewn with diamonds. Allegedly it is 'patrolled by birds of prey in the air, and guarded by snakes of murderous gaze on the ground'.

CENTRAL ASIAN LEGEND

Contents

Prologue: 1857

Cutting from the *Meerut Gazette,* 15 May 1858. Article by Captain James Carwardine. Found in the effects of Mr Anthony Hodder and sent to his son, Mark Hodder, by Dr Mackenzie, Resident Doctor, Ghora Gali, Murree District, Punjab, India.

THE WOMEN OF MEERUT

There is an aspect of the Mutiny which, for reasons of chivalry or from a natural distaste to speak ill of the weaker sex, has been largely unreported. In all the tales of carnage and of selfless heroism, of divided loyalties and courage beyond belief, writers have treated the Mutiny as a struggle confined to the outraged sepoys turning upon the officers who had forced them to use the fat of defiled animals to grease their cartridges. No one has seen fit to report upon the myriad stories of the warlike womenfolk, whose deeds of crime and violence are the more horrible, being perpetrated by the hand that rocks the cradle and feeds the family.

On the evening the Mutiny began I was dining with a fellow officer and friend, one James Bulstrode-Henshaw, and his wife and sister-in-law. There were present two other officers from the regiment, and a gentleman from *The Times* newspaper who had entertained us greatly with his reminiscences of life in the front line at the Crimea Campaign. After dinner, the ladies having retired, we were engaged in conversation over our port and cigars when there was a loud commotion in the hallway and Mrs Bulstrode-Henshaw burst into the room, so pale and distraught that it was evident something was wrong. As she spoke in low tones to my friend, I first noticed outside the window the orange glow of fired buildings, and a distant humming sound, as of bees swarming.

My friend's concern was obvious and we were all gravely

11

attentive when he held up his hand for silence. He told us that a crowd was advancing upon the bungalow, that the servants were loyal and to be trusted, and that the memsahibs would be safe in the attic with the khansamah and the chokra standing guard with jezails. As for us, he knew that no subject of Her Majesty would be afraid to face the Ignorant Saracen with an unsheathed sabre in his hand.

Mr Bessemer, the gentleman from *The Times*, said that he was distraught he could not fight, but he had a heart condition and was afraid that he might hinder us in the execution of our duty. I was surprised to hear this after the tales of his Crimean exploits, and as he had eaten and drunk with the best of us with no previous sign of ill-health, but he was dispatched with our hostess to keep the ladies company.

Bulstrode-Henshaw then furnished us with fowling pieces and set us to the windows, extinguishing the lights. As we waited, the firelight flickered luridly on the wall and the heathenish chanting grew louder. I recollect our host saying, in most heartfelt tones, 'Thank God that Harry and Sam are safe at Eton,' and my own heart felt heavy to see us in such bad case. Captain Ratchet then discharged his piece through the window, and the yelling outside grew in intensity. I recall James saying, 'Hold your fire until I give the word,' and then I felt a violent blow upon the head and fell beneath the casement, where I lay dazed for some time.

When I opened my eyes again it was to see a sight so fearful that it has haunted my dreams ever since. The wooden verandah was on fire and, by this light, I could see the bodies of my companions lying about the room. By the door I could just make out a figure dressed in black holding a kukri in her hand. When I looked across at the body of my poor friend James I was transfixed with horror. The figure kneeling over him in a burquat was a woman also holding a kukri, and she was carving from his body his manly appurtenances, cackling in inhuman glee to herself the while. I tried to move, but could not, and no sound would come from my throat. When she stood up, holding her grisly spoils triumphantly aloft to show the other woman, I saw that the creature had carried out the same gruesome and barbaric rite upon my other fellow officers, and carried the parts at her belt. From above there came the loud screaming of the

12

Englishwomen in the attic, and the hiss and crackle of the flames. A She-Devil had begun to advance upon me when a burning rafter fell athwart the table and set the curtains alight. From the door the other figure in black beckoned, and in a moment they were both gone, leaving me in the funeral pyre with my unhappy friends.

The story of how I alone escaped the inferno and made my way to safety has been told in official records, and in Colonel Earnshaw's historic account of the Mutiny. But the scars I shall always bear upon my flesh from the flames are as nothing to the scars I shall bear within my soul, having seen my poor friends thus killed and dishonoured by these She-Devils of Meerut.

A learned mendicant Saddhu, or Holy Man, of my acquaintance tells me that these parts are used in secret rituals to draw strength from the enemy, and to curse their line in perpetuity. Notwithstanding his learning, this is ignorant superstition. For, as with mythical transgressors of old such as Medea or Messalina, there are certain women who betray their gender by indulging in behaviour of such depravity as to put themselves beyond the normal considerations of society towards the fair sex.

Prelude: 1930

One

It is only when things are lost forever that their memory attains the flawless, golden perfection of a dream.

It was hard, even in the early 1930s to imagine that life would ever be different. In a world of change the Colonial masters of British India were privileged to live in communities where change was almost unknown. There were servants to cope with the household tasks, and a hectic social life which strict protocol did little to dampen. The list of active pursuits was endless; from walks along the forest paths within sight of the mountains in the North-West Frontier Province to the good-natured polo and racing of the plains. Everything combined, then, strand by strand, to reinforce the myth of endless youth, of sunladen days to be plucked and savoured and thrown away, prodigally and without care.

Buildings were important to this feeling. They epitomized the British presence in India, in all its self-important arrogance. Every trader who had done well with the East India Company, every second son who had unexpectedly received an inheritance after serving his time in the Indian Army, every box-wallah who had managed to disguise the source of his wealth and enter society, all had made their marks with great houses, usually set among annexed acres of reclaimed forest and tended by toiling malis who received a pittance but whose families, like all the servants, lived upon the memsahibs' unwitting bounty.

15

These houses, in red brick or faced with Augustan sand-stone, comprised perhaps twenty or thirty rooms. Their styling was eclectic, departing from their Inigo Jones or Vanbrugh models in the addition of skylights for coolness and verandahs where the landowner's friends could share his drink and envy his possessions. Above these again, in the self-conscious hierarchy of social affairs, were the greater houses built by the Viceroys or, further back, by Clive's captains and lieutenants whose blood had grown too thin for them readily to retire to England. And at the summit (though there were those who could not accommodate this view because of their owners' race) were the great palaces of the Indian princes, which reared massively upon the southern plains and the burgeoning hills of the north and north-east.

When visiting princes returned from Europe they professed their disappointment in the meanness of scale of Buckingham Palace, the Royal Palace in Madrid, even Versailles. Hari Singh, ruler of Kashmir, had shown some admiration of Nero's Domus Aurea, built on the verge of the Stagnum Neronis beside the Colosseum, but his gardeners had advised against the construction of such an underground palace as a feature of his parks and his interest had lapsed.

For those English people who were privileged to visit the native palaces of Gaekwal or Baroda, Calabagh or Mysore, it became a matter of honour to find some way to restore the English to their position at the apex of the hierarchy. Ultimately, however, there could be only two grounds upon which they might retain their precarious pride. First, that the architecture should have all the unmistakable echoes of Britain. Secondly, that these dusky rulers, giving their vast armies of relatives and retinues of servants shelter within their dank and mould-

16

ering rooms, were intrinsically inferior to the British by virtue of their colour and their polyglot cultures and pantheistic beliefs.

The idea of hierarchy, of class, position, role, station in life, were exaggerated copies of English society, permeating every corner of the Empire in India. There was precedent in everything, from the correct way of inviting guests and seating them to more nebulous but no less rigorous mores governing every aspect of behaviour. Eton and Harrow, Marlborough or Winchester, gave their old boys immediate access to every club and every social gathering, providing they did not commit any glaring solecism. A further handful of schools was sufficiently acceptable to confer only slightly less honoured status. A grammar school education, often not admitted once the poor wretch had realized the stigma, was considerably worse than a bar sinister on a nobleman's escutcheon, rendering the unfortunate possessor virtually invisible on all social occasions. Men ruled their families with a firm but kindly hand, played bridge and pontoon, joined Masonic Lodges, took part in polo, shot, and got drunk at Mess dinners without incurring any hint of disapproval. Mistresses were acceptable, providing they were not the wives of friends. Sexual dalliance with ladies of a lower class or even Indian women was tolerated on the firm understanding that such liaisons were casual and merely to relieve physical desires which, it was generally accepted, wives were no longer obliged to accommodate once the early fires of marriage had died down. Gunevati, the whore who plied her trade in Murree, was much in demand. On his infrequent visits the Bishop was sometimes taken to her quarters in the bazaar, once his pastoral

17

duties were dispensed with. There was no conflict between this manifestation of virility and his ecclesiastical role.

It was a society which distrusted intellectuals. The overriding emphasis in all things was on *doing*; and conversation, at dinner or in the Mess over a drink, tended to be anecdotal. Cleverness, too, was distrusted and 'too clever by half' carried censorious overtones reaching far beyond the mildness of the description.

Women took the lead from their husbands. They ran their households and overpaid the khansamahs. They polished their accomplishments – a modest voice or an ability to pick out a tune with both hands – to bolster their husbands' reputations at dinner parties. When the occasion demanded that they entertain Indian dignitaries, they offered the correct degree of glacial politeness. When they were entertaining friends, they allowed themselves the precise extent of decorous flirting permitted, and excused themselves from the room after dinner with some arch comment, retiring with the ladies and leaving the men to smoke their cigars, drink brandy and tell their risqué stories.

Politics were not generally discussed. The Viceroy, the Regent for the King Emperor, had everything well in hand. All was organized for their comfort and well-being. Above all, everyone, from the Viceroy, through the ICS and the Indian Army, the tea planters, the box-wallahs, to the humblest mali or chokra, knew his allotted place and had learned, through honourable tradition, those things which were and were not permitted.

Perhaps the beginning of change, in the late 1920s and early 1930s, was too subtle to grasp readily. True, the English at home, ever the leaders, had revised their attitudes in the wake of Mrs Pankhurst and Mrs Pethick-

Lawrence. True, voices had been raised, posing difficult questions about the morality and wisdom of colonizing. True, there had been increasing commentary about self-determination. But it was hard to imagine that the demands of Gandhi and Bhose, Birla, Menon, Jinnah and Nehru could be taken seriously. Hadn't these, who towered head and shoulders above their colleagues, been educated at the Inns of Court and universities of England? It was impossible to think they would truly want change. When they had passed their hour of glory they would sink back, and things would be as they always had been.

Each small change within the mechanical structure promotes other changes, other stresses. The process was infinitesimally slow. On the whole, it seemed that the women, less encumbered by the outmoded furniture of antiquated chivalry and strongly drawn rules, fared better with the changing regime and began to thrive.

By the mid-1930s, those who needed convictions handed down through the generations like obiter dicta began to enter a stressful time of their lives. Those whom the world saw as amoral, who had eschewed the rules in any case, and those who were strong enough to reforge their own rules, felt freed.

It was a confusing time to be young.

Ghora Gali, Punjab: 1931

Two

There is a golden age in every life. Often it arrives unexpectedly, the product of innumerable small things which contribute to its delight. It cannot be grasped and held, and its very ephemerality is itself part of the pleasure.

Always, afterwards, those years at college with Roger returned to haunt Anthony with their recall. There was nothing magical to recount, no stories which could convey the flavour of the time to others. Anthony's pleasure in Roger's company came from some deep separate spring. Just to drink coffee or whisky on the verandah while they talked late into the night. To know, from his face glimpsed across a crowded dance floor, the precise nature and shape of the thought in his mind. To go fishing (where for once they were equals) and to see Roger's genuine pleasure in his trophy. To observe the passion with which he expounded his views, so overpowering that Anthony could not argue against him. Once, to Joginder, their Indian friend, after the Founder's Day Dinner, Roger had burst out: 'Why do you ape the British? We only exploit you with our vices. Our affection for meaningless ritual, our snobbery, our dependence on drink and puerile games. Yet you, who possess a reality which stretches back far beyond our Romanized culture, trade everything for a share in our second-rate customs. We only laugh at your attempts to wear our clothes and copy our accents.

But it reinforces the myth of our superiority . . .' It was only much later that the cynicism had come upon him. 'It's a matter of national identity, I suppose. The Germans see themselves as the master race, the Indians as the servant race. It is beyond changing, from outside, at least . . .'

Anthony's excitement came from some ill-defined knowledge that to Roger nothing seemed impossible, and, by some fortunate accident, that he had been chosen as the co-conspirator, the witness who would follow safely and be part of thoughts, events, perceptions which would have been denied him alone by himself. From Roger's shelves he gathered armfuls of books and first encountered Hobbes and Bentham, Mill and Marx, read Livy and Herodotus, and Tacitus and Pliny. 'Immortality is the passing on of valid ideas. I would be gladly dead to have written this,' Roger said once, holding up a copy of *The Nicomachean Ethics* of Aristotle.

Years later, with the hindsight of maturity, Anthony recognized the theatricality and pretensions. The aphorisms had dulled and lost their edge, and the fine clarity of the ideas they had discussed had tarnished with experience. Yet what remained like a permanent striation in the layers of experience was the memory of affection without possession, of communality of feeling.

For when the golden age has left, it goes beyond retrieval.

The goat wandered to the end of the tether, cropping the grass methodically. Occasionally it paused for a moment appraising some noise from the deep forest beyond the clearing before it resumed feeding. It was thin, and its rank smell hung in the air so powerfully that a stir of wind would sometimes bring a brief hint to the three men concealed in the machan in the oak tree at the other side of the clearing.

It was an honour that they had been chosen to hunt the maneater. The villagers had lost a number of bullocks and, far worse, two children had been carried off during the past four months, their remains found days later when the jackals and kites and ants had taken over after the tiger had eaten its fill. The village council had wanted Jim Corbett to hunt down the tiger, but Feroze Khan, supported by Constable Anwar, had persuaded it that Roger Henshaw was the right man. Walid Khan, the Headman, had protested, 'But he's only a boy of twenty or so. How can he have the experience?' Feroze had stood up and the talking had stopped. He said, 'You know me, brothers. My father and I have gone with the Ingresi to fish for mahseer and to hunt leopard and panther. Truly we have never met a better man than this.' His father, sitting with the village elders, had nodded his agreement and so the thing was settled. Walid Khan had donated the goat, under pressure from Feroze.

'Why do we have to go so early?' Joginder Singh grumbled, pulling the goat behind him on its tether. He was more used to riding, a big man with regular, handsome features, a laughing mouth, and a relaxed attitude to life which was reflected in his casual gait. He was five years older than the others and an early marriage and considerable inheritance had already given him perspectives different from his friends.

Roger Henshaw stopped and waited for them to catch him up. 'It will only come when it thinks that there are no humans near. We will have to lie on that platform for hours, so enjoy the walk . . .' He smiled widely, starting up the khud again with his forceful stride. The sun blazed down out of a cloudless sky, and the village in the valley far below shimmered under the heat.

Anthony Hodder brought up the rear. By the side of his friends he seemed slight, though he was not a small man. He had a rifle over his shoulder, and his khaki bush jacket was already stained with sweat at the armpits.

Anthony and Joginder had grown up together, and it was Anthony who had befriended Roger when he had first come to Murree a couple of years before. 'I'm grammar school, you know,' Henshaw had warned when they first met, with a curious truculence underlying his smile. Anthony had shrugged and said, 'So what?' and they had laughed. At college Roger had far surpassed all others both academically and on the games field. It was not so much through natural intelligence, though he did have the quality which Anthony remembered his father calling 'gutter sharpness', but rather through a single-minded will to win which could not conceive of failure.

Roger's evasiveness about his childhood was marked to the point of caricature. Early in their acquaintance Anthony had teased him, pretending to have met someone from England who had known his family. In the unexpected face of Roger's complete loss of composure, he had to admit, with the best grace he could muster, that it had been a rather poor joke. Once, in an unguarded moment after a dance, walking down the pine-possessed paths back to the college, Roger had said with an uncharacteristic gloomy introspection, 'After some time with a girl I remember *her*, and that destroys everything. No wonder he couldn't wait to die . . .'

Anthony walked on without words, aware that no enquiry could prevail but assuming that Roger was referring to his parents. Roger's resentment at his grammar school education, at the grinding poverty in which he was raised, were matters which might be inferred from certain comments; there was nothing to grasp – no facts – as though Roger had arrived newly-minted on the earth aged twenty. But he possessed the quality which Anthony imagined to be immanent in all leaders. Possessed (in Anthony's imagination) by Cardigan, who willed his men into the defile where the Russian guns cut them to pieces, this quality was not intelligence but the capacity to inspire hero-worship and belief which sometimes transcended reason. Roger, who reminded Anthony of a younger Colonel von Stomm from Buchan's *Greenmantle*, had some intrinsic quality of power which rendered unimportant his rather ugly vulpine features, the thin cruel mouth, and the cropped black hair which sprayed angrily erect from a trapezoid head. Anthony confessed to no one, least of all to Joginder, his growing affection for and dependence on his new friend. In later years he saw the line which led from his father to Roger, the same absolute certainty, the same overwhelming belief in the validity of his own observations. To a young man who had found the tenets of his childhood beliefs eroding despite himself, there was a relief in finding such a replacement. And knowing so little about his friend, he could invest him with whatever qualities he wished.

They reached their destination by noon, and Roger took a stake from his rucksack and banged it into the earth in the centre of the clearing, tethering the goat firmly. In the machan they ate the sandwiches Joginder's wife, Sita, had prepared and talked idly. The tiger would not come until much later when the heat of the afternoon had gone. Anthony was curious about Jane Porter, one of the trainee teachers from the local training college whom Roger had taken out a couple of times, but Roger refused to be drawn about her, turning the enquiry deftly aside.

24

'I hear you've been playing tennis with Diana Fairfax. Bit of a goer as I hear it . . .' He and Joginder laughed at Anthony's disclaimers. 'Only tennis, eh? Not what I heard,' Roger said, relishing the last pieces of sandwich from his pouch.

When they had loaded up and got themselves comfortable for the long wait and the shadows had begun to lengthen, Anthony said anxiously, 'We won't let it kill the goat, will we?' glancing down at the animal which had now begun to gaze uneasily at the darkening jungle. Roger looked down the barrel of his rifle, pulling it to his shoulder and taking imaginary aim. 'Oh yes,' he said. 'The tiger will be concentrating on eating. It could give us another shot – make all the difference.'

Behind them on the platform Roger had set up a battery of torches on a board. Joginder's job was to pull the switch if the tiger came after sunset, though the clearing was open enough for the moon to give some light. Three days before, Roger had spent the afternoon at the clearing with Feroze Khan and Constable Anwar. Roger had stayed into the night, sending the two Indians back to the village. 'We were afraid, so he told us to go,' Anwar said to Anthony when they went to collect the goat. It seemed to Anthony that his friend knew every twig and blade of grass, every angle of the sun and moon. He felt again a familiar half-resentful admiration.

Anthony was almost asleep when he felt Roger press his arm. He could see nothing and moved his head carefully, looking at the other man for confirmation. Roger put his hand up to his ear. At first Anthony heard little: twigs cracking and the distant, sleepy chattering of birds. Then he felt cold. There was a noise like the distant guttering of thunder, growing closer. The thicket crackled with the approach of a huge body, and the goat began to

25

back away to the end of the rope. From the shadows there were a couple of coughs from the still-unseen tiger. The smell of the goat, now some twenty feet from the platform, was overpowering. It was still possible to see blades of grass at the other side of the clearing, though the sun was settling towards the rim of the horizon. Anthony raised his rifle into position and held his breath. He could feel his heart beating hard against his chest.

Suddenly the thicket parted diagonally across the clearing and a massive head appeared. The goat began to whicker, pulling at the stake with frenzied efforts. The tiger leaped into the air and bounded towards it. At the same moment Joginder threw the light switch and Anthony fired. He saw the great body check and knew that he had missed. By his side Roger shouted, 'Bloody fool,' and fired. The animal took two more strides and then rolled over, clawing and biting at itself. The goat danced at the end of the rope, bleating with terror. Roger moved swiftly to Anthony's side and fired again, so close that Anthony felt his head would burst with the sound of the shot. The tiger thrashed around and then its body straightened out, twitching in its last convulsions.

Anthony was trembling. He laid his rifle on the platform, wiping his wet hands on his shorts as he got to his feet. Roger sat back against the trunk with the rifle across his knees. 'A fine pair,' he said, and his voice was amused and something else besides. 'One tries to save the goat, the other puts the lights on without a signal . . .' Joginder switched the lights off and said awkwardly, 'Sorry. It was the shock,' and Roger said, 'Never mind. The main thing is we did it.'

By the time they climbed down the goat was already grazing again. The tigress ('They'd even got that wrong,' said Roger, busy slitting through the inside of the massive leg) was over twelve feet long. Eventually he put his knife away. 'I can't do it until morning. Will you send Feroze and a couple of men up with poles and ropes tomorrow?' The eviscerated stomach gleamed blackly in the fading light, and Anthony felt his stomach heave. Roger went over to the goat and cut it free, handing the end of the tether to Anthony. 'I'll stay here to keep off the jackals. You can tell Walid Khan he's in your debt.'

On the way back, the goat kept stopping to graze on thistles. Even with Anthony pulling the tether and Joginder pushing, it stood its ground stolidly. Anthony began to feel an unreasonable urge to give it a sound thrashing. Behind him Joginder began to laugh. 'The grammar school boy is ending up the burra sahib, while you and I are demoted to goatherds.'

When the feowls began to howl the goat lost his appetite for thistles and they made better time. Joginder said thoughtfully, 'I may be old-fashioned, but I prefer you public school chaps. You're less frightening, somehow.'

It was a week before Anthony could hear properly again. 'Hunter's ear,' said Dr Mackenzie briskly, 'you'll get over it in time.'

It took much longer to rid himself of the feeling of having failed his friend. He wondered if he would always feel like a child in Roger's presence.

Roger left college a year before Anthony and went to work in 'Pindi. Joginder's father died, and he too left, to devote himself to his estates, his wife and Guruchunder, his young son.

Though all three met from time to time, for picnics or at dances at Sam's or Lintott's, the quality of their relationship had changed. Anthony missed the evenings

27

when they had sat out on the verandah under the storm-dark skies, watching the lightning flicker as they talked with the confidence of the young and untested about the great matters of the moment. Of the rumours of impending war in Europe, of the growing threat of Japanese nationalism, of the campaign for Independence in India. He missed the closeness of those times, the boisterous high-spirited suppers to celebrate their winning of the hockey cup again, and the walking back, pleasantly mellow, down the moonlit path from Murree after a dance or a film at Baghwan's Silver Screen where the lights came on while the projectionist changed reels.

Sometimes he joined Dr Mackenzie for a whisky on the balcony of his bungalow at the edge of the forest. Mac was a link with the past, having known Anthony's long-dead parents, and in time Anthony grew accustomed to his habits of obliqueness. He learned never to ask a direct question about anything, knowing that Mac would divulge only as much as he wished through a series of tantalizing hints. There was a ritual. Mac would fill his pipe with careful deliberation, turning it in his fingers to examine it carefully, and tamping it down with his flat-ended silver penknife. His wife never joined them on these occasions, and Anthony would hear her moving about inside as she ceaselessly carried out the smaller domestic tasks, the rearrangement of ornaments, the filling of flower vases. Mac would then reach for his matches and fix Anthony with a look which he held just long enough to ensure he had his attention, before glancing down to see how the ritual of lighting was proceeding. 'Hrrm. Your friend Roger Henshaw seems to be getting serious about Jane Porter.' Anthony knew better than to venture any comment in the silence that followed. 'Been seen riding together twice at Nathia Gali, and she's been down to

'Pindi to visit him.' Anthony felt suddenly hurt that Roger hadn't contacted him, and angry with Jane Porter. He had met her twice and found himself unwillingly attracted by her. She was not conventionally pretty, but she had a level, direct gaze and a spirited quickness which he found unusual. There had been no overt signs of mushiness between her and Roger on the two occasions he had seen them together, and Mac's comment had come as a surprise. But he had schooled himself to betray nothing and merely nodded in response, enjoying his newly formed ability to play Mac at his own game.

Mac had been the main source of companionship since his friends had left, and through these oblique conversations he had built a patchwork understanding of the district. How Joginder's father had used mercenaries to protect his cattle and his land in the bad old days. How one of the invading tribesmen had been Feroze Khan's father who had decided to settle in the village, and had married a shop keeper's daughter from the bazaar so that he now ran the shop. How the local Nawab had killed his own father in a dispute about money, but was permitted to roam freely during the day providing that he returned to the custody of his own house-guest and private guard, Constable Anwar, every night.

Once or twice Anthony had dinner with a lecturer from the college, Simon Preston, and his wife Margaret. Simon was only a couple of years older than Anthony, a febrile, neurasthenic man who was racing towards premature middle-age. He had a dry wit and an enormous fund of anti-Indian stories. It took Anthony some time to divine his intense hatred of India, and even longer to understand that he had come away to escape parents who had pushed him through a scholarship to Winchester, a First in

Classics at Balliol, and had pursued their active interest in promoting him ever further after he had come down.

Anthony had, briefly, fancied himself a little in love with Margaret Preston. She had a pre-Raphaelite beauty, with striking bronze hair piled atop a high white forehead and a classically proportioned face. She was always teasing Simon, good-naturedly, with, 'There speaks my Lord and Master,' or 'You can see my husband is the sole bearer of The White Man's Burden.' She had, too, a habit of laying a white hand, with opalescent tapering nails, on Anthony's sleeve when she asked him a question, or wished to enlist his opinion. 'There's no point in asking Simon, because to him this whole country is benighted, but do you agree with Mr Gandhi's views?' She never seemed to notice that she reduced Anthony to a blushing schoolboy, nodding gravely at his broken responses as though they contained seeds of great wisdom. Sometimes he imagined standing on a balcony with her after a dance, and then kissing her, and she responding. There were other thoughts, too, which he felt ashamed of and suppressed. It was all right to think thus of Gunevati, the strident whore who sold her well-displayed charms in Murree bazaar, but not of a woman like Margaret Preston.

Not surprisingly, his occasional outings with Diana Fairfax were uncomfortable and frustrating. He had kissed her after the cinema one night, but in his mind's eye it was Margaret Preston he held in his arms. Later, walking back after a dance, she had taken him by the hand and led him off the road. After they had lain on the grass kissing for a few minutes she had put her hand inside his trousers, and he had been shocked to see her swollen lips and flushed cheeks. She had taken his other hand and guided it to her thigh under the voluminous

30

petticoats, saying urgently, 'Come on. What are you waiting for?' She had laughed at him when he stood up, but it was an angry laugh, without humour. 'Yet another public schoolboy who believes that nice girls have no sexual appetites,' she said, pulling down her skirts, and they had walked back in silence. He had thought a lot about her comment, and had been surprised when she accepted another invitation to a dance with him, and even more surprised when she refused to return to the clearing on their way back. 'Oh, Anthony,' she said reproachfully, looking at him with mock chastisement, and he had felt like a gross importunate beast. Along with everything else, he had much to learn about revenge.

Anthony had finished his exams and was due to begin his familiarization tour in two months, after which he was to be posted to 'Pindi. The most exciting part was the prospect of being reunited with Roger again, and he was bitterly disappointed to find that his friend had been posted to Murree and would be taking up his new job there in a month. 'Think of it as a promotion for me,' Roger said, uncorking the bottle of whisky and pouring them each a measure for the toast. 'We'll see each other from time to time. It's only forty miles. Cheer up.' He brought such an ebullient massive energy into the room that it was impossible to feel downcast.

Roger was staying the night, so they went up to Sam's for the evening. 'You don't want to dance, do you?' said Roger, looking disparagingly at the girls sitting in groups on the plush-seated gilt chairs at the end of the floor, and they sat and drank whisky over a curry while the orchestra played a medley of popular tunes and couples swept round the floor. Anthony felt overwhelmed, as always, by Henshaw's prodigal energy, his single-minded pursuit of some secret atavistic goal. Later his friend hailed a tonga, and they rode down the long road back to the college. 'One day I'll do this in a car, from the finest house in the area,' Roger said, taking a swig from the bottle in his pocket.

It was past three when Anthony yawned and said, 'Well, I'm for bed.' He picked up the glasses from the table and put the bottle under his arm. When he was at the door from the verandah into his quarters, Roger said, 'Anthony,' and something in his voice, a quality near to tears, made Anthony turn. Henshaw said haltingly, 'I know I'm hard to take, sometimes. I have to do everything better, you see. Because I can't change the past, and it is always there no matter how well I do, I need to do better. You do see, don't you?'

Anthony nodded mutely. His throat felt swollen and he was unsure that he could trust his voice. He nodded. 'Of course,' he said. 'Goodnight.'

Simon Preston rubbed the blackboard clean and picked up his lecture notes. As always he wore his Balliol gown, greening with age and frayed around the sleeves. He stopped by Anthony and said, 'No more Principles of British Law as modified for Heathens, the use of, eh? Now you can play God for a few years until you begin to question your qualifications . . .' His delivery, and the smile accompanying it, relegated Anthony to the role of a child. 'You free for dinner tonight? About eight then.' He moved down the aisle, his gown billowing behind him.

With a week to go the college had already assumed an abandoned air. Students from the South, whose journeys would take several days, had left already. The dining-room was almost deserted and the groundsmen had begun to dismantle the goal posts on the hockey pitch and take

32

down the nets on the tennis courts. Only two weekends, and then he would be going to Rawalpindi. He felt disorientated and unable to settle to anything. After lunch he took his collection of Tagore's poems and walked to the boundary of the playing fields, where he fell asleep.

Dinner was an uncomfortable affair, and he wished he had turned the invitation down. His face was flaming red from his long sleep in the sun, and the lassitude of the afternoon had grown. There was, too, some hidden dissension between Simon and Margaret which seemed to edge many of the remarks, ostensibly addressed to Anthony, but with some hidden, half-venomous import intended for the other. This evening there even seemed to be some disagreeable aspect to Margaret. For once he felt unmoved by the shadow between her breasts and the beating pulse at the base of her slender throat.

'Do you regard Indians as inferior to the British, Anthony?'

There it went again. She was smiling faintly, toying with the stem of her glass, but her eyes were serious.

He said, slowly, still unsure in himself of how he felt, 'I don't think so. Their culture is far older than our own. The Hindu demonology which we affect to despise is echoed in every branch of Anglo-Saxon society. All our primitive superstitions . . .'

She laughed, and the timbre grated on some nerve. 'People who dress up feelings in long words avoid the real issues. Do you think coloured races inferior to white?'

'No,' he said, unwilling to discuss the matter further.

'That's just as well,' she said. 'You cannot work effectively here except upon the basis of a truly felt equality.'

Later she said, 'Simon is going on leave to England by himself. His mother has died so there are some family matters to take care of. You'll have to come and visit me.'

33

Her green eyes danced at him over the rim of her glass, and he smiled back awkwardly. The invitation, issued in front of her husband, killed a hope he was surprised to find still existed. He was just a boy to her. 'Yes, of course,' he said, knowing that he would not.

In the garden, after dinner, she took his arm and walked down the long vista to the summer house. 'Tell me about your friend, Henshaw,' she said. 'I've heard he is a Great White Hunter and more besides.'

So Anthony smoked a couple of cheroots, a new habit which made him feel older, and talked about Roger until Simon came out and all three walked back to the house.

The light hurt Anthony's eyes, sucking the colour from the grass and trees with a white intensity which made it impossible to look out at the scorched maidan for more than a few moments. He went back to his room, oddly naked now with the walls revealing untanned patches where the pictures had been removed, and finished his tardy letter of thanks to the Prestons. When the chaprassi had taken it, he lay back on the bed with his hands above his head and stared at the ceiling. He and Dr Mac had put away a lot of whisky last night. Small wonder he had felt so queasy that he had slept with the chamber pot by the bedhead. Unused though, thank God. Mac would have been out doing his rounds for the past hour. To his mind, the doctor shared some mythic quality of indestructibility with the rocks and mountains and the very earth.

Joginder had dropped by during the week and had invited him to come over for a picnic and a ride. 'Roger will be there, too, in honour of your passing out. I'm afraid he's bringing Jane . . .' and he had laughed at Anthony's involuntary grimace of disappointment. Sita sent her love. Gur had his own pony and was learning to ride. Joginder had responded to an appeal by Feroze Khan and had arranged for his father to be taken to hospital for a cataract operation at his own expense. 'Beware the sin of hubris. Aspiring to sainthood in your twenties,' Anthony had said mockingly, and Joginder had laughed. 'Even barons and zemindars have an obligation to their peasants,' he had said. It was an unfamiliar world now, and everything spoke to Anthony of the decay of some old bond, the loosening of the carefree comradeship of their student days together.

Now it was the day of the picnic and the schoolboy feelings had returned. This was the last bulwark before the unknown. The last lunch, the last walk round the college, the last look at the ignored, familiar objects of everyday life, their very staleness rendered precious by the sense of imminent loss.

He walked up the road with the bottles of Murree beer clinking noisily in his knapsack. The road had long since fallen into disrepair, harbouring huge boulders dislodged by the monsoon from the hills above. Below the road their broken paths showed for hundreds of yards through the dense pine and spruce clinging tenaciously to the precipitous shoulder of the mountain. From the forest above the sound of woodcutters' axes carried faintly through the birdsong. Beyond the Grange, he passed Karam Deen, the gorah wallah, leading a halting pony. They exchanged salaams and he could hear the man talking tenderly to the horse as he walked up past the Convent.

Gur was being led around the garden on a small pony by the syce as Anthony walked down the path. Despite the ring saddle, Anthony could see his apprehension and the way he held on to the neck of the beast. Sita stood by, frowning with concern, and Joginder, by her side, was

35

shouting encouragement. 'Shabash. You can come hunting with us soon. Well done, my son . . .' Roger sat on the steps and Jane Porter stood above him in jodhpurs, her fists on her hips. She looked like a proud Valkyrie, her black hair lifted from her face by a sudden wind. Gur began to cry and Sita ran to him. 'That's enough, Jog,' she said reproachfully, and Joginder spread his hands in a gesture of mock despair and said, 'That's what is happening when women become involved in men's things . . .'

Roger ran to meet Anthony, and hugged him so that he felt his ribs would crack. Again, Anthony was struck by a febrile perception of change, some nuance of mystery in the massive confidence of his friend. 'God, it's good to see you,' Roger said, and Anthony felt warmed by the affection and a tremor of fear again, at the unknown. Roger gripped his shoulder hard and shouted to Joginder, 'You see, late as usual. Been dawdling up the road reciting poetry to himself I daresay.' Jane Porter turned and smiled. She appeared startlingly beautiful for a moment, and Anthony looked past her to Joginder, who waved and walked forward to greet him.

The servants had already begun to file out with the hampers. Food and wine (nobody else whom Anthony knew had wine), napkins and tablecloths, cutlery, china, crystal glasses, rugs, the black wind-up HMV gramophone and a pile of 78-records. Four cocker spaniels ran between the servants and Joginder in agonies of indecision. 'We're only going to 'Pindi Point so that we can come back to pick up the horses afterwards,' said Joginder. Gur, still slightly tearful, said, 'Can I bring my gun please, daddy?'

The forest path was cool, green dappled. Ivy-clad trunks sprawled where they had fallen, rotting their bleached chips on to the mossed floor of the forest. The pine needles gave under their feet, thinning to a patch of bare earth here and there where feathered ferns bowed gracefully to their approach, or deadly nightshade thrust out of the soil. At the top of the tall pines the wind swayed the branches, hissing the needles together like beads slithering on to a cushion. Beyond, a light cloud blew past, whitening the cobalt blue of the midday sky. Gur ran ahead, pointing his gun at imaginary enemies. 'Bang! Bang!' in a little boy's voice. Sita and Anthony followed behind the others, talking idly. It was this he would miss, Anthony reflected. This permanent landscape with its prodigal resistance to change, its capacity to absorb the devastation of storms and earthquakes without lasting effect. There were places in the forest which he loved, which seemed to him to summarize all the mystic yearning he could barely admit to himself for fusion with this earth, these mountains, these accepting forests.

Ahead of them Jane lifted her arm to point something out and a moment before Sita spoke Anthony saw it, a livid purple bruise which ran from inside her elbow up her arm. 'Oh, I took a toss from the mare. You should have seen it when it first happened,' she said, in response to Sita's question, and Roger turned aside from his conversation with Joginder briefly to touch her hair.

After lunch Roger took the gun from Gur. 'I'll show you how to shoot,' he said. Joginder levered himself onto an elbow and said, 'Uncle Roger is a burra shikari, my son. You listen to what he has to say.' Sita put *Pale Hands I Loved* on the turntable. Down by the stream the servants sat and talked, squatting on their haunches with their knees under their arms. Jane lay on one elbow watching Roger teach Gur how to use the gun. She had a frond of fern in her brown hands, stripping the leaves from it with slow, deliberate gestures.

Roger straightened Gur's right leg and said, 'Now make

37

sure the thin blade at the front sits in the middle of the vee here,' and he touched the back sight, 'and that both line up at the top.' Behind the hands held up to his eyes, Joginder murmured, 'That's right, my son. Listen to the great shikar,' so softly that only Anthony heard. He sensed some wearied disaffection in the tone, but there was a report and the pine cone spun a yard to the left. 'I did it, daddy. I did it,' Gur shouted, and Sita clapped. 'Again,' Roger said. 'Again.'

Karam Deen had brought two horses to make up the number. Anthony looked at the great dappled hunter and said with exasperation, 'Why did you bring Kali, Karam Deen-ji? You know she has a will like iron and a mouth to match? Why didn't you bring Piarath?' Karam Deen looked at him without expression, stroking the mare's grey velvet muzzle gently. He took the bit in his hand so that the horse jerked her head, opening her mouth to show large yellowing teeth. In a soft, wheedling voice he said, 'All the Ingresi want horses now, sir. But Kali is gentle with someone who knows how to ride.' He shot a quick glance to assess the effect of his subtle flattery. 'Besides . . . I have honed the bit so that it cuts her mouth. A few tugs will calm her down.'

Roger said, 'I'll take her,' and the old man looked at him gratefully. 'She will respect you, Sahib. Feroze says that you ride like an Afridi.' His tone suggested some flattering association of manliness between them.

They rode towards the Galis where the diverted stream water filtered and plashed hollowly into the great concrete cisterns which supplied the estate. On Camel Rock a falconer whistled his bird, holding the great gauntlet to the sky and swinging the lure. But the bird wound ever upwards in the gyre, beyond recall. 'She'll stoop,' said Roger, reining in, and they sat their horses, watching.

'There she goes,' Joginder pointed and they saw the bird drop like an arrow. There was a scream of terror from the scrub below the rock, abruptly silenced. The falconer began to move down past the crag with exaggerated caution, and they cantered on.

It was Joginder who began it. 'Last one to Endor's Crag pays for drinks at Sam's,' he shouted, and spurred his chestnut forward into a gallop.

The horses began to stream over the open ground towards the forest path which led to the great crag which dominated the valley, a mile to the south. Roger reached the gap just before Joginder, turning in his saddle to shout something which was lost in the wind of their passage. Fifty yards behind, Anthony let his mare make her own speed just ahead of Jane. Jogging up and down, he had to concentrate to avoid the whipping ferns. He was surprised to see Joginder at Roger's shoulder, rowelling his horse. But the chestnut was no match for the big grey and Jog began to fall behind. The path had narrowed now, and the ground was rougher, so that the ponies closed together in single file. The only place where Roger could be passed was the last open clearing before the final narrow path to the Crag. There was no doubt in Anthony's mind that Roger would win.

But as they burst into the clearing Kali stumbled and Joginder went past. Anthony followed him too swiftly to hear anything beyond a muttered curse. A second later he glanced over his shoulder to see the big grey gaining on him, and a few strides later she went past. Joginder made the gap first with Roger just behind. Roger hit Kali across the crupper and she jerked forward, stumbling into the ferns before righting herself.

A hundred yards down the path Anthony saw Joginder throw up his arm and rein in his chestnut. A huge tree had crashed athwart the path, its jagged broken branches standing out from the bole. Joginder's horse stumbled, almost sitting in the bracken. With horror, Anthony realized that Roger was going to attempt the tree. He shouted, 'Stop,' his throat already dry with fear, but he could see Roger rowelling the mare with his spurs, dragging her terrified head straight with the muscles of his arm standing out like ropes. There was a moment when it seemed Kali might baulk. The black jagged thrust of the tree stood like a massive bulkhead against the sun. Then they were in the air together.

Kali's front hooves cleared the trunk. Mare and rider hung in the air for a moment. Then her rear hooves caught the trunk and she fell sideways onto a protruding shard of wood. Roger pitched over her head and the mare slipped slowly over on top of him. Blood had already begun to gout along her coat and splash over the silver lichen. The horse began to scream.

Anthony dismounted and ran to the tree. He hauled himself painfully up, followed by Joginder. Roger lay under the mare which was struggling to rise. His face was contorted, though it seemed with rage and not pain. His legs were trapped under the horse's withers, and he put his hands under the animal's body, heaving himself free with tremendous effort, and stood up. His jodhpurs were torn and blood was seeping slowly through the cloth on his right thigh.

The horse whickered softly. Her back leg was bent at a sharp angle and splinters of bone showed through the flesh. Her viscera had begun to ooze through the great wound in her stomach. 'It's all right,' Roger said softly. Joginder said, 'I'll get home and send someone to put her to sleep. Are you OK?' Roger held up his hand, looking down at the mare. 'Kali's in pain. It must be done now.

Besides, I must do it myself.' He motioned them to go back and they climbed over and remounted. No one spoke.

There was a gurgling sound, and a few moments later Roger climbed stiffly over the trunk. Jane said, 'What did you do?', and Anthony was amazed at how calm and level her voice was. 'I cut her throat,' Roger said. 'The jackals will do the rest.' He leaned against the fallen tree and tore the sleeve of his shirt open, breaking a twig from the trunk to twist the tourniquet on his leg.

At first he refused to accept Anthony's awkward offer of his horse. He walked ahead and the rest followed silently. Once Joginder started to say, 'We'll have to tell Karam Deen . . .', but his voice trailed uncertainly away. As they filed across the open plateau where the race had started by Camel Rock, the swallows had begun to take the midges and the light had dulled to orange. It had taken an hour at the funereal pace imposed by following Roger, who was favouring his injured leg increasingly, but they had walked their horses meekly behind, each afraid to challenge his curt refusal again. Now Anthony diffidently offered his horse, and to his surprise Roger accepted. It took both Joginder and Anthony to man-oeuvre him into the saddle, but he made no sound even though Anthony could see that his lips were white with pain. He settled himself and then gave Anthony the reins to lead the horse, saying with a crooked smile, 'Just in case you feel I might do the same again. I'd forgotten that public schools invest people with a love of animals. Never trust a man who values goats and horses . . .' He laughed harshly and Anthony took the reins and led the horse forward at a brisker pace.

It was dark when they arrived. An ambulance was summoned and Roger was taken to Murree Hospital.

Karam Deen left, highly satisfied with the price he had agreed with an exhausted Joginder for the grey mare. While the women changed, Anthony and Joginder had a subdued drink on the balcony.

Joginder said, his voice flatly dismissive, 'I'm sorry. I really don't want to see anything more of him,' and Anthony nodded without speaking. The incident had robbed the past of some magic and made the prospect of Rawalpindi more attractive.

Anthony took Jane back that evening. Over the next few months he saw her increasingly, and when he took a shooting holiday with a couple of friends he was surprised to find that he missed her. She came to dances with him, and they played tennis with Mac and his wife, and dined together with his new colleagues from the Mess. There was nothing dramatic in their growing intimacy but gradually everyone tacitly assumed – even before the idea had occurred to Anthony himself – that they would get married. When he had met her family on a trip to Mysore and had formally asked for her hand and been accepted, he was a little surprised that this outcome had seemed a foregone conclusion. He felt disappointed by the lack of excitement, by his friends' lack of surprise at the announcement.

He had one secret concern. When he asked her about Roger, she would change the subject, or wave dismissively and say, 'But that's in the past. Before us, I mean.'

At first, this was enough to calm his incipient fears. But later, when their honeymoon idyll on Hari Singh's houseboat on the Shalamar Gardens was over, he found he could no longer reason away some elusive unease, and Jane would not give him the assurance he needed for his peace of mind. When it finally came to a head, after months of covert questions and evasive replies, she had looked at him with her brown open eyes, hunching her slim shoulders over the dinner table as though hugging some past memory she did not wish to share with anyone. 'Why? Because he is . . . was exciting, unpredictable, powerful? I felt half afraid of him . . . but he made me feel alive.' Anthony felt sick to see the passionate tension with which she struck the table with her small fist. Contrite, she looked across at him, her face softer now in the glow of the candles and said, 'I'm sorry. I wish I could tell you something else. But you know him. It wasn't love . . .' she shivered at some memory, 'but fascination.'

He had got up from the table and walked out to the verandah. Yes, he remembered what it was like to be with Roger, though they had not met for almost four years, since that fateful picnic. He felt diminished, unable to compete, and when she came out later and put her arms round him and her cheek against his and said, 'But I married you, didn't I?' he felt impotently angry, as though she had chosen him only as the safe familiar harbour against the dark storm beyond.

Alone among his acquaintances he tried to join up in 1938 when the rumours of impending war in Europe became stronger. Such a course presented a clear enemy, and the chance to become absorbed again in a community he nostalgically felt would restore all the hopes and sense of purpose of his college days. Against Jane's anger he offered only the stubborn thesis that it was his duty, and then silence. For the greatest part of it would be to restore some sense of being a man to himself.

Commissioner Pogson had refused to release him.

Pogson was kindly enough, even flattering, but he made it clear that he would not even consider releasing Anthony when the department was so hard pressed. Anthony applied for leave, deciding to press his case in Delhi. Anne was dispatched to stay with her maternal grandparents, and Jane, with every show of indifference now, announced that she would visit a friend in Peshawar.

But when he got to Delhi, it was only to find that Pogson's benign and rather stupid appearance disguised a shrewd mind. His letter, arriving well before Anthony had left, was a model of cogency against which Anthony's reasoning and pleas seemed thin and self-serving. There was an over-abundance of qualified recruits, but few people who could replace him in India, he was told. His interview had been delayed for over a week and he suspected Pogson had engineered this as a mark of his understandable displeasure at the course his subordinate had chosen.

When he came home again, and the servant had taken his case to unpack, Jane only said, 'You weren't successful then?', looking at him with a curious pity. Later, it was that comment he remembered more than anything. The journey, the stay in the dak house, the first disappointment.

Mark: 1984

Three

When a victorious Roman General was given a triumph he would be paraded through the streets in a garlanded chariot. As he acknowledged the roars of the crowd, a slave stood by his side constantly reminding him of his mortality. It is fanciful to think of Andrew Carew as a slave to anything beyond a late conversion to convention, but the conceit pleases me.

It was, after all, Carew who started the whole process. I was in my Chambers, trying to devise a defence for Regina v Duffy. I'd spent the morning with Walter Schnafel and his client in my chambers. As with most of Walter's briefs, I found the clients repellent but the challenge fascinating. It is hard to stand outside and evaluate my ability to reassure clients, but Duffy, a stout perspiring gentleman with pebble glasses which gave his eyes a strangely dishonest look, seemed well-satisfied. 'We'll stitch them up, Mark, won't we?' he said, exuding beery bonhomie, and I was aware that Walter's lizard mouth twitched briefly with rare private amusement. Of Duffy's guilt I had no doubt. In my experience, no one with three homes, a private jet, a yacht and three ex-wives is ever honest or in a position truly to plead ignorance – which, in any event, as everyone knows, is no defence. It was only lately that I had occasionally felt the immorality of such situations. As a QC I should have learned the limitations and approximations of my trade, but I had been too often aware of late that the fees washed by the Walters of this world which came to me in such gratifying abundance were from sources which would prove to be dirty on a true evaluation.

I felt a sneaking envy for Carew. He was amicably divorced with a daughter upon whom he lavished every imaginable present. He had never lived up to the early promise of a First in Greats and pupillage in the best Commercial Chambers, but he really didn't seem to care. I met him, from time to time, at the homes of mutual acquaintances. He invariably had in tow some nubile girl, with an impeccable accent and the permanent exotic sun-tan of a rare visitor to our rain-sodden land. He came into my Chambers that grey August afternoon, perched on the corner of my desk, and held his wig out towards the pale afternoon light filtering through the long window.

I'd asked him about his holiday, glad of a break from the papers littering my desk, and he'd waxed enthusiastic about Pakistan. 'Go back before it's too late, old man. Everyone says it's changed already beyond recognition.' I felt suddenly afraid, looking at Carew's uncaring, preoc-cupied profile with the cow-lick of blond hair flopping loosely across the pale forehead. Oh lucky man, my effortlessly stylish friend, with your Eton education and country-seat childhood in Georgian splendour amidst loving and still present siblings. It was in part the certainty which I felt all this produced in him which nurtured my affection for him. In the end I said, 'Oh, go away. I'm fearfully busy,' and he walked off twirling his wig on the end of a forefinger. Three days later I lost the case, and knew that it was due to something his careless remark had begun in me.

* * *

Carew's remark had against my will reopened the closed doors of childhood.

Over the next weeks I thought about going back to Pakistan and the idea nagged me, disturbing my sleep and upsetting my daily routines. There was another factor (beside the fear of what I might discover) which I recognized with a slight sense of shame. I could not come to terms with the unconventionality of the idea. The Ironsides, who lived two houses (and seven acres) away from us, always went to Florida for a month on a house-swap every summer. The Raynors took a gîte, driving down to the south of France in the latest model in their series of ever-new estate cars, with their two spoilt children quarrelling in the back. There was some subtle definition in what would be acceptable in the neighbourhood, and an odyssey in Zia's new Pakistan would not, could not, prove acceptable to my liberal acquaintances. Even to me, the thought seemed at odds with the greyly conventional image I had built up over the years, reading *The Times* Law Reports on the same seat on the same train amid the same silent commuters, morning after morning; a sidesman at the local church, with a wife involved in fundraising for underprivileged children and a son at public school. Side by side with this, the memories returned. Importunate visitors. They pursued me on the train, or as I mowed the lawns, and I only realized the extent of my preoccupation when I overheard Susan remark to Mollie Ironside, sotto voce, her concern that I didn't seem to be myself lately. I had, in truth, found myself pursued by fragments of childhood. Splinters of memory, prompted by the smell of dust rustling against the sun, brought with them a tantalizing incompleteness.

For the first time in twenty years I took down the old biscuit box from the attic, one Sunday afternoon when

47

Susan had gone to help at a church bazaar, and felt again the distant shapeless lappings of memory on some remote shore. Together with Mac's letters and clippings they made an odd collection, and I felt a tremor of the strange feelings of childhood when the rituals governing the opening of the box had been precise and magical in their mysteriousness. Five black crow feathers, a piece of snakeskin, dry and transparent as tissue, two used cartridges from an army issue Colt 45 and some yellowed, fading newspaper cuttings. Mac's letters had meant nothing to me at the time, arriving periodically over my first three years, from 1950 to 1953, at public school in Somerset. Along with the paraphernalia of fagging, of Commemoration Days and Founder's Days, and of the orotund speeches in Chapel at the beginning and end of term, they had seemed only another facet of an incomprehensible system which demanded subservience but offered no understandable explanations. There was one letter, I remembered, which seemed to offer some code, and I re-read it now, still unable to grasp the oracular truth it seemed to promise:

'I knew your father well. In common with other men like Simon Preston, Roger Henshaw and Andrew Prescott (just names to you, I'm sure) I always felt Anthony was a victim of the new consciousness. He was too gentle, too immured in the social traditions of India. I believe, too, that Roger had a profound effect upon him, despite the coolness between them after those years at college. I could say nothing, seeing how your father secretly hero-worshipped and admired him, but Roger seemed to me from the first to be unstable – a judgement which later events endorsed. Like most obsessions his had begun as a child and been fed and exaggerated in secret. He felt that his mother had been responsible for his father's premature death, and afterwards had resented her for what he saw as her attempt to diminish him. I tried to suggest that she was only concerned, as

48

any mother might be, that he had a job and an income at a time of recession, but Roger wouldn't have it.

'Nobody can say what happened at the end, and I know that you will become more troubled about this as time goes by. I hope you will keep this letter until the time comes when you may find comfort in it. Of course nothing is final, or absolutely known. Only fiction offers us the consolation of a completed pattern of pat conclusions. We have to live with approximations to the truth.

'I have written now while these things are fresh in my mind and the future is uncertain. In the end you may find, as I have, that beside human relationships everything else becomes unimportant.'

I pulled the stepladder over and cached the box in the topmost tea-chest. When I'm anxious I tend to sweat, regardless of the weather, and I felt clammy and a bit sick. I caught myself at my usual trick of trying to find a physical cause (had Mollie prepared the mussels properly? was I sickening for 'flu?) before having to admit that it was something else. Sitting on the floorboards, surrounded by my moth-eaten teddy bear and several dolls, failed pieces of electrical equipment, furniture which we had replaced but still kept for some reason, I knew that I would have to go back.

It was an odd afternoon. The casement flapped a little in the wind and the pyracantha lashed across the window like a giant trying to climb in. Being alone in the house gave me a luxuriant, almost wicked sense of forbidden freedom. I had opened the box and now a strange recklessness overtook me. The sickness had gone and my hands were dry. For the first time, looking through the old albums (a lock of my black hair, my Birth Certificate in Urdu), I let childhood steal over me. The feathers! I remembered a pet bird. That's right . . . I could remember myself at eight or nine, the dry smell, the heap of

49

feathers. I was upset, and so were Rod and the servant . . . Samuel . . . yes, that was it . . . The snakeskin. I could remember peering through legs. A snake had got into the godown and a servant was sent in with a lathi to kill it. I remember the thumps of the stick on the earthen floor. The coherence was hard to retrieve.

I distrusted the memories, a little. Most of my professional life is occupied in dealing with memories. Even when people are being honest they select, distort. Duffy's case, the one I had lost the week before, was typical. Uncharacteristically, he was being honest. 'I never wrote such a letter, Mark,' he said, almost crying at the injustice of it all. Too late now, I realized, looking across at Mr Justice Blackstock, and I said to Duffy, as gently as I knew how, 'No. You don't *remember* writing such a letter, which is something different.' At least *I* wouldn't get five years if my memories were faulty. Though maybe, on reflection, that would be preferable.

At about five Susan creaked up the stairs. 'Oh, there you are,' she said, sounding oddly relieved, 'I've been yelling for you downstairs for simply ages.' She put one elegant leg over a pile of papers, and looked about her with that feminine curiosity which always gave me the feeling I was doing something unimportant, childlike. She picked up the bear and sniffed it, wrinkling her nose. 'Sawdust fatigue. He'll have to go,' and I said, almost from panic that she would spoil some memory with a careless comment, 'I've been thinking. I'd like to take a holiday in Pakistan. See how it's changed.' She wandered round for a few moments, touching an old table, picking up the lamp base we'd brought back from Seville. 'All right,' she said, 'why not?' and I felt something relax in my stomach.

* * *

She did the planning and I got on with my clients. Carew took a couple of cases off me. He seemed to have got ambition (rather late) from somewhere. I had noticed that his latest girlfriend had stayed around long enough for her tan to fade. One morning, by chance, I was in Conduit Street and happened to see them walk into Collingwood's, the jewellers, together. She had a firm grip on his arm and it clarified things for me. Circumstantial evidence only, but I was fairly certain I was right. Along with the other signs (clean shoes, replaced buttons, reasonable haircut) I could think of no other explanation that fitted the facts.

As the time drew nearer I felt a strange excitement growing in me and steeled myself against expecting too much. Though I say it myself I had tackled the visit with meticulous efficiency, culling information from every source available. I was aware that this was partly so that I could build myself a protective carapace. Against what, I was not quite sure. Jean Mackenzie replied to my letter, as did old Parsons. I could almost smell, seeping from the paper, lives caught in a bleb of time in the 1940s. From that vantage point, they wrote of the encroachment of new roads, the deforestation of the wooded slopes, the great commercial factories which had sprung up around Islamabad. Friends who had taken tours tried to help, seeking to divine my needs over the rim of their gins and tonics. Carew was the only one who saw the fallacy immediately. 'No point in even trying, old man,' he said, draining his claret and looking at his watch. 'All of us went as tourists. You're going back as someone who wishes to rediscover his childhood.' He looked at me and tapped the side of his nose. He was my closest friend, and I admired him greatly. Despite that, I had never realized how foxy and alien he could look. 'Only remember there are no absolute answers. Our memories of childhood are inaccurate at best. You might convince Blackstock of your case. Be satisfied with that . . .' He threaded his way through the tables consulting his watch. I knew he was serious about the girl.

At first my mother had been enthusiastic about joining us on the visit, and I had presented Susan with the fait accompli of her proposed presence on the holiday, ignoring Susan's pursed look of disapproval. As the time grew nearer (my palms were never dry now) I called the doctor who attended my mother at the home only to be told that she would be too frail to make the arduous journey to Murree. (It made no difference to Susan. I had committed the unforgivable sin of asking without permission.)

A week before we left I drove dutifully down to Torquay to see Mother. 'You must bring me back lots of photographs. Promise,' she said, craning her head awkwardly to look at me as I wheeled her along the front. When the wind blew up and the sea began to buffet the groynes in a grey and white fury, I took her back to the home for tea. Over the lawns nurses wheeled their elderly charges towards the portico, and the gulls swooped and darted in the last rays of the October sun.

When we arrived at her room, I helped her into the faded chintz armchair, feeling a hopeless tenderness to see her look so old and wasted as I covered her legs with the rug. Mac had been right in one thing at least. There was no rancour now, only the sad recognition of impending death as I looked at her face, the eyes momentarily vacant as she remembered some unspoken preoccupation. As always I had to remind myself that I was paying, that she constantly professed her happiness in these surroundings, that there was no need to feel guilty because we had all decided she would be better living in the Home than with us.

She picked up the silver-framed photograph of my father from the bedside table and looked at it with a sad smile. I used to think it was an act, but she was beyond such artifice now. The thin smiling face, and the casual stance of the figure standing with a hand on a younger more vivacious mother's shoulder, bore no relationship to the father I carried in my memory. Again mother said, as I had heard her say before, 'He was such a gentle man.' She put the photograph down carefully. 'If only Anthony and Roger had never met . . .' I had learned never to ask what these occasional comments meant. Now that she was old and confused she might have told me, but I could not bring myself to press her. She mused to herself, half smiling, and then fell asleep as I watched her. I put my cup down carefully to avoid waking her, and covered her with the blanket. In the corridor I put my finger to my lips to warn the maid bustling down the corridor on her way to prepare the bed.

A week later I was in Murree with Susan. The air was so thin that my head had ached from the time we alighted at the hotel. I felt oppressed by something which I could not define. I slept badly the first night, waking with the phrase, 'Where is the body buried?' ringing in my mind. Beyond Susan, standing in her negligée at the window, I saw that the scale had changed. The mountains still reared massively into a white blue sky, but the houses were more pinched and huddled than I had remembered.

Over chota hasri I suggested diffidently that I would like to look around on my own. 'You and your bloody childhood. Go by yourself, then,' Susan said, and I could see she was half-amused, half-hurt by the exclusion. When

I left in the hired car she was trying to arrange the trip to Jaipur with a smiling but uncomprehending Pakistani reservations manager. Confronted with this pomaded midget with his permanent smile I could see the colour travel up her neck. There was a reassuring familiarity in the sound of her raised voice as I left the lobby.

Joginder's estate seemed to have fallen into decline. The long drive was now lined on both sides by barbed wire, beyond which the woods had been replaced by fields. Several women were working, ankle-deep in water, gathering some crop. A fierce-looking old man sat on a charpoy in the corner, watching them work. I waved as I went past but there was no response. The drive had long since lost its macadam, and was mossed and embroidered with dense woods. The lawn was unkempt, and the summer house derelict. The sightless busts in the embrasures beside the massive door were cracked and cobwebbed, and the stucco walls wept yellow and brown stains. Finally, in answer to my repeated ring, an ancient woman shuffled down the marble hall and opened the door a crack. A smell of damp wafted from behind her, carious and gloomy. 'Gone to Lahore. All gone,' she said, closing the door firmly. I could hear her footsteps shuffle away down the hall.

I did not know what I had expected to find, but there was so little resonance there that I felt depressed. As I drove through the rusted iron gates, hanging drunkenly from long defunct hinges, I had to brake sharply to avoid a figure standing in the road. I checked the impulse to swear and saw it was a Saddhu, a holy man. Though his hair was white his face had been destroyed by leprosy, and it was impossible to say how old he was. One hand was a smooth pad and he had lost all his toes. But what eyes! Black, lustrous, angry. He must have stood looking at me for twenty seconds before moving aside. There was something about him which arrested my impatience. Perhaps the lack of oxygen, or the strangeness of everything, affected me.

I drove over the brow of the hill and down the wooded slope to Roger Henshaw's bungalow. This was where it had happened, according to the yellowing paper in the biscuit tin. (I remembered the phrase, *Superintendent Anwar was called from his bed by the chowkidar . . .*) I stopped outside the gate and was fervently sick into the bushes. My chest hurt and I found it hard to breathe. I sat for a few minutes, reassuring myself that this was only fear, that I was not terminally ill. I felt the sour taste of bile in my throat.

A little Pakistani sat under a sun umbrella on the lawn, reading the paper. A middle-aged woman, gathering her brilliant orange sari clear of the ground in one hand, dead-headed the roses with a pair of secateurs in the other. Behind her, a man perhaps in his forties mowed a lower lawn. There was something strangely familiar about him; the set of his shoulders, the way he walked, stirred some memory. When he turned I realized with a shock he was a mongol.

It is condescending to remember the little Pakistani, Malik, as charming, since his appeal was based upon something tremendously humorous. He was a retired lawyer, he told me in his ponderous archaic English, standing very stiffly to his five feet to introduce his wife, Premla. Now that the sun no longer blinded me I could see that they were much older than I had supposed at first. I had to take tea with them, and eat chilgozas, the small pine kernel nuts which we had loved so much as children.

He insisted on talking politics as we sat, while I looked

surreptitiously past him at the grey corrugated iron roof which had replaced the pink tiles, noting with relief that only details had changed. I knew that I would still see, beyond the sharp edge of the house, the thin line of trees and the purple hills beyond. Malik talked while his wife looked at him with ironical affection, reminding me curiously of Walter Schnafel with one of the old lags he insisted on defending time and again. 'You know,' Malik confided in a whisper, looking theatrically over his shoulder, 'this bloody country has gone to the dogs since Zia took over. Ayub, even Yayha, were all right. Bhutto was brilliant, really one of the old school,' he absently fingered the knot of a non-existent tie. 'Soon we will be back in the dark ages again, like Iran,' he said mournfully. 'Even now Feroze Khan's brigands own all this land,' he waved his hand towards the hill.

I couldn't put the moment off any longer. 'Of course, of course,' Malik said, gesturing me expansively towards the house. When I stood on the verandah I could see his wife talking rapidly to him, and his little nods of response. I walked around the perimeter to the side. Under the trees the shade struck cold. The gravel crunched with each step. In the end I had to force myself towards the verandah at the side. It was here that Superintendent Anwar had come, over thirty years before. The body had lain here. I leaned against one of the pillars trembling. There was a blandness I had not expected. Two chairs stood by a table. Nasturtiums straggled over the edge of the verandah cloying the air with their heady smell. There was nothing there, any more.

I walked round the front of the house, out into the sunshine. Malik and his wife stood by the steps. He looked hard at me and said hesitantly, 'Hodder? Wasn't your father . . .?' and coughed behind a small, neat hand to cover his confusion. Behind him Mrs Malik stepped to one side. With the light on her face I saw, with a shock, that she was almost blind, both eyes milky with cataracts. I fancied I heard pity in her voice. 'Nobody knows what happened any more. Superintendent Anwar is very ill and Dr Mackenzie is dead . . .' Her voice was very gentle. She put her hand on her husband's arm.

We were three awkward strangers. I bade them farewell and climbed into the car. Truth, like justice, is a fiction. We must reach conclusions based upon the available evidence. We must reach conclusions to put old ghosts to rest.

I felt profoundly tired when I got back to the hotel. The pomaded clerk shot me a brilliant smile and ducked down beneath the counter. I walked slowly up the giant staircase, hung with portraits of the great Mughal emperors and stumbled down towards our room. Susan looked up enquiringly as I came in, but I could think of nothing to say. 'He finally got the message. We leave tomorrow,' she said, moving from the wardrobe to the case and folding our clothes before putting them neatly away. A little later she said hesitantly, 'Was it OK then?' as though enquiring how a case had gone. I felt a little ashamed of my boorishness. 'I only wanted to find something,' I said. 'But there was nothing there.' It was one of those moments when words seem inadequate to express any of the essentials. I sat on the bed recalling Roger Henshaw's bungalow. Susan walked across and touched my cheek and said, 'That's all right then, isn't it?' in her condescending adult-reassuring-child voice.

For the rest of the visit I was a tourist again, touched lightly by the beauty of the great palaces, the temples; all too often glad to be back in the luxurious anonymity of an air-conditioned hotel.

At Heathrow there was a message for me to call my sister Anne. It was years since we had last spoken and I knew, without being told, what she would have to say. The chill in her voice was an unmistakable warning against intimacy. I turned into the perspex booth, trying to shut out the bustle of the crowd. Susan was waiting by the luggage, looking at her watch, impatient to be off. She exonerated me from blame for the delay with a smile and I smiled back, even as Anne told me that Mother had died in her sleep two nights before. Later, I felt guilty to recollect my first reaction to the news – that there would now be no interested audience to hear the conclusions I had reached. And later still, even as I felt the beginnings of a deeper sense of loss, it was ameliorated by a transient insight. It seemed to me then (that night, when I had come down to the darkened drawing room unable to sleep) that I had broken the patterns of inheritance, the repetitions I saw so clearly in the lives of my friends. During those hours it seemed to me that I was now free, beyond the reach of the chimaeras which had remained with me as an ever-present reminder of the apprehensions of childhood. There was a strange emptiness to those hours, before I had begun to grieve. As though empty vistas, robbed of fantasy, obligation, desire, comradeship, want, need, stretched endlessly ahead. It seemed then that India had finally delivered Nirvana to me in a strange guise, unwanted and unsought.

I felt oddly unsettled to be back. I couldn't raise much enthusiasm for Duffy's appeal, though he seemed satisfied enough after my visit. 'Walter Schnafel said you were the best,' he said fixing me with a proprietorial look through the pebble lenses, and I said, 'We'll have to see what we can do.' But walking through the great quadrangle back to my Chambers under a sullen November sky, I had already thrown the appeal in my mind. There was no doubt of Duffy's guilt and I found myself thinking that truth and justice should not be on hire to the highest bidder. A late conscience. Irritably, I hoped it would go away. As I was soon to discover from Carew, it wasn't infectious.

There had seemed a paucity of promising cases on my return. Mr Henderson, balding, fifty-ish, richer than me, our Managing Clerk, was a shade evasive. Clearly all the interesting cases had been unable to wait for my return. Even more clearly, Carew had done me a favour in taking them over. 'Getting married in a month's time,' Henderson ventured, glad to escape my probing for a moment.

On the third day on the stairs I met Carew, carrying a bundle of ribbon-bound affidavits, his dress agreeably askew like an untidy schoolboy. I fancied he had the grace to look sheepish, though he put a good face on things. 'Hm. Not as you remember it?' he said, more as a statement than a fact, trying to look shrewd and wise. I felt obliged to be enthusiastic for a few moments. 'Really. Really,' he said, irritatingly unconvinced. I couldn't resist saying, 'I see she's forcing you to work hard,' and felt immediately contrite, seeing his face fall. 'Well,' he said. 'Gilded youth must turn to sober age. It happens to all of us.'

Over the next few weeks I knew that the change was fundamental. I no longer found the old comfort in the prosaic conventionality of my former life. When the Raynors came to dinner and Harold, his face covered by the fine broken lines of rich living, extolled the virtues of their holiday, I murmured polite responses, but was desperately aware of a profound sense of boredom. One Saturday, listening to Mollie Ironside arranging the details of a bring-and-buy sale, I was surprised to find myself reflecting uncharitably on bored well-to-do housewives trying to find some justification for their existence. There seemed no further pleasure in discussing opera with the Wyndhams, or inviting any of our acquaintances in for a bridge evening. I recognized this, like my thoughts on guilt and justice, as part of a dissatisfaction which went beyond a mere ennui with our social life, to some more basic recognition that I had cut myself off from my past in a way that was no longer tenable.

It was, and is, all in the mind. Susan suspected an affaire, and I had to curb my tongue when she used to arrive unexpectedly at the Chambers. For some weeks she examined my lapels for alien hair. Other things, too. No. What she couldn't recognize and even I couldn't articulate for a long time was something new. I could see, now, that we are all cannibals, preying upon one another. At work, in marriage, between siblings, the principle holds to a remarkable degree. Most of all it seemed to me, in marriage. I was too passive to pursue any dream of solitude, though the dream is there. Who would wash and iron my shirts, or accompany me to the theatre when I was in need of stimulation, or accommodate with mutuality my infrequent lust? Marshalling my facts, I concluded that my losses were Carew's gains, or Susan's, and my gains their losses. There was a tolerable equilibrium, a balance, and while there was no soaring joy, neither was there raging despair.

A sad footnote to the Duffy case, from which I cannot entirely dissociate myself. I had forborn to help Carew on the appeal, partly from pique at his taking the case over, and partly from a conviction of Duffy's guilt. Two days before the appeal Carew dropped by and said, 'Have you heard? He's hung himself.' It took me a moment to realize he wasn't making another half sick, half wishful-thinking comment about our indolent Head of Chambers. We sit far enough from the real flesh and blood to dismiss such things, to lie abed easy, but I could imagine, all too graphically, that overweight figure strung lifeless from the bars of a prison cell. He probably used his belt, not being considered a high risk. 'The irony is,' said Carew, 'that we had new evidence which made it ninety per cent certain that it wasn't him.' I couldn't tell whether his melancholia was for Duffy or for the loss of a lucrative case. So much for my intuition and circumstantial evidence!

My instinct (my Head of Chambers used to say, 'Lawyers don't follow instincts – only facts') told me that something perverse – even evil, if that is not too fanciful a word – lay at the heart of what happened. I did not think my parents were involved, not from the blindness of filial obligation, but because the clear, pure apprehensions of childhood sometimes visited me with a sort of truth. From them I knew, beyond doubt, that in the imperfect way of human beings, Jane and Anthony had once loved and been concerned about each other. I knew this in the same way as, without employing specious reasoning and tortuous legal semantics, I was convinced of my own fundamental decency, and of my affection, au fond, for Susan and our son. Despite those other thoughts which were still true fragments of my belief, this was the cohesive force which made life tolerable. And I believed that this decency and affection came from them, and their possession of it would, in itself, have prevented their involvement in those events which took place under the cover of Partition.

Evils often lie within systems of thought which create, through the abstract beauty of their logic, a moral blindness. Nazism, Apartheid, the Stalinist purges ignored or justified the immediate and specific suffering in apparent pursuit of some general ideal. Those tired old words trotted out ad infinitum: the end justifies the means; you can't make an omelette without breaking eggs. Each generation wreaks upon the unmoulded clay of its successors in turn what has been wrought upon it before. There is continuity. The child is father to the man. The central dilemma is the correct way of feeling and acting towards those who are trapped by their inheritance. The old morality has gone and good and bad gone wandering in the void. Nor is there any virtue in sterile judgements, although, to children, they afford security.

There were those whom I knew with certainty, again, as children know such things, had grown up and escaped their pasts. My uncle Vincent, my Aunt Angela, perhaps (though then I was a child indeed) Joginder and Sita. They seemed to see with clearer eyes, to feel with hearts which had recognized that life is a solitary business whose responsibility cannot be shared or passed to others. About the others I was not sure. Grandmother, Uncle Rod, Aunt Patricia, Doctor Mackenzie. In the absence of facts, of crucial evidence, my doubts remained, and I could not exonerate them entirely from some complicity in what happened.

I have done something which it is beyond my own powers to fathom. The first evening of the Christmas holidays, after our son Andrew had finally gone to bed, Susan came in and sat on the arm of my chair, where I was going through some papers. She smiled and ruffled my hair, leaning against me so that I could feel her ribs against my shoulder and her warm flank against my forearm. (There's life in the old dog yet.) 'That boy,' she said, her brown hair falling across her face, and her lips amused at some memory. 'He wants to get a pet. I've told him he can have something provided it doesn't need too much attention. After all, we'll have to look after it while he's at school. What do you think?' She stooped and kissed me on the forehead.

Suddenly, unaccountably, I felt happy. 'I'll think of something,' I said, already picturing the grass snake in the aquarium in Andrew's room. 'Leave it to me.' When I kissed her she broke free, smoothing her hair nervously and holding out her hand in an unconscious gesture of rejection. 'Remember we're not alone,' she said warningly, and for a moment I recalled the taste of her sunwarmed hair in my mouth on a deserted beach in Cornwall so many years before. When we were young.

The pet shop tried to persuade me to take a lizard, but three weeks later I took home a reticulated python, paid for by the foot. Susan won't come into the room, and I must confess I have to turn away when he (I always think it is a he) eats his live white mouse. It is inexplicable, though. I can sit for hours watching him. He lies, coil upon coil, almost immobile, in one corner of the glass case. His eye fixes me unwinkingly, glossy, black, alien. Sometimes a vibration disturbs him and his head comes slowly up, and his tongue flickers between his lips. Then he brings his head down again. I feel some strange affinity, beyond words, with him. What are his thoughts? How does the world seem to him from behind that glass wall? I can only speculate. There is something in him which stirs some dusty primitive imagery in my brain. In his presence I can venture to a surreal imaginary world, where I am no longer bound by narrow habit. He has the power to release dreams in me.

Lastly, conclusions. We all live by selective fictions. Andrew Carew (now proud father of twin sons, a pillar of the local church, his Mercedes Sports traded in for a sober Daimler, ha! ha!) was right. I have become used to sitting in the cave and drawing my conclusions from the flickering shadows on the wall. It is too bright to look at the fire in whose heart Reality lies.

I am constantly aware that there could be – is – more in the sum of the hidden parts between Susan and me than we are capable of expressing now. We devalue each other in our summary judgements. Mine, at their most extreme, being that her preoccupations are materialistic and petty (though I know this is a partial and unfair view). Hers that I have abrogated ambition and responsibility for some mystic and unproductive communion with my past. Yet, buried under the trivia of mutual annoyance, the detritus of everyday living, the caps I leave off the toothpaste tubes, the briefs she tidies away into a drawer, there is somewhere that sharp, pure apprehension of how it all once was. The synchronization has gone so that the moments which unexpectedly restore that first tenderness to me have no resonance for her; and I, in my turn, can only show my hard exterior at times when I can see a vulnerability from long ago in her face. It is the accept-ance of the trivia which, paradoxically, giving us an apparently clear representation of the way things are, makes life both easier and less rewarding. But it is the waste that remains and kills.

When these thoughts come round, usually in autumn with its melancholy darkness and russet leaves, I am reminded of some friends of ours. It was Raymond's fourth marriage, and a late one for him, and when we met they had had the love child who had finally led to Gillian's break with her first husband. Already there were the small signs of wear and tear. Her lips tightening when he nodded off for a moment once after dinner. His habit of saying patronizingly to her, 'Well, as you'll find out in due course . . .' Within three years it had developed into a full-scale war carried on indiscriminately wherever they happened to be – all too often, it seemed to me, in our living room during a party or after dinner. Then, one November evening, Gillian came round on her own. She was a large blonde girl with rather pasty, bland good looks, and a usually ebullient manner. That evening her manner was overlaid with something graver, and her eyes seemed bruised and full of pain. She'd sat for a while at the edge of the chair, twisting her ring nervously with her untouched sherry by her side. When she spoke her voice was shocked, disbelieving, as though we could reassure her that what she was saying must be untrue. Raymond had gone to the doctor for some tests a few weeks previously. They had completely forgotten about them and she had been surprised when the doctor dropped round in the morning while Raymond was out. Terminal cancer, he had said, upset by his own directness but seeing no other way. She would be the best judge of whether or not he should be told.

She had decided not, though it seemed most likely to me over the next few weeks that he knew. But what happened then was like a miracle. It was as if that great shadow had purged all the pettiness from them at a stroke, so that they existed again in some pristine state of mutual

65

dependence. His patronage disappeared and she seemed to welcome the chance to minister to his infirmities. 'The time I have wasted in useless anger . . .' she said once, when he had left the room.

In the last few weeks, even concerned visits seemed like an intrusion. They spoke little, to each other or in response to our standard fractured news of the outside world. Whatever the vision he saw with his dimming eyes which grew remoter from us at each visit, she saw it also. When she looked at him there was a new acceptance in her face of him in his totality. He no longer attempted to hide his frailties from her. Now, seven years after his death, his grave always has fresh flowers upon it, and she has never remarried. It is always the best she remembers, expunging those years before. But who can disentangle where love ends and guilt begins, or state with certainty the composition of a feeling? And must we wade through years of indifference before the advance battalions of mortality call forth these responses from each other?

I have decided I cannot be a Judge. That would require me to be the Court of last resort, and play the game with belief, without a confessor to bear away my doubts. It is the last mystery which has shown me my frailty. I worry about it as I prune the roses and trim the box hedge. In church I even sometimes remember St Paul's saying, Nunc videmus per speculum in enigmata. Tunc, autem, facie ad faciem. The thought of an ultimate almost restores my faith, for I wish to believe in absolute answers at the last.

When I think of my father, still, I cannot do so without weeping. That is, when I really think of him. On those picnics where the sun shone through the giant trees as through a great cathedral's clerestory and the stream laughed beyond the clearing, growing louder as we approached along the needled floor. He seemed a god, a friendly earthbound god. Did he really know everything? Could he really beat all the other fathers? It doesn't matter. I knew, beyond words, that he would always value me, whatever I might do. At the first, as far back as I can remember, there was that feeling of absolute safety. It was in Mysore that the change occurred – or perhaps just a little before. There was a day in Mysore that I remember now. Perhaps it was my last day with my father.

When he left, I saw it as a betrayal, unable to comprehend that there might be circumstances beyond even his power to control. I can only think, now, that there was some struggle which defeated him. What happened when he returned to Murree is something for which even I, skilled advocate that I am, can offer no reasonable conclusions. I wish that I might have attended a decent funeral. Stood over the open coffin, I would have seen the dead face for the last time, and the terrible process of grieving and separation could have begun. That was denied; and I never could believe my mother's idealized suggestions, nor understand Dr Mac's veiled hints. All I can divulge with certainty, is my own never-ending, private sense of loss. Why did you leave me, Father? Why did you leave me?

Murree, Punjab: 1940

Four

Gunevati, the whore, walked slowly up the path from the village. It was Saturday, and she normally stayed at home and cooked for her elderly mother and aunt. But business had been slow the past few weeks and on the previous day she had only had three clients: the boys from the school, and a visiting Eurasian trader who had turned out not to have enough money to pay her the full rate. Like her mother and aunt before her, she often dreamed of retiring, of buying a field from Feroze Khan and keeping a few goats and a chicken or two. She daydreamed thus on her way up the path, fixing her property up in her mind as she went. Young Afzal could put the fence up. Hosein, the builder, could mend the roof where the last monsoon had torn a hole in the thatching. She could relax and tend the animals and the crops.

She stopped and rested on the path at the corner where it had a vantage point over the entire valley, a plump, handsome woman of almost forty with thready marks at the corners of her eyes and mouth from grimacing against the white sun. The water here, ten yards from the path, threw itself in an arcing cataract down the mountain-side. Idly she imagined assigning the building of her own private irrigation channel to another young workman. Over the years she had developed in her mind a complex picture of her property as it would be.

This was her favourite spot, and she always stopped

both on the way up and the way down to look across the valley to the mountains. From the room rented from Feroze's father in the bazaar she could see the mountains. She still remembered a trip to Rawalpindi ten years before. It had been so exciting to think of it, but when the day came she had felt her spirits sink as the bus wound its way down the hairpin bends to the level plains below. The traffic, and the houses huddled all together without enough space in between, and the noise! She shuddered to remember it, hauling the bottom of her sari up again and rehitching it into the waistband before she turned to resume her slow walk upwards. The path meandered ahead, past monolithic boulders and into the dark wood which sat in the collarbone of the great crag, before it resumed its erratic winding out the other side and up towards the houses hanging from the towering rim of rock. It was hot now, and she grumbled to herself, mopping her face and between her pendulous breasts with a soiled rumal. Once in the woods it was cooler. The wind shirred through the pines and the bushes danced endlessly reflecting the light in points from their shining leaves. Lizards scurried ahead across the path lifting their prehistoric heads and vibrating their tongues to assess her approach.

When she reached the rock by the stunted pine she sat down and removed her sandals. She took a drink from the lotah she carried at her waist and sprinkled the remainder of the water on her feet. Behind her in the forest a twig cracked and she turned to look into the grey-green interior. She could see nothing but the tree trunks receding into the distance and, beyond them, the sun burning the yellowed grass. She took a piece of chapati from the bag at her waist and began to eat, her throat hurting as the saliva flowed into her mouth.

The first blow hit her behind the right ear and she felt the thick taste of blood in her mouth. There was no pain, only the sensation of falling and a singing in her head. With surprise she recognized the figure standing above her, and, still unable to understand what had happened, tried to speak. Her tongue felt thick and swollen. The man was fumbling at her clothing and she tried to smile through blood-caked lips, to say that it was all right. The sound of her own voice croaking frightened her and she began to fight.

She felt nothing after the second blow. Behind her eyes the red slowly faded. Briefly she remembered her father looking for her in the garden. I was how old then, five? six? she wondered. 'Guneeee! Guneee!' he called, and she felt a strange excitement in her stomach as he walked towards the bush she crouched behind. The scene faded to black.

Superintendent Anwar led the way down the path. He walked delicately for such a bulky man, lifting his arms to balance himself with oddly feminine gestures. Behind him Roger Henshaw followed, still in the tennis whites he had been wearing when Anwar had arrived at the Club. There were no replays or delays allowed under Club Rules, so Dr Mackenzie would probably win the tournament.

There was a group of villagers standing on the path watching the two constables who guarded the blanket-covered body on the ground. Anwar broke into a run, flourishing his swagger stick at them. 'Go back to the village. This is nothing for idle curiosity.' His voice trembled with disgust. When one of the constables moved towards them, one of the older men signalled them to follow and they began to walk down the hill. Anwar watched until they were out of sight and then gestured the other man to remove the blanket from the body. The eyes were open, staring sightlessly at the sky, and the flesh had been torn from one arm, possibly by jackals. Ants swarmed blackly by the wound on the head. Her sari was drawn up to her thighs and her legs splayed apart. Henshaw felt his stomach heave. He looked at Anwar and thought, My God, he must have to do this all the time. 'Who found her?' he said, and Anwar gestured towards the valley. 'One of the young men was coming up to buy ghee. She must have been here two days by then.'

Roger saw Anwar's hand shaking as he tried to light a bidi. He put a hand on the other man's shoulder briefly and said, 'Have you begun your enquiries?' Anwar nodded, drawing until the cheroot showed a red, even tip. 'The police doctor is coming to look at the body in situ. When we have an approximate time of death we can start to reconstruct her last hours.' After a while Roger said carefully, 'I'm still not completely sure why you asked me to come. This is a police matter, isn't it?'

Anwar stubbed his bidi out on the rock, flicking it in a high arc into the ferns below. He took a handkerchief out of his pocket and wiped his hands. 'I brought you here because it seems to me that there are unusual features to this case,' he said carefully, removing a shred of tobacco from his lip with his forefinger. 'Murders of this type are extremely rare within our own community.' His voice took on a pleading, embarrassed tone. 'I have to consider the possibility that this crime may have been carried out by . . . er . . . one of the other racial groups from this area.' He looked down into the valley, avoiding the other man's eyes.

Henshaw said easily, 'Of course, Superintendent. Nobody can be excluded from such an enquiry unless they could not possibly have committed the crime.' He looked back at the blanket-swathed body and said reflectively, 'I'm sure Dr Aziz will find evidence of sexual molestation. That offers a lead, doesn't it?'

One of the constables shouted, pointing his lathi up the hill. Dr Aziz was stumbling down, carrying his battered Gladstone bag. He really was the most unco-ordinated man, Roger reflected, momentarily diverted by the sight of the doctor tripping erratically down the hill, mouthing curses at the rocks and shrubs which barred his progress. Aziz was more English than the English, only really at home in the house incongruously cluttered with English nineteenth-century water-colours and ornamental bric-a-brac. He fell and the sound of a shouted curse came faintly down the valley.

Anwar's voice was troubled when he spoke, and it took Roger a moment to remember what they had been discussing. 'Everyone knew that Gunevati only charged a few annas. No, this is about something else . . .' They waited in silence for the doctor to arrive.

Rawalpindi, Punjab: 1946

Five

It was evening before Anthony had sufficient leisure to read his copy of *The Times of India*. Late summer evenings in Rawalpindi always produced a torpid relaxation in him. He spread out his long legs with a sigh of satisfaction – a tall, diffident, blond man in his midthirties with the unremarkable good looks of a school games captain, the years sitting lightly on him. As a boy his mother had often said, with loving disparagement, 'You'll never be a leader like your father, Anthony,' and he had accepted the slight with his customary appearance of equanimity. But under the passive mask and the self-deprecating manner which had acted as a protection all his life, a little canker of anger at being thus categorized had burned for year after year.

That morning his Brahmin administrative assistant, Guruchunder Singh, had brought him the news of the riots. Gur, son of Anthony's old friend, Joginder, had fallen silent over the bitter coffee and then added with characteristic wryness, 'Now you will see Mother India devouring her sons.' But outside the traffic still droned lazily past, and the malis toiled over the sun-drenched flower beds, and Anthony had turned back to his work and forgotten both the news and Gur's comment for the rest of the day. Only now, on the verandah, with the stengah the house servant, Lal Deen, had brought him on the glass-covered rattan table by his side, did he sense that something he had denied, even to himself, had begun, and there was no going back.

The muezzin had sounded and, beyond the white paling fence which demarcated the edge of the compound, the sunset had begun to suffuse the pale horizon in a reddish glow, lighting the edges of the thin, trailing clouds with a brilliant golden nimbus. The heat was dying too, minute by minute, and a light breeze threatened to snatch the paper so that Anthony had to fold it to prevent it blowing away.

On the edge of the verandah his eight-year-old son, Mark, sat propped against the white stucco wall reading *The Jungle Book*, his freckled brown legs stretched in front of him. He had the olive skin and black hair of his mother, and something of her quick instinctive movements. Anthony watched him for a moment, envious of his complete absorption, before turning back to his paper. The Moslem League had proclaimed 16 August 1946 'Direct Action Day', intending to prove by their actions to both Britain and the Congress Party that India's Muslims were prepared to create their own territory, Pakistan, Land of the Pure, by force if necessary. The paper carried feature articles on the ensuing massacres. There were even some blurred photographs.

Anthony took a sip from his glass, wiping the bottom with a forefinger to remove the rim of moisture. Looking across at Mark, still engrossed in his book, his mind wandered. In three months he would be thirty-six, but the knowledge of the impending changes which had filtered into the office and were discussed in the club had begun to affect him. He felt like an old man, destroyed by uncertainty. Pull yourself together, he thought crossly, aware that the obiter dicta from his childhood were meaningless and impotent, but afraid, presented with matters beyond his control.

He remembered his colleagues at the office and their conviction that these riots were only a temporary disturbance. Roger Henshaw had dismissed any suggestion that anything would change. 'They'll break a few heads, burn a few houses, commit a few rapes. Then it'll all be over. You'll see,' he had said with the absolute conviction he brought to everything, and Parsons had nodded his agreement. It was only in Andrew Prescott that Anthony had felt a reflection of his own unease.

Anthony could no longer shake off the feeling that a way of life, which had continued unchanged in all its essentials since his grandfather, James Hodder, had come out to work for John Company, was now under threat. Though Anthony had suggested half-heartedly to Jane that they should go to England when Mark went to public school it had been a diffident gesture, without substance. Home to him was Simla in the hot weather and Rawalpindi when it was cool; bridge, polo, racing, and the comforts of the European Club when the round of dinners and dances began to pall. Now, with the shadowy prospect of loss ahead, it suddenly felt dear to him, artificially dispossessed of the host of minor irritations it had in real life.

Anthony's own childhood in Simla had been imbued with a flavour of moral definition which had assumed a greater reality than the prosaic details of life in the bungalow, sheltered in the lee of the great hill. True, he remembered the faded tapestry cushions, the parquet flooring, the primitive sanitation, the zinc baths which would be full of beetles and moths, and the mosaic of details which made up lives lived at the fringes of Empire, where sophistication was his father having a drink on the verandah with his friends after a day's work, and luxury a second-hand iron bed with real springs which the coolies had brought laboriously up the hill when he was six. But far more than that, it had been a childhood of aphorisms, of moral parables, and hints at some eternal and immutable laws which conferred certainty and safety, but in the course of so doing removed responsibility and free will from the individual. From his father, out riding or walking the cocker spaniels, the phrases came from the Bible or the classics. 'Man must suffer to be wise,' he would say to Anthony, looking down at his son, struggling up the steep hill path beside him or trying to check the prancing iron-mouthed pony. Or, upon hearing of some local tragedy, he would shake his large head, the brown hair grizzled with grey at the temples, and assume a look of self-conscious melancholy while delivering himself of some phrase such as, 'Call no man happy until he is dead.'

These phrases, reverberating with the echoes of profound thoughts, conferred a mythic quality to his father in Anthony's eyes. These tenets, and the more homely adages dispensed by his mother about stitches in time or the devil finding work for idle hands, entered into the warp and weft of his life. He had accepted them with the uncritical belief of a child and, together with his own perceptions, they formed a coherent but rigid view of life in which each action, each thought, was referred automatically to some internal moral arbiter bearing a passing likeness to his father, whose iron precepts defined the only path to the good life.

Even the sudden death of his parents had not shaken the sure foundations. Later, at public school in England paid for by the Freemasons, he found the codifications endorsed and expanded. Dr Hammond, his housemaster, made no secret of his aversion to women. 'He's queer,' said Anthony's friend, Wilen Minor, disgustedly, after they had attended a compulsory tea with Dr Hammond in his study. 'Dirty old bugger,' and they had indulged themselves in a few coarse jokes and sniggers at Old Ham's expense. But Anthony still felt that Hammond, as a grown up, was the possessor of some vital insight which approximated closer to the truth in things than Wilen's dismissive evaluation would allow of. 'He pees all down the front of his trousers. Didn't you see?' said Wilen. 'That's not tea. It's where he shakes his knob,' and he gave a graphic exhibition of Dr Hammond urinating, grasping his trousers and swishing an imaginary spray of urine up and down the panelled wall of the corridor, until the games master, with a bemused glance, hurried them down the corridor.

As the years passed, the theorems had lain dustily in his mind, unacknowledged in discussions with others, or even in his everyday consciousness. That love between the sexes was war. That bitter medicines were good. That there were correct and proper places in life for men and women, and that men were superior, more ethereal and closer to the angels. He hid these burdens in the subtle recesses of his mind, and people said he was 'a good sort', and that he had 'his head screwed on right', and one or two of the ladies secretly fancied themselves a little bit in love with him.

At thirty-six his boyish, worried good looks and the diffidence of his manner only increased his attraction for the ladies of the Tennis Club. His wife, Jane, reprimanded him once or twice, with a guarded crossness, for his politeness. 'It's 1946 not 1916 you know. All this leaping up and down every time a woman comes into the room. It really isn't necessary.' But he had persisted, unable to rid himself of the ingrained habit, and eager to please and pacify and be thought well of. Occasionally he surprised in himself an unexpected anger with Jane, or with Mark or his daughter, Anne, which frightened him by its violence. But it always passed quickly, never breaking into open argument, or an unpleasant scene.

Mark put down his book, breaking his father's reverie. He put his knees up, making a bridge for his chin with his arms, and looked across at Anthony. He loved this time of day when he sat with his father on the verandah in a companionable silence. The book was all right, but really part duty, part family tradition. 'If you don't read Kipling you'll never understand India,' his grandmother had written in her neat, crabbed writing. So, he had sat down each evening for the past fortnight to read at the edge of the verandah while his father worked or read the paper in the cane chair by the front door.

He heard his mother call the servant inside the house, and he saw his father sigh, momentarily disturbed by the noise, and then resume his melancholy, abstracted perusal of the garden.

From the corner of his eye Mark saw a movement, just where the rounded bevel edge of the verandah had crazed and cracked in the earthquake three years before. At first he thought it was a lizard, as the pale head came into sight moving with rapid, darting movements from side to side, the thin black tongue flickering like a tuning fork. But when the head cleared the edge of the concrete and the reptile began to move he realized it was a snake. It moved slowly, with a winding motion, towards Anthony's brown Oxford shoe, and Mark said urgently, 'Daddy, daddy!' He pointed towards the snake and Anthony nodded, smiling, sitting completely still. When he spoke his tone was light and conversational. 'He won't harm me. Don't worry.' The snake moved forward, winding awkwardly over the concrete until the curve of its throat rested on Anthony's shoe, and Mark held his breath.

Behind Anthony the door opened and Jane came out on to the verandah with a drink in her hand. She started to say something and then stopped, following Mark's gaze. 'Oh, my God,' she said, putting her hand to her mouth. She moved swiftly through the door and Mark could hear her calling Lal Deen in panic-stricken tones. The snake moved unhurriedly away and slowly, like a drop of water suspended from a gutter, hung for a moment on the edge before sliding out of sight into the pelargoniums.

Lal Deen came to the door with a lathi in his hand, and Jane peered fearfully out behind him. 'Where is it?' she asked, and Anthony waved the servant away with an irritated gesture. 'Gone,' he said, and then, looking at her, 'Why do people need to kill things they don't understand? As I've told you before, they're harmless unless you hurt them.'

Jane looked at him for a long moment, and Mark could see her mouth tightening into a thin, grim line. 'You might at least think of the safety of our son,' she said, and Mark could feel the anger in her. She went inside, banging the door behind her. There was an unpredictability about her which went with the gipsy colouring, the quick, controlled gestures.

It was almost dark. Anthony lit a cheroot and blew the smoke towards the house, stretching luxuriously. 'He is the house god,' he said, 'and he is here to protect us.' He smiled, and Mark knew that it was a grown-up smile, containing some meaning inaccessible to him. 'But snakes are male gods, and some women don't like them.' On the road the cars had begun to use headlights, crawling like glow-worms, too far for the sound to carry.

Mark said, 'It was a poisonous one, wasn't it, daddy? Do people worship them?' and Anthony nodded, grinding out the cheroot in the ashtray. 'In Egypt snakes were so regarded that the cobra – the uraeus – formed part of the Pharaoh's double crown. The Romans used to put food out for them and let them live in their houses and sanctuaries. In Bangkok there is a temple where the snakes are allowed to roam free, and the priests feed and protect them.' He gazed towards the faint red line of the horizon, intent to catch the last gleam of twilight. From the garden a nightjar began to call, and inside the dinner gong sounded its muffled note.

Mark got up, dusting his shorts free of the concrete dust which lay like chalk along the creases. He said carefully, persistently, 'But snakes can kill you, can't they, daddy?' Anthony levered himself up from his chair and put an arm around the boy's shoulder.

'So could your closest friend, if you hurt him enough,' he said, and Mark could see in the waning light that his face was serious.

Roger: 1921

Six

The boy walked down the hill past the row of huddled houses to the butcher's shop. Hardly houses, but tenements, pebble-dashed in brown with identical unwashed lace curtains behind the dirty panes. From Scarth Nick, towering above, damp, woody, secret smells drifted down to mingle with the oily smell of fish and chips. To the north the clouds brooded massively and he felt slicks of rain against his face.

His clothes were too small, his arms hanging well beyond the cuffs, his top shirt button undone, three years too small for the man's body. Cuckoo, his mother used to call him, frequently wondering aloud how he could grow so fast on 'the sort of food we can afford'. This with a sideways look at her husband who would always say mildly, 'Leave the boy alone. He can't help it.' But the boy, with the wisdom of youth, knew that she only used him to express her disappointment with his father.

He stood outside the shop for a moment, watching his father serving a large woman in a fur coat with a boy in Rydal School uniform. When she turned to point at a great carcass hanging from a hook at the back of the shop, he recognized Mrs Whiteoak from the big house on the Bolton estate. 'I don't want that tired-looking meat, Mr Henshaw. All that dried blood. Cut me a piece from that leg.' Her voice was assured, imperious. Beside her James snickered. His blazer and flannels were immaculate. Mr

Henshaw turned to take down the carcass, and beckoned Roger to come into the shop, out of the rain which was now coming down in earnest.

Roger stood in the corner by the white-tiled slab covered in dried blood. The visceral, bloody smell disturbed him, and he averted his eyes from the two scrawny chickens hanging by their feet above the counter. '. . . take you to Paris with us . . .' Mrs Whiteoak was saying to James, but the boy was looking at Roger, smiling with derision. In the back, there was the dull thump of the chopper cutting into meat. Mrs Whiteoak stopped talking and looked round, and Roger saw her eyes look him over as though he were a member of some other species. She bent her head and said in a stage whisper, 'James, you mustn't stare at people less fortunate than yourself. That poor boy is to be pitied. He'll never have your opportunities . . .' but James, with the innate savagery of small boys towards those who don't conform, began to laugh, pointing at Roger and saying, 'He looks like something from the circus. Look at his trousers.'

From the back room, Mr Henshaw's voice sounded hollowly. 'I'm sorry to take so long, Mrs Whiteoak. I won't be a minute,' the words had a pleading deference, distorted by the echo. A car coughed laboriously past, scrabbling over the tarmac in first gear. Something provoked James Whiteoak to fresh laughter. It was suddenly intolerable and Roger ran down the length of the counter towards his tormentor. Mrs Whiteoak screamed and tried to interpose her bulk between the two boys. Her feet went from under her and she fell heavily on the sawdust-covered floor. Even as she slid away to land against the counter with her hat askew over her eyes and her plump, bestockinged legs spread in obscene display, Roger had hold of James's neck in both his hands and had begun to beat the boy's head against the desk on which the cash-till stood. The till rocked precariously, then fell, showering the two boys with coppers and silver, clinking across the floor. It could only have been a few seconds before Roger felt his father's hand on his collar, and the quiet voice saying, 'Come on, lad. That's not the way to do things.' Getting to his feet he was gratified to see James had a black eye, and blood running from his lip.

The two boys glared at each other while Mr Henshaw lifted Mrs Whiteoak to her feet. 'That boy,' she said, when she stood up, pointing her finger with venomous exclamation, 'is worse than an animal.' She beckoned James and walked out of the shop, and the boy scooped up a couple of coins from the floor and ran to the door, pausing to look defiantly at Roger before he left.

His father's hand tightened on Roger's shoulder. 'Let him go. It doesn't matter,' Mr Henshaw said quietly.

Roger's father got down on his knees and began to collect the coins. In a few moments he began the racking cough again, and the big shrunken face became pale and sweaty. 'Pick them up, will you, lad? I'll just sit down and get my breath back for a moment.'

It was half an hour before Mr Henshaw's colour was better. Guilt-ridden, Roger had cleaned the shop up for the night. The carcases, red and blue-veined with the terrible nakedness of death, went into the cold room. Hanging them took all his strength, his breath spurting like hoar frost into the dim grey light. Sponging the slab so that the congealed blood slipped down crustily in the pinkening water to the draining runnel, sweeping the sawdust, muddied to mire grey from trampling feet, into the corner and then using the rusted dustpan and brush to tidy the floor, he looked surreptitiously at the figure slumped in the chair fighting for breath. He spread Dusmo over the floor in brown heaps, sweeping with furious, jabbing strokes, as if to expunge his guilt, until Mr Henshaw said, 'That's enough, son. You'll wear the floor away,' laughing in breathless gusts.

Afterwards he locked up the premises and walked with Roger down to the chip shop. He waved Roger's apologies away. 'They're no loss, son. She comes in mebbe three times a year and it's always trouble.' He sucked his fingers appreciatively, delving into the sodden newspaper cornet until the vinegary crumbs were all gone. They walked slowly up the hill. The rain had stopped and small flies hung above their heads. The dying sun like blotting paper drew the light from the sky beyond the elms on the hill ridge, and the field below, covered in rosebay willowherb, cowslips and vetch, gave up its colour slowly to the dusk. At the gate he paused and said apologetically to Roger, 'We would have sent you to one of those places if we could have afforded it, son. There just wasn't the money. Now, this had better be our secret. No point in upsetting your mother.'

When later, he heard their voices in the next bedroom, he shut his ears. He had finished his book about the mutiny from the library and he imagined himself as an officer in the Indian Army. The voices faded into the background as he left the village behind, and, once more, rode ahead of his patrol into the waste of the North-West Frontier.

Rawalpindi, Punjab: 1946

Seven

By September Anthony had begun to feel that Henshaw and Parsons had been right. There had been little further rioting and the news from England, culled from the yellow-covered monthly compilations of the *Daily Mirror*, was that Churchill was implacably opposed to Indian Home Rule, and that Attlee's administration was too insecure to contemplate forcing the Act through in the face of inevitable Conservative opposition. With the notable exception of Andrew Prescott, the workers who toiled in the Administrative Buildings had begun to return to their habitual complacency.

Roger Henshaw, who was now an occasional colleague of Anthony, as his contemporary and Collector for the Murree District, arrived in the office on the last Thursday of September for the monthly meeting in which difficult cases of law and administration were discussed, and said bluntly, 'They'll piss around for years playing this game. Gandhi controls Nehru and Patel and the Congress Party and he told us in 1942 he wouldn't accept the permanent vivisection of India. Jinnah wants separation on any terms – but the rumour is he's dying and there isn't anyone else with the stature to conclude the separation issue. People like Liaquat Ali Khan are all right, but,' he grimaced, spreading his hands, 'it'll be years before they get it together, if they ever do.'

It was hard to remember their college days together.

But, now, Anthony was relieved at Henshaw's certainty, even as he felt a renewed tremor of unease. Sometimes he thought uncomfortably that the dislike for Henshaw which had grown over the years had some connection with an envy for his complete certainty. There was something fleshy about him, something overblown, condescending, self-important. On the way to tiffin, down the featureless cream corridor along which the servants cleaned listlessly, sliding deferentially aside to let the Burra Sahibs past, Henshaw put his beefy red hand on Anthony's shoulder.

'You know, old man,' he said confidentially, blowing a whisky-laden breath in Anthony's direction, 'I think you should have a word with young Reeves. I'm told he's seeing a young Indian schoolteacher.' He took his hand from Anthony's shoulder and made a suggestive, pumping gesture with his right forearm, holding the bicep with his other hand. 'We're all broad-minded about a bit of fun, but he seems to be getting serious. Turned down an invitation to the Commemoration Ball because he couldn't take her.' Anthony felt a momentary disgust. He said stiffly, 'He's going on his familiarizing tour in a month's time. It will probably bring things to a natural conclusion without any fuss.'

Henshaw pushed open the door to the Mess, ushering Anthony through. He nodded vigorously. 'Good. Good,' and Anthony felt again the vague dislike and a brief sadness. Walking to an empty table in the corner, he saw once more how popular the man was, and felt a sneaking contempt for Parsons and Major Lawrence and the others for their lack of judgement. Only Prescott cast a cold eye over Henshaw and resumed reading his papers over his coffee with no sign of recognition.

Anthony had watched Roger Henshaw dispensing

judgement at two Durbars. Though he had been unable to fault the other man's judgements or the skill with which he had uncovered the kutchanal of the cases, he could see now an arrogance, a dismissiveness in his manner towards both plaintiff and defendant; it had seemed that his beady eye, resting unwinkingly for a moment longer than was required upon each speaker in turn, gave the game away. I'm British, the glance seemed to say. This may be life or death to you, but it's small beer to me.

As Roger walked through the tables in front of him, occasionally stopping to exchange a word here and there, Anthony looked at the massive head thrust forward belligerently on the short, bull-like neck and thought: I'm becoming priggish and unfair. We've just grown apart, that's all.

They sat at a table at the end of the panelled hall, by the side of the long windows giving out upon the rose gardens. The malis moved systematically down the beds, scraping the friable earth with their koorpis. In the room, motes of dust danced in the rays of the sun whilst overhead the three-bladed fans rotated slowly, cutting through the spirals of cigar smoke which rose from the crowded tables. Anthony saw Gur and waved involuntarily, cursing himself inwardly a moment after. But it was too late. His assistant was going to join them. Anthony stood up and Roger, too, rose reluctantly to his feet.

Gur was dressed impeccably in a white linen suit. Though in his early twenties he gave the impression of being much older. There was a wariness in his manner, and the boyish enthusiasm which Anthony remembered in him had been modified by a reserved watchfulness, a tendency towards hesitancy which had only grown upon him since he had worked in the predominantly British-staffed Administrative Offices.

Anthony indicated Henshaw and said, 'Gur, you remember Roger Henshaw? Collector, no . . .,' he corrected himself, 'I'm sorry, District Commissioner, Murree District. My assistant, Guruchunder Singh.' Gur smiled widely, showing white, even teeth, and held out his hand. After a moment's hesitation Henshaw took it, and Gur said, 'Murree, eh? I remember you coming to meet my father, Joginder Singh.' He laughed deprecatingly, adding, 'The zamindar. He lives on the Mall just below Lintott's Café.' His manner gave no sign that he remembered the picnics, or Henshaw's visits.

Henshaw nodded coolly, and Gur pulled a chair up to the table. Over pilao, sag gosth, dhal and chapatis, the talk turned to political matters. Henshaw was dogmatic in his assertion that neither Home Rule for a unified India nor Partition were possibilities. He sat forward on his chair, pushing the food aggressively down his throat. When he talked Anthony could see the grains of saffron rice spray on to the cloth and down the linen napkin tucked into his collar. In the face of Gur's insistence that both Home Rule and Partition were historically inevitable after the ignominious fall of Singapore, Roger's tone became louder, more hortatory.

'It can't happen,' he said stubbornly. 'The British and the Indian have lived in a mutually beneficial symbiotic relationship for three hundred and fifty years. First, India is not ready for self-governance. Second, Quaid-e-Azam's vision of separate Muslim and Hindu areas simply ignores the logistics of moving generations of polyglot communities who would be living in small, alien enclaves on the "wrong" side of the border.' He concentrated on tearing his chapati apart for a moment, laughing to himself as if at some private joke. 'So the Muslim League will provoke further riots and the Sikhs will counter-attack, and in the end the British will be the only force capable of dealing with the chaos.' He called imperiously to the bearer, 'Chokra. Finger bowli laow,' and sat with his fingers outstretched. Anthony shifted uneasily in his chair, concerned that, in the passion of his argument, Roger might have forgotten Gur's presence at the table.

'These people,' said Henshaw contemptuously, gesturing with an outflung arm to indicate the world beyond the window, 'have been policed, controlled, mollycoddled by the British since 1660. Even they will realize in time that self-government involves more than the mere shrugging off of imperial shackles.'

There was an awkward pause. Gur stood up abruptly. Anthony was horrified. He felt protective towards Gur, the feeling he might have were Anne or Mark to be subjected to an unfair attack. Some convention held him paralysed, while Roger dried his hands on the towel the bearer held out to him. Henshaw said, 'Goodbye, Mr Singh,' making no move to stand or to offer his hand. 'I should recommend that your parents move to somewhere like Amritsar. Even though nothing is going to happen I would agree that zamindars are unlikely to be popular in Murree.' When he smiled the corner of his top lip snagged temporarily on a tooth.

Gur bowed and clicked his heels together stiffly. Anthony wanted to put an arm around him, to absolve himself from blame, to distance himself from Henshaw. He put a hand on Gur's sleeve awkwardly and said, 'Come up with us for a picnic with your parents this weekend, eh? We'll arrange it.' Gur nodded gratefully, but the hurt was still in his eyes.

As Gur walked away, Henshaw looked speculatively at

Anthony, the syrup from the rasa gula he was eating leaking from the corner of his mouth. 'I can see I chose the wrong person to read Reeves the riot act,' he said.

Anthony said, 'You went too far again . . .' and was embarrassed to see several people at nearby tables turn curiously around to peer at him. Henshaw looked up and slowly wiped his face with his napkin before letting it slide to the polished floor. With his eyes still fixed on Anthony, he clicked his fingers and the bearer came over. He said peremptorily, 'Coffee laow,' glancing impersonally at the waiter before looking back at Anthony.

'Time you went Home, old man,' he said. 'When you start treating blackies like your own kind you let us all down.'

When Anthony got back to his office he felt ashamed. He had reached out instinctively to hit Roger and had slipped on the fallen napkin. Henshaw had helped him up with solicitous concern. 'You all right, old man? They certainly polish their floors well.' The sense of indignity displaced the momentary anger.

Out in the blinding sunshine, Henshaw had shouted for his syce to bring the jeep, and had left, waving, in a cloud of fine dust for the thirty-mile drive into the mountains. Walking back to his office down the long corridor, Anthony had felt the bruise on his hip and flushed at the memory.

All afternoon he felt hot and angry, reliving the scene. His anger came partly from a recognition of his own unwilling complicity in Henshaw's attitudes. His father's Fabianism, and the moral hypocrisy which he now recognized had imbued both his parents, had ruled out any direct comment on the segregation of the races. But it had been implicit in the fact that their parties were only attended by colonial neighbours, and veiled references to 'people being happiest with their own kind', and the now half-remembered memories of his father applying Darwin's theories to the development of separate races. He hated himself for holding such attitudes, but found them still too strong to set aside almost thirty years after his parents' deaths.

Gur came into his office at teatime and stood awkwardly in the doorway, sipping tea from a fine, bone china cup. 'Usual time on Saturday?' he asked, and Anthony said abstractedly 'Yes. Will you 'phone them and let me know if there are any problems?'

Gur paused by the door for a moment and said diffidently, 'Major Lawrence told me what you did. Thank you, mere mabap.' He joined his hands in the gesture of namaste, bowing with self-mocking deprecation.

Anthony had the sensation of something unfinished and was unable to settle to anything for the afternoon. The incident at lunchtime had induced a state of introspection, of dissatisfaction with himself. He picked up the papers relating to the following Friday's Durbar and was struck, for the first time, by the predominance of cases in which the plaintiff was a Sikh or a Hindu and the defendant Muslim. He felt suddenly hypocritical, placed in the role of prosecutor, defendant and judge. Outside the window four ayahs wheeled their charges in prams over the yellowing grass towards the summer house. The doves sat on the paving fanning their wings and spreading their tails in the sunshine. One or two, unaffected by the lassitude of the hot afternoon, strutted to and fro with swelling crops. Something in the sheer normality of the afternoon made Anthony feel momentarily afraid. He turned back to the papers on his desk wondering uneasily about the quality of the justice he had dispensed with such blithe self-confidence over the past six years.

He remembered the first Durbar he had attended on his familiarization course. It had been a murder case, involving a farmer who had beaten an intruder to death with a lathi. The District Commissioner handling the cases had been a burly Scotsman named McEvoy, with the florid complexion of a heavy drinker. Though he had confided that he was thirty, he had seemed much older to Anthony, with his dewlapped chins and dour, humourless expression. He and Anthony sat at a folding deal table whose legs were propped with stabilizing pebbles, in the open, under the spreading branches of a banyan which offered some welcome shade. Beyond, the heat shimmered from the whitewashed huts with their discoloured roundels where the cowpats had dried before being stored for fuel. McEvoy had listened to both sides without comment, making notes from time to time on a sheet of foolscap on the table before him. When the prosecuting counsel had finished he raised his heavy-lidded eyes and looked up at the farmer, a stocky, grey-bearded man of sixty-odd.

'Did you kill the man?' he asked, and the farmer cried angrily, 'Of course, Sahib. He was stealing my chickens. I hit him on the head with the lathi and he fell down. Then I hit him again and again when he was lying on the ground until the blood ran from his head.' The crowd of villagers nodded and muttered their approval. They seemed as uncomprehending as the farmer, who listened impassively as sentence of death was passed on him, walking away quietly between the two policemen.

McEvoy dealt with some administrative matters after that. When the Durbar was over Anthony walked with the burly Scot through the ambling crowd. 'He didn't seem to mind,' he said, wonderingly, still trying to come to terms with the farmer's fatalistic acceptance of the sentence. McEvoy walked ahead, his voice trailing back to Anthony over his shoulder. 'That was a straightforward one. There was no tetul gach shaksi – that is, a Bengali saying meaning a tamarind tree witness, one coached on the spot. There was no dastur – that is, bribery. There was no breach of the phal-phul rule . . .' Anthony had caught up with him now, and saw that he was crying soundlessly, the tears running down his big face. 'This bloody, bloody country,' he said with quiet vehemence. 'Let's go and have a drink.' Anthony had felt embarrassed then, ashamed to be associated with a man who let his feelings show, who ignored the rules. After ten years he was surprised at the clarity of the memory.

That night he lay awake. Jane had asked him if they could go down to Mysore to stay with her mother for a long break over Christmas, and he had said abstractedly, his mind full of other things as he looked out over the garden, 'I can't leave now. I have a duty to carry out here.' She had been angry then, the colour mounting hotly on her neck and face. 'You have a duty to your family, too,' she said, and had walked indoors to finish her coffee. He had watched her sitting in the lounge, apparently engrossed in her book, with the feeling of impersonal concern which shielded him still, as it always had, from a too direct confrontation with the untidiness of feelings.

When she walked out of the lounge and put the light off, he sat in the dark and finished his coffee, looking out over the dim, moonwashed shapes of the sleeping city. Much later, as he lay in bed unable to sleep, with his hands clasped behind his head, he heard her move and some quality in the action made him realize that she was awake. He slipped from his bed and knelt by the side of hers, impelled both by some compassion and a slow-firing lust, and he put his hand on her shoulder. In the darkness he could see that her eyes were open, and he stroked the damp hair behind her ear with hopeless tenderness. Her voice was unmoved, almost dismissive. 'It's too hot, Anthony,' she said, and he ran his hand slowly over the blanket covering her in a valedictory gesture before going back to his bed.

Mysore, South India: 1946

Eight

Arline Porter sat by the window watching the dudh wallah milking the cow. Outside the window Mysore had begun to shimmer with heat though it was still early. At almost seventy Arline made no compromise with the years, sitting straight-backed in the hard chair. As usual, she had watched him wash the udders and hindquarters, grumbling to himself as he did so, had checked the bucket to see that it was clean and had no water in the bottom, and had made him remove his loose jacket to ensure that he was not carrying a skinful of water with which covertly to dilute the milk. The cow stamped her feet, switching her tail over her back against the persistent settling of the morning flies. Arline could hear the milk hit the pail as his hands squeezed against the swollen udder, forcing the flesh in a rhythmic motion.

She sat with the letter in front of her and turned her attention to the mali. He smiled up at the window, squatting on his haunches, and drew the tines of his trowel lazily across the clover sheltering under the azalea bushes, raking the weeds into a neat mound. He could make out her figure through the hazing reflections of the large window, her black dressing-gown ruffed at the shoulders, and the heavy, grey hair piled in a knot at the nape of her neck, and turned so that his face was visible from the window, chewing on his forefinger thoughtfully for a moment. He inserted the forefinger deep into a nostril, manoeuvring it round and round, his face distorted in a grimace of concentration. When he looked up again there was no one at the window, and he picked up the trowel and resumed his weeding humming to himself.

Sam, the Dravidian house-servant, was in the kitchen cutting up raw meat for William. He moved crab fashion, with small, darting actions, still lean and spry at seventy-six. For forty-one years, since Arline had joined this household as Mr William's bride, he had shared this first hour uneasily with her presence. When William Porter had first brought her home in 1905, she possessed a glacial, tight-lipped beauty. In those first months she had said little, but Sam from the corner of his eye, had often seen her watching him as he shuffled around, still doing the chores as he had when it was a bachelor household. Her first comments had been diffident, soft-spoken, suggestions rather than commands. 'Don't you think it would be a good idea if . . .?' or 'Have you ever thought of doing it this way?' Now, after all these years, it was difficult to recollect the steps by which her iron dominion had reached into every part of the household and beyond. There were incidents Sam remembered. William's shame-faced acquiescence when she had brought out his old boots for disposal and Sam had looked to him for confirmation. Sam's trips with William to the races, which had become fewer and fewer and then ceased altogether. The Maharajah's invitations to strictly masculine dinners and shikars which were increasingly turned down. Sam would hear Arline arguing with William. 'You've got responsibilities now, William. A family. These games are all right for young bachelors. You've had your fun and now it's time to settle down.'

Sam could understand Vincent's birth, for that first year had held some illusory promise of happiness. It was harder to understand Jane and Angela and Patricia, born against a background of successively more bitter quarrelling, of longer silences, of harsher words. Though the quarrels stopped immediately Sam came into the room ('Not in front of the servants, William,') he could not help hearing them through the thin walls. 'You're not a man at all . . . Look at the beautiful house Mr Bulstrode-Henshaw has built for his family . . . If you were man enough you would demand a salary increase.'

The litany of hate was endless, a variety of themes which in all their multiplicity only underlined her growing contempt and frustration. Cutting the meat into slivers, Sam reflected again that she hated men because she had the misfortune to be born a woman. He remembered how William would sometimes invite him in for a late-night drink in the study. William would lay the old album down on the tooled leather desk and they would look back through the browning photographs. The ceremony for the death of the King Emperor. The expedition to shoot ibex and black bear in the Himalayas the year the Great War had begun. 'Look. Look,' William would say. 'God, man. You could be the Abominable Snowman himself,' and Sam would feel tears of loss pricking at his lids, looking at the pictures in which a younger, more upright version of himself stood holding William's rifles, his foot on the bear's throat and the black blood staining the snow. William would smile at him, the skin stretched tightly over the bony jaw and prominent cheekbones. Sometimes they drank too much, and would giggle helplessly at pictures of William sitting on a howdah on the back of Ranee at the tiger shikar the Maharajah used to hold two or three times a year. William would hold his fingers to his lips, saying, 'Shhh. Shhh!' his face suffused with blood, his eyes bulging. Once Arline had banged angrily on the wall, and William had looked instantly worried, haunted, the pleasure of the evening immediately drained away.

On a few occasions at the beginning, William had joined Sam for a trip to the bazaar, and it had seemed for a while like the carefree bachelor days. But after they had returned from the third or fourth outing, he had heard Arline say to William, using the arch tone she used to hide her dislike of visiting children who were infringing her rules, 'Honestly. You two are so irresponsible. Sam knows as well as you that you must take care of your diabetes, and yet you still go to Bapu's sweet stall. No, don't bother to deny it.' It was true, of course, and the next time Sam had presented himself in the study with his shopping basket, William had shaken his head sadly.

One November Sunday, ten years past, William had gone out to read the papers in the garden. Sam remembered the bells for the morning service tolling as he set out his master's chair with the small folding table by the side. At one o'clock Sam had rung the dinner gong, but William hadn't moved. He seemed to be looking out over the maidan where the boys were flying their kites against a livid sky. When Sam had come out and touched him on the shoulder he fell sideways and lay on the gravel with his open eyes staring sightlessly into the brilliant sky.

He had never forgotten Arline's reaction. She had come out to help him carry the body indoors, only saying, almost to herself in a tone of abstracted exasperation, 'I could never understand why he persisted in wearing that holey pullover.' That was all.

When Arline left the window, disgusted by the mali's performance, she came into the kitchen, where Sam had finished preparing the meat, stacking the bloody slivers on a plate. 'That mali will have to go,' she said, ruminatively, standing with hands on hips looking out into the back garden, where the crow sat, sharpening his beak on a branch in the guava tree. Sam gave her the plate and began to sort out the place settings for breakfast.

She took the meat and stopped by the door, as though a thought had just struck her. 'By the way,' she said, 'I've had a letter from Miss Jane this morning . . .' (he noted that she had used, as always, the title to emphasize his separate position as a servant) 'they won't be coming to stay just yet. So it will be only the family for Christmas as usual.' She looked at him for a moment, the black eyes malicious and young in the powerful, lined face, and then went out. She moved like a girl still, strong and sure.

William flew down on to the parapet and sat looking at the plate Arline had placed next to her, his head cocked on one side and his feet moving in a restless dance. His black beak was worn to white at the end and his glossy blue-black plumage with the handsome grey hood shone in the sun. 'Mere piarath. Mere butcha,' she crooned, laughing approval as he tore the bloody strips from her strong fingers. Beyond the wall a train whistle shrilled, and the goods wagons began to clank their desolate refrain across the points.

Sam finished laying the table – an extra place for Vincent who was off-duty from the hospital this morning – and went out on the patio to watch. He reflected, not for the first time, that he had only ever witnessed Arline show affection for one living thing. William. She showed a pride in ownership of her family, and he had perceived the subtle signs that Angela and Patricia had failed to escape her influence over the years. Her face was animated now as she watched the crow, bending forward to offer him the last scraps from her beringed fingers. The dudh wallah brought the milk bucket round the corner of the house and swung it on to the patio, making his salaams. Cowbells tinkled, growing fainter as man and beast moved towards the front gate.

Over the neighbouring wall, through the thinning hedge of the bamboo thicket which divided their houses, Indijeet Bhose sat at her dressing-table, frowning as she looked at the effect of her golabi lipstick, first this way, peering to the right to catch the three quarter profile view, then to the left, lips pursed into a Cupid's bow. Her husband, Nathoo, had gone off to his work at the bank, and her sons were out, Raju at some political meeting, and her younger son, Zia-Ula, at school. The long day stretched emptily ahead. She daubed some soorma on the end of her forefinger and opened her eyes wide, bending forward until her face was a few inches from the mirror. In a few moments her breath had clouded the surface and she clicked her tongue in irritation, wiping the condensation off with her powder puff. Small grains of powder clung to the moisture. Holding her breath she leaned forward again. She couldn't come to terms with growing older. In her mind she had remained twenty-eight for the past ten years.

In the Porter household Angela had come downstairs, dressed in her white uniform with the blue cape over it. 'We're not in the Officers' Mess here,' her mother had remarked acidly when she had sat down once without the cape. Angela remembered such things. Everything went in and was remembered, but little came out.

Her brother, Vincent, was already downstairs, lounging elegantly in an easy chair in his dressing gown, reading a week-old copy of *Hindu Rashtra* which his friend, Major Majid, a fellow doctor at the hospital, had brought back from Poona. 'Just to stop you feeling complacent about the future, Porter,' he had said, stabbing a stubby finger at the editorial.

The editorial, written by the editor, one Nathuram Ghodse, proclaimed the 'scientifically provable' racial superiority of the Hindu over the 'bastard invaders'. It went on to expound the doctrine of Hindutva – Hindu racial supremacy – promulgated by Vinayak Damodar Veer, 'The Brave' Savarkar. 'With the help of the RSSS – the Rashtriya Swayam Sewak Sangh – we shall rebuild the Great Hindu Empire from the sources of the Indus to those of the Brahmaputra.'

Vincent read with snorts of derision and whinnies of despairing disbelief. 'Oh God. I don't believe it. The man must be mad. Who reads this rubbish?' He pounded the cushion on his chair-arm with a clenched fist, raising his eyes to the ceiling in mock despair. At forty he still had the lean, hard figure of an athlete, and good looks of the sort which may have seemed feminine in another man. Brown eyes, deeply waved black hair, and a generous mouth bracketed with laughter lines.

Angela ignored his outbursts, working on some papers at the escritoire. A few seconds later Patricia came down the stairs. Ten years younger than her brother she had the fragile beauty of a child and with it the uncertain hesitancy of movement and gesture. She hadn't taken off her make-up from the evening before, and her mascara had run under one eye, leaking down her cheek. Her fine chestnut hair stood in disordered stooks on her head, and her pink seersucker dressing-wrap had powder round the collar. She caught sight of herself on the mirror landing, paused self-consciously. Her husband would be home soon and she would have to attend to her make-up. Patricia was unable to conceive of a relationship between a man and a woman which was not firmly predicated upon sexual

101

attraction, nor of one which could survive a degree of naturalness.

Arline sat on the parapet with the crow perched on her hand. William's black talons had left livid scratches on the back of her brown wrist and on her forearm. She brought the bird up towards her face, scratching into the feathers on the back of his head with her free forefinger. Behind her Sam said, 'Everybody is down, ma'am. Breakfast's ready.' Arline turned her head. As she did so William's beak scythed across her cheek and she gave a great cry, turning her head from the bird. William launched into the air as she clapped her hand over her cheek, flapping lazily in a dipping, languid flight before he settled on the back wall. Sam stepped forward to help Arline, but she waved him back with her free hand. Drops of blood fell on the mossed paving slabs. Sam said, 'I've told you to be careful. He's vicious, ma'am,' but she only laughed. 'You know nothing about love, Sam,' she said, and got to her feet.

Indijeet Bhose opened her bedroom window. Her voice carried faintly, full of confected concern. 'Are you all right, Mrs Porter?' And Arline called back, affecting an exaggeratedly saccharine tone, 'Perfectly all right, thank you, Mrs Bhose. So nice of you to enquire.' She turned her back deliberately on the small figure at the open window, and Sam held the kitchen door open for her.

Rawalpindi, Punjab: 1946

Nine

At 6.30 A.M. on the Saturday morning after his brush with Roger Henshaw, Anthony heard the bheesti open the bathroom door and pour the hot water from the ghee tins yoked over his shoulders into the zinc bath. Jane had already gone to the bathroom and he could hear her voice, softened to avoid waking the rest of the household, 'Thik hai, Mazuffar. Shokria.' Anthony lay for a few minutes, sunk in the illogical thoughts of semi-consciousness, reluctant to emerge into the new day.

Since the evening when the snake had visited them he had discerned a new tendency beyond his conscious control. His thoughts often returned to the past, but without the pleasure-seeking selectivity of previous years. There was a darkness, and an obscure urgency in the visitations now, and he was uneasily conscious of a restlessness, and a seeking, which was all the more irritating for seeming to have no precise focus.

He remembered his mother, years before in the bungalow, brushing the slick of hair off her sweating forehead one evening as he argued with her about going to bed. 'One day, my son, you will learn the pleasure of going to bed early to sleep. Hard to imagine now, I know, but it will happen.' It was only in the last couple of years that he had come to appreciate the truth of her words, in this and in other things. He remembered many things she had said to him on those long, sultry evenings when he sat with her on the verandah and it seemed that this life would go on for ever. Kajan, the man of all work, would squat on his haunches by the door whittling a boat or a figure from a piece of layered pine bark. His father would have been on tour for some months, a distant memory, barely recalled by the infrequent letters which his mother read to him, with their complaints of falling standards in the dak houses and the rigours of his working life.

Just before the hot season began there was always an evening when his mother used to say, 'Your father will be home soon,' with a small sigh. Anthony had never known whether it indicated regret or relief at his anticipated return. As the last evenings wore past and the blue-white storm lightning flashed fitfully, night after night, illuminating the gaunt pines for a moment, she would come to life. 'When your father gets back we'll go rambling.' He would feel, then, an uncertain conviction that she must love his father, though she never said so, because he would notice a new animation in her as the time approached for his return. She would look down the darkening valley, as though she expected to see his car moving along the winding road towards them. On the hill above them a few lights shone amongst the rustling pines, but when his father was away he and his mother were the last to go to bed. Sometimes she would talk to him about the stars: the Pleiades, the Plough, Orion the Great Hunter, Ursa Minor. But mostly, while the lights flickered out over the deep valley, it was the events of the day, comments on the books she had been reading, little things. He would try to follow the thread of her thoughts. It was endlessly fascinating that she could, at one moment, be talking about what old widow Milchrist had been saying to her that morning and then venture, after a silence, 'It must be terrible for your father. We live secure lives, you at school and me enjoying my bring-and-buy sales, my social meetings, my coffee mornings. He has to go on alone, day after day. I can't help him.'

A picture of his father as a heroic figure came into Anthony's mind. He said curiously, 'Now what made you think of that?' admiringly, like someone seeking the raison d'être of a particularly recondite crossword clue. She only said, 'The literal is unimportant. It is only the dressing, the outward show of things. It is the inner life that matters, the secret connections.' He had instantly remembered the half-understood phrase, and it came back to him now again, imbedded in these new, uncomfortable memories of childhood.

When, now, he began to remember again – the servant bringing the news of the accident on the road as they returned in the car together – he got up, trying to escape. After his parents' deaths life had assumed a terrible impersonality. The hushed kindness of people who didn't know what to say, and the awful charity of the Masons in sending him to public school in England. He didn't want to think of that.

Waiting for Jane to come out of the bathroom, he sat on the window-seat and looked down over the garden. By the summer house a movement caught his eye, and he turned to look, still half-asleep. His breath caught in his throat for a moment, and he rubbed his eyes carefully to wipe away the glottal sleep accumulated at their inside corners. His fifteen-year-old daughter, Anne, was walking in the garden in her white nightdress. Her feet were bare upon the dewy grass and she carried a chiffon scarf self-consciously in the hand she held above her head so that it floated behind her on the morning breeze. She was singing to herself, but though he could see her lips moving it was too far for the words or melody to reach Anthony. As he watched her self-absorbed grace in the sunshine, she began a hesitant dance, looking down at the pointed foot poised in mid-air, and he was reminded of Jane when they first met.

Behind him the door opened and Jane came in, wrapped in her white towelling robe. Her damp hair lay down her cheeks and on her neck like Medusa's ringlets. She looked out of the window over Anthony's shoulder. 'The little minx,' she said, and there was a calculating, combative edge to her voice, 'we'll have to watch her.'

Mark watched Lal Deen making the toast over the charcoal. When the fire burned too high and the toast began to smoke Lal Deen said, 'Aiee. Ban chod. Theire ma ki . . .', picking up the blackened pieces and putting them on the plate. With long, unhurried strokes he scraped a knife across each surface, covering the white porcelain sink with a fine black dust. Mark didn't dare to tell him that the toast didn't taste the same when it had been scraped. It was difficult to talk to Lal Deen these days. He no longer laughed and joked as he used to. He had become surly and uncommunicative. He no longer came out to play marbles with Mark, or made him tops, or cooked special surprise dishes on Sundays. When the toast was scraped Lal Deen put it into the worn silver-plated rack and set the kettle carefully on the grid over the glowing charcoal. Without speaking he gave Mark a piece of toast, the thick butter clarifying at the edges as it slid over the surface.

Gur arrived by tonga as the family was finishing break-fast. Anne said eagerly, 'I'll let him in,' and ran from the table. Jane frowned briefly across at Anthony, engrossed in his copy of *The Times*. Mark sniggered behind his hand, and she said sharply, 'Why are you laughing?' Mark looked up at her, trying to judge her mood. 'She always gets excited when we see Gur,' he said, 'haven't you noticed?' Jane looked hard at him, and called Lal Deen to clear the dishes.

When Gur came in, talking animatedly to Anne, Anthony took him out on the verandah while Jane went into the kitchen to pack the cold-bag, and Anne and Mark went to collect the things they would need.

When they were on the verandah Gur said anxiously to Anthony, 'Please don't mention Henshaw or any of that taking flight to Amritsar business to Father. It's become a bone of contention between my parents. Mother wants to move to Bangalore to stay with her family. Father says he has no intention of moving and wouldn't be able to sell his land and horses now.' He laughed ruefully. 'You know what they're like. It's hell when they start on this discussion.'

Anthony lit his first cheroot of the day and walked to the balustrade. He said, 'And you? What do you feel? Despite what Henshaw said, Partition *is* going to happen. Then you'll be surrounded by Muslims, cut off from your own kind. Won't you feel isolated?'

Gur looked up at him seriously from the chair in which he sat. At such moments he seemed to leave his youth entirely behind. He said, 'You've known me since I was a boy. I am a Brahmin, though caste and religion mean as little to me as they do to my parents.' He cleared his throat and began to pick at a splinter on the arm of the chair. 'I am born from Brahma's mouth. I eat mutton and have never venerated the Sacred Cow. I do not believe in idolatry, or that God is immanent in all things. I do not believe in the Hindu pantheon of gods – in Brahma, Shiva, or Vishnu. But I believe in the principles encoded in my religion, and I believe that those people closest to my family espouse those same principles – whatever their professed religion.'

As Gur talked, a focus in Anthony's mind twisted. He saw, uncomfortably, that his love for Gur was qualified in a number of ways. By the colour of Gur's skin, by a sense of the alien Dravidian culture from which Gur had sprung, by a modified version of the same supercilious colonial contempt for the Indian which he affected to despise in Henshaw and in the British members of his community. In the past, when he had briefly had this insight, he had blamed his parents, thus avoiding any personal responsibility for the attitude. For the first time he was forced to acknowledge that the distaste was in himself. It was not a comfortable insight.

From inside the house Jane's voice sounded briefly. 'Lal Deen. Roti kidre hai?' and Lal Deen's guttural reply, 'Idre, Memsahib.' Gur smiled faintly. He gestured towards the pale mountains, almost hidden from sight in the haze of morning. 'This is our home. Nothing can change that.' Anthony looked at him, thinking, At least I can feel affection. He set aside his other thoughts. Gur had surprised him again with the tolerant maturity of his views. There was a certainty, too, which was beyond Anthony. He felt, momentarily, the presence of some relationship between Gur and the very earth which made his own tenancy ephemeral.

He envied Gur.

Gur sat in the front passenger seat, and Anthony drove. Jane, Mark and Anne sat in the back and the hamper was wedged in the boot which was secured to the bumper with a dressing-gown cord. 'Hardly dignified for a person in your position to drive around in a glorified rag-and-bone cart,' Jane said, and Anthony laughed. You mean hardly dignified for you, he thought.

The sky was a brilliant cerulean and as the car laboured up the winding road the resinous smell of the pines huddled on the hills above the road hung on the air. The road surface was pitted, and the holes had been casually filled in with stones and mud. The edges had broken under the weight of innumerable lorries and buses, and the macadam was rough and serrated. The canvas hood flapped in its housing in the bodywork and, with the loud burring of the tyres, made conversation impossible. The Brewery buildings stood in the lea of the huge hill, almost three quarters of a mile ahead on the straight road. The road now ran into the hill's shadow, with the gentian-clad slopes to the right rising steeply into a dense forest of Douglas pines, while below to the left there was a steep slope, covered in scrub and heather, scarred by the passage of great boulders on their thundering flight down into the vast valley. The gradient steepened and Anthony changed down into second gear. Half a mile ahead now the road turned sharply left, following the contour of the huge spur which continued the shoulder of the hill down into the valley. Farmer Thorne owned the spur. His cattle provisioned the local communities from Ghora Gali, through Lower and Upper Topee to Murree, and as far away as Nathia Gali.

The gradient flattened slightly, and Anthony changed up to third, feeling a vague, unidentifiable unease as he did so. At the corner, just past the Brewery, the road turned steeply westward, still in shadow. The red mud had bled over the road in the rains, and the dried runnels now sprayed a fine powdery dust into the air behind the car. As the car turned the corner Anthony realized what seemed strange: there were cows in the lower pastures and the pigs were rooting round their vast muddy pen; but there were no men in the fields. No tractors or machinery. And there was no fire burning in the lower field. Farmer Thorne's fires were a local legend. 'How was the Eternal Flame today?' Sita used to ask when they arrived, rolling her eyes to heaven in mock exasperation. When the fire was stacked high the smoke could be seen in Murree, ten miles away and three thousand feet further up the mountain.

The engine began to labour again, pinking metallically, and Anthony changed down, double declutching to keep the revolutions going. Beside him Gur pointed and shouted, 'What are those men doing in the road?' In the mirror Anthony could see Jane shift forward in her seat, narrowing her eyes as the car moved into the sunlight again. There were a group of labourers ahead. They seemed to be carrying pickaxes and lathis, and one of them was limping badly. For a moment he thought they were returning workers, crossing the road to take the path down the khud to the farm. Then, with the unreal clarity of a nightmare, he saw that two of the men carried jezails, and that the stumbling man had his wrists bound behind him. One of the men hit the prisoner on the back of the head with his lathi, and the man fell across the road. When he looked up and saw the car coming towards him he tried to move, and his assailant hit him again. There was a dull, popping sound, audible even above the noise of the labouring engine, and the man lay still. In that instant Anthony had recognized the victim's face. It was one of the Hindu boys who worked in Farmer Thorne's abbatoir.

Anthony was suddenly aware of Jane gripping his shoulders. 'Are you crazy?' she shouted. 'Turn around. Oh, *please* . . .'

He could not stop. With some part of his mind he calculated the space between the man's head and the edge of the soft overhang of earth bordering the steep drop. It was enough, he thought, and forced his foot down on the accelerator. The engine note rose to a scream. The two men closest to the recumbent figure leaped aside as the car veered towards the edge of the drop, seeming to hang over the edge for a moment before the wheels gained purchase and began to haul the protesting chassis back on to the road. Anthony felt that everything had slowed almost to a standstill. In the mirror he saw one of the men raise his jezail and he opened the throttle wide, frantically shouting, 'Down. Down, everybody, *down*!' There was a sharp crack of the report and then the clang of the bullet hitting the car followed by the whine of its flight out of the valley. Then they were round the corner, protected by the rock-ridged slope of the hill. He eased off the accelerator. Jane said, 'You stupid fool,' and he felt, again, a sharp anger. In the mirror he could see she had her arm around Anne who was crying. He drove on. Nobody said anything else.

Sita and Joginder Singh lived in a huge bungalow, set in an estate of lawn and woodlands extending to some three hundred acres. It had been built for one of Curzon's staff as a summer residence. The pink roof tiles, diagonally hung, had been specially ordered and shipped from Brixham. The verandah floor was faced with an Italian hunting scene in marble based on the floor of the Roman Hunting Lodge in Piazza Armorina. The stable block, where Joginder kept three mares, was built in thin red Roman brick, arched and supported by slender pillars of granite faced with marble. The wall which ran out from the wing to the stable block, demarcating the servants' quarters, was crazed and cracked by the slow constriction of a huge Virginia creeper. Joginder was a wealthy man, and he and Sita had carefully restored the house over the years. In embrasures on either side of the Lebanese cedar doors sat sightless busts of Augustus and Marcus Aurelius, and the verandah wall was lined with Roman stelae and turbe from Turkey. The interior of the house was rich with Russian ikons, Hindu gods and temple carvings, rugs from Persia, glass from Murano, ivory carvings from Malaya. There were four malis, three house servants resplendent in green and gold uniforms, a syce and a chokra who performed all the menial tasks of the household.

Anthony teased Joginder sometimes about being a despot. 'The only man I know who gave up religion and embraced Carlyle at the age of seven. It may be benevolent, but it is paternalism nevertheless.' Joginder had laughed a trifle uncomfortably, but it was open to Anthony to make the joke without rancour, knowing his friend's open-handed generosity to the workers on his estate and to the villagers. Since Feroze Khan had told Joginder that his father was going blind with cataract and Joginder had arranged and paid for an operation in Rawalpindi, sending the old man down in his own car, he had done many other unsung kindnesses. Anthony knew there were people living rent-free in the houses Joginder owned, many of them receiving presents of food from Sita. Yet, almost because of his generosity, there were many who muttered about the zamindar, Feroze Khan prominent among them. Ten years before, when Anthony had indignantly reported an overheard criticism to Joginder, his host had smiled gently, and said, 'It is only a reflection upon them, and not upon me.'

The gates were open as Anthony turned off the road and into the drive. He was aware of the tension still in the car. To him the incident had already begun to fade, to assume the surreal proportions and blurred definitions of a dream. He saw that the gardeners had cleared the brambles away, and that the grass underneath was sere and yellow. Ahmed was walking across the rough grass with a gun over his shoulder, dragging a piece of sacking behind him upon which lay the body of a white dog, its paws lolling from side to side in the progress over the bumpy ground. Anthony cut the engine, and braked, and behind him Gur said sadly, 'Did you see? That was Sheba.'

Joginder was still a handsome man at forty-two, with only a trace of bulk around his waist, and a dusting of white in the hair at his temples. He had long since discarded the turban and beard of his religion. By his side, Sita seemed like a child. Anthony kissed her, noticing the puffiness under her eyes. Joginder too was subdued, and after the greetings were over he said heavily, 'Sheba ran with the jackals some weeks before. A couple of days ago she began to act strangely. When Henshaw told us there was another outbreak of rabies I am having no option . . .' He trailed off helplessly.

Anne began to cry and Sita put an arm around her shoulders. 'I thought it was too cold for a picnic. Come and help me with the lunch.'

Mark stayed with the men, sitting on a low chair by the door while they settled down with their stengahs. Anthony told Joginder of the incident on the journey, making light of it as if to defuse its seriousness, and Mark thought, That's not how it was at all. Shifting guiltily in his chair at his unspoken disagreement with his father.

Over the stable block the doves wheeled and swooped out of sight over the roof. Joginder rested his drink on the balustrade, hunching his shoulders. 'That's not all,' he said, looking at Mark for a moment. 'In the last two months four girls have been found dead in the woods below Murree. Assaulted, their throats cut . . .'

There was a silence and Mark heard his mother's voice, too low to carry to the men, saying to Sita, 'Anthony keeps going on about his duty, his work. How he must stay and carry on. He doesn't seem to have the faintest idea of what is really happening. It's all a game to him. Today I finally realized that I will *have* to make us move.' There was the sound of pans scraping and then her voice again, 'My mother always said that women were the stronger sex in everything that counted.'

In the kitchen the stone flags gave off a slightly musty coldness. Jane stood back to look at the salads and wiped her hands on her apron, turning to call the others in for lunch. Sita said, 'There's no hurry. Give them a minute,' and Jane caught an unease, a desire to prolong the moment's intimacy with her friend. Saeed looked round the door and she shook her head at him so that he withdrew. The servants could never understand why the memsahibs wanted to prepare the food themselves when there were servants to do it for them. Sita picked at the salad bowl, averting her eyes, and said in a low voice, 'I wish Jog would listen to Roger Henshaw. He thinks it may be dangerous for us to stay here with all the uncertainty about Partition. But Jog just won't listen.' She looked so distraught for a moment that Jane was genuinely concerned until Sita laughed, saying, 'Oh, don't pay any attention to me. I'm just being silly, going on like this.' But her eyes were still troubled.

* * *

Over lunch they talked idly of friends and local matters. 'I am gathering young Richard Reeves is joining you,' said Joginder. 'You may be having some difficulties with your colleagues. He's seeing a lot of a young Indian schoolteacher.' He smiled widely at Anthony, aware of straying into an uneasy area. Anthony shifted in his chair, uncomfortable again. Over his friend's shoulder he looked for relief at the pastel horizon, where layer upon layer of mountains rose against each other in sloping graphs until they blurred into the white-blue sky. Against them the trees stood like paper cut-outs, riffled by an idle breeze which picked up the fir tassels for a moment and then left again.

When they were having their coffee Saeed came and whispered in Joginder's ear, and Joginder got up, putting his starched linen napkin on the table. 'Time for one of the seigneurial duties I am inheriting with the house,' he said, beckoning Anthony to go with him, and together they strolled up the gravelled drive.

Around the corner, hidden from the house by a dense bramble bush growing through and around a massive oak, stood a group of beggars. There was the blind man who haunted the Mall, his sightless washed-out eyes turned up to heaven. He held on to the ragged clothing of his companion, whose legs were gigantic scaly trunks, brutalized by the ravages of elephantiasis. By the side of them was a torso on a cart. It was a man without legs, with massive shoulders and over-developed arms. His hands, with which he propelled the cart, were bound in coarse sacking stained with black deposits of dried blood. His face was extraordinarily beautiful, with light brown eyes, luminous eyes, fringed with long lashes, and a fine aquiline nose. But it was the fourth member who caught

Anthony's attention, stirring some dim memory which he could not immediately place.

He was a man of considerably over six feet, dressed in a loin cloth and carrying the mendicant's begging bowl in his right hand and a staff with the remains of his left hand. His body was silver white with leprosy scales, and he had no nose. His mouth was a ragged tear through which the saliva bubbled and dripped with his breathing. Only his eyes seemed still alive, black, fierce, angry.

When Joginder and Anthony appeared all the other beggars began to plead for alms. 'Baksheesh, Sahib. Bahut gareeb hai. Baksheesh.' Only the leper stood silent, looking at them with unreadable intensity.

Anthony felt unreal, and the hair on the back of his neck began to prickle. He was suddenly aware that perspiration was running down the front of his chest, soaking his shirt. He took out his wallet and Joginder took the proffered money from him, adding some more before putting the notes on the ground in front of the beggars. They made no move towards the money, looking at the leper who still stood impassively apart.

The leper made the sign of namaste and looked at Anthony for a long moment and then at Joginder. He addressed himself to them, speaking in a deep resonant voice, in flawless English. First he indicated his companions, saying, 'You see here the poor of India who must be counted fortunate against what is yet to come.' Then, looking at Anthony, he said, 'You will go away, but you cannot escape your future. That waits wherever you may go. You will need strength and courage, but these may not be enough and you may fail. You must remember that what you may see as failure, another may see as success.' He paused, looking at the sky, and his eyes seemed vacant now. 'I cannot see further.'

116

He turned to Joginder, and his voice seemed to carry a valedictory sadness. 'You have always been our friend. It grieves me to tell you that you will stay, and the sadness which will befall you will come from an unexpected place. Nor can it be avoided now, for the actions which will bring it about have already begun. I grieve for you, my friend, and am truly sorry.'

When the beggars had picked up the money, and begun to follow the leper up the drive, Anthony said, half-laughing, 'Now what did you make of all that?' and Jog responded, with an attempt at lightness, 'I am learning that people compensate for their physical defects by claiming impossible powers.' But then he stopped, looking out to the horizon, and said in a low voice which would not carry to the verandah where the others watched with interest, 'That was the Silver Saddhu, who has the reputation of a seer. He has been in these parts as long as I can remember. The legend runs that he killed a man for going with his wife, but the police would not touch him because he had the divine madness.' He sighed heavily, and they walked back to the house in silence.

Karam Deen's son had brought down three more horses, as arranged, and a pony for Mark. Despite Mark's objections the syce had orders to keep his mount on a leading rein. 'Perhaps you can have a little canter on your own, later,' said Anthony, ignoring Jane's fierce headshake and mouthed 'No,' and Mark submitted to being led, half-mollified by the promise.

Joginder and Anthony rode ahead of the others, galloping down the woodcutters' path towards the first clearing in the pines. Joginder reined at the edge of the plateau overlooking the valley, and Anthony pulled up beside him. From the next clearing they could hear the sullen, muted roar of the cataract, throwing the icy water over the jagged, grey rocks. Behind them the forest looked black and mysterious in the afternoon sunshine. Joginder leaned forward to pat his mare's neck, saying thoughtfully, 'Henshaw's proving a bit of a problem. He's been round several times to try to persuade us to move. He always manages to get Sita very upset.'

As though reminded suddenly he smiled at Anthony and said, 'Oh, by the way. Gur was telling me about the incident at the Mess. If it didn't sound patronizing, I'd add my thanks.' Anthony, embarrassed, made a gesture to indicate it was of no consequence, though he felt, instantly, a shadow of the anger he had felt towards Henshaw. He said, carefully, determined to be fair, 'I do find Roger Henshaw most unpleasant now personally, but I must say that he does seem concerned about your safety here.'

Joginder laughed drily, seemingly amused by his friend's innocence. 'There's rather more to that than meets the eye, I'm afraid. I went for a midweek ride in the forest at the beginning of the summer and came upon Roger and Margaret Preston, in flagrante by the third clearing. I am pretending not to notice and rode on, but two days later she met me – by design, I think – on the Mall and she came right out with it. I mustn't think badly of them. They had tried not to see each other but had found it impossible. How Roger's wife had gone back to England six months ago, and refused to return and how he was planning to write to tell her the marriage was over. I am a little embarrassed to be receiving these confidences from a relative stranger, and am trying to walk on, but she is pursuing me. Richard Reeves is her nephew. Now she is saying that Richard, unfortunately, had taken violently against Henshaw and there had almost been a fight. She ended by saying that she and Roger would appreciate it if I kept their secret for the moment, and I am saying, a little pompously, that I felt it didn't concern anyone else but the two of them. I am thinking she'd rather hoped I would go down on my knees there and then and swear eternal silence upon Bramah.'

In the undergrowth something started suddenly, crashing through the dry thicket in headlong flight. An eagle wheeled far above them in a slow gyre, sailing the wind with unmoving wings. Joginder's horse champed at the jingling bit and scuffled her feet against a gnarled root.

Anthony felt a disquiet, obliquely raised by Joginder's story: a sensation of some breakdown of the sense of moral order which he had held since childhood. He found that he had begun to construe everything that happened in relation to a dimly realized sense of the prevailing order of things: Reeves and the Indian schoolteacher, his own feelings about Henshaw's attack on Gur, and now this discovery of Henshaw and Mrs Preston coupling like animals in the forest. He recognized the presence of some vast, permanent, potent mystery, of which Joginder and Gur were a part, which could afford to tolerate the facile arrogance of the English in the certain knowledge that its silence and certainty would overcome. He felt, for a moment, a sense of the massive brooding indifference of India, the stone gods guarding their ruined jungle temples, feeling, as he did so, a frightening desire to look further into the darkness.

Joginder said reflectively, as if there had been no break in his monologue, 'Henshaw's been edgy, too, about the unsolved murders. "I'm not Sherlock Holmes you know," he is saying last time I asked about them. I suspect on all counts he would be happier with me out of the way.'

Anthony laughed, responding to the lightness of his

friend's tone. 'There's nothing so perverse as an English hypocrite.' He had refrained from commenting on Henshaw's attitude towards Reeves and the girl, but told the story now. Joginder gave an exclamation of disgust. 'She and Reeves are enjoying classical music and poetry. I'm sure there's nothing in it. In fact I caught Henshaw eyeing her at a Lintott's dance himself, and rather thought he had taken a fancy to her.'

There was the sound of horses behind them and Anthony turned, still half-smiling at the thought of Henshaw's lust in the staid surroundings of Lintott's. He saw Anne and Gur ride up. Their horses were very close and Anne put her hand on Gur's arm as if to steady herself, looking at him with shining eyes.

When they went to the car, Anthony looked back at the tall bulk of his friend, standing with his arm protectively round Sita, and wondered when they would meet again. With a feeling of surprise he realized that he had decided already that he would take the family to Mysore for a holiday. Now it was a question of putting it to Jane in such a way that she could not triumph. As he began to drive through the hoary mists which rose from the gravelled road he realized, with a cruel insight, that his decision to go to Mysore after all had been prompted by seeing Anne and Gur exchange that one glance in the clearing. And again a shame at his own littleness rose up in him, and a desire to be better. He put the thought out of his mind and drove on steadily.

Beside him, Gur looked out of the window, immersed in his own thoughts. Behind him, he could see in the mirror that Anne and Mark were asleep. Jane looked straight ahead and each time he glanced at her he could see her fearful eyes, straining to see what lay behind the yellow headlights of the car.

120

Anthony: 1922

Ten

Anthony stood awkwardly outside the study door and knocked twice. There was silence for a moment, and he looked down the long, polished corridor, wishing that his ordeal was over. He heard the housemaster's voice say, 'Yes,' on a rising note of query, and he pushed the door open and went in. The first thing he saw was the sheaf of canes, stood in a cylinder of linseed oil in an umbrella stand by the roll top desk. Outside he could see the first XV playing Blundells. They were pressing hard on the right wing, and the Blundells pack were covering fast across the field to cut off the winger. The shouting of the crowd rose and then fell, disappointed, as the winger was brought down and the ball went into touch.

Dr Hammond took his half-glasses off, and laid them on a pile of papers on his desk, rubbing his eyes. He had the cynical, tired look of a man who had taken up teaching as a refuge rather than a vocation, and had long since lost any belief in the efficacy of education. 'Ah, Hodder.' He indicated the armchair. 'Sit down for a moment.' He paused, looking up at the ceiling with his mouth open, evidently uncertain of how to begin.

When he had walked round the room a couple of times, paying a close attention to the carpet as though he had never seen it before and was intrigued by its pattern, he looked out of the window and said vaguely, 'I don't understand you, Hodder. I was told you had been seen escorting a girl – holding her hand if I remember the story correctly – out of bounds and without your school cap.' He looked at Anthony in sorrowful reproach, clasping his hands in front of him. Anthony nodded, looking down at his hands, and Hammond sighed heavily. He had the air of a man defeated by the small decisions of life, ground down by uncertainty about what he should do next. When he spoke his voice had the tremulous, unctuous cadences of a vicar delivering a sermon. 'Those of us old enough to have experienced the Great War will never forget the young men who went out to die for our freedom in Passchendaele, the Somme, Mons, Ypres . . .' His voice trailed away and Anthony sat still, mildly intrigued despite his fear, to see how Old Ham could make all this relevant to his misdemeanour.

Dr Hammond went to the window and looked out at the rugby. For a few moments he seemed to forget about Anthony, gnawing the end of his ginger moustache which he pushed into his mouth with a forefinger. Then he turned back into the room and resumed his monologue. 'Some of the bravest and best were those who had just started down the road to manhood, whose ideals were still the pure and visionary ones instilled in them by institutions such as this. They were inspired by the vision of masculine good comradeship, which you too will find in the years ahead to be the highest form of relationship, more valuable and deeper than anything which can exist between a man and a woman.' He paused and looked at Anthony crossly. 'You've had a good career here, Hodder. Don't spoil it all for a few moments of sinful pleasure with a worthless tart.' He walked briskly over to the umbrella stand, taking out a long cane which he wiped with a duster before testing its flexibility with both hands. 'You're an intelligent boy, and I'm sure you've learned your lesson. Nevertheless, I'm afraid I shall have to beat you.'

There was some echo of his father in the polemic. From his father it had been less direct, inclined towards statements such as 'Men exist upon a higher plane than women,' but the puzzling antagonism was there, no less for being oblique, veiled. She is a tart, he thought, despising himself as he remembered the compliance with which she had moved her hips so he could remove her knickers, down by the dark brown flowing river. He knelt on the edge of the armchair, gripping the arms tightly and tensing himself for the blow. Now it was a consummation devoutly to be wished, a means of wiping the slate clean and beginning again. Hammond walked up to him and, almost gently, raised up the jacket so that it was free of the boy's bottom. He walked back a few paces and from the corner of his eye Anthony saw him raise the cane high in the air. When the blow fell the pain was exquisite. After the fourth blow he could feel the wetness begin to trickle down his leg. He gritted his teeth, forcing himself to remain silent. Hammond's face was very red and his breathing had become stertorous and laboured. When he had given Anthony six strokes he stopped, and said with an old-womanish, spiteful acidulousness, 'That will help you remember one of the fundamental lessons of life.'

As he walked down the corridor Anthony was aware that Hammond was watching him from the study door. It was painful to move, and he could feel the tears pricking against his eyelids, but he walked steadily towards the stairs, determined not to let Hammond see him show the pain he felt. That, too, was part of the way the game was played.

When he took his shower the following day the young games master, Mr Martin, called him over. 'It's nothing, sir,' he said, realizing from Martin's face that the teacher had seen the welter of bruises and welts lacerating his buttocks. Martin turned the boy's back to the window and examined him, grave-faced. One of the prefects was dispatched to take Anthony around to the sick-bay. Sister Hampson looked at the thin buttocks, black with bruising. She called the nurse over and they dressed the contusions with iodine and lint held in place with plaster. 'This will hurt,' she said briskly before starting. 'Was it Dr Hammond?' and Anthony nodded, feeling guilty at this betrayal. Sister Hampson said to the nurse, 'This time we *will* do a report for the Head. We'll list all the occasions.' To his surprise, Anthony felt no pleasure at the prospect of Old Ham being arraigned in front of The Beak sensing, in part, that, much as he might relish the revenge, he would rather the instrument of it was something removed from him.

Four days later one of the younger boys ran into the Senior Reading Room. His high-pitched voice was almost inaudible with excitement. 'I say, you fellows. Have you heard the news? Old Ham's dead. They've just taken him away on a stretcher under a blanket.' As the hubbub of excited voices broke out Anthony stared at the wall, knowing beyond doubt that Old Ham killed himself. He felt he would do anything to put the clock back. He remembered Old Ham saying, 'The ayenbite of inwit, my boy,' about something else. Yes, that was it. From time to time over the years, it returned with savage force and he remembered the incident as if it had just occurred.

The Punjab: 1946/7

Eleven

Christmas had a peculiar character that year. In retrospect, Anthony attributed the hysterical gaiety to people's subconscious realization of impending change, and their consequent determination to wring as much good fellowship as possible from the festive season. The carol singers raised over five hundred rupees for Father Eusebio's soup kitchens, and the Howrah Traders were amazed at the returns they took in exchange for food and shelter from their ragged hordes of halt, and maimed, and blind.

Christmas had always been a time of refuge for Anthony. He had never thought of himself as a religious man and his attendances at church were – in the normal course of the year – motivated by the same urge towards convention as were his acceptance of invitations to bridge evenings and dinners. But he had always felt at Advent the approach of some uncontrollable mystery which would touch him in passing. It was incomprehensible in rational terms, but it spoke to some depth in his nature which craved a deeper commitment than was offered in his ordinary life.

The tree was brought down from the hills. It was too tall to stand in the hall so the mali took it upon himself to cut three feet from the top. Jane's Urdu was inadequate to express her anger, and the mali remained mystified when Lal Deen translated her comments. Surely the object was to place the tree in the hall. He had made that possible. Why was the Burra Memsahib so angry with him? Anthony laughed when he came back from the office and saw it standing, broad-shouldered and headless in the crepe-covered tub, and Jane saying crossly, 'It's not funny. Just look at it.' But the tinsel fairy gave it height and Mark and Anne covered it inexpertly in wads of cotton wool to represent snow, and hung the rooms with paper chains they had made years before, hand-coloured and stuck together with rice and water paste.

On Christmas Day they sat solemnly in their paper hats, and the debris of wrapping paper from opened presents, and listened to the King's speech. The lame duck for the year, Jane's seasonal act of conscience, was Grantham, a junior member of Wavell's staff exiled by stand-by duty from his expected leave in his Kent village, homesick for England. He was a phthisic youth, pale and studious with Dickensian illusions about an English Christmas, gravely tired despite his age. It was a malaise d'esprit, not the superficial weariness which would respond to the customary panaceas of rest and a shooting holiday in the mountains. 'The trouble,' he confided to Anthony as they scrambled up a hill path in the forest to walk off the effects of guinea fowl and vegetables, followed by Christmas pudding and port, 'is we've had years of watching the dream dissolving. The old man says there will be bloodshed. He feels there is nothing we can do except ship our own people out and leave India to civil war.' Anthony held out his hand, helping Grantham up the loose shale of the rock face. 'You're a young man. In a couple of years you'll be deeply involved in something else.' He felt irritated to be reminded of what was happening.

Grantham stood with a hand on his knee, breathing heavily. He looked bleakly at Anthony. 'I hope you're

126

right,' he said, but his voice lacked conviction. When Anthony heard that Grantham had died of pneumonia barely three months later he remembered the boy's hopelessness, and wondered if there was such a thing as foreknowledge of death.

Mark's bicycle had been brought in by the mali, as planned, after Christmas lunch. The mali felt that the waves of approval and warm good humour which greeted his arrival were a sign of forgiveness for whatever he may have done, and backed from the room, making namastes to Anthony and Jane in jerky, alternating bowing motions.

Until that moment Mark had smiled mechanically, pretending that he was enjoying Christmas, and that the presents on the tree were precisely what he wanted. Inside he was weeping. They must have known . . . he said to himself bitterly, and hated them while suffering a not wholly disagreeable sensation of martyrdom. It never occurred to him, afterwards, to question the mildly sadistic nature of the deception. When the bicycle finally arrived he looked at his parents in turn and they smiled back at him. He noted, with dazed wonder, that it had gears and the new brakes. Wordlessly he hugged his mother and went over to shake hands with Anthony. Anthony said, teasingly, 'Bet you thought we'd forgotten?' and ruffled his hair, and Mark said, 'Thank you,' over and over again in a trembly voice, his eyes bright.

While Anthony and Grantham were climbing the hillside, Mark was riding round the streets near the house. 'I'll be careful,' he promised. Anthony had pleaded with Jane. 'It's a bit contradictory to give him a bike and then confine him to the compound.' Jane let him go, but she was unhappy, going out on to the verandah to watch him at frequent intervals.

Grantham was staying a further night before reporting back for duty, so there was no hurry to return. They drove back through the greying city amid a light flurry of snow. The car headlights occasionally picked out a sacred cow, wandering forlornly in search of new pastures, or a sleeping form swathed in rags lying in a shop doorway. From the end of the drive the house looked warm and welcoming, the light from the windows showing yellow on the grass. The tree lights glittered through the window of the drawing-room where Jane and Anne were listening to *Stille Nacht, Heilige Nacht*, the sound coming faintly out into the garden. Jane put the porch light on and came out to greet them, kissing Anthony warmly, to his surprise. Cynically, he thought, That kiss is for show only. Nothing's changed, aware, for a moment, of the quality of the estrangement which had grown between them.

When Anthony had poured them a drink Jane said casually, 'By the way, dear. I had to clean up Mark's knee with iodine. He came off the bike on the Mall.' She seemed somehow triumphant, justified in the correctness of her view. Anthony said defensively, 'He could as easily fall off in the compound,' but she had her answer ready. 'It's not so dangerous when there's no traffic about. I've suggested he rides around the garden until he's more in control of the machine.' She looked at him with the straight-backed stance which was part of her preparation for battle, but Anthony merely nodded and changed the subject. It would be ill-bred to expose a guest to family disagreements. There was, too, a fragile feeling of well-being which he wanted to preserve. When Anne and Jane followed Mark up to bed he stayed with Grantham, talking of England. Anthony listened well, trying to comprehend Grantham's enthusiasm for grey skies and drizzle, and the hopfields with their witch-hatted oast houses. He remembered only the rain and the greyness of winter, without affection. Above all, he remembered the darkness and the unheated corridors of school. But, as was his fashion, he agreed for the sake of comradeship, and it was well after midnight when they retired to bed.

During the holiday he had deliberately avoided the news as much as possible. Joginder had dropped in unexpectedly on Boxing Day, bearing presents for the family, and had told him that two more girls had been found strangled and assaulted. Anthony had almost convinced himself that the riots and looting had been an isolated occurrence. The murders were something else – disturbing, certainly – but evidently the work of some deranged person who would eventually be caught when the police drafted in someone capable to carry through the enquiry. He had felt admiration for Henshaw who had taken control of such enquiries as were being made.

The first day back at work Anthony dictated a number of letters and had begun to work out a schedule for the next few weeks when the chaprassi came in and stood by his desk.

'Sahib. I wish to go to see my parents at Tippera.'

Anthony vented his exasperation at being back at work guiltily aware that he was over-reacting. 'Oh, Wahid. Why can't you wait for a month or so? You know how busy it is always at this time of year.' The man stood by the door, looking down at his feet and waiting until Anthony had finished.

'There has been a massacre, Sahib. I want to see if my parents are alive,' he said. And Anthony signed the chit, contrite and embarrassed.

In the mess he came upon Andrew Prescott, one of the political officers. They had met a number of times before, at dinners or at bridge evenings, and Anthony was aware that his colleague had a reputation as an eccentric. Prescott was a languid, blond, Old Harrovian of Anthony's own age, who affected a drawling delivery and whose manner suggested a profound boredom with everything. He yawned heavily behind his hand from time to time and, even as he spoke, his heavy-lidded blue eyes scanned the room in seeming search of something more interesting. He had a reputation for being over-sympathetic to Indians, and there had even been a rumour voiced at a Tennis Club party of an Indian mistress. Not that Anthony paid much attention to Tennis Club gossip, fuelled by the malicious inventions of the idle colonial wives.

He asked Prescott about Tippera, recalling, even as the other man started talking, that Reeves had left for Srirampur for his familiarization course two days after Christmas. Srirampur was very near Tippera. Reeves wouldn't be thinking much about poetry or music or pretty young Indian schoolteachers now, Anthony thought grimly.

Prescott sat back in his leather chair, telling the story in the desiccated, dry tones of a professional historian relating the battle order at Marathon or the effects of Vesuvius erupting upon the inhabitants of Pompeii. That's the trick, Anthony thought, if you divorce disasters from the individuals it robs the incidents of any pain.

From time to time Prescott paused and took a long draught of his beer, his Adam's apple bobbing as he swallowed. 'Srirampur, as you probably know, is in the region of Noakhali, a water-logged settlement on the delta of two of the holiest rivers of India, the Ganges and

130

the Brahmaputra. What the primum mobile of the whole shooting match was, God knows,' and here Prescott permitted himself the brief rictus which passed for a smile.

The Muslims had turned on the Hindu population, raping the women, burning homes and temples, killing the men. The news had taken some time to filter back. 'There may well be some connection between the rioting and the fact that the half-naked fakir, the Blessed Mahatma, is living in the area and trying to reconcile both sides with each other.' For a moment his expression was passionate, concerned, and Anthony glimpsed a side of Prescott he had never suspected. The well-bred indifference was gone, and Prescott pounded the chair arm with his clenched fist. 'God preserve us from idealistic visionaries. Wherever they sow their discontent and their vision of heaven upon earth they only promote war and destruction.'

'What do you think the long-term prospects are?' Anthony asked.

Prescott drew a hand over his face in a gesture of weariness. In sharp contrast to the gesture his words were venomous, spitefully delivered. 'That wizened fart Attlee has some bee in his bonnet about people's right to self-determination. If they can persuade Winston, who seems a spent force since the war, they'll probably promote some bemedalled hero with the impeccable credentials of complete ignorance to preside over the dissolution of India. Let's face it, there are very few people they could choose who do have a knowledge of the place. Cripps might have been a possibility. But it seems our colonial past has made our rulers incapable of understanding that dealing with flesh and blood, with land, and water, and arable and arid soils, requires someone with wisdom and compassion and the ability to analyse the whole complex problem and to reach equitable solutions . . .' He trailed off, shaking his head.

Parsons, one of the older Assistant Collectors, who had brought his drink over, stood by them nodding his undershot jaw and said in mildly remonstrative tones, 'Come on, old man. We haven't done too badly here, or in Malaysia or Rhodesia . . .' His voice had a soft Yorkshire burr, and the conciliatory cadences of a father talking to his unruly son.

Prescott turned his cold blue eyes on Parsons. Anthony could see that Parsons' manner had irritated him, and held his breath as Prescott spoke.

'Dear boy. You were fortunate in being spared the celebrated English public school system. Only those less fortunate than you are in a position to appreciate the Establishment's unique ability to destroy all that is original, alive and individual in the cause of their concept of progress. Misconstrued Marxism is the new fashion. You know the sort of thing – workers controlling the means of production, the suppression of any differences which may disturb the smooth, newly socialized order of society. Not that the grammar school system works much better if your friend Henshaw is a typical example.' He yawned suddenly and smiled at Parsons. 'I'm sorry. I shouldn't have said that. I've only had a couple of hours sleep over the past two nights.'

Parsons' face was a dull brick red. He shrugged his shoulders, affecting nonchalance, and said with awkward kindness, 'My bungalow's just around the corner. Why don't you get your head down for a couple of hours?' He looked quickly over his shoulder to ensure that Prescott's words had not carried to the other occupants of the mess hall.

Later, when Anthony was leaving, he bumped into Parsons in the car park. The Yorkshireman was in a state of massive indignation. 'D'you know what the bugger's done?' he asked incredulously. 'The Memsahib just called to say that he's absconded with a bottle of my best Glenlivet.'

Anthony couldn't help smiling, and Parsons finally managed a rueful laugh.

'That's the trouble with nursing vipers,' Anthony said. 'They make very bad house guests.'

Driving back, he reflected that Harrow hadn't managed to turn Prescott into a colourless member of the Establishment.

Twelve

The mahseer felt the hook bite deep in its gullet. From instinct it began to run, out from the rocks towards the centre of the pool where the water ran fast and deep. As it seemed that the safety of the grey rocks on the other side was almost achieved, it felt, again, the fierce barb bite its throat and the tug of the line. Unknowing, fearless, it began to fight.

Roger Henshaw stood in the shallows, the line running taut from the bent rod held in his powerful hands. He watched the line slit clear of the water, about three feet from the white froth of the fish, and let the reel click out a few notches. The mahseer surfaced briefly, arched silver in the sunshine for an instant, and fell back, fighting against the line. He let it run further, giving the fish a short illusion of freedom. Then, conscious of the breaking strain, he began to play the fish. It was fighting well, and he felt the same excitement as he had when he went on shikar for tiger or on sambhur shoots. 'Not quite one of us. Grammar school, y'know,' he had heard Listowel mutter behind his hand to Toby Rendell when he had gone on his first expedition to shoot snow leopard. He had secretly practised using the rifles, taught by Feroze Khan, and had confirmed his reputation for bravery and for sportsmanship by killing two man-eating tigers in the district.

He knew that he was not fully accepted at the Murree Club, nor by people like Listowel or Andrew Prescott. Though he had made District Commissioner on merit early, by dint of hard work, and ambition, there was some indefinable, ineradicable nuance which marked him down and set him apart. His family's poverty had not even the virtue of being genteel. Though he daily fought to maintain a fragile dominance over his colonial acquaintances, he had long since realized that he would never really be one of them. Even Joginder Singh possessed some unknowable superiority over him. Because of all these things, he exulted in his coarse and brutal strength, and when a black buck fell to his gun at three hundred yards or he tracked a wounded leopard into a thicket where no one else would follow he felt a scorn which, for those brief moments, gave him the impression of soaring effortlessly.

He played the fish viciously, winding the reel and watching with a practised eye the line tauten and thrum. The struggles were getting weaker now and he waded in to avoid the tackle snagging on the grey rocks as he brought the fish slowly in. His khaki shirt was stained with sweat at the armpits, and his hairline leaked moisture over his low forehead, and down past the hooked, predatory nose and the thin-lipped mouth.

* * *

Feroze Khan sat on a rock above the waterfall. He watched what was happening, noting the cruelty in the play, and Henshaw's excitement, without judgement. He used to come out with his father in the 'thirties to show the English the pools where the great fish rose. He had first seen this excitement then, and his father had said, 'It is the way of the Ingresi. These are games to them; they could buy these for food in the market.' The humorous contempt stemmed from his father's security, his knowledge that he and his kind were the true owners of the land, and that the English, for all their apparent superiority, were merely temporary guests whose departure must surely come. Feroze Khan felt more sharply than that. The English were a violation of his land, almost, though not quite, comparable to the Hindus and Sikhs who were still permitted to own land and property on the great crag above the valley. It was a feeling within him which nothing could change: he could not willingly cede any hold upon the mountains or the forests to the Hindu zamindar who had saved his father's sight, nor to this Englishman who had made veiled promises to him of land and cattle and wealth in return for certain favours.

When the Englishman had brought the fish on to the rocky bank and begun to gut it expertly, Feroze Khan called, 'Shabash,' and picked his way over the scrub and boulders to sit a few feet from Henshaw and to watch the operation with his flat, unwinking gaze.

When Henshaw had finished he plunged his knife into the sand at the water's edge before washing it and putting it in his pocket. Then he wrapped the fish carefully and put it into the knapsack with precise, careful movements.

'I have nothing for you, yet,' Feroze Khan said.

Henshaw looked across at him for a moment. He said carefully, as though instructing a child, 'You know that it is only small things I want. It is easier to move stubborn people with many small things than with one great one.'

Khan nodded, and blew his nose into his fingers, flicking the mucus expertly into the river.

'By the way,' Henshaw said conversationally, 'Walid Khan tells me you have purchased Gunevati's land?' He looked up sharply but the other man made no sign.

Feroze watched as Henshaw dismantled his rod and carried his equipment to the jeep. Then he stood up, hitching the rifle slung over his shoulder into a more comfortable position. He looked up the great escarpment of rock now half in shadow, the rest rosy in the light of the westering sun. Far above, the Union Jack fluttered from the flagpole at the edge of the school playground. Feroze said, so softly that the other man had to strain to hear the words, 'In this matter of the girls who have been found dead and dishonoured, my people need a culprit. They are only happy when these things are solved.' He didn't look at Henshaw, but began to walk up the narrow path into the fissure between the rocks. The quails strung together at his waist had bled upon his white trousers.

Thirteen

The letter came out of the blue. His mother-in-law's letters were like military campaigns; never undertaken without prospect of gain. Anthony was glad that, for once, she was only pressing him to take a decision which he had already taken for his own reasons.

34 Kipling Road
Mysore   25th March 1947

My dear Jane

Every time we get news of what is happening on the border I
wish that you could persuade Anthony to bring the family down
until the troubles are over. You were the only one of the family
to leave home and it is natural for a mother to feel concerned
for her daughter at a time like this.

We heard the news about Dickie Mountbatten's appointment.
One can't help remembering the rumours of Queen Mary's
concern about the Prince of Wales being in Paris with him, and
be a little worried about his enthusiasm for Hollywood too. We
must remember that he is of German extraction, however much
of an Anglophile he may seem. Still, I suppose we must accept
what we cannot alter, though there seems little chance that one
man can stop these terrible riots and disturbances that we hear
about every day. Vincent has got his promotion. He rang from
the hospital to tell us, and sent on the letter of congratulation
from Major Majid. I remember thinking when he first came
back from Burma that it was the end. He used to sit in the
bedroom with the curtains drawn and just a dhoti round his
waist for hours on end, looking vacantly into space. He was skin
and bone. Sometimes I used to go in and find him crying, though
his face didn't look unhappy, just blank. There was nothing I
could do. You know how I hated him going back to the hospital,
but it *was* a relief when he started to show interest in something
again. To celebrate the great occasion we went to dinner in
Bangalore with Bob and Daisy Farris. The restaurant is called
the Maharajah and the cook is rumoured to come from H.E.'s
kitchen. It is very beautiful, one of the mid-Victorian houses
situated on the edge of the Old City. Duck, fresh from the
jheels that morning, sorbet from England. Lots of familiar faces;
the brigadier and his wife, Listowel and a party who are staying
at the palace for a shikar, and old Bulstrode-Henshaw down
from the Nilgiris still wearing his Edwardian evening clothes. I
remembered the young man you'd introduced to me when last I
visited, and it appears that there is some distant connection
going way back. It was a splendid evening, just like old times;

linen and crystal on the tables and everyone properly dressed. Afterwards we had champagne at the Gymkhana and I met some of Vincent's English colleagues. Very rowdy and high-spirited, but such nice boys nevertheless.

Rod is due back in a couple of months. I don't know whether to be pleased or sorry. He was always prone to drink too much and his experiences in the Burma campaign seem to have pushed him further down this road and made him even more sullen and morose. It seems to me it is time he grew up a little. No good playing the baby at forty-one. But Patricia is counting the days. She said to me the other day, 'I wish I could have a child for him,' and I felt sorry for her. If only she knew, as you and I do, that it is no such great thing. That the pride of authorship quickly fades, and soon they are irretrievably lost and one is alone once more.

I had to have a talk to Angela. The Saturday after Vincent's dinner she asked if she could bring someone home for the evening. She was very secretive, as only she can be, and I was rather hopeful that she would be bringing one of the older officers from the mess. You may imagine my surprise when the door opened and Sam ushered in Major Majid. After the initial shock, which I suppose he must have spotted, I was quite polite to him, and the evening was fairly jolly. I've had to make it absolutely clear to her that we can't have this sort of thing happening again. Given half a chance I think she'd be inviting the Bhoses in for tea!

I'm well, but forced to recognize that I'm getting older. I really feel that I would like my family round me once more and where I can appreciate them. D.V. I will remain active for some time yet, but I find that I am appreciably slower than I was in the mornings, and my hearing is giving me trouble.

Your room is waiting for you and Anne can have the small boxroom. Mark can have the dressing-room at the end of the landing. Remember, Janey, what I told you as a little girl. I had to make sure your father followed the diet for his diabetes, stopped going to those ridiculous shikars, and didn't let the beggars take advantage of him. Men never really grow up. They have Masonic dinners, and dress up to play strange games at Mess stag evenings. We have to make the real decisions, the ones that count. And we have to do it without them knowing. I know that you, as a daughter of mine, understand this and will do whatever is required. Write soon. Our thoughts are with you.

Your loving Mother.

Anthony put the letter down by his plate, willing himself to speak calmly. 'I could do without her bigoted philosophizing but I had already decided we should go down south for a spell . . .'

'When?' said Jane, and Anne and Mark looked at him enquiringly. 'There are a few things to arrange first. I'll sort them out over the next few days.'

By the time he got to the office he felt calmer. If only, he thought, I had suggested it before the letter came. It felt now, as if he were giving in, and he cursed himself for drifting, for his indecision. He had become so used to the details of his domestic life being organized by women – first by his mother and now by Jane – that it was hard to impose his own wishes. Covertly he sometimes envied Henshaw's strength and Joginder's absolute assurance. It was hard to imagine that they could ever be dictated to by anyone else.

He sat at his desk and breathed deeply. His stomach pressed against the waistband of his trousers and he slapped it disapprovingly once or twice. He had opened all the mail left by the chaprassi. Two petitions: a request for money in aid of the lepers of India, a gratuitous circular (unordered) offering rabidly Muslim League views on a variety of social topics. He sipped his coffee, grimacing at the gritty residue in the bottom of the cup. It had been impossible to get proper coffee for months. He lit a cheroot and glanced at his watch. Reeves was due. Anthony got up from his desk and stretched, looking out across the parkland.

Reeves looked absurdly young when he came in. His blond hair, slightly dishevelled, stuck up at the crown so that it imparted an urchin innocence to his face. The blue eyes were like china, bleached and bleeding off into the whites, wide, ingenuous, unseeing. Even as Reeves said, 'Good morning, sir,' his voice faltered and tears began to spill down his cheeks.

Anthony said, 'Sit down, Richard,' using his kindly voice. He was embarrassed. He hated these discussions in which he felt uneasily that he would be afforded a glimpse of another human being whom common compassion would force him to recognize, in which things would emerge which couldn't be tidied away, left at the office, filed and forgotten.

Gur had met Reeves two evenings before and had reported to Anthony that the experience of Srirampur seemed to have devastated him. 'He has that peculiarly European attachment to the idea that individual life is important. All those bodies. He can't help thinking about them, imagining their bereaved relatives, the empty houses.' Then Gur had laughed, looking at Anthony, and had said gently, 'And you, too. You don't know what I'm talking about either.' And Anthony had looked back at Gur's clean-shaven face and conservative English suit, and had felt, again, the sense of something beyond his comprehension.

Now Reeves accepted a whisky, and Anthony poured himself a generous measure, topping it up with cool water from the lotah. Drinking before lunch was a breach of one of his private rules. As he finished pouring, he could see from the corner of his eye Reeves' hand gripping the arm of his chair. The knuckles were white under the pinky brown tan. Anthony forced a lightness he didn't feel into his tone.

'So, I gather you had a few teething problems.'

He still hoped, knowing it to be vain, that the interview would be a conventional exchange of clichés following the accepted rules.

There was a knock on the door and the chaprassi came in to collect the letters. Anthony gave him the post, indicating that he should close the door behind him. Reeves was now slumped in his chair with his hands over his face, weeping bitterly. Anthony sat down and waited, looking out of the window. With part of his mind he remembered the meeting with Henshaw, but instantly dismissed any thought of saying anything to Reeves about the Indian schoolteacher. Reeves took a crumpled handkerchief from his pocket and blew his nose noisily.

'I'm sorry, sir. It was terrible. So unexpected. We were going into a village to hear a case involving a land dispute between a Sikh farmer and a Muslim small-holder. When we drove down the road in the jeep it seemed misty, but after a while I realized that it was smoke . . .' He paused, searching for words, calmer now as he attempted to remember the scene. 'The first figure we saw was a woman. She was walking by the side of the road. It wasn't possible to see if she was a Sikh or a Muslim. Her hair had been cut off so badly she was almost scalped. Blood was running down her face and on to her sari and her arm was hanging at a strange angle. She just walked past us and carried on walking. She didn't seem to register us at all.' He looked at Anthony, but the older man was looking down at the blotter on the desk, distancing himself from the appeal in the pleading eyes. Again, Reeves pulled his handkerchief from his pocket and blew his nose violently.

Anthony searched for something to say which would return the interview to some more conventional exchange. It was, as always, the specific, anecdotal narrative which worried him. He said helplessly, aware of the emptiness of the platitude even as he uttered it, 'We must accept what we cannot change, Richard.' He felt a moment's rising panic, a sense that such phrases carried no force nor meaning in such circumstances. Outside, the abdar was haranguing one of the buddis as they walked down the corridor. His voice echoed loudly, fading as they walked past the door and down towards the mess hall.

Anthony said, 'We cannot deny the Indians swaraj any more. The days of colonial possession and the Great Game are over.' As he went on, he felt surprised by what he was saying, as if the traitorous words were being dictated by someone else. 'We've patronized and used the people of a culture two millennia older than our own. But we have been too arrogant to attempt to understand them. Since the military passed out those bullets greased with cow or pig fat in 1857, the writing has been on the wall. At that moment we displayed what had always been there – our fundamental ignorance of their most profound beliefs. It has taken almost a century for Gandhi and Bhose, Nehru and Jinnah, to complete the process that started then.'

He thought to himself, My God, what am I saying, both surprised and curiously elated by the words he had spoken. But when he looked at Reeves the boy had noticed nothing. He sat gazing at the ground with the tears streaming down his face. Anthony looked at his watch as unobtrusively as possible. It was almost tiffin time. He began to feel comfortable, the sense of control and detachment and understanding returning to him as he spoke.

'Richard, we are powerless to prevent or subvert what is happening here. This has its roots in events which took place long before the East India Company arrived on

Indian soil. In the oppression of the Dravidians by Tamerlane and Genghis Khan; in the fundamental differences between the Islamic canon with its precise structure and Hinduism which has no founder nor revealed truth, nor dogma nor churchly establishment.' Watching Reeves as he spoke, he sensed suddenly that something might happen which would break through the conventions and codes that must govern the relationship between a man and his subordinates. He started to his feet, intending to offer Reeves tiffin in the Mess where the presence of others might inhibit any further outbreak.

Reeves hit the table with the flat of his hand. His glass leaped on to the parquet flooring, shattering into fine shards which spilled across the floor like ice. His face was distorted with pain and rage. At first his voice was low and controlled, crawling with loathing. 'My God, you're even worse than Roger Henshaw. At least he has passion. Don't you understand that I'm not talking about some academic historical problem?' He swung his head wildly from side to side, sawing the air with clutching gestures. 'I'm talking about men and women and children dead – rotting in the sun with the vultures pecking out their eyes. Have you ever seen a body which has lain in the sun for a few days? Smelt it? Have you? *Have you*?' His voice cracked with emotion and he rose from his chair and stood over Anthony with his hands on the desk. The child's face was puzzled, questioning.

Briefly, irrationally, a picture came into Anthony's mind of himself sitting on his mother-in-law's verandah sipping a stengah, and he wished they had already left for Mysore.

He stood up and said quietly, 'That'll do, Reeves. Sit down,' and Reeves obeyed, suddenly deflated. 'I'm sorry, sir,' he said in a chastened voice, suddenly completely calm and abashed by his own outburst. It was strange how manners and custom took precedence over all. Anthony walked over to the duty roster and said, 'I'll make a few alterations here. You'd better go off on leave for a few weeks.' He affected a light jocular tone. 'You've got an aunt in the hills, haven't you?'

Behind him Reeves said desperately, 'Sir, please don't send me on leave. I'd like to work now.'

But the boy seemed a stranger to Anthony suddenly, an administrative problem which could be solved by some simple rearrangements. A couple of weeks should do it, he thought, blur the edges and consign the memory of what had just taken place to the embarrassed past. 'Nonsense,' Anthony said briskly, 'a couple of weeks in the mountains will make a new man of you. You start immediately. That's an order.' He stopped and said, 'Use my phone to call your aunt. And get a syce from the pool to drive you up.'

He heard Reeves say, 'I wish you'd let me stay, sir,' but he walked on down the corridor, relieved that the inter-view was over. He was uneasily aware that Reeves' accusation had found a mark, and that his mysterious progress towards some hidden end, suspended during the days at home over Christmas, had begun its wormlike movements deep within. When he arrived home in the evening, still troubled by Reeves' comments, Jane met him at the gate as the office car rattled away. He could see immediately that something was wrong, and his mind leapt to Mark and the bicycle. Jane opened the gate and said incredulously, like a woman in shock, 'Lal Deen's been arrested. You'll have to do something.'

He felt a surge of relief and an incongruous desire to giggle. Instead he took Jane's arm and began to walk up the drive with her. 'What's the charge?' he asked, part of his mind still preoccupied with anticipation of his customary stengah on the verandah. He imagined some trivial traffic offence; Anwar Khan's men had become overbearingly punctilious of late. When Jane said, 'Murder,' just the one word, before her lips closed tightly, he felt a coldness come over him, and the anticipated pleasures of the evening began to disappear. He clutched her arm for comfort, but she moved away, shivering and drawing her cardigan over her shoulders.

He stopped by the rhododendron bushes, not wanting to take this thing into the house. 'Tell me,' he said, and listened while the sun died on the pink-tiled roof of the verandah and the muezzin came and went and the sounds of traffic grew fainter as the evening rush subsided. Superintendent Anwar Khan had come to the house himself. Anthony could picture him as she spoke, tall for an Indian, with features of simian, long-upper-lipped dignity and an expression of permanent sadness. He had culled a report from bystanders and Jane retailed this, unconsciously adopting some of Khan's mannerisms as she did so. The open, splay-handed gestures to accentuate a point, the theatrical pause before a dramatic moment. Her near perfect memory was based on a frighteningly intense concentration on whatever she observed, a facility Anthony had often envied.

It had been Lal Deen's day off and he had gone down to the bazaar with a group of friends. 'Two of them members of the Rashtriya Swayam Sewak Sangh, it appears,' said Jane grimly, looking at Anthony as if to imply that he should have known the company his servant kept. They had been drinking (and here again Jane looked at him meaningfully, and he remembered how weak some of his stengahs had seemed recently) and were behaving rather noisily, ('larking about like a band of goondas,' was Khan's description) when they had met up with a group of beggars.

As Jane continued, Anthony felt a sick certainty that he knew how the story was going to end. The wind came up briefly and he shivered. 'Do you want to go in?' Jane asked, but he shook he head mutely, and she carried on. According to witnesses the beggars had been walking up the street with the leper known as the Silver Saddhu at their head. As was the custom, people had fallen back to allow the beggars to walk up the narrow alleyway. But the leader of Lal Deen's band, known to the police as the Cobra, had stepped in front of the group, pointing with his lathi at the Saddhu. He had made some mocking references to the beggars. 'You see what the corruption in our blood has produced,' he had said, pointing his stick, and people in the crowd had begun to laugh and jeer.

Then the Saddhu had stepped forward, and the voices had fallen silent. He had slowly raised his staff until it pointed at the speaker, and said in a loud, clear voice, 'You and your brothers will murder the Great Soul of India. The Jackals will bring down the Lion.'

There was a moment's electric silence in which nobody seemed to move or speak. Then the Cobra had shrieked an obscenity and leapt forward, hitting the Saddhu on the head with his lathi, and his followers had joined in frenziedly. It was all over in a few seconds. When the police arrived the Saddhu had been dead in a pool of blood on the cobbles.

They began to walk towards the house and Anthony said heavily, 'I'll see what I can do.' Jane stopped, remembering something, and he waited, dazed with shock. She said, 'I knew there was something else. The Cobra is Feroze Khan. But the Superintendent had telephoned Roger Henshaw's office and was told that Feroze was with Henshaw and both were away fishing for the day.'

Anthony was silent and preoccupied all evening. He tried to enter into the dinner conversations with their guests, the Parsons, but could not stop himself going over the events of the day – the interview with Reeves, the prophecy, the death of the Silver Saddhu. From time to time he remembered Saddhu's words to Joginder and himself on the day of the picnic with a sense of unease. But the greatest sense of unease came from a thought which persisted against all reason and would not go away: that the Saddhu was not, could not be dead.

Three mornings later, Mark came out on to the verandah where his father was finishing his breakfast. It was a bright morning with the light haze which promised a perfect day. Anthony had visited Lal Deen the previous day and accepted his assurances that he was not involved in the incident, but had just been carried along in the rush. He couldn't confirm exactly what had happened, and the papers, so busy with the news of the rioting, had ignored the incident.

Mark sat down on the concrete with his back against the wall and his knees drawn up, looking across the garden with an expression of such unhappiness that Anthony finally felt prompted to ask what the matter was.

'The mongoose man comes today. The new bearer arranged it for mummy,' Mark said glumly, rubbing the dust into whorls with his forefinger.

Anthony felt a twinge of annoyance that Jane had arranged this without consulting him. It seemed, in some obscure way, an act which carried some hostility towards him. The new bearer, Mazuffar Khan, came through the door with his obsequious shuffle and took the tray away, holding the door open on his return so that Jane could come through.

'Isn't the driver here? You'll be late.'

She wants me out of the way while the deed is done, he thought, looking at his watch. It was true that the traffic had been particularly bad in the mornings recently, and he saw that he would be late for the office again. His annoyance grew, became displaced. He said, 'Why didn't you tell me you were bringing in the mongoose-wallah?' And Jane abruptly took her hand from the back of his chair and moved away. Her voice was hostile. 'You've never shown the slightest interest in domestic matters since we got married. Why are you so interested now?' Anthony shrugged his shoulders and raised his hands to indicate that the matter was unimportant, unable to sustain the confrontation.

Since reading her mother's letter, he had recognized, as he saw it, the patronage of the women of his acquaintance towards their menfolk. Sometimes it manifested itself in open dislike. Julia Howard had once stood up after dinner and looked at her husband with a jaundiced eye, saying 'Can you stand?' and the phrase and its method of delivery had evoked a whole life of hatred, of hopes blighted and love destroyed, which had briefly united Jane and Anthony, almost in a common fear that it might happen to them. More often it was expressed in smaller and more subtle ways. The incident of Mark's bicycle, and now this of the mongoose, were merely part of a many-stranded web. There was still a dependency upon him but despite that, or perhaps because of it, there was also a permanent subtle disagreement which made every discussion and every exchange a conflict of wills. In the subculture of the Club, blessedly relieved by stengahs under the slow fans, slumped in the battered leather chairs, it was an accepted reality. Over a certain age the men joked of their wives' convenient headaches, their resentment at the men's nights at the mess, their dislike of polo and other all-male pursuits. Under the casual badinage it was possible to discern, sometimes, a real desperation, but the shared joking made the situation tolerable in a society where divorce or open separation spelt the end of a career. 'If a man can't stick with the woman he chose, what chance he will prove fit to carry the responsibilities of this job?' It was not the social aspects of his growing estrangement from Jane that worried Anthony, but the daily erosion of the small, shared intimacies he remembered as the texture of the first years. Each day brought some small new evidence of her movement away from him and towards her mother. Sometimes he surprised contempt upon her face, immediately masked when he looked at her, and it was against this, and to establish a place of his own beyond the conflict, that he had first let the snake go unhurt. He had known, as he spoke to Mark, that the seeming victory would be finite, and that she would seek some way of re-establishing her dominion over the household.

His equanimity didn't return until half way through the morning. The news on the radio and in his paper had been about the rioting, again, but over the months he had prepared himself for the worst, so that any indication of orderly progress of structure gave him a feeling of security, of rational decisions taken by wise men in panelled offices. As he had endowed his father with superhuman powers as a child, so he endowed these men with the same qualities, only half aware that they could not really possess the attributes he gave them. This morning one of the inter-office memoranda carried the heading 'Not For Dissemination' and detailed the information that India and the new state, Pakistan, would remain within the Commonwealth, and went on to say that informed sources indicated that Churchill had reluctantly agreed to persuade the Tories to fall in with Attlee's grand design. Someone had scrawled in pencil at the bottom, 'Typical British politicians playing God in other people's lives.'

At eleven o'clock Gur put his head around the door and said, 'D'you have a moment?' His usually cheerful face was grave. In response to Anthony's nod he came in and sat down, carefully lifting the creases on his grey flannels so that the knees wouldn't bag. More English than the English, Anthony thought affectionately. He remembered that Gur had been home over the weekend, and he asked after Joginder and Sita.

'Oh, they're fine,' said Gur, smiling briefly. 'Father fell off his new mare and is hobbling round with a stick. Grumbling a lot but I think it hurt his dignity more than anything else. No. What I wanted to talk to you about was Reeves.'

Anthony sighed and sat back. The last person he wanted to talk about was Reeves, but Gur's mention had made it semi-official and thus unavoidable. The story Gur had to tell was brief and inconsequential enough in itself, but Anthony sensed uneasily that it was not an isolated incident, but a flaw in some pattern whose shape would only become apparent in the future. As always, faced with some imminent disclosure, he felt a premonition of disaster coupled with an irrational belief that there would be some avoiding action he could take if only he knew what the action was. Some primitive belief in magic, a residue of childhood, worked on in him unchecked.

Apparently Reeves had arrived unexpectedly at Joginder's house the previous Sunday morning, riding a rangy cob. He was sweating heavily, and evidently distraught about something, but had accepted Joginder's invitation to join them for a drink. When Sita disappeared into the house and the bearer left to get the drinks he had suddenly shouted, 'I'll kill the man. I'll kill him,' and both of them knew immediately he had been talking about Roger Henshaw.

Roger had dropped round to Reeves' aunt, Margaret Preston for coffee the previous morning and had told Reeves that his friendship with the Indian teacher, Premla Purveys, was embarrassing to Margaret and would destroy his career. 'Everybody knows about him and my aunt,' said Reeves bitterly. 'How dare he say that I am embarrassing the family?' He was beside himself with rage, unable to talk of anything else. But by the time Joginder enquired if he would join them for lunch he was able to smile apologetically. 'I say, I am sorry to have lumbered you with all my problems. I seem to have been doing this a lot since Srirampur.' He had declined with his disarming little boy's smile, and had ridden slowly through the pines out of sight.

That was all, but Gur was worried too, with the same ill-defined, unplaceable concern. Anthony said, 'He'll be all right. He was just upset by the massacres.' But Gur wasn't convinced. He picked up a pencil from the desk and twirled it between his fingers, looking at it as at a prism which might reveal some new dimension. By a trick of the light his face seemed suddenly old.

'Henshaw went to see Premla some time ago. She was very upset, but wouldn't tell Richard what had gone on.'

There was a long pause, with only the soft creaking of the fan and the distant voices from the gardens to break the silence. Then Anthony said heavily, 'Nothing we can do about it. I've got to get to Lahore for a Durbar tomorrow afternoon.' He gestured towards the papers in his tray. 'If the workload seems heavy now, just wait until the relocation starts. Can you imagine what that will do to land disputes?' He felt guilty that he was leaving as the work increased and continued ruefully, 'I'm throwing you in at the deep end, I'm afraid.'

When Gur had gone he was restless, unable to settle. He felt a nagging resentment at being drawn into these matters which could not be solved by the application of a set of rules; it was as if the conflict which lay at the heart of his marriage, forcing him into a reluctant recognition of his own involvement in a situation where feelings and not reason held the primary place, had now spread, so that he was being forced towards a re-evaluation of his attitudes, not only to his own family, but also towards Reeves and Lal Deen, and who knows what else besides. It was a process which he seemed powerless to reverse. At least, he thought, it will be like old times tonight, treasuring in anticipation the imperial anonymity of dinner alone and the hotel suite awaiting him.

At four o'clock he set off for Falletti's Hotel in Lahore. He could have stayed at the Punjab Club, but he shrank from the prospect of the boozy bonhomie and another evening of speculation about what was going to happen. The dusty roads were thick with oxen carts, trundling their loads of firewood on slatted carts mounted on wooden, steel-bound wheels; with women leading donkeys whilst their menfolk rode in somnolent comfort; with patient, grey water-buffaloes trudging ahead of their keepers, scything their long, curved horns to and fro over their backs to dislodge the swarms of clustering flies. On the long downhill stretches, the syce cut the engine and put the clutch out, a heritage of his previous job driving

152

the ramshackle bus between Rawalpindi and Murree. Anthony had remonstrated with him many times, but Afzal seemed incapable of learning, and now Anthony ignored it, giving himself up to his pleasure in the passing scenery.

When he had unpacked and changed after bathing, he had a modest dinner in the vast, ornate dining room. About thirty servants in immaculate gold, green and white livery stood around. There were only four other diners. A Parsi businessman at a table on his own ate curry and rice while reading the *Lahore Gazette* propped on a wooden stand at the table. Three Bengali traders talked noisily in the far corner, drinking Vimto from gaudy glasses.

After dinner he went for a walk, too preoccupied to take much note of his surroundings. The beggars huddled on the pavement murmured, 'Baksheesh,' half-heartedly as he went past, but he was oblivious. Jane had talked every day for a week about going to Mysore. There was a permanent wariness about her now, and Anthony would sometimes lift his head from the paper or from a book to find her looking curiously at him, as at a stranger. They no longer made love. After three occasions when he had recognized the anger within her, and had felt ashamed of his importunate desire, she had said to him in the darkness, 'I suppose you think that everything would be all right if I just lay on my back and let you do whatever you wanted?' He had been stung by the anger and contempt in her voice. Since that night he had ceased to approach her, and soon even the desire had ended and there was only a dull sadness when he remembered from time to time how it had once been between them.

He had been so preoccupied with his thoughts that he paid no attention to where he was walking. He had left the vast square which Arungzeb's Mosque dominated with vulgar splendour, its terraces and ledges illuminated by strung bulbs, and the road he was now in had narrowed to an alleyway, punctuated by dark doorways. Above him the moonlit sky was bright against the dark bulk of the buildings. He passed a couple doing something frantic with each other in a doorway. The woman gasped, 'Nay, nay,' but her sari was above her waist and she plucked her companion's clothing with frenzied fingers. Anthony looked away and walked on. The traffic noise had died away but he could hear the faint sound of voices. They seemed to be coming from the upper storeys of the buildings around him, but when he looked up he saw only a flash of white which may have been the loose end of a puggaree floating in the wind; then nothing. It was only when his ear became accustomed to the noise that he could suddenly hear what the voices were saying. 'Beware. Beware,' and the sound was like an echo repeated over water. Anthony began to run, panic-stricken suddenly by the dark alley, by the absence of people. His foot hit something and he stumbled, grazing his forearm on the cobbles. The object he had kicked rolled along the ground unevenly, coming to rest in the gutter where the lights from the main thoroughfare caught it. It was the head of a middle-aged man, severed neatly at the neck. He got up and began to run, and the warnings stopped. Someone began to laugh.

By the weekend the memory had the blurred definition, the distance, of an evening at the theatre. Mark had recounted how the mongoose had found three snakes and had killed them, describing the event with such morbid relish that Anthony had felt wonder at the fickleness of the young.

Mark said, 'What did you do *then*, daddy?' The horses came into view round the curve of the track, far to the right, and Anthony put his binoculars to his eyes, carefully adjusting the knurled knob between two cylinders to focus the lens. He affected nonchalance. 'I reported the incident at the police station and walked back to the hotel, son,' but he saw the look in Mark's face from the corner of his eye, and felt diminished. Even as he thought it was time the boy learned that adults weren't omnipotent, he felt a sense of loss. It had been hard enough to acknowledge to himself that he could no longer control the circumstances in which they lived. He wished that Mark had remained a hero-worshipper a little longer.

Despite what had happened it was hard, on days such as this, to give credence to the shrill editorials and daily reports of disaffection and violence. Dr Mackenzie had joined them in the Mess box. An inveterate gambler, he was senior enough to arrange that his two assistants took the surgeries and rounds which conflicted with race meetings. He had inveigled some sort of unofficial consultancy with the Managing Stewards of the race-track to endorse his presence, and cheerfully dispensed burra pegs from his medicinal whisky bottles, leaving the official race-track physician, Dr Ayub Khan to treat the rare cases of sunstroke or minister to the bruises and cut knees of children. He had a mordant wit, mildly melancholy and preoccupied with mortality, and laughingly confessed himself the worst advertisement for his profession. Something about Mac, his refusal to take anything seriously, his never-failing fund of gossip and louche stories, gave Anthony the feeling that time, the causal dialectic of events, and the grimness of life were suspended. That fear of the savage riots, of the future and the encroachment of the unknown, were rendered unimportant in the face of this laughter and good fellowship. He had never understood the central paradox: that Mac created laughter out of a bleak and pitiless view of life which contained no sentimentality or bathos.

It was for these reasons that Anthony was concerned to find his friend genuinely sombre, his usually mobile face set and humourless. Anthony went down with him to Motilal's kiosk by the finishing post to collect their winnings. Motilal complained bitterly in his customary way, 'Aiee, Sahib. Yay quothia ne sir ke ghora. I'm sorry, sir, but this bloody horse should not have run. Jockey was telling me that horse fell in training yesterday morning. Owner too lazy to cancel. Then horse wins . . .' His chins wobbled with emotion. Mac leaned through the kiosk window and patted the fat man soothingly on the shoulder. 'Come on, Moti. You know better than to be taken in by those stories.' Motilal gave a painful smile, a martyred saint in a cruel world, showing several gold teeth black rimmed with betel nut stains. Mac counted his winnings as he walked back, smiling gently to himself as he smoothed out the notes and put them in his wallet. 'What are you smiling at?' asked Anthony and Mac said, 'Everybody's acting all the time. Moti always enlists your sympathy so you don't spot his extra commissions. Lazy man's way of covering bad debts.'

As they walked up over the stepped concrete towards the box, through the crowds of Indian punters, Dr Mac said, 'I'm a little concerned that your friend Henshaw seems to treat the Murree District as his own personal relief. He spends a lot of time with that villain, Feroze Khan, who has the reputation of a political agitator. Even stood alibi for him over some recent charge . . .' He vaulted over the wooden fence into the box while Anthony walked more sedately round. 'He hasn't managed to get anywhere in solving the murders either . . . If he's allowed to carry on unchecked God knows where it will end and I, for one, have no faith in natural justice.'

Lal Deen's trial began on a blustery day in June at a Durbar held on the outskirts of 'Pindi in a ramshackle Victorian house which had once been used by the Bishops of Lahore on their fruitless tours to gather in the faithful. Anthony took the day off work to give his evidence of good character.

Lal Deen stood among the other defendants under police guard, looking impassively ahead. As the proceedings wore on, Anthony stopped glancing across at his former servant for evidence of contrition, feeling himself to be in some way the guilty party. Under the new policy, the case was presided over by a Muslim judge, and the sentence, when it came, was brutally severe.

Gur had come along. It was a rest day for him, but he had said he would attend 'to see if justice is still being dispensed in the time-honoured way'. Anthony was grateful for his support, but they disagreed subsequently about the verdict. Anthony had felt that the evidence against Lal Deen and two other defendants was largely circumstantial and unsafe, but Gur had only smiled and said, 'Better a little good-hearted justice for all, than no justice for most. You should see how they deal with such matters amongst the tribes . . .'

The judge had refused to entertain any plea in mitigation afterwards. Seated at a battered school desk in the small, whitewashed room which passed for Chambers, he had halted Anthony's speech with an upraised hand. 'We are the masters,' he said, and then smiled gently at his own intentional phrasing 'of our own destinies.' When they walked out into the now blinding sunshine Gur said, almost apologetically, 'He's right, you know. There must be no feeling that once the British have gone law and order will cease.'

When Anthony arrived in the Mess for a late lunch he was surprised to see Andrew Prescott sitting with Parsons. Parsons was laughing, slapping his knee and throwing his head back. Andrew Prescott sat in his customary, indolent pose, his eyelids half-closed over the bored eyes.

Anthony joined them and the bearer took his order. Prescott said languidly, 'Just been telling friend Parsons here the news. That little bugger Corfield has given orders for all the Maharajah's records to be destroyed. All those marvellous stories of rape, murder, bestiality, lost for ever . . .' He snapped his fingers with a look of mock regret.

'Typically enough,' he continued, 'they've announced the date of Partition as 15 August, and there is already an outcry from the astrologers who consider the date inauspicious. Can you imagine that happening in our benighted country?'

Parsons laughed dutifully, but Anthony could see that Prescott was serious, and he felt, again, an unexpected warmth towards him.

They talked idly. Prescott commiserated with Anthony's disquiet over the trial verdict, but said gently, 'One cannot judge these matters entirely by European standards. First, there cannot be impartiality in this climate with a Muslim judge and a Hindu defendant – more particularly since the judge will have been all too aware of the British observers. Second, you will have reckoned without the fatalism of the Indian. He will accept his fate without a great sense of injustice. It is his karma . . .'

Prescott was being posted to Amritsar. Now that the arrangements accompanying Partition had begun, the Army were in a quandary. Though it still continued to operate in the way it had always done, there was now a manifest confusion over its precise role, its exact powers. In the background the property settlement between the emergent nations was being worked out between Chaudhuri Mohammed Ali and H. M. Patel. Now that the costs were being counted, they included Britain's two billion pound debt to India as the costs of war. Though it had been agreed that Pakistan would receive seventeen and a half per cent of the cash and sterling balances and that Pakistan would cover seventeen and a half per cent of India's debts, these were agreements between politicians only, and the agreements themselves were provoking dissident groups to acts of violence. Already the signs of division and over-reaction were becoming apparent. The Muslims wanted the Taj Mahal broken up and shipped to Pakistan for reconstruction because it had been built by a Mogul. Hindu Saddhus insisted that the Indus, flowing through Muslim India, should be theirs because the Vedas had been written by its banks. Sir Cyril Radcliffe had been summoned from Lincoln's Inn to delineate the boundary lines dividing the provinces of Bengal and the Punjab. Nehru and Jinnah both felt that his complete ignorance of India would be a proof of disinterest. The Maharajahs were unhappy with the offer guaranteeing their titles, privy purses, immunity from arrest, quasi-diplomatic status on condition that they joined one or other of the new states. Everywhere death stalked the countryside, often unreported, crowded from the newspapers and radio by the sheer volume of events. In March a Sikh leader had hacked down a pole flying the Muslim League banner with a cry of 'Pakistan murdabad,' and had started a riot in which more than three thousand Sikhs had been killed, but there was a numb dullness to

159

the times. When a cry was heard in the night, people bolted their doors and windows and tried to sleep.

Anthony was surprised to find how depressed he was to learn of Prescott's imminent departure. Now that the cloistered blinkered cosiness of the colonial community had begun to disintegrate under the pressure of events, he had begun to see, with clear eyes, that there were rare exceptions such as Prescott who had elected to join in a wider life. Divorced from the parochial considerations of the colonial community in 'Pindi, the trivializations of local concerns and Messroom gossip, Anthony sensed that Prescott saw more, and more clearly, than any of the other Europeans. His intelligence was undimmed by blinkered patriotism, and unbowed by any guilt-ridden wish to excuse the past.

The Mess Hall was almost empty when Anthony reluctantly rose to his feet. Prescott stood up and shook his hand firmly, and Anthony fancied there was a genuine and much-needed friendship in the clasp. 'You will come to Amritsar and look me up,' he said and it seemed to Anthony afterwards, watching the tall figure walk languidly through the tables and out through the door, that it had been a statement of certainty and not a polite farewell.

With only a week to go before their planned departure for Mysore, he could not imagine how he would finish the work to be done. He had taken to going to the office early and leaving late, ignored Jane's recriminations and spent his weekends working. 'We can't treat our friends like this,' she had said, and he, touched by a feeling of guilt, had retorted angrily that he had a duty to his work as well. Now Prescott's departure had stirred up a feeling of loss and disintegration and he was glad that he was so busy. He worked methodically through the afternoon.

When he had begun to tidy his papers, he heard swift steps in the corridor outside and a peremptory knock. Before Anthony had time to answer, Roger Henshaw pushed open the door and came in. He looked tired and his cotton suit was covered in fine dust. He was carrying a brown leather briefcase under his arm and Anthony noticed that, for once, his manner showed no bluster or superiority. He seemed almost humble, uncertain of himself.

'May I speak to you alone?'

Anthony gestured to the clerk to leave and shut the door, and motioned Roger to a chair, trying to instil some warmth into his manner. Henshaw eagerly accepted a whisky with water, sucking half of it down immediately with noisy, smacking gulps and wiping his mouth with the back of his hand. 'God, I needed that. Something terrible has happened.'

Even before Henshaw said, 'Richard has shot himself,' Anthony had known.

He looked at the other man in silence and Henshaw looked steadily back. A bead of perspiration ran down his forehead on to his nose and again he rubbed the back of his hand across his face.

'What happened?' said Anthony. 'Tell me.'

Henshaw seemed more at ease now. He settled himself comfortably in the chair and held out his glass for a refill.

'You know how upset he was about the massacre? Deranged almost. He wandered round for days on his own. He was very sharp with Margaret and when I tried to intercede he attacked me . . .' Henshaw sounded indignant for a moment. 'Yesterday he didn't come back from a ride. I went out to look for him. He was in the copse by Holly Stream.' His voice shook and he took a quick sip from his drink. 'He'd made a good job of it. There was nothing left of his face.'

Anthony opened his mouth to speak, but Henshaw carried on. 'It wasn't only the massacre,' he said. 'This morning I went to interview Premla Purveys, his school-teacher friend . . . When I told . . . told her that Richard was dead she started to laugh hysterically. I had to make her a cup of tea and wait for her to calm down. She kept rocking to and fro with her head in her hands, saying, "What am I going to do? What am I going to do?" I tried to comfort her by saying he wouldn't have suffered and must have died instantly and she shrieked at me. "Don't you see? I'm expecting a baby. I told him yesterday."'

Anthony sat still, stupefied.

Henshaw helped himself to a cheroot from the packet on the desk, and poured himself another whisky. His self-confidence seemed to be growing by the second. He said conspiratorially, 'I hope I can rely upon you in a couple of matters.' He looked across at Anthony but there was no response. He sighed heavily. 'For a number of reasons I feel we should keep these conclusions to ourselves. It would certainly reflect very badly on the English commu-nity here, for a start. Then Reeves has a widowed mother who lives in Kent. She dotes . . .,' he corrected himself, 'doted on the boy. I wanted to save her and Margaret from knowing what really happened. Anwar Khan is prepared to go along with a story about Reeves being attacked and robbed by goondas. There are so many incidents at the moment that it will be easy enough . . .' He got up and walked over to the window, and then back again. There was an impression of enormous reserves of

162

trapped energy in his movements, carried out with the exaggerated care of a drinker who has exceeded his limit. He picked up the battered briefcase from the side of his chair and took out a brown hopsack bag. 'Would you look after Richard's gun for the moment? Just until matters are sorted out?'

He proffered the sack across the table and Anthony picked it up gingerly by the drawstring. It weighed heavily. He stowed it in his briefcase.

'What about the girl?' he asked, Henshaw smiled confidently. 'She'll get over Reeves. Her panic is about the baby. Don't worry, I'll take care of her.'

When he was gone Anthony finished arranging his papers. He felt defiled and dirty; and part of those generations of merchant adventurers he had always despised, those who had taken from India with scorn and given nothing back.

Already, as his syce drove him home, he felt the beginning of a new and unfamiliar order of experience and, with it, an unreasoning conviction that the trip to Mysore could only be a temporary respite before he would return here to fulfil some unknown destiny. His feelings of helplessness grew with the realization that the old order, the unvarying rhythms of life, had been changed irrevocably, and so had the feelings associated with those comfortable habits. His acceptance of the revolver, which now weighed heavily in the bottom of the case, was part of his own unwilling complicity in the new order, an obscure symptom of the disease which had touched him in passing, and whose stain he could never now escape.

Mysore, South India: 1947

Fourteen

Samuel Julius Faraday met the Hodders at Mysore Station in the old shooting brake. He wore one of William Porter's old black suits, cut down to fit and shining with use on the lapels and cuffs and, incongruously, a pair of brown chuplees on his horny brown feet. In his top pocket he carried a fly whisk to swat the flies, and a slightly crumpled top hat shaded his ebony head from the sun. 'Miz Porter thought you'd have lots of luggage, sir,' he said, eyeing the three modest suitcases and one cabin trunk with surprise. 'She's waiting to welcome you at home.' He surprised Anthony by picking up one end of the canvas-bound cabin trunk with a strength unexpected in one so apparently frail, and dragging it to the car. Anthony helped him load it into the wagon, which settled lower on its leaf springs, groaning with the weight.

It was a month since Anthony had seen the Commissioner. 'At least three months, Hodder. You deserve it,' Pogson had said expansively, and Anthony had felt a little hurt by the casual manner in which his request for leave had been accepted.

Sita and Joginder had come to Lahore on the eve of their departure, and had joined them in seeing the sights. They were all unwilling to talk of the impending separation. They had visited Akbar's fort with its enamelled terraces and lacy marble grills, wandered amongst the three hundred fountains of the Shalamar Gardens, and seen the Tomb of Anarkali, 'Pomegranate Blossom', the girl from Akbar's harem who had been buried alive for smiling at his son. Once, driving past Falletti's on their way to lunch, Anthony had remembered the severed head rolling away from his feet and suddenly shivered. When they were walking down the wide boulevard of the Mall after dinner, flanked by cafés and shops, theatres and restaurants, Joginder put an arm around his shoulder and said, 'Do you remember the words of the Saddhu? You will go away, but you cannot escape your future. That waits wherever you may go. Better to face it here among friends, whatever it may be, than in the company of strangers.' Anthony had turned away to hide his tears.

As the car crunched up the gravelled drive Arline stood in the doorway of 34 Kipling Road to greet them. On the white stucco wall beside her, the moths clustered thickly round the light. 'How you've grown,' she said, embracing Anne, and to Mark, 'I can still smell that terrible journey on you.' She put her arms around Jane and they stood a long moment in silence. Then Vincent came out and after him the others – Rod, Angela and Patricia. Anthony felt moved. Why have I held out so long against this? he thought, watching the new softness in Jane as she talked animatedly to her sisters. Sam brought out a lantern and placed it on the parapet. When they had each drunk a toast from the sherry glasses laid out on the tray, Arline said briskly, 'You know where everyone is sleeping, Jane. I'll take this young man off for a good wash.'

Mark felt shy, shut in the bathroom under Arline's unwinking gaze. 'I daresay you've got lice as well,' she said disparagingly, helping him pull off his shorts and vest. She had rolled up the sleeves of her black dress to the elbows, showing muscular arms flecked with brown liver-spots. When Mark was naked he stood in the sink, an area of the floor demarcated by a low concrete plinth, which drained into a small hole in the corner. Arline soaped him with carbolic soap on a loofah, rubbing him fiercely until he glowed before pouring a bucketful of cold water over him. She pointed to his penis with the dripping loofah in her hand, laughing so that he could see her strong, yellow teeth.

'I've got a pet crow who's partial to unconsidered trifles. You'll have to be careful,' she said, laughing, her ample black-clad bosom wobbling with the explosions of her breath. When she moved back, pushing a strand of hair from her face with a wet forearm, her hair hit the naked electric bulb which began to swing. Even after he had gone to bed in the unfamiliar room it was the image which remained with him. Arline's face, alternately lit and then in darkness, laughing uncontrollably at some adult joke which was beyond his understanding.

Anthony stood at the drawing-room window watching Mark playing with Zia-Ula, the little boy from next door, on the concrete apron in the corner of the front garden upon which his father-in-law, William had been gathered to his Maker. Beyond the white paling fence the road ran past, edged on both sides with swamp grass and wild hedge flowers. Beyond that stretched the maidan, a vast open field pitted with hidden mine shafts and bordered on three sides by a dense layer of trees. On the second day Arline had told them the story of a youth who had fallen down a mine shaft and died, six months before, and Anthony had reluctantly conceded that Mark should be confined to the garden. Mark had looked mutinous at first, deprived now of his treasured possessions including the bicycle (all stored in the godown in 'Pindi), but had accepted the verdict of the determined adult faces around the tea-table. 'You'll be at school soon,' his mother had said, in tones which suggested that this was something to look forward to. 'There'll be plenty of space and lots of children to play with there.'

The two boys were unaware of Anthony watching them from the window. Mark pointed to the dense copse of bamboo and said something to Zia. His face was animated, but Zia shook his head and, after a moment, they resumed playing marbles on the concrete apron. Anthony thought, Time to be thinking of his common entrance exam, his mind ranging for a moment over the list of English public schools he could afford. He smiled wryly to himself, remembering how a few months before in Rawalpindi he had been planning to break with tradition and send Mark to the Lawrence College or to Rajkumar.

When the bell rang for tea Jane and Angela were already sitting on the verandah. Vincent was working, and Rod and Patricia had gone off to the bazaar. Arline came out on to the verandah and called to Mark, 'Time to wash your hands for tea,' and Anthony felt a tremor of irritation as he saw his son stand up and walk towards the house. Over the wall Indijeet Bhose's voice sounded faintly. She spoke in exaggerated, over-enunciated English, the accents falling heavily on the first part of her words. 'Zia. Zia. You must be coming back and doing your homework now.' Arline smiled thinly, silently, watching like a great predatory bird as Zia went through the gate and closed it carefully after him. When Mark returned she caught his hands and looked at them, and then motioned him to sit down.

Jane and Angela had finished their conversation about the forthcoming dance. Angela was on the Organizing

167

Committee. Despite her prettiness, Anthony recognized the self-contained, desiccated preciousness of the spinster by necessity rather than choice. Like some great tree, Arline sucked the moisture from the soil and denied her daughters the sun. Angela rearranged her lists carefully, pinning them together with paper clips which she attached to a board before putting everything back in a large manila envelope. The sun slanted yellowly through the banyan and on to the corner of the verandah almost without heat now, and the maidan whose sere grass seemed to shimmer in the heat at noon looked grey and cool in the long shadows cast by the buildings and the far line of trees.

Jane said quietly, looking at Arline but addressing her oblique comment to Anthony, 'I don't know if it is a good idea for Mark to spend so much time with Zia. Have you noticed how he has begun to speak in a chi-chi way?' Anthony saw Mark wince and caught a grim satisfaction on Arline's face. Angela said heatedly, 'That's a bit harsh . . .' but Anthony stopped her, holding up his hand.

The comment had touched upon something in his mind and he felt suddenly furious, both angry and helpless at the same time. He knew that this had been discussed and considered behind his back many times, and felt a sense of fury at the covert, insinuating suggestion. His hands were shaking and he clasped them together resting his elbows on the arms of the chair. He said carefully, 'You have stopped him playing on the maidan, and I am sure he is tired of washing his hands at your command every few minutes. I would like to make something absolutely clear. I am delighted that Mark has found a friend so quickly and, as far as I am concerned, Zia is welcome here whenever he wants to come.' In the silence that followed his words he was aware of his heart beating furiously. He looked at Arline and saw that she was smiling to herself, and found himself wondering how long he could continue the battle.

Mark looked at him gratefully, and he gave his son a small, pinched smile. Nobody had heard Anne come through the gate. She stood on the gravel path at the bottom of the steps. 'Bravo, Father,' she said without malice. When Arline said, 'And where have you been?' in a jocular tone, she walked up the stairs and across the verandah, swinging her jacket on the end of her finger.. 'Oh, here and there,' she said, turning her brilliant smile on them before going into the darkness of the hall. Over the wall Indijeet Bhose's voice came faintly. 'Oh, there you are, Raju. You're late. Can you give your brother a hand with his mathematics homework?'

Murree, Punjab: 1947

Fifteen

Long after Margaret Preston had gone to bed Roger Henshaw sat out on the verandah, looking into the night. In the distant forest a hyena sobbed its sad, cackling cry. The villagers thought it was the cry of a churail, the unquiet ghost of a woman whose soul could not rest. Well, there had been four of those in the past year, he thought, remembering his visit with Anwar to the make-shift morgue where the sixteen-year-old body of the first girl lay on a slab of melting ice. Tears had rolled down Anwar's cheeks and he said uncomprehendingly, 'I have seen the tribes make war on each other, but that is a clean thing, between men. I have never seen such things as this . . .' and Roger had put a hand on his shoulder and said, 'The times are out of joint, my friend,' and gestured the attendant to cover the body.

He felt tired, and his big body sagged in the chair. The heavy scent of rotting undergrowth, dew-damp, hung on the air. A mosquito whined by his ear and then stopped, and he slapped his hand against the back of his neck. Twenty years, he thought, and now this. He could hardly remember England now, the small house, pinched and grey with factory smoke, the rotting lino on the kitchen floor and the permanent smell of overboiled greens. His father had continued to run the butcher's shop despite the lung complaint which gave his voice the hoarse whispering quality of a gangster in a Hollywood film. During the day

170

his mother cleaned for people, and in the evening she took in washing. She would stand over the copper with her hair tied in a bandana and a cigarette in her mouth, her arms red to the elbows from the heat. Night after night she harangued them, in a monotonous rancorous stream of hatred. Sometimes his father would beckon him upstairs and tell him stories of the past.

He remembered those times most of all. They would flick through one of the fraying, cloth-bound albums and look at the sepia photographs. His father in the desert in Mesopotamia. A picnic with Bombardier 'Chalky' White, posted missing two days before the end of the war ('Reckon he couldn't face coming back to live with Helen,' his father used to say winking at him conspiratorially.) Roger at six years old with his arms around Toby, the Jack Russell; behind him the gasworks. Even one of him and his parents on the beach at Clacton, laughing at some long-forgotten joke.

From the first time he saw the yellowed cuttings and his father had told him about the Mutiny, he had felt that he must go to India. It promised a release from the grey skies, the eternal drizzle, the endless raging monotone from the kitchen. He saw a means of escaping the prison and he began to work hard at school, holding his secret vision inviolate from everybody, a talisman which protected him when the worst times came and his father was dying. Even at the funeral his mother's caustic bitterness had numbed his grief. 'Feckless like his father before him,' she said, and the rain dripped down her face, hiding the tears if there were any.

When he was seventeen, he came home one day and his mother announced that she had arranged an interview with the Manager of the Co-op. 'They need a bright boy to work in dispatch,' she said, and he took a deep breath, seeing his favourite tea laid out on the table. She wouldn't believe him at first, sitting with her mouth half-open so that he could see the top of her ill-fitting dentures. Even as he left the house with his small case she harangued him disbelievingly. 'You can't do this. You're only a child.' His hatred had strengthened his will, and he had signed on at Liverpool. Much had changed in twenty years, and he had never tried to contact his mother again.

Even here he didn't fit. He knew that. It was not possible to overcome deficiencies of birth and education in India, any more than it had been in England. But here, at least, he had made progress, and he belonged to the same clubs as the other colonials, even though they didn't invite him to play bridge or canasta or have dinner with their families.

Now, it was his meeting with the Commissioner that weighed him down. Even when Roger had finally accepted that change had to come with the Partition, he had never contemplated for a moment that it would make any difference to *him*. But Pogson had said lugubriously, 'Don't you see, old boy? Already there's talk of an Indianization policy and a lot of our boys are having to train Indians to do their jobs. You may be able to stay on in some capacity, but it won't be anything like this. It won't bother me too much. Only two years to go before I retire on full pension to my cottage in the Cotswolds.' He had stared into the middle distance with a vacant smile, and Henshaw had forced himself to be deferentially polite while he stormed inside at the injustice.

He knew that his late night thoughts were not always logical. A plan so bold and so incalculable in its effects as to take his breath away had come into his mind. He tapped his front teeth with the nail of his forefinger. If he felt the same in the morning he would take Feroze Khan fishing. There would be no harm in talking about it. Suddenly revitalized he got up and folded the camp chair, looking once into the darkness before going into the house. It is action that makes one feel better, he thought, plans and ideas beginning to form and modify in his mind almost of their own accord.

Mysore, South India: 1947

Sixteen

During the day Indijeet Bhose had little to do. Her husband, Nathoo, was out at the Bank, and though Raju, her eldest son, wasn't working yet he seemed to spend most of his time with his political friends, and ten-year-old Zia was at school until three o'clock. Indijeet's father had always said to her, 'You should marry a Maharajah, mere piarath,' and sometimes, after an afternoon spent dreaming of the life she should have had (nestling upon a cushion on the verandah with her women's magazines and her chocolates within easy reach), she would think of Nathoo with affectionate contempt. He was a good man, but so dull. In her day-dreams the Maharajah would come to her couch, dressed in white satin, his features (bearing a remarkable resemblance to a dusky Lex Barker) working with uncontrollable passion. He would hold out a blood-red ruby to her, his kohl-rimmed eyes gazing fiercely at her face, and then gather her into his powerful arms and she would surrender herself voluptuously to his embrace. Though she sometimes felt guilt about the lust these dreams engendered for her ghostly surrogate lover, her guilt changed to self-righteous justification whenever Nathoo approached her in the dark. She would sense his tentative, crab-like movements across the bed, and grit her teeth, crying silently to herself, 'It shouldn't be like this.' Reality was not her strong suit.

In the evenings she would sit with Nathoo on the

verandah sipping tea and talking loudly about her garden, the events of the day, and political matters in her fluent, swooping English. She knew that the Gopals, her neighbours on the other side of the hedge from the Porters, could hear her, and she felt they must be impressed by her command of the language and customs of colonial society. Part of her was anguished at the thought of the Raj leaving. She felt dimly that her accomplishments would be devalued, and her place in society diminished, and already she could feel the sense of loss. But there was another part of her which remembered the dense rituals of her family childhood – the darshans with Kali or Vishnu or Shiva, the retailing of the complex mythology of gods and goddesses, of epic battles of cosmological importance, and these memories invested her with a sense of being part of a much greater and more significant process than the superficial, day-to-day social round. These latter thoughts only came to her in the moments of despair; when she had inadvertently taken the mirror in the bedroom too close to the light and, before she could close her eyes, had seen the seaming round her mouth and the threaded crows' feet around her eyes. Sometimes, when this had happened, she would take her mirror into a darkened part of the room and whisper to it, 'Fierce as first love, and wild with all despair,' thinking of her Maharajah until the illusion was restored once more. She nurtured hopes, still, after many years, of being invited by Arline to tea and picnics and shopping expeditions. She felt obscurely resentful of Nathoo and Raju and even Zia. It was to do with their freedom from the ties of home, their inevitable assimilation into a society whose demands diminished the strength of her hold upon them. It was, above all, to do with her feeling that men had the best of some divine bargain, that their attractiveness did not necessarily decline with the passing years.

She heard Anthony's voice raised in anger, but the bamboo thicket dulled the words. Then the gate catch clicked and Raju started to walk up the drive, the gravel spurting from under his chuplees. She looked at her watch, holding her plump wrist away from her so that she could make out the gold lettering. 'Oh, there you are, Raju. You're late. Can you give your brother a hand with his mathematics homework?'

Raju didn't reply, throwing himself down on a cushion on the top step and running his fingers through his black, oiled hair. He was like a fierce young hawk. But there was something about his eyes, dark and troubled and shadowed with violet, which made him seem much older than twenty. 'Have you been with your friends, my son?' she asked, and Raju said wearily, 'I've spent the afternoon with Nathuram and a couple of the others.' He leaned forward and chewed a knuckle pensively. A bullock cart creaked past the gate, stacked high with fodder. Raju said, 'There are some people coming from the Punjab. Perhaps they will teach us to grow up. We are appealing for a restitution of our birthrights and all the others can think about is daubing slogans on Imperial buildings.' He made a disgusted sound in his throat.

Indijeet said uncomprehendingly, 'Is that so?' but he was engrossed in his thoughts. She sighed. He never talked to her in the evenings now that he had become involved in these politics she didn't understand. She felt the sense of loneliness which had begun to return now that Raju was away so much. Even Zia had his homework now. When Raju got up she asked, 'Have you had darshan recently, my son?' and he stopped for a moment

176

before turning to her with a smile. 'Yes, mother,' he said, 'I have had my darshan.'

When Nathoo came back carrying his ledgers in the bag slung over his shoulder (like a common coolie, she thought), Indijeet beckoned him over to sit on the cushion beside her.

He unslung the bag carefully, cursing the Bank which gave him so much work to do that he could not spend as much time as he would like with his Indie. 'What is it, my butchee?' he said, feeling a sense of mild lasciviousness at the invitation to sit so close to her. But she firmly removed his hand when he placed it gently on the plump roll of flesh which bulged over the waistband of her sari, giving him a brief, exasperated glance. Nothing else on his mind, and so bad at it.

She dropped her voice. These were matters which had nothing to do with the Gopals. 'It's time Raju got a job and settled down,' she announced firmly, and Nathoo nodded his head. He sometimes felt half-envious of his son. Raju lived at home and, on Indijeet's insistence, received a small allowance which paid for his bidis and the glasses of Vimto he and his friends consumed under the trees on the waste ground by the bazaar. Also, he was convinced, Raju was seeing a girl. Night after night the boy went out in the direction of the maidan, often not returning until after midnight. He said, 'I talked to Mr Bulstrode-Henshaw already,' glad to be ahead of Indijeet for once. 'They are a little worried about the company he keeps.'

'What do you mean?' she said indignantly, turning to look at Nathoo with an expression of disbelief. He sighed gently. It was hopeless to talk to Indijeet about their sons in terms other than extravagant praise. 'I'm afraid he spends rather a lot of time with those hot-heads from the

RSSS,' he said gently. 'Bankers, people in business, are notoriously conservative. They don't want to take on potential trouble makers.'

Even before she started to upbraid him in a passionate whisper for his disloyalty to his own son he knew he had made a mistake. 'Yes, yes,' he said abjectly, listening to her oft-repeated, fervid defence, aware that he had miscalculated his path in the intricate business of preparing a suitable ambience to approach Indijeet later that night. 'I know, I know,' he said mechanically, later, when the stars had begun to show and the traffic on the road had ceased, and Indijeet was exhaustedly muttering the last of her repertoire. It was the same as it had always been. 'You told me I was a goddess. How can a goddess produce imperfect offspring?' As always, he felt defeated. How could he tell her that he had been wrong? That she was not a goddess, and that he was afraid of their son and his friends?

Murree, Punjab: 1947

Seventeen

Margaret Preston said, 'But why Mysore?' and then, with quick nervousness, 'I'm sorry. I shouldn't have asked.' She poured herself another measure of gin, and he steeled himself to say nothing. The level had gone down considerably since the morning.

Roger said, 'Official business. I won't be gone long, and perhaps we can have a holiday when I come back,' trying to infuse a sense of gaiety into his voice. If he could get her away for a while she might forget about Richard. Kashmir on a house boat he thought. Hari Singh would let them have one of the Royal Boats. His spirits began to rise again and he thought, This is only a phase. She'll be all right again. Give her time.

She walked to the french window, hugging her shoulders as if it were cold, and looked out across the lawns. Sunset hung, gloriously blood-red and gold, on the hazy hills in the west, and the trees had the crepuscular round-shouldered look of old men. The crows flapped noisily round the elms, settling and resettling for the night, and the lights in the valley began to wink on, one by one. In repose her face softened and lost its worried look, and he felt again, looking at her, a sense of loss and the unbridgable separation of her despair. For an instant he knew the appalling certainty that there was nothing he could do to help, before hope sprang mercifully to his aid. Yes, he would contact Hari Singh. Everything would be as it was before.

When she spoke again her voice was uncertain, and he heard the slurring vowels with sadness. 'There's a rumour that you are investigating Guruchunder Singh about the deaths of those girls . . .' she began, and he said firmly, 'You know I can't talk about these things, Margaret. Anyway, you mustn't listen to idle gossip.'

She set her glass down and put her arms round his neck. He smiled at her, smelling the gin on her breath, and she said, as if she were a supplicant, 'It couldn't be him, you know. He's far too gentle. Whoever did those things must be crazy.'

He held her stiffly for a few more moments. Then she moved away and picked up her glass, moving with the dreamlike motions of a sleepwalker. 'I'm so lonely, so lonely,' she said, almost to herself, in a whisper. 'You have your work and I . . .,' she gestured hopelessly.

He stood and watched her, and the sun went out.

Mysore, South India: 1947

Eighteen

By the beginning of June Mark had been attending the Convent of the Sacred Heart for almost a month. When Sam dropped him at the gate each morning he would stand on the dusty verge watching the car drive out of sight, wishing he was sitting by the old man and on his way back to Kipling Road. He felt a fear which he could hardly bring himself to acknowledge because it seemed so absurd: that he would return one day on the bus to find the house razed to the ground, just a pile of rubble and destroyed furniture; whenever he came back there was a moment before the last bend when the image of the destroyed house came to him unbeckoned, and was followed by a sense of relief. The tranquil, unreal calm of the nuns in their white habits, and the mandatory ritual of mouthing responses whenever the bells rang, filled him with an obscure anger. He was glad when he caught a summer cold and his mother grudgingly said he must stay at home.

Rod had been ill too, with some adult illness which involved many knowing glances between the grown-ups. Mark had noticed that his Aunt Patricia had been crying on a couple of occasions but Rod seemed quite cheerful. Perhaps she had been crying about something other than her husband.

This morning Mark had been barred from going out of the house ('I'm not having you treat this as a holiday,'

181

Jane had said grimly) and he remained in his room reading until he heard the car taking Arline, Jane and Patricia drive down on to the road. He felt an unformed resentment against his mother and grandmother, a sense of his own weakness and dependence upon them, and the presence of some injustice. In some way that was not entirely clear he saw the anger between his parents reflected in the way women in the house treated him. It was nothing overt or substantial, but he felt that he did not, could not, conform to some ideal pattern.

He had to knock twice before he heard Rod say, 'Come in,' and he pushed the door open and went into the bedroom. The curtains were partly drawn, and Patricia's clothes were scattered on the floor by the dressing-table. A light sprinkling of talcum powder bloomed the sheen of the wood and had spilled over the purple dress crumpled on the floor below. There was a strange, sickly smell in the room, sweet and decaying.

Mark sat on the bed and Rod raised himself on the pillow and put his hands behind his head. He was unshaven, and his face had a sweaty pallor. When he spoke, Mark noticed that his head shook all the time, but his voice sounded light.

'How are you, old son?'

Mark put his hand up to his head. 'It aches. My nose keeps running.' He tried to look ill.

Rod laughed and took a swig from the bottle by the bed. Liquid ran out of the corner of his mouth and dripped on to his pyjama top. The hard smell of whisky hung in the air.

'Better than going to school, eh?' he said slyly.

There was a revolver by the whisky bottle on the bedside table, lying with its chamber broken and six rounds of ammunition by the side. There was an oil can, and a roll of white lint. Mark said curiously, 'Is that yours, uncle?' and Rod picked it up, squinting down the barrel before clicking the chamber shut and handing it to Mark. It was heavy, and the boy had to use both hands to bring it up to aim.

'It's your father's,' said Rod. 'I said I'd clean it for him.' He watched the boy walk round the room, aiming with narrowed eyes at various objects.

Mark looked at him suddenly and said, 'Have you ever killed anyone, Uncle Rod?', and Rod seemed to falter before saying, 'Not with a gun,' holding out his hand to take the weapon back.

When the gate latch sounded, Mark got up and looked out of the window. 'They're back. I'd better go,' he said and Rodney, his face so serious that Mark knew that he was giving some deeply-felt advice, though he could only guess at the meaning of the words, said, 'Be thou like th'Imperial Basilisk, killing thy foe with unapparent wounds.'

When Mark stood, puzzled but poised for flight down the landing to his own room, Rod smiled and gestured towards the hall where women's voices had begun to echo. 'They don't mean it. But until you are beyond their reaches you must preserve yourself against them.'

Walking back to his room, Mark remembered, 'Oh, I could eat you,' Arline had said once, and he realized with surprise that a kind of love lay behind everything.

Alone in the dark now Rodney knew that the memory was coming back, that there was nothing he could do to keep it at bay. He took a deep draught from the bottle, recorking it and putting it carefully by the bed. It always began so, with a sense of guilt at misleading the innocent, at involving others in wars which were not of their making. The scene came back, as it always had, like a tableau in which he observed himself as one of the players. In the background the buildings blazed fiercely against the night sky. Men ran past, crying names, or doggedly, silently. Rod sat in the lee of a ruined building, holding Rissaldar-Major Afzal's head on his lap. Blood was soaking blackly through Afzal's uniform front, and Rod had given up his attempts to unbutton the tunic to see the extent of the damage. The man stirred and said, 'Tunda hai, Sahib,' and Rod took his greatcoat off, moving as little as possible, and covered him with it. 'Ubi so jaow, Rissaldar,' he said, trying to make it sound like an order, while the tears coursed down his face. The fighting went on round them, with wild figures appearing and disappearing through the smoke and flames, and the cracking of shots and the smell of smoke and cordite. He had cursed fate, for showing him, so inescapably, his own collusion in the conspiracy. Impossible to think of the man dying in his lap as a servant, or an equal partner in some mutually beneficial cause. He wept for the life ebbing away on his knees, for the Rissaldar's uncomplaining stoicism, but above all for his own part in this colonial conspiracy which used innocents with such callous disregard.

Before dawn it had been quiet for a short time and he must have slept. He moved involuntarily, stiff and cramped, and the Rissaldar-Major said, 'Sahib, sahib?' in an enquiring tone and then his head fell sideways. Rod held him for half an hour until he was sure he was dead, while the sounds of battle rose once more around him.

When Patricia came in he was asleep. She took the gun gently off the bed and put it carefully down on the bedside table. When she covered him up she saw that he had been crying and stood by the bed looking down at him for a few moments. She saw the bottle, half-hidden by the trailing sheet and picked it up. She put her hand on his head for a moment and then went quietly out, concealing the bottle under her coat.

'Come on,' said Mark impatiently, grabbing Zia's arm, but Zia hung back. Mark taunted him. 'Fraidy. Fraidy,' and Zia's brown eyes filled with tears and his lip trembled. There were heavy blue-black clouds, and the air crackled with electricity. Everyone was out, except Sam, sleeping on his charpoy until the alarm woke him to drive out to pick the family up from the Bulstrode-Henshaws. William sat on the side wall with his head hunched into his neck feathers. The tegument flicked over his eyes every few seconds.

Mark threw a scornful glance at Zia and stepped into the edge of the bamboo thicket. Dried bamboo husk popped and rustled in the dark green shade. He had made himself a little shelter where he could hide from everyone. When he looked out he could see Zia standing anxiously at the edge of the concrete apron, trying to peer in. He felt a sense of power, of possessing a potent secret which made him feel grown up. He parted the bamboos nearer the wall carefully, until he could see the snake lying, coil upon coil. It lifted its head and looked at him, its tongue trembling in and out and the flanges on either side of its head flaring. It remained motionless and he watched it for a while, and then slowly let the bamboo press itself upright against his fingers.

When he came out Zia looked at him fearfully. 'It's our secret,' Mark said aggressively, afraid now that Zia might tell someone. 'Cross your heart and swear to die if you tell.'

185

Zia said seriously, 'I won't tell,' and crossed his arms over his heart.

At the far side of the house Sam appeared. He saw William and picked up a pebble, weighing it speculatively in his hand, but before he could throw it the crow lifted lazily into the air and swept out over the fence and across the maidan. When Sam saw the two boys he looked embarrassed, letting the stone drop from his fingers as unobtrusively as possible. 'What are you two up to?' he asked gruffly, and Mark said, 'Just playing,' looking at Sam with a slight smile. When Sam got the car out of the garage they opened the gates for him, swinging back on them until they crashed shut against the stop.

It was the end of July. Rumours abounded. A colleague of Major Majid knew Jinnah's personal physician, and the word went round the Club that the Quaid-e-Azam was fatally ill and wouldn't last another month. 'Only if the RSSS kill him,' Vincent said. 'Fanatics never die of natural causes until they have achieved their purposes.'

Anthony, still beset by the feelings of doubt which had started in 'Pindi, chafed at the inactivity and lack of purpose of this enforced idleness. He envied Vincent, whose periodic visits to Kipling Road brought a scent of the real world, and felt sorry for Rod, who was companionable enough, but broken-backed, even in his periodic remissions. At the Mysore Club Rod would say, 'Don't worry, old man. You go ahead,' his pallid face yellowed by Mepacrine, but Anthony would see him grimacing over his tonic and feel guilty about his own strength. Their relaxed former friendship had come to an uneasy stewardship. Every time he looked at Rod he was reminded of his own mortality. When he drove back from the Club, mellowed by a couple of drinks, he was always aware of

Rod's straight-backed and faintly disapproving figure by his side. And when Rod fell, as he did with increasing frequency, Anthony was aware of Rod's despairing envy.

There was one thing he saw in Rod which he envied, and strove to emulate. Though it was never spoken of openly, he knew that Rod made no distinction between himself and his Indian friends. In himself, Anthony still felt the condescension, ameliorated and mellowed since his youth, of a sense of superiority. It was mainly dormant and unobtrusive, but sometimes, talking to Major Majid at the Club, or to Nathoo Bhose over the garden wall, he caught himself being overly concerned and polite in compensation.

In the house he felt uneasy. It was not so much that Arline usurped his role as head of the household, more his shadowy apprehension that she and her daughters were conniving together in a conspiracy which involved Mark's and Anne's futures and which was conducted in secret between them. He had once hesitantly hinted as much to Vincent, who had at first laughed with genuine amusement, and then, seeing the concern in his brother-in-law's eyes, said seriously, 'The only way to deal with Mother is to ignore her. Once you acknowledge her authority you're lost.'

'That's easy enough for you to say,' retorted Anthony. 'You're her son and you don't live in the house.' Vincent looked wryly at him and said lightly, 'And *you* don't have to endure her attentions as a matchmaker. Tea with unsuitable etiolated faded English roses . . . her avid expression as she watches me . . . and her disappointment when I don't follow it up. Much as I love her with true filial devotion, I saw her geld my father over twenty years as surely as if she had operated on him surgically. And seeing that, I could never contemplate marriage . . .' and he spread his hands with such a comical gesture that

187

Anthony had to laugh at his rueful expression, his attitude of mock despair.

Anthony had taken to spending a large part of his days at the Mess. The masculine company and the political speculation at mealtimes had fostered the illusion that he was still involved in the wider community in some meaningful activity. But it was an illusion he could not sustain to himself. He managed to arrange small administrative jobs for himself at the Club. Finally, furtively, with a sense of guilt, he wrote to Gur and asked him to see if it was possible to arrange an official request for his return. For a few days he felt ashamed of what he had done, but then the increasing chaos reported daily in the papers began to lighten his spirits. He felt justified in his feeling of being out of joint with the times, as he read and heard about what was happening on the subcontinent.

Despite the gloomy prognostications of the astrologers, the date of Partition had been set for midnight on 15 August 1947. The arbitrariness of the time on a landmass where hours separated sunrise and sunset from one corner to another reflected the ad hoc nature of all the arrangements. It was common knowledge in the Mess that Nehru had pleaded with Mountbatten to stay on as administrative head of the transitional government. As all the old India hands professed to have foreseen, Radcliffe's division had certainly been disinterested in the worse possible sense. Inevitably, following from the primary misconceptions held in England, he had chosen to divide the nation along religious boundaries. But his formulae seemed to the armchair philosophers at the Mess recipes for economic ruin. They nodded their heads sagely to one another, each agreeing with the previous speaker, with no one suggesting how matters may have been arranged differently.

Bulstrode-Henshaw was one of the foremost critics of the plan for Partition. His great-grandfather had been killed in the Mutiny under the most horrific circumstances, which he never quite felt able to divulge, and successive generations of his family had lived and worked in India since the days of Clive. He was semi-retired, and his love of pontificating and his expansive personality had overcome, at least for this period when he sensed a captive audience, his concern that the Indian clerks were not to be trusted without his own personal supervision. He was always immaculately dressed in a cream linen suit, and invariably carried white kid gloves and a silver-topped malacca cane. His hair was a startling white against the leather tan, and at over sixty he walked with the vigour of a much younger man. Since his wife had died in a tragic car crash fifteen years before, an Indian housekeeper ran his house with reclusive efficiency ('and does other things besides,' observed Majid drily). His spinster sister, Daisy, usually accompanied him when a partner was mandatory. He was an agreeable, if garrulous, companion, and Anthony had spent many hours in his company, fascinated by the stories of an India that had long vanished. Once, walking across the parade ground, he said musingly to Anthony, 'The Englishman cannot understand that his is a matriarchal society. That men do, and are seen to do, but the underlying animus of his country is female, and primitive.' When Anthony mentioned Roger Henshaw he was uncharacteristically reticent. 'Ah, yes,' looking with brilliant blue eyes across the polo ground. 'A very distant relative. Came here once when he first arrived. Wanted to know all about the family, particularly James who was killed in the Mutiny. I didn't take to him. Felt there was something unsound . . .' When Anthony started to talk

189

about Henshaw the older man cut across, deliberately changing the conversation.

With an audience he was inclined to be bombastic. He prided himself upon his encyclopaedic grasp of statistics, lugubriously retailing his version of the litany of disasters to the younger men around the bar. That eighty-five per cent of the world's jute would be produced in the new Pakistan, but that they would have no processing mills, while India would have over one hundred jute mills and the shipping port of Calcutta, but no jute. That Amritsar was to be given to India despite housing the Golden Temple, Sikhism's most holy shrine. As for Kashmir (and here he spread his hands to demonstrate the hopelessness of the situation and sank his head on his chest in a theatrical gesture of despair for a few moments before resuming), Radcliffe's failure to make a clear-cut decision one way or the other would ensure a bitter legacy of disagreement. 'Hari Singh is a maniac,' he said portentously inviting people to mark his words with a raised forefinger. For the first time Anthony saw Bulstrode-Henshaw as a bit of a mountebank, and felt mildly irritated. But these comments, and the daily gossip in the Mess along similar lines, paradoxically helped him to feel better. It gave an external focus, an objective correlative, to his discontent and justified his feelings of frustration. The neurasthenia, the irritation, the sense of impending doom were, after all, the product of a deeper malaise in society and not in himself.

When Sam brought the letter requesting his return to the breakfast table his jubilation overcame the mild feelings of guilt. He was to use his own judgement about the safety of travelling over the border but, aliis aequis, it would be appreciated if he could resume his duties by first September. An accompanying note from Gur, couched in official language to avoid the censor, carried a cryptic nota bene. 'Be nice to have you back. Pertelote and partners ruling the roost.' Only later Anthony remembered that Gur had called Henshaw Pertelote.

Jane said incredulously, 'But you can't go back now! There's rioting and looting, and besides, your place is here with your family.'

The secret knowledge that he had engineered his own return made Anthony pompous. He said stiffly, 'A man has a duty to do his job.' Arline looked up at Jane and smiled drily, and Jane said vehemently, 'God, you're absurd. I'm your wife and these are your children. Don't *we* matter?' She walked out on to the patio and stood with her back to the kitchen, her arms folded, watching William who was gorging the last of his breakfast. Anne got up from the table and kissed Anthony lightly on the cheek. 'I understand, daddy,' she said defiantly and left the room. Mark sat miserably between his aunts, looking down at the table.

On the patio Anthony put his arm round Jane's shoulder, but she walked away from him. 'When will you learn what really matters?' she said bitterly, and he felt defeated.

In the dining room Patricia had prepared a breakfast tray to take up to Rod. 'At least he'll still be here for the dance,' she said brightly to no one in particular. Mark slipped out of the room to collect his satchel for school. He felt lonely already.

Nineteen

By night the bazaar seemed infinitely more exciting, imbued with a feeling of grown-up mystery. Mark spoke in whispers, until Vincent laughed and said, 'It's all right, old man. Nobody's going to hear us now.' Mark felt a warmth steal over him, an enormous gratitude towards Vincent walking by his side and exchanging banter with the shopkeepers. 'Array, huzoor, kithre jatha hai?' 'Abdul, barfee wallah ko.' Salaams were made from every side where the teeming hucksters carried on their trading, and the fat banias sat making their deals with worried-looking men. Some shops boasted an electric bulb whose anaemic light cast a feeble glow over a group sat under their carpets hung over lines, bubbling breath through their hookahs and exchanging soft, monosyllabic conversations. Chickens pecked among the cobbles, flapping furiously in flight from passing feet. The sounds and smells of night reeked into the narrow alleyway. Pots clinked and jangled; from the maidan the sound of cowbells signalled the herd's slow ascent to the sheds; a muezzin sounding far to the east was ignored. On the pavements, under the listless sacking blinds, old men sat on charpoys looking with uninvolved, cataract-ridden eyes at the bustling activity.

They stopped at a stall. 'Char pakora,' Vincent gestured. 'Acha, Sahib.' Mark ate his pakoras contentedly, aware suddenly of a potent compact with his uncle which echoed his affinity with his father, and Rod. It was a thrill to think that the household was asleep while he walked with his uncle through these crowded streets.

It was when they were coming up the street again, and Mark felt a little sick of the deadly sweetness of barfees, and more than a little tired, that he suddenly saw the two men. He pulled at Vincent's sleeve and said, 'Look, uncle. It's Raju and Mr Henshaw. What's he doing here?' He ran up the street, scattering pigeons into the sky. 'Mr Henshaw. Mr Henshaw.'

The man looked round, his scowl relaxing into an uneasy smile. When Mark had introduced his uncle, and they had shaken hands a little stiffly, Henshaw smiled crookedly and said to Vincent, 'I'd appreciate it if you didn't mention this to anyone. I'm here on business, but unofficially.' His expression and the movement of his shoulders suggested a complicity, a certainty that Vincent would understand. Raju stood silently with his eyes downcast. Vincent nodded, and Henshaw ruffled Mark's hair and said, 'You too, young man?' with the question in his voice betraying his anxiety.

Behind Raju a thin man with glasses and a lean, ascetic face stood by a storm lantern hanging from the canopy rail over a bric-a-brac stall. Mark looked at Raju, and then beyond him towards the still figure. He knew the man's face from somewhere. Henshaw repeated his question with a touch of urgency and Mark nodded, abstractedly.

He followed Vincent up the alley. The pleasure had drained from the evening. The smoke from the fires stung his nostrils, and the lights glittered tawdrily. He wished he was at home, in bed. Vincent walked ahead very fast and he had to run to keep up. When they came to the car, parked on the dusty ground above the bazaar, he saw his uncle's face was set and serious. Vincent said, 'We gave our word so we must say nothing. But the man they were meeting was Veer Savarkar who runs the RSSS. What can they be doing with him?'

They didn't speak on the way back. In the dark hall Mark bumped into a chair and the echoes reverberated down the hall. But no one came. Silence descended once more.

Murree, Punjab: 1947

Twenty

When Feroze Khan and his men had left, Joginder walked across the room and put his arm around Sita. She held on to him tightly, and he stroked her hair, rocking her gently until the incoherent sobbing became quieter. Over her shoulder he looked at the devastated room. The Aubusson carpet was strewn with splintered shards of Meissen china. Feroze's lieutenant had slashed a great rent in a Fragonard landscape and the head of Apollo, purchased on a long-past holiday from a vendor in El Djem, lay shattered on the floor.

'This is only the start, zamindar. Next it will be your son . . .' Feroze Khan had said as he left the room. Sita had looked at her husband with wide terrified eyes and said, 'What does he mean about Gur? Why are they doing this to us?' and he said wearily, 'I don't know. It is part of the madness inflicted by the British. After all these centuries they hate us now . . .' For the first time since it had started he felt his spirit failing. It seemed as if, in their wanton destruction of these ornaments and treasures he and Sita had collected over the years, Feroze Khan and his men had invaded and despoiled a private sanctuary which had belonged to them alone. Thinking of the operation he had arranged and paid for for Feroze Khan's father he remembered, bitterly, an old Frontier proverb, 'No good deed goes unpunished.'

Sita knelt on the carpet and began to put the fragments

195

of porcelain into a pile, brushing back a strand of hair with the back of her hand. 'We should have listened to Mr Henshaw,' she said, and when he didn't answer she said vehemently, 'I wish that Anthony and Jane were here.' Looking at her he felt moved again, knowing that Sita, like so many of his friends, still clung to the false hope that their way of life had not vanished forever, could still be brought back so that things would be as they had always been. He said gently, 'There is no one we can turn to. Henshaw has gone away and besides he and Feroze have some arrangement. I knew that Feroze Khan wasn't fishing with him when that riot occurred in 'Pindi. But I didn't say anything, didn't want to be involved. As for Jane and Anthony . . .,' he shrugged his shoulders, straightening up to rest his back for a moment. 'In the end they will cleave to their own kind. It would need a strong man to take our side in these matters and, though I love Anthony as I would a brother, he is not such a man.'

When they had cleared the room it almost seemed as if nothing had happened. Dost Mohammed came shame-facedly into the room and said, 'Huzoor, I was afraid, and hid in the godown.' 'There's nothing to be ashamed of,' Joginder said, and Dost Mohammed smiled his thanks. When the servant withdrew and they sat on the chaise longue together it was in Joginder's mind to give up, to move to the South, but as he started to put the thought into words Sita put her hand up and said, 'I know what you are going to say. We have gone too far to run away now. Besides I would have to live with you knowing of your shame and regret at running away. No, we will stay.' A little later she said, 'Besides, we must be here for our son's sake. I wonder what Feroze Khan meant . . .'

In the gathering dusk outside the window a light flared

suddenly where the mali had begun the bonfire. Against the light his figure assumed monstrous proportions as he heaped brambles upon the flames. Joginder said lightly, 'It's just loose talk. He wants to frighten us.' But he felt a new uneasiness, an inching forward of the recognition that he could no longer control the events of their lives. He turned and smiled at Sita and saw her face relax. At least there is something I can still do, he thought.

Mysore, South India: 1947

Twenty-one

Mark stood in the doorway watching Anne brush her hair. She put her head first to the left and then to the right and brushed with long strokes, the light giving an incandescent glow to the edges of her hair. She wore a broderie anglaise wrap which fell open as she leant over, exposing one small firm breast. Mark felt hot and confused, unable to tear his eyes away from the dark aureole and the blue vein which showed faintly through the pale skin. Anne caught his eye in the mirror and said, 'Come in and shut the door,' with a peremptory, adult delivery and carried on with her brushing as he dutifully came in and sat down on the end of the bed. Since he had heard that his father was going back, he had felt an uneasy sense of being betrayed, abandoned. Since they had left 'Pindi, Anne had stopped playing with him and begun to assume that remote mysteriousness which he associated with his grandmother and the women of her family.

Anne said nothing further and after a little while he said, 'What's this secret you're going to tell me, then?' half hoping to be drawn into a conspiracy which drew them closer against the others.

She turned to look at him, her hair slowly falling across her face in wisps and strands. 'I don't know if you're old enough to keep a secret properly,' she said in the grown up, half-teasing, half-cogitating voice which he hated. 'Of course I am,' he said indignantly, flushing a deep, dull red. He hated her at that moment, thinking to himself, Girls are so stupid. Anne had turned back to the mirror and resumed her brushing. The fine hairs at the nape of her neck glistened like white gold and her mouth had an amused secretive smile.

He felt an inconsequential moment of pure happiness that it was Saturday and there was no school. Outside the window he heard the noise of a funeral procession moving down the road on the way to the Christian cemetery. The sheer spectacle robbed the scene of any mordant overtones. 'Oh, come and look,' he called to Anne, and she joined him at the window. The corpse was propped cross-legged on a palanquin covered in flowers. He sat in front of a table on which was perched an ancient Singer sewing machine, his far-staring, glassy eyes giving him the appearance of a man who has suddenly been struck by some profound philosophical insight. A gaily dressed crowd of relatives followed, wailing and beating their breasts in a ritualized depiction of grief. Anne said, 'He was a tailor. I wonder if they bury the sewing machine with him?'

'Do you remember the Mohorram tiger?' Mark asked, and Anne laughed, sitting down at the dressing-table again. One of the Mohorram tigers this year had been a young Anglo-Indian Railway employee who had been disowned by his relatives for 'going native'. Very drunk, he had run up and down the Mall, leaping out at people with ferocious roars to the accompaniment of much appreciative laughter, until his frenzy had overcome his good sense and he had stabbed a bheesti's water skin. In the resulting fracas he was arrested and taken to the cells to cool off. He had a broken collar bone, and Bulstrode-Henshaw, sitting in for an absent friend on the Bench, handed out an unexpectedly severe fine. 'Bad enough for the boy to be taking part in this native mumbo jumbo without misbehaving as well.' Anthony had nodded, wondering if Majid's suspicions about the housekeeper could be true.

Mark waited, but Anne seemed to have forgotten he was there. She wasn't going to tell him any secret, he thought glumly, and he moved to the door, intending to see if Zia was free for a game of marbles. Before he got to the door Anne said, 'Do you promise not to tell anyone?' and he turned and nodded. She took an envelope from the drawer and looked at it, and then handed it to him, saying, 'Can you get this note to Raju?'

'Is that the secret?' Mark said incredulously, and Anne nodded. 'There may be more notes, and I don't want anyone else in the family to know about them. Can you make sure of that?'

His disappointment was displaced by a feeling of pride. 'Of course,' he said. 'I'll give them to Zia and make him promise, too.' The thought of implicating Zia in a conspiracy with himself and his sister was strangely satisfying. He felt in some undefined way that it would make him safer.

He put the note away and asked curiously, 'What's it about?' and he saw the colour rise into her cheeks. 'Nothing really. We're just friends.' He looked at her speculatively for a moment, feeling the shape of the letter in his pocket, but her lips were pursed. She wasn't going to tell him anything more.

By tradition the men were dispatched from the house on the day of the ball. 'For which relief much thanks,' said Vincent fervently, sprawling comfortably on the chipped blue-green Lloyd Loom chair which creaked and chittered with his movements as he watched Mark and Anthony finish their breakfasts. Patricia had already started to parade her dresses before her sisters, and her voice echoed down the stairwell and through the hall. 'Is this one too daring?' followed by a burst of laughter from Jane and Angela and then, again, Patricia's querulous voice, full of resentment. 'I don't see what's so funny. Oh please tell me what you think of it.' She sounded on the verge of tears. Rod came grim-faced into the room shutting the door behind him and the voices faded to a muted whisper.

It was over a week since his last relapse and he had lost the sweaty, red-veined, unshaven appearance which was characteristic of his drunken episodes. He looked tired, and much older than his forty-two years, but there was a tenuous air of tranquillity about him. It seemed to Anthony the terrifying calm of a man who had witnessed the loss of every possession dear to him, who looked upon the void and whom nothing further could touch. Rod gestured upstairs with a mock grimace of despair. 'The sooner we go the better,' he said, pouring himself a black coffee.

The Maharajah of Mysore had invited them to a shikar on his estate being held in honour of Conrad Corfield, who was acting as the intermediary between the Rulers of the Princely States and the Viceroy's Office. The Maharajah was an enlightened despot, proud of his Science Faculty which, due to the huge endowment from his prodigious fortune, was the best and most modern in the subcontinent. As a child, Vincent had gone with his father, William, on a number of shoots, and had later advised the Maharajah about the purchase of equipment, and suitable research projects and staff for the faculty, and the Maharajah had been intrigued and amazed when Vincent refused not just a fee for his services, but also an offer to become the ruler's personal physician. They had

201

been walking through the twenty of the six hundred palace rooms which were devoted to the collections of tigers, panthers, elephants and bisons killed by three generations of princes in the jungles of the estate. The Maharajah had paused under a massive bison head, looking at Vincent with genuine puzzlement.

'I don't understand you, my friend,' he said. 'Your countrymen have never been backward in extracting their tolls from my country. And even any one of these . . .' and he gestured with a wave to the following attendants who smiled ingratiatingly or bobbed their heads at this sign of recognition, 'would immediately have told me that the honour of serving me was enough while they gave themselves time to work out how much they could ask for . . .' He fell silent for a moment, looking at Vincent. 'One of my ancestors was told by a Chinese sage that an application of crushed diamonds was the most efficacious aphrodisiac in the world. So hundreds of stones were crushed in the mills and in celebration of his new-found virility dancing girls were paraded through the state on elephants whose trunks were studded with rubies and whose ears were covered in the surviving diamonds. If you had wanted . . .,' he gave these last words an individual emphasis in his accented English, 'you need never have worked again.'

Vincent had laughed easily and said, 'India is my home and your people are my people. I am ashamed of our colonial domination. Besides I enjoy my work and there is nothing I need that I do not already have.'

From then he was invited to all the major functions of the estate as an honoured guest. At dussehra, when a thousand elephants in elaborately woven blankets of flowers, their foreheads studded with gold and jewels, paraded through the city, Vincent followed the procession in a royal palanquin, discreetly curtained from inquisitive eyes. Through the chink in the curtains, he had watched the huge bull elephant carrying the Maharajah's throne, its gold pedestal was draped in brocaded velvet, and surmounted by an umbrella, the symbol of princely power, followed by two beasts with empty howdahs symbolizing the spirit of the Maharajah's forbears. He had dined at the palace off gold plates, under elaborate crystal chandeliers, side by side with officers of the Eighteenth Lancers who had helped to defeat Rommel in the Desert Campaign, with men whose grandfathers had been members of Hodson's Horse or Skinner's Yellow-boys. Sometimes, on such occasions, he had seen the Maharajah give him the same quizzical glance, a mixture of puzzlement and disbelief, and he saw, too, the same unspoken question upon his face to which the answer would always be the same.

Once Rod had said to him, genuinely exasperated, 'I don't understand you, Vin. It's not as if he would even notice . . .' and had stopped, suddenly aware that he was trespassing upon some private preserve, some decision taken alone and in silence, long ago.

Vincent had said conversationally, almost casually, 'When I was first taken prisoner by the Japs in Burma, a guard kicked me on the shins, laughing as he did so, and I was then forced to march twenty miles with a fractured leg. When we arrived, the camp was a barbed wire enclosure with barely adequate room for two hundred. There were over a thousand men, women and children in the compound and no medical supplies. They were suffering from dysentery, pneumonia, malnutrition, scurvy, worms. In some of the makeshift huts they had died during the night, propped up until morning by the press of bodies . . .' His voice was still light and relaxed, but his eyes were dead, as if looking upon some private horror. Rod shivered. 'We ate whatever we could. Rats. Cats. Once even a human liver. Anything to keep alive. And day after day I saw my skills break before reality.' Vincent had looked at Rod then, but his eyes were still vacant. 'I realized then that there was no shoring up the ruin. That possessions, wealth, power, mean nothing. That we are all equal in the path of death. That nothing matters except people and each moment . . .'

Rodney had felt embarrassed at Vincent's candour, understanding suddenly what had obsessed the Maharajah: that he had met a man who was genuinely indifferent to all he had to offer. Such thoughts would be an almost intolerable reminder to a prince of the limitations of his power.

So this morning neither Anthony nor Rod voiced their disappointment over missing a shikar in their own howdah. At least Vincent had asked if they could take a picnic in the palace grounds, on a high hill overlooking the shikar route, and had managed eventually to dissuade the Maharajah's Estate Manager from supplying a banquet and a host of servants. The man had been almost tearful with concern, and Vincent had eventually given him a note for the Maharajah which exonerated him from all blame for the meagreness of the arrangements.

They went to the bazaar first, parking on the Mall under the brilliant shade of the flame of the forest trees. (On picnics with Arline, supplies always came from a large emporium run by one of Bulstrode-Henshaw's nephews. 'So much more hygienic than trusting those stalls,' she would say, entirely disregarding the fact that Sam went from morning to night without washing his hands, regardless of the activities he may have pursued during the day.) Mark wandered down the rutted cobbles, avoiding the constant stream of dirty water which flowed down the central declivity, stained red with the juice of betel nuts. The men meandered behind, purchasing food for the picnic.

From half way up the hill Mark looked towards the waste ground and felt a tremor of delight. A large crowd had gathered to watch an itinerant circus which was setting up on the mud-baked earth. It reminded him of going to a circus in Murree with his father and Joginder before everything had changed, and he felt anew, as he had since morning, a return of his sense of wonder and some apprehension of continuity. If there was still magic, then the India that he loved still lay under the surface of events and would return.

There was a collection of jugglers, firewalkers, trapeze artists, a nautch bunder (periodically scratching its mangy coat) and a snake charmer. A thick pole, some twenty feet high, was sunk into the fissured earth and secured by three ropes attached to steel pegs in the ground. Outside the perimeter of the circle described by the pegs a man smeared with white ashes with darts stuck in the skin of his back walked somnambulistically through a bed of glowing coals. A woman in a brilliant golabe sari trimmed with gold squatted by the bank of earth on the far perimeter with a lotah by her side. Periodically she poured a few handfuls of water from the lotah into an earthenware chattee over a few handfuls of uncooked rice which she rubbed in her hands, before throwing out the starch-laden water and starting again. By her side the snake charmer removed the round lid from his basket and began to play a reedy, hesitant tune. A man clad in a dirty loincloth with a puggaree wound round his head stepped forward. He was skeletally thin, with the blue-black skin of the Dravidian. He looked at the top of the pole and spat on his hands, rubbing the palms together. Then he squatted on his haunches and took three juggling clubs from a gunny sack on the floor, securing them together with a piece of sisal which he then took in his teeth. He began to climb the swaying pole.

Mark had squirmed almost to the front of the crowd. In front of him stood a stout European woman. She wore a solar topee with a white linen flap which rested on her ample neck just above the collar line. Her bare freckled arms sagged with burned pink flesh and the armholes of her gingham dress were stained with sweat. Her companion was a desiccated colourless man of fifty or so, with sparse black hair spread carefully across his bony scalp. He wore khaki shorts and knee length socks secured with green scout garters. They were both watching the snake charmer from whose basket the cobra had begun to rise slowly, spreading its hood. 'Look at that, David,' she whispered to the man and Mark could see her mouth tremble with excitement.

Meanwhile the juggler had reached the top of the pole and was standing gingerly upright, his leg muscles taut and striated with the strain of keeping his balance. He held his arms out until the swaying of the pole stilled, then, taking the clubs from his teeth, he began to juggle.

The crowd clapped desultorily, and a few coins chinked in the brass collecting bowl. The woman in the sari looked up briefly. Once again the juggler gathered the clubs together and put the strings in his mouth. He lowered himself until his head rested on the pole. On the khud a man began to play a small drum with his fingers, chanting as he did so. The plump European woman shifted, pushing Mark heavily into the crowd behind, seemingly unaware of his presence. With sudden anger he pushed back.

He always remembered her face afterwards as she began to fall. Her mouth was open and there was a pig-like stupidity in the faded blue eyes. She seemed to topple in slow motion, like a giant tree crashing to earth, scattering the crowd around her. One of the ropes securing the pole whipped loose, carrying the securing peg with it. Even as the woman's shoulder hit the ground and she cried out in pain, Mark could see that the pole had begun to lean. The juggler, upside down, hung on desperately. The woman in the sari ran forward, knocking over the lotah whose contents spilled over the earth. She called 'Ram. Ram,' harshly, running to try to prop the pole. The juggler fell and the clubs rattled together furiously for a moment as he hit the ground. He didn't move.

The white woman's companion went to help her, pulling her awkwardly by the armpits so that her dress rode up to expose ample mottled thighs. Her arm was skinned and bleeding and she looked at Mark saying in an incredulous voice, 'It's his fault. He pushed me.' All round him dark faces turned towards Mark. He said hotly, 'You were squashing me so I pushed back,' and the man gave him a sneering, adult look and said, 'Where are your manners, boy?'

Mark felt an enormous relief when he saw Vincent's face and then his father and Rod at the edge of the crowd. Over the babble of voices he heard Vincent say, 'I'm a doctor. Let me through,' and the crowd parted. The Englishman stood up, holding out his hand with an expectant smile. 'I'm David Lassiter,' he said, but Vincent went straight past without pausing, towards the group surrounding the still body of the juggler.

Lassiter went a dull, brick red. 'Is he with you?' he asked Anthony and Anthony nodded. 'Well,' said Lassiter nastily, 'I'd like some details about him. I'm on the

Viceroy's staff and I find his behaviour extraordinary. He must have seen that Sarah was hurt.' He managed to invest the words with the menace of a man accustomed to being obeyed.

Rod had pushed his way through and put a comforting arm round Mark's shoulder. Mark was surprised to hear the hard edge of contempt in his voice. 'He'll attend to your good lady in due course. If I'm not mistaken he's dealing with a matter of life and death at the moment.' The woman had stood up and was leaning heavily on Lassiter's shoulder, carrying her weight on one leg. Her solar topee was askew, and her dress dusty and creased. She said unbelievingly, 'But he's only a native,' and Mark saw his father put a restraining hand on Rod's arm. 'Not worth it, old boy,' he said quietly.

They stood awkwardly while the mob chattered and speculated around them. An ambulance clattered down the alley and came to rest by the maidan. When the stretcher bearers returned, the figure on the stretcher was covered over in a red blanket, one brown arm trailing limply over the side. Vincent followed behind and beside him walked the woman in the golabe sari. When they got to the ambulance she took the hem of the sari away from her mouth for a moment and said, more in confirmation than as a statement, 'Murgyaha, Sahib?' and Vincent nodded mutely. Without a word she climbed into the interior and the stretcher bearer pulled the doors shut and the vehicle clattered noisily away.

When a taxi had come to take the still-glowering Lassiter and his companion to the hospital with a scrawled note from Vincent, Rod said, 'Sometimes I'm ashamed to be English. We call the Japs barbarians and then . . .' He made a disgusted sound in his voice, turning to Vincent. Vincent said, 'He was killed immediately. One of the

208

clubs had crushed his head. It's the poor woman and her family I'm concerned with now.' The circus folk were packing their belongings together, and the crowd began to drift away.

Mark walked alongside the men up the hill, still dazed with shock, Vincent's words gave a reality to what had happened, and he suddenly felt overwhelmed by grief. He began to cry, with great choking sobs. Anthony said awkwardly, 'You mustn't blame yourself. It wasn't your fault. She only accused you because she was upset.' But Mark only cried harder, wishing again and again that he could expunge the moment when he had lost his temper and pushed back, now more than half-convinced that the man's death could be laid directly to his account. A terrible apprehension had come to him. The magic had gone, and when he remembered the sunlit forest glade which possessed and held his most secret heart, the mist had risen through it and would not be dispelled. Vincent said to the others, 'You go on ahead and load the car. We'll follow in a minute.'

They sat down on the crumbling stone and mud wall while the indifferent crowds seethed past. Rod and Anthony, carrying the shopping, were soon lost to view. Vincent waited patiently until his nephew had stopped crying. He said gently, 'Things just happen sometimes. They are nobody's fault. They are not the consequence of some planned action undertaken with a deliberate end in view. And there comes a time in our lives when no one else can carry the burden of forgiving us, or of telling us how things work . . .' Mark sensed that his uncle was offering him something he could take or reject. Part of him wanted some easy salve, his uncle's grown-up judgement that nothing that had happened was his fault. But stronger than that, he felt he was being offered an equality if he could accept the terms.

He wanted to believe Vincent, to feel that there was no connection between his anger and the still figure on the stretcher. He remembered the woman's face and her accusing comment. 'She thought it was my fault,' he said, with renewed hurt, remembering that she, too, was an adult whose words carried weight, and Vincent shook his head patiently with a sigh. 'Some people make value judgements about everything in life. Bad consequences are punishments, good consequences rewards. They have a child's view of life, believing that everything is controllable, that good will be rewarded and evil punished.' His face in the sunlight seemed tired, dispirited by some secret sorrow. A herdsman shooed his flock of bleating goats past, raising his whip to his forehead in salutation and Vincent waved. 'But the truth is that there is no divine justice. Things just happen. Just are.'

They sat for a few moments in silence. Mark felt older, already distanced from his first instincts to cry. Is this how it happens, he thought wonderingly, suddenly aware of a new world in which right and wrong were overtaken by a vast impersonal force which gave no credence to such things.

Vincent started to laugh and Mark looked at him, puzzled. 'They'll be coming to the ball, I'm sure. I specifically gave instructions in the note to give her anti-tetanus jab and to paint iodine on her arm. It stings a lot and leaves a heavy orange stain.' Mark giggled, and they started together up the cobbled alleyway towards the car.

Twenty-two

In the valley the elephants moved ponderously forward in line. James Bulstrode-Henshaw sat in the howdah perched atop the third beast, maintaining the dignified monosyllabic semi-silence he had decided was the correct response to the affront to his dignity. Colonel Fawcett, spending his leave at the palace, was talking to the Dewan at the front of the howdah. Snatches of conversation drifted back over the noises of the creaking howdah and the constant 'Hut,' 'Juldi,' 'Ubi, ubi, ubi,' of the mahout. 'But Listowel doesn't have the power . . .' Fawcett said patiently, resuming to the uncomprehending Dewan some explanation which had continued since they had stopped for lunch.

Every time James Bulstrode-Henshaw looked ahead and saw Roger Henshaw with the Maharajah, deep in conversation on the leading beast with Corfield in the back, he felt aggrieved. He had always ridden in the first howdah with the ruler. Now Roger, who had been staying with him for a week on 'confidential government business', had persuaded him to introduce him to the Maharajah and had established such a rapport that they had been talking and laughing together like old friends all day. (At first Bulstrode-Henshaw had felt a little flattered and young again. Not too old to still have a part to play in events, he had thought, hugging his secret to himself in the Mess.) Now the elephant broke into a lumbering run, and his back began to ache. He felt old.

In the leading howdah Roger Henshaw sat sipping champagne with the Maharajah. The smell of patchouli hung heavily on the air and the cushion upon which his head rested was pure silk. Behind them Corfield slept, his head propped with a cushion. Until the moment when Henshaw had shot the tiger (after Corfield's first shot had missed), peering through the shimmering haze and the deceitful undergrowth, he had begun to despair of achieving his goal. His host hadn't seemed interested, waving a bejewelled hand dismissively. 'Conrad is making the representations. They cannot take these ancient rights away from us . . .' he had said and, though he listened further, it was with such an air of lack of interest that Henshaw had lost heart. But when he had shot the tiger and the mahout had quietened their disturbed elephant, so that they could watch the beaters strapping it on to the pole, the Maharajah had put a hand on his shoulder and said, 'We must see you here more often,' and Henshaw had seen his opportunity.

He had talked about Hari Singh's opposition to the British proposals and the rumours that an army of Sikhs was being prepared to overthrow Kashmir by force. About the Nizam of Hyderabad's attempts to buy off the British. About Bhupinder Singh, powerless to prevent the diminution of his power although he was a friend of the King Emperor. And, now that the Maharajah saw that he was a man to be reckoned with, he had talked about his own opposition to the imminent division and its likely consequences. That he was in Mysore to meet with a group whose aims were, by peaceful means, to prevent Partition. In the end, when the Maharajah had murmured that he should see the Chancellor to arrange a contribution, which must be anonymous, of course, and had said queryingly, 'Peaceful means, my friend?' Henshaw had looked him in the eye and said, 'I only make war on shikar or when pursuing a woman, my lord.' His companion had laughed uproariously, slapping his knee and shouting, 'When pursuing a woman. Very good. Very good.'

Now he needed to persuade Savarkar and Ghodse that holding rallies and defacing colonial buildings were minor irritations. The real targets must be Jinnah and his lieutenant, Liaquat Ali Khan. With them out of the way, the Muslim League must lose direction, and the tide must turn. He felt sure that in such circumstances the Viceroy would persuade Attlee's government to leave things as they had been.

What a way to hunt, he thought contemptuously, looking down from his high perch on to the lines of beaters who moved forward in close formation, shouting loudly. On the hills above, the light glanced red-gold, and he could see tiny figures watching from the plateau. Their beast plunged into the thicket, and the light was greyish and murky once more.

Once on the hill, the events of the morning seemed to Mark like the fading memory of a bad dream. They had driven up the winding track, in some places brushing through the dense encroaching foliage. At times it had seemed that night had fallen, as the car moved through ambuscades of huge, luxuriously leafed branches which joined fingers across their path. Once a ruined wall pouted its distended belly covered in lultus which scurried to find sanctuary at their approach. A bird of paradise pursued its ungainly flight across their path, trailing its sumptuous tail and uttering its strange, desolate cry. Now, on the level, the engine note changed to a flatter, smoother register and they could hear game crashing away from the road through the undergrowth. When the clearing was in sight they came across three hyenas ripping open the corpse of a sambhur, their muzzles caked with blood. At the approach of the car they stumbled clumsily away on drunken legs, watching the vehicle warily.

In the clearing, the grass reared up in tufts of brilliant green. 'Careful, Vin. The car will get bogged down,' said Anthony anxiously, but Vincent only smiled and jolted the car over the tussocks to the shade under the spreading banyan. While the men unpacked the food and laid it out on the picnic spot, Mark walked over to the rim of the plateau and looked down into the valley. Below him the khud fell away steeply, torn from the flat hill top by the last rains and scarred with a jagged rim of red earth upon which the vegetation had already begun to take its green hold. In the valley far below the purple haze was interspersed with trailing mists.

Movement caught his eyes and he shaded them against the sun with his hand. A line of beaters came into sight and he could just hear, so distant as to be barely audible, the faint sound of trumpeting. When the leading elephants came into sight he called the men. Anthony said, with a catch of sadness in his voice, 'Corfield's leaving present, I suppose,' and Mark looked at his father, disturbed to feel some tremor of uncertainty about the future. He remembered suddenly that his father would be leaving them soon.

There was a flurry of movement and the beaters ran to and fro. Now the shrill trumpeting of the elephants was much clearer. Rod said, 'There it goes!', pointing over Mark's shoulder, and the boy could just make out the striped form moving through the panicking beaters and making for the heavy cover further up the hillside. There was the loud boom of a shot, but the tiger continued unchecked and was lost to view. Beside him, Vincent let out a long, thankful breath. Below, the beaters reassembled, and the procession began to move slowly out of sight into the heavy cover. As they turned back towards their picnic, Vincent pointed upwards to the vultures moving in slow gyres on the thermals. 'Uncanny the way they know, isn't it?' he said.

After lunch Mark dozed in the sun. The adults seemed to have been talking interminably about political matters, and exchanging anecdotes about the massacres at Lahore, Amritsar and Sheikpura, taking an obsessive interest in the precise details of the incidents. Occasionally, when the conversation drifted into familiar channels, or dealt with people he knew, he half-listened for a while. Vincent had laughingly said, 'Typical of the English. While war is waging they organize a ball. When it can no longer do any good, they throw the invitation open to the Indian community. The Maharajah has always had a dispensation but I gather that the Bhoses and Majid are coming this year. Mother will have a cardiac arrest.'

Rod said maliciously, 'I think Angela's had that in mind since that sticky dinner party a year ago.'

Vincent looked across at Anthony. 'She certainly wouldn't have invited the Bhoses but for Anne's persistent nagging.' Though his voice was as deceptively casual as before Mark realized that he was trying to communicate some message, and he remembered the meeting in the bazaar. 'Don't get me wrong. I've nothing personal against the Bhoses, but Raju seems a bit of a hot-head. Intelligence have been keeping an eye on members of the RSSS because of rumours of a plot on Jinnah's life, and I gather that young Raju has been present at a couple of meetings with Veer Savarkar, who runs the party, and his lieutenant, Nathuram Ghodse.' He laughed. 'Apart from anything else, their sexual proclivities are a little unusual – not that I think young Raju could be in the least influenced in that direction,' here he levered himself on

215

to his elbow and looked slyly across at Anthony again, but Anthony lay with his arm across his eyes against the sun and made no rejoinder.

The conversation died away and a valedictory melancholy crept over the party. The birdsong muted, and a light wind scuffled the dust into little eddies. Mark watched the Coringa ants carry the crumbs which had fallen from his plate, fascinated by their determination in dragging their gargantuan loads. From time to time he had thought of the juggler, but the memory was muted now, and Vincent's words had comforted and released him from some immediate and causal connection with the tragedy.

He fell asleep, waking suddenly to the sound of Rod's voice. Rod was standing on a tussock with a bottle in his hand. Mark heard him say, 'With a whimper,' and saw him carry out a crazy jig, like a whirling dervish. Watching his uncle, Mark felt unreal. Some faraway divinely ordained structure shivered to its foundations. Rod stopped and said belligerently, addressing himself to Vincent, 'We can't pretend that everything is the same any more. Go to dances . . . act as if nothing is happening. This is the end of it all.' The men observed him in silence, and Rod began to wave his arms about. 'We're dinosaurs, extinct, useless. They don't need us any more . . .'

Vincent began to clear the detritus of the picnic, collecting the dirty napkins and bakelite plates and putting them methodically into the centre of the checked cloth. Something in the deliberation of his movements seemed to infuriate Rod and he ran down and placed himself in front of Vincent, legs apart, hands on hips, his face working with anger. There was something comical about his posture, stood like a mandrill contemplating a banana, and Mark began to giggle.

Rod yelled at Vincent. 'Nothing touches you, does it, Vin? Your mother . . . what's happening here . . . you don't become involved, don't suffer like the rest of us?' Anthony gave an embarrassed cough, but Vincent only said sadly, 'I know,' kneeling before Rod for a moment like a supplicant before a god. Anthony, as if in recognition of their shared state, touched Vincent briefly on the shoulder.

When they began to load the car, Mark said, 'I won't be long,' and ran to the edge of the plateau. He heard Vincent laugh gently and say, 'No one to see you here except the vultures,' but, driven by some need for privacy, he scrambled down the hillside ignoring the brambles which scratched his legs until he reached the base of an old pine, obscured from the plateau by a ridge of grey granite rocks. It was impossible to understand grown ups. They always seemed to live in the past or be thinking about the future. No one lived in the present. He braced his legs apart, suddenly aware that there was no sound save for his urine dully plashing on the spongy pine needles. When he had finished he was seized by a feeling of unaccountable panic, that they had left without him, and he ran breathlessly up the hill, falling and skinning his knee in his haste to reach the top. When he saw that they were still there, loading the car, he felt the same private mixture of relief and embarrassment at his own feelings as he did when he returned on the school bus to find the house still standing.

Vincent walked to the edge of the plateau and looked down through his binoculars. 'They got it after all,' he said, sighing, and handed the binoculars to Mark. The boy could just make out the tiger hung from two poles carried by the beaters. As he watched, an elephant moved in front of the tiger, its howdah swaying as it navigated the slope. He was taken by surprise to feel tears pricking at his eyes. Vincent took the binoculars from him and said gently, 'There won't be many more of those, old son. It won't be all bad if this is coming to an end, too.'

Twenty-three

Henshaw ran for the last half mile, cursing the brambles which tore at his trousers and swung across his face. When the ruined outline of the temple appeared, swathed in ivy, he slowed to a walk. Dusk. A cicada shrilled and far to the right where the tributary forced its sluggish way through the jungle, the bullfrogs boomed and gurgled.

The temple always filled him with uneasy awe. The glow from the lanterns of the waiting group lit up the stone figures around the walls: Ganesh, Hanuman, Hathi trampling Gunevati. But their figures were dwarfed by the representation of Kali in her image as Destroyer, six-armed, dancing in her circlet of stone flames.

Savarkar sat to one side of the effigy, a rumal containing some salt and sugar on the ledge by his side. Raju squatted by his feet and another man, grave and plump in formal white clothes, stood incongruously eating peanuts from a paper bag. The floor round his chuplees was covered in shells.

Henshaw stepped over the low stone parapet into the courtyard. 'I couldn't get away before,' he said, and Savarkar said in a harsh voice, 'Well? Did you succeed?'

Henshaw sat down in an embrasure and leaned against the wall, feeling the perspiration drying on his face. He nodded. 'The money I am arranging over the next few days. It will be paid into the account of the Hindu

Rashtra, as you directed. I have also got supplies. Food, clothing, medical supplies.'

'What about weapons?' said the man chewing peanuts, spitting a piece of pith on to the ground.

'No weapons. He wishes his hands to remain clean. So I talked of defacing buildings, peaceful demonstrations, editorial pressures. Any attempt to push him would have resulted in nothing.'

Savarkar said in his dry, distant voice, 'I think you should know that our thinking has changed as to the best target. Gandhi's wish to appear even-handed has led to his lending weight to causes which can only damage and defile the Congress Party and, more importantly, every devout Hindu.' He spread his hands looking for a moment like a Holman Hunt representation of Christ. 'We realize the dangers of martyrdom. We realize, too, that in this our aim might not be the same as your own.' He fell silent. The plump man, Nathuram Ghodse, threw his empty peanut packet into the wild vetch growing in the corner of the temple and said, 'Jinnah is too well-guarded.' His voice was high and childlike.

Roger leaned forward, fixing Savarkar with a direct look. He said passionately, 'Jinnah is the key. He will be taking a ceremonial ride with Mountbatten, and I can give you all the details. There is no one, *no one*,' he emphasized, banging the heel of his hand against his knee, 'who is pursuing Partition with the same single-mindedness as he is. If we can only delay events, he will die. He takes no sustenance apart from whisky, and he has incurable cancer. At least think of what I have said.'

Later, Roger said to Raju, 'Guns are difficult, I know. It may be worth cultivating the Hodder girl. Her father has a gun . . .'

By the time the meeting had broken up, Roger felt they

might reconsider. The trouble was that Savarkar was a complete bigot. Despite his undoubted intelligence, he showed an inability to consider means and ends; his obsession with some obscure religious slight offered Hinduism by Gandhi's concession to 'Congress or Gandhi's espousal of the Harijan cause, blinded Savarkar to the strategic end they should be pursuing: the maintenance of the status quo. Already, in Roger's mind, he was coming to terms with the new circumstances: Gandhi's death would not deal Partition an effective blow, but it might considerably delay the progress of Partition and remind both parties of the advantages of retaining the structures and personnel of pre-Partition. The ceremonial, the meaningless treaties enshrined in archaic language in Government House were unimportant.

'You'd better go now,' Roger said to the three conspirators. 'There will be very few police on duty tonight because of the ball. I've arranged with the Dewan that the first supplies will be delivered to the safe house by cart.' He felt tired, watching them leave in single file down the narrow path where the smoke from the woodcutters' fires hung upon the branches and in the clearing like ghostly fog. The moonlight was bright now, throwing Kali's shadow across the broken paving slabs. Above the marble columns bats squeezed out of a hole in the trabeated cross piece, which depicted Lord Vishnu carrying out the Sacred Hunt. They wheeled in erratic flight, twittering and squeaking as they took the late flies. A crackle of thunder sounded and abruptly stopped.

A brick fell on the floor, echoing hollowly around the walls. When he looked up she was standing by the broken doorway, her face ghostly in the moonlight. She ran to him, putting her arms round his neck, and kissed him on the face with little breathless kisses. 'Oh, quick, quick,' she said, moving back from him to remove her dress. 'I had to say I needed something at the bazaar. I've run all the way from the taxi . . .'

He moved towards her and saw the fear and desire in her face. 'Don't hurt me,' she said in a wild, broken voice, but he saw her unfocussed eyes and felt exultant and refreshed to know that things were as they had always been.

Afterwards, lying in the crook of his arm and watching his chest rise and fall, Jane remembered what her mother had said.

'You never told me that you'd met my mother at Mr Bulstrode-Henshaw's?' she said on a note of enquiry, her voice sounding slightly aggrieved. It had worried at her, from the moment that Arline had drawn her aside, a couple of weeks before, when the house was quiet. Jane had been afraid at first, afraid of being found out. When her mother spoke she had felt disgust at the prurient interest, the animation, the flushed face. Her mother had met Roger several times at Dr Mac's and Joginder's years before. 'He was the one I hoped you would marry,' Arline said.

Jane had been shocked, realizing her mother both knew of the liaison and was actively encouraging it. 'Roger Henshaw has ambition,' Arline said, and Jane had felt a sudden, sad protective instinct towards Anthony. He was so passive, so trusting, that he made her feel guilty.

By her side Roger stirred, levering himself on to one elbow. He looked down at her and said, 'So she guessed, eh?' He picked a twig from the ground and snapped it between his fingers. 'Well, that doesn't matter too much. I don't want my visit shouted from the roof tops . . .'

When they were dressing Jane asked, suddenly anxious,

'But *why* are you here?' Roger didn't answer. He looked round carefully to make sure they had left nothing behind. 'You'll be late,' he said, looking at his watch. 'Better run.'

It was only in the taxi that she wondered, again, why Roger had come down. She knew it hadn't been only to see her.

Twenty-four

It was one of James Bulstrode-Henshaw's agreeable failings that he felt bound by an almost religious fervour to show visitors round the sights of Mysore. His spinster sister, Daisy, was convinced that he would rise, Lazarus-like, from his deathbed if news of a fresh party of uninitiated visitors came at the apposite moment. It was a tradition that she accompanied him on these occasions but, less involved than he, she had long suspected that his passion for imparting statistics and detailed information on every facet of Mysore's history and social life proved boring to most, and positively risible to a few. Even if she suspected that the handkerchiefs produced so regularly by visitors were not to stem the sudden symptoms of a summer cold, but to stifle some access of hilarity, she bore the knowledge in a loyal silence, knowing that James' nature was incapable of change, and unwilling to hurt him with the truth. For, in his own portentous, waistcoat-and-fobwatch way, he was a likeable man who lived his life according to a generous interpretation of the Christian principles of his Presbyterian forefathers. Though his adherence to those principles did not prevent him indulging himself heavily on Masonic dinner and Mess nights, it did prompt him towards unexpected and lavish acts of generosity and a benign and charitable disposition. Too charitable, sometimes, she thought grimly, remembering Roger Henshaw, their guest.

Bulstrode-Henshaw had taken a party round the Hall and through the splendid state rooms only that morning. Whenever he took people through he felt, anew, a sense of pride in being British, and his memory stirred with half-forgotten lines and phrases from *The Charge of the Light Brigade* and Newbolt's *Vitae Lampada*. They never ceased to move him when he walked through the great formal gardens or the imperial rooms. He would imagine himself trotting steadily behind Cardigan under the volley and thunder of the Russian guns, or remember the second stanza of Newbolt's poem, which began 'The sand of the desert is sodden red,' and feel a gratifying sense of deep emotion.

The building was quintessentially English in his eyes, a symbol of the enduring power of the Raj, of the undoubted benefit the Creator had conferred upon all those He had chosen to be born English. It had been built in the early nineteenth century to the plans of an English architect fresh out from Berkshire with a passionate enthusiasm for Robert Adam. It had been commissioned by a wealthy English merchant who had willed it, together with a considerable sum for its upkeep, 'to be used in such manner as they will by the Committee and Members of the Mysore Club,' doubtless assured by such provision that the hallowed rooms would only ever be employed by the English for entertaining the English.

It retained the original square plan of an Elizabethan house. The principal apartments were on the piano mobile and the ground inside the court was raised to that level, providing a wide flight of steps as an approach and throwing an Ionic portico across the open side of the

223

square. The ballroom and hall floors were of fine, inlaid oak splines, and the upper rooms had been refloored with narrow deodar boards. 'It cost eight hundred pounds to send three workmen to England for three months to learn how to lay this floor,' Bulstrode-Henshaw said proudly. (For the umpteenth time, thought Daisy through mentally gritted teeth.) Her brother fingered the fob resting on his waistcoat, totally unaware of the open giggling of some of the younger members of the party.

Daisy sighed and wished it were all over so that they could go up to the Club for a stengah. But it was no use trying to hurry her brother. Never had been, since nursery days. There were still the low reliefs, the friezes and painted ornaments, the stucco in the grotesque style, the portraits of European royalty by Hoppner, and the Gobelin tapestries. All of which (she sighed again as she consulted her watch) represented at least another forty-five minutes.

She smoothed her spare ginger hair with a nervous gesture and hurried after the group on her thin legs. Through the great windows she looked out on the magnificent formal gardens stretching out towards the promontory as she rushed past. If only he liked gardens, she thought wistfully, dismissing the disloyal thought immediately.

When they got to the great portico Jemadar Akbar was waiting, immaculately dressed as usual in white baggy trousers and black top, with his pariah bitch at his heels. Bulstrode-Henshaw gave him a smile and a half salute, in recognition of the service Akbar had done the State, but the man continued to stand in mute supplication, and James realized, with a frisson of impatience, that Akbar wanted to talk to him. He noticed that the bitch's dugs hung heavily down and thought uncharitably that there would probably be further 'accidents' on the immaculate gravel until the puppies had been trained. 'What is it, Jemadar Sahib?' he asked, surreptitiously looking at his watch and trying to hide his annoyance.

Akbar stood stiffly to attention. 'If I may take up a moment of your time, Sahib,' he said, beginning to walk away. James gave an apologetic glance to the gaggle of tourists and followed the old man. This had better be important, he thought to himself, already resentful at being late for his pilao lunch at the Club.

At first he couldn't see anything when Akbar pointed into the shadowed wall where the wing began its traverse from the portico. Then, as his eyes became accustomed to the shadows, he saw that someone had painted in large red letters the words HINDOSTAN ZINDABAD PAKISTAN MORDABAD and beneath it a swastika. For a moment he felt ill, unreal, and he put out a hand against the wall to steady himself.

Jemadar Akbar was almost in tears. His old eyes, milky with cataract, were screwed up against the sun, giving him the appearance of a sightless statue. 'Who would do this, Sahib?' he asked plaintively. 'Those buggers from the RSSS – that's who,' Bulstrode-Henshaw said distractedly, already thinking of how he could ensure that the matter was taken seriously enough for an official enquiry. 'Now get a couple of men on to cleaning it up.' He reflected for a moment, one hand on his pudgy lips. 'If it won't clean up, paint both the bricks and pointing in the same colours again. Do you understand?' Akbar nodded miserably, still looking at the words with a hurt expression. At his heels the bitch whined softly.

When her brother got back to the party, Daisy realized that something was wrong. He made a few mechanical observations and answered a couple of questions but he

225

was not his usual loquacious self. Even she, knowing him so well, could not know that something had been destroyed for him forever. He had been able finally to come to terms with the fact that Indians had been invited to the ball. But now he knew that, however well Akbar's men did their work, he himself would always be aware that the building had been diminished. She did not divine before, or suspect afterwards, that it was the end of an absolute certainty in her brother, that he would often lie awake and wonder to himself in the dark, What will happen to us all now?

Twenty-five

Akbar's men had done their work well. As the rickshaws came up the hill, their guttering cressets barely illuminating the road, the great house was outlined by the lights from the chrags burning on parapets and window ledges so that it stood in monolithic splendour against the night sky. The Jemadar had inspected the cutlery, the linen and crockery, and had then turned his attentions to the buddlis, masalchees and chokras. They passed the test of his critical eyes. The crystal chandeliers illuminated the tables laid with fine linen with Lord Curzon's crest picked out in drawn threadwork. The white uniforms, trimmed with green and gold in a Greek key design, were starched and brilliantly creased. 'Baht uccha,' he had said after the inspection, smiling at the ranks of servants, his memories of the desecration of the morning temporarily in abeyance.

As each rickshaw or car drove up to disgorge its load in front of the huge portico, he stepped forward stiffly, merely opening the door to some while to others he offered a rigid arm to the memsahib stepping down from the conveyance. His features remained impassive as the Indian traders and merchants began to arrive, hiding his disapproval of the break with tradition. Only when the Maharajah's Rolls appeared, and he and his guest, Sir Conrad Corfield, stepped out to be greeted by Brigadier and Mrs Dawnay-Smythe, did he permit the stern lines of his face to relax for a moment.

Sam led the Kipling Road contingent. Arline sat in front in black bombazine, the collar standing stiffly up under her chin, and her hair held in a chignon. Anthony and Jane sat in the back, a certain stiffness apparent in their manner towards each other. Vincent drew up just behind, with Anne sitting beside him. She wore a white halter-necked dress, and her hair was swept up behind her ears, hanging upon her slender neck in a coil of white gold. When Vincent first saw her that evening, standing poised in the hall under the lamp, gravely listening to the adults talking, he had felt hurt by her beauty. It was an abstract appreciation, or so he had to remind himself. 'My beautiful niece. You'll be the belle of the ball,' he said, and she smiled gratefully at the compliment.

Now, as they alighted, Arline took Jemadar Akbar's proffered arm and smiled at him. 'How are your children?' she asked in her heavily accented Urdu, and he nodded gravely, 'Thik hai, Memsahib,' aware of and yet participating in her patronage.

When they had gone into the great hall and Sam had driven off to park round the back and join the servants, Akbar helped Angela out. He said urgently to her, 'Miss Sahib, we tried but we couldn't clean up the stonework,' she looked at him uncomprehendingly for a moment and then said soothingly, 'It's all right, Akbar,' not knowing

227

what he was talking about but only concerned to relieve him of whatever anxiety he felt. He smiled, relieved now, and ushered them into the hall to meet the Brigadier.

Twenty-six

When they had left the house Mark watched the cars drive out of the gate, listening to the car engines dying away along the road. Mrs Farris' housekeeper was dropping by, despite his protests, to see that he was all right, but that would be later and for the moment he was alone. He felt full of an un-nameable delight, a sensation of real freedom which he had not experienced since they had come to Mysore. Slowly the euphoria of feeling that he could do anything ebbed. He sat down for a while at the window, watching the stars over the maidan, and the gharries rushing past with their storm lanterns flickering with the motion. It took him some time to pluck up the courage to take the action which had formed in his mind. He tried to read his book for a few minutes, but the words had no meaning. He put the book down and walked out on to the dark landing. The familiar furniture seemed alien, somehow hostile, and he was glad when he was in his parents' room and had the torch in his hand. He went back to his room to pick up the rest of the equipment.

He propped the front door open with a cushion. When he was outside, the yellow hall light seemed comforting and he almost stole back inside. But something in his mind would not let him stop until he had done what he had set out to do.

The thicket, too, was different at night. He placed the torch between his knees, adjusting it so that the beam was at the right height, and parted the bamboo shoots with his hands. He felt a sense of relief when he saw the head come up, and the shiny black eyes looked unwinkingly into the torch beam. He manoeuvred the beam upwards, shifting in pain as he knelt upon a shard of bamboo. At the sudden movement the snake struck, and Mark was surprised at the strength of the blow as the head hit the torch. He withdrew cautiously, holding the torch steady, and watched the head go down again, slowly. It should not be tonight after all, he thought, not knowing from where the certainty came.

With all that happened afterwards Mark only remembered the dream much later. He had gone to sleep immediately, immersed in a strange calm, unafraid now of being alone in the old house. Despite the distortions of the dream, he knew that the train he was travelling on as the only passenger was the one in which the family had come to Mysore. He saw himself as a player in the scene. Through the train window the desert swept by, half hidden through the golden motes of swirling dust. The train drew to a standstill and Mark saw himself get out. Fifty yards from the track a gaunt tree, bare of leaves, stood stark against the yellow sand. As he walked towards it he saw that what had at first seemed like a bundle of rags was the body of a boy. A crow sat on the child's head, tearing at the eyes with strong, pulling movements of his beak. When he came near, the crow flew into one of the branches of the tree, slowly dropping its head into its ruffled neck feathers as it watched him. He looked at the body for a while. In the background he heard a noise and turned to see the train moving down the track towards the horizon like a great snake, with the smoke streaming over its long back. He was left with the crow, and the body of the dead child.

Then the voices in the hall and the crying woke him up.

Twenty-seven

Nathoo Bhose shifted uncomfortably in his chair. He was possessed with a vague feeling of wrongdoing which he had not felt since he was a child. When the invitation had come Indijeet had been happy for days, singing around the house, and even submitting twice to his tentative embraces with a simulacrum of ardour. He had paid for it, of course, horrified when she had come back from Henderson's Fashions with not one but two new dresses. 'I couldn't choose,' she had said coyly, clasping them to her ample bosom with a loving possessiveness and making a babyish moue at him to defuse any rejoinder. When she had eventually told him how much they had cost (lopping, he suspected, several rupees off the actual cost), he had striven to keep his face from recording the shock. More overtime, he had thought glumly, and that would make Indijeet angry about being left alone in the evenings. In the circumstances he felt even more irritated by his inability to enjoy being at the ball. He sighed and picked up his lemonade.

By his side Indijeet was sipping her third – or was it fourth – pink gin. She and Nathoo had discussed this aspect of their social life early in their marriage, and now Nathoo accepted her drinking without comment. He wondered if her dress was perhaps a trifle too bright, too many sequins covering the gold cloth. Even to his untutored eye the dresses worn by the European ladies seemed much more restrained. He could see her eyes gazing around the room and her mouth smiling vacantly in profile.

Raju sat the other side of Indijeet, wearing an ill-fitting, borrowed dinner jacket in honour of the occasion. He had brought some Abdullah cigarettes, eschewing the bidis he customarily smoked, but Nathoo could see from his occasional grimaces that he was not enjoying them. He, too, was drinking, and Nathoo seethed inwardly. The boy was a law unto himself and every day brought fresh evidence of new habits he was learning from his political friends.

Arline Porter sat with her daughters at the next table. She had voiced her disapproval of the Indian guests, sotto voce, to all the acquaintances who had come to their table to pay respects. Bulstrode-Henshaw had responded with unusual acerbity and Daisy, sitting quietly by his side, had prayed inwardly that he would take it more calmly, would just agree with Arline in the manner decreed by polite society. 'We've got to get used to playing second fiddle now, Mrs Porter. It's their country, after all. We're only here on sufferance.' As they made their farewells Daisy wondered at some new humility in his voice. Bulstrode-Henshaw bowed and cleared his throat with a hrrmph and, trailing Daisy behind him, bore down like a man o'war in full sail to pay his respects at the next port of call. 'Old fool,' muttered Arline viciously under her breath.

At the bar Vincent said a little sadly to Anthony, 'A week and you'll be gone. Why don't you leave it until after Partition?' Anthony, precariously balancing the drinks which they had decided to take over to the table themselves, felt under siege. It was a question to which he knew the answer, but he felt unable to discuss with Vincent his growing estrangement from Jane. 'There's going to be a lot of administrative work in connection with the changeover. Best I'm back before the paperwork builds up too much.' He could see from Vincent's direct gaze that he wasn't convinced.

After receiving Gur's letter Anthony had cabled to say he would be in Amritsar by 14 August; and a couple of weeks later Gur had cabled his delight and the information that he would travel down to Amritsar on the Ten-Down Express from Lahore the following day so that they could return together to Rawalpindi. Anthony was touched, knowing that Gur was giving up part of his precious leave.

As Anthony and Vincent traversed the floor, crowded with dancing couples, Rod and Patricia danced past. He was playing a Spanish dancer and Patricia, in a flame-red decolleté dress was laughing wildly with a touch of hysteria. 'Must keep an eye on him,' said Anthony, anxious to avoid any further outbursts like that of the afternoon.

Unexpectedly they bumped into the couple from the bazaar as they made their way back to the table. She was wearing long white gloves, entirely unsuitable for the rest of her outfit. Lassiter bowed stiffly, his face registering disapproval, and Vincent said genially, 'I'm glad the hospital fixed you up,' moving past so that they were out of earshot in the hubbub before either of them had time to reply.

Once at the table Vincent took Jane off for a dance and Anthony sat down. In the corner the Maharajah and Corfield sat in a curtained banquette. Corfield was speaking urgently, but the Maharajah was watching the floor with every appearance of lack of attention. Anthony felt the evening slipping away, remembering Jane in the black dress, standing in front of the mirror with her arms above her head as she arranged her hair. For a moment he had remembered his feelings for her at that first dance, the breathless tightness he had experienced. He sighed. It had been a pleasant illusion, but the coldness of months now lay between them, and he had noticed that Jane never looked at him any more. She sometimes straightened his tie or flicked a hair from his lapel, but the old directness had gone. She had seemed even more edgy and distant the last few days. Perhaps it is my leaving, he thought abstractedly, watching the dancers assemble for the Gay Gordons; but rather the sense she gave him was of looking over his shoulder at something in the shadows behind him. Back at the table, she leaned forward, laughing, and he felt a vague sense of pain, and unwilling exile. It had been a mistake to come to Mysore, though he knew that there had been little choice. Idly he thought of Rod's outburst. Yes, there was a chauvinist absurdity about this evening. He remembered the importance Angela, the whole family, had attached to this; the arguments over who should and should not be invited; the agonies over what should be worn; the protocol; the food. To his mind it was no bad thing that the British pink was slowly fading from the map everywhere. Malaysia in 1942, Burma, now India. He realized, with a start of surprise, that what had always angered him was the superficiality of the British presence. Angela was leaning across the table and saying excitedly behind her fan, 'The Maharajah's here. He's with Corfield in the curtained alcove over there.' Her eyes were shining.

India was not, could not be, for him, merely a comfortable place to live. The social round of dinner parties, bridge and polo had possessed a limited appeal, but not as an end in itself. It was the mountains and forests which had caught him with their beauty first. There had been, of course, those student days with Roger and Joginder, when that friendship had transcended everything. (Despite all that had occurred since, his feelings for Roger

233

were from that time.) Later, when life had begun to sort into the patterns of maturity, he had started to feel ashamed of the British arrogance, to recognize that his Hindu friends, with their syncretist polytheistic religion, and his Muslim friends, who prayed towards Mecca five times a day, had forged a closer relationship with these snow-swathed mountains, this incandescent sun, these huge rivers drifting their detritus and their burning ghats on silted flood tides to the sea, than could be possible to those who were bound by rules and regulations. A maimed Hindu had once seen the look of pity on his face and laughed. 'This is only one existence,' he had said, touching his fingers to his forehead in thanks for the alms. 'It matters not at all. I shall eventually attain Nirvana.' He had hobbled to the edge of the Ganges where the rising sun burned the water to molten gold and lowered himself into the holy water with the other pilgrims.

Anthony was suddenly aware that Raju was standing at the table. 'Good evening, Mr Bhose,' said Arline and he inclined his head nervously, the quiff of blue-black hair falling for a moment forward over the smooth olive forehead. Anthony noticed that the boy was sweating profusely and clasping his hands together nervously. He addressed himself to Arline, with a look of apology at Anthony. 'May I have this dance with Miss Anne?' Beyond him, Anthony caught Indijeet and Nathoo looking fixedly at them.

Arline picked up Anne's card from the table. Anne sat absolutely still, looking at Raju with an unreadable expression, but her face had taken on a deep flush which was distinguishable even in the low lighting in the recess where they sat. Anthony could see that her card was blank. Arline looked up at Raju, smiling, 'I'm afraid my granddaughter is taken for every dance, Mr Bhose,' she

234

said emphatically, replacing the card face down on the table and turning dismissively aside to resume her conversation with Angela.

Raju bowed, and Anne made an involuntary gesture with her hand towards him. Anthony was surprised to find himself saying, 'Of course you may have the dance, Raju.' Arline sat like stone as he got up and took Anne by the hand to lead her around to Raju. She gave her father a distant fleeting smile as she took Raju's arm, and said something inaudible, and then they were threading their way through the tables towards the dance floor. As Anthony sat down, Angela glanced at him briefly and he fancied he saw approval in her face. Arline looked straight ahead, with an expression of ironic, detached amusement.

Indijeet was smiling triumphantly across at the table. At last. She had always known that one day acceptance would come, but she had never envisaged how absolute and at the same time how simple it would be. She allowed herself to speculate about the future. The parties at which she would discuss intellectual subjects while the port flowed. The picnics ('Another cucumber sandwich, Indijeet?' 'Oh, thank you, Arline.' Lifting a wafer-thin sandwich from the plate with a bent little finger.) The race meetings – she saw herself in pink with a parasol, leaning prettily from the box with a pair of ladies' binoculars.

By contrast, as Nathoo watched the couple dancing, he felt afresh the sense of guilt and of being implicated in some monstrous social gaffe – like farting during a formal dinner. Over the next half hour, as he watched them, a suspicion he had held for a few days and frequently dismissed, took hold of him with such force that he felt he must go to the lavatory merely to perform some action which might alleviate his mounting sense of unease.

On the way he met Patricia on the edge of the dance

floor. She seemed distrait, wringing her hands together and looking wildly round the hall. 'Mr Bhose,' she said fearfully, putting one slim hand on his sleeve, 'have you seen my husband?' He wished he could help her, touched by her waif-like panic and the muted hysteria in her voice. He was forced to confess that he hadn't, squeezing his thighs together to alleviate the pressure on his bladder of copious draughts of lemonade. As he walked towards the cloakroom he saw her talking to the Brigadier who was shaking his head with a troubled look.

He felt relaxed for the first time in the evening, standing with his hands in his pockets as he sprayed up and down the porcelain stall, playing the familiar game of trying to wet the entire surface before the supply of urine ran out. He washed his hands in the warm water and dried them on the linen towel, smelling them appreciatively afterwards. He looked at the toecaps of his shoes and polished each in turn on the back of the other trouser leg. From under his brows he examined his thinning hair in the mirror, peering anxiously to see if there was evidence of further loss, before combing the greasy black strands carefully over the bald patch. With a sigh he prepared to leave the safety of his haven. As he opened the door the noise from the dance hall hit him with an almost physical force.

As he walked away from the lavatory down the corridor towards the dance hall, he glanced through the half-open door of the men's cloakroom. His mind didn't immediately assimilate precisely what had caught his attention. He pushed through the door. There were row upon row of capes hanging from metal hangers on long frames. For a moment he forgot what he had come in to investigate, entranced by the sight of so many splendid garments. Then he saw the pair of feet protruding from under the capes in one of the long rows. His first impulse was to leave quietly and pretend that he had seen nothing, but even before he had turned towards the door his conscience was railing at him. Is this a responsible attitude for a senior clerk at the Bank? it said; and reluctantly, almost against his very will, he returned to be faced with a dilemma. Should he heave the person out by the legs? No. Any Englishman (and he was sure this was an Englishman and not one of his countrymen) would take it very amiss to find himself grasped by the ankles and pulled over the floor for the purposes of identification by a diminutive Indian.

He decided that the only way was to part the cloaks and identify the sleeper from above. Taking a deep breath he pushed the capes over the figure, standing astraddle the legs by this time, and plunged his head into the soft material. An overpowering smell of mothballs almost overcame him, and he fought back a moment of panic as he struggled to draw breath. It was harder than he had anticipated to part the heavy coats. A sepulchral voice came welling up through the heavy folds. 'Oh God. Leave me alone,' it implored in tones of abject supplication, and Nathoo recognized Rod's voice. He had no wish to thwart Rod's wishes. When he had got to his feet with some difficulty, just avoiding falling to his knee upon Rodney's unsuspecting crotch, he stood back and paused to consider his next move. Why do these things have to happen to me? he wondered wildly, discarding on some instinctive basis his first thought of asking Indijeet's advice. He knew, beyond reason, that Arline would always blame him irrationally for having seen Rod in this state, just as he knew that there was nothing else he could do but tell one of Rod's family.

As he made for the table, pausing to side-step a dancing

couple who whirled past almost knocking him over in their mutual absorption (noting in a bemused way, for further examination later, that his son and Anne were still dancing together cheek-to-cheek to an old waltz), he was suddenly reminded that the gods were just to the devout. In his mind's eye he had already told Arline the news in several ways, none of them acceptable, watching in his imagination her lip curl and her eyes harden against him. He almost cried with relief to see his salvation in the forms of Vincent and Anthony walking between the tables towards him in the direction of the bar.

He told them his story and Vincent thanked him, putting a hand on his shoulder and saying, 'You've done well, Nathoo. We've been looking for him.' His lack of embarrassment made Nathoo feel accepted, almost a friend. Happy with the knowledge of a job well done, he went back to join Indijeet.

Vincent whispered to Anthony. 'Just tell them Rod's not very well and I'm taking him home. See you in the cloakroom in a few minutes.'

At first Patricia wanted to come too and Anthony was surprised when Arline supported him in dissuading her. 'You must stay here,' she said sternly. 'Nothing you can do anyway,' settling back in her chair and continuing her conversation with Jane with an air of finality.

As he started for the cloakroom Anthony was furious with Rod. Though Major Majid had said alcoholism was an illness, he found it hard to take it as anything but self-indulgence. In the cloakroom he found Jemadar Akbar and Vincent standing on either side of a pair of legs protruding from under a coat rack. Akbar was saying doubtfully, 'We won't disturb the sahib too much if I move all the coats.' Anthony's anger boiled over. He said, 'Leave this to me,' and bent down, grasping Rod's ankles and pulling him out across the polished floor. He resisted an urge to kick the recumbent figure, just saying, 'Christ', vehemently as he thumped his fist into his open hand.

The Jemadar went ahead, looking conspiratorially around when he reached the side exit before he beckoned the group forward. They bucked and swayed down the corridor like a pantomime horse. Rod had begun to sing, both words and tune indistinguishably slurred, and Anthony felt thankful that there were no witnesses to the scene. Vincent began to giggle.

When they propped Rod against the car and Vincent leaned into the back to arrange the rugs, tears of maudlin self-pity ran down Rod's cheeks. He seemed suddenly sober, looking solemnly into Anthony's exasperated face. 'It's women, Tony,' he said with the surprised air of a man who has just stumbled across some profound insight. 'They cannot rest until they have destroyed us.'

Vincent emerged from the car, his hair dishevelled, and put his arm round Rod, saying with a chuckle, 'Only some women, Rod. It's known as penis envy in the jargon these days.'

In the back of the car Rod fell asleep immediately, jammed on the floor between the front and rear seats. With both back doors open they tried to get him on to the seat until Anthony felt a sudden twinge of pain in his back and said irritably, 'Oh, let the sod suffer. Serve him right,' and Vincent gave him a mock reproachful glance, easing himself into the driving seat.

Anthony stood watching the red tail lights move down the road. Many of the chrags had given out, so that the house bulked ragged and half-lit against the night sky. He thought bitterly, What a send off, pitying himself already for the imminent separation and the work that lay ahead of him and more than half-afraid that he had taken the wrong turning in the myriad pathways lying ahead.

The Bulstrode-Henshaws helped ferry them back. Nathoo, prompted by Indijeet, who had got the story out of him and had watched the subsequent proceedings avidly, diffidently offered places in his car, hired for the evening complete with driver from Mehrabani Transporting Facilitations. Arline had dispensed with even the niceties, turning regally away from him and smiling at Jane with a shared complicity as she said, 'I don't think we need to put you out at all, Mr Bhose,' and Anthony, by this time immersed in depressing thoughts of the future, felt too despondent to say anything to Nathoo in amelioration.

When Bulstrode-Henshaw drew up in front of the house there was a black car by the gate. Sam, who had driven some of the party in the other car, was fumbling with tired fingers at the catch when a man walked over from the parked car and spoke to him for a moment. When the gates were open and Sam got back in to drive them up to the front of the house, Arline, wrapped in her coat in the back, asked peevishly what 'these men' were doing and Sam said deferentially, 'It's an Inspector Faroukh, madam. He wishes to have a word with you inside.'

Bulstrode-Henshaw, bid goodnight to Anthony and Anne and drove away. In the hall the family waited for Faroukh. Patricia was wide-eyed, ghostly, and Jane had an arm around her shoulders. When Faroukh had said, 'It was one of the palace ox-carts delivering late for some reason, the driver was killed, but the passenger seems only to have bruises and a broken arm,' Pat said involuntarily, 'Oh, thank God. Thank God.' There was an appalled silence. Patricia buried her head in Jane's shoulder, sobbing violently. The Inspector stood awkwardly with his hands clasped in front of him. Arline looked at Faroukh for a moment and then bunched her fists and raised them towards the ceiling. Anthony half stepped forward, convinced for a moment that she was going to strike the Inspector. Instead she said in a deep, resonant voice, rippling with unshed tears, 'You bastard. You bastard.'

Then the women began to cry. When Mark appeared on the landing rubbing his eyes Anthony went up the stairs. He looked back before taking Mark to bed. It was only his daughter he saw, and it seemed to him then, though he could never quite recapture the insight later, that her face showed a bacchanalian, debauched aspect which was totally at odds with all else, the weeping women, the impassive Police Inspector, the whole tableau.

Twenty-eight

Vincent's funeral was held two days before Anthony was due to leave.

Rod had been brought back to convalesce at home. 'But,' Majid said, 'no questions. No discussion about what happened. He is still in shock.' So there had been an artificial interregnum since his return and everybody had tried to pretend that nothing had happened. It had helped, and they had continued the charade out of Rod's earshot, by unspoken mutual consent. Nothing was said about Vincent. It was as if he had never lived. Mark, watching Arline feed William, said unguardedly, 'When we were on the picnic . . .' and only remembered when

Arline cut across him and said to Sam, 'Some more liver please, Samuel.'

Anthony had been totally unprepared for the crowds. Jemadar Akbar had walked, starting out on his feeble legs at 5 A.M. When Anthony passed him, walking with the family down the long road to the Christian cemetery, Jemadar Akbar touched his arm and gestured to the crowds, saying with tears in his eyes, 'He was loved, Sahib. You can see that he was loved.' Anthony saw among the grief-stricken faces the juggler's widow from the bazaar. On impulse he walked up to her and said, 'Did you know the man who has died?' and he saw the grief-paint on her palms. She said, 'He did not know me but he gave me money for my children. And when he told me that my husband was dead I saw that he would have changed things if it had been in his power.'

When the service was over, they looked at the wreaths and flowers. Arline walked away leaning heavily on Jane's arm while she talked to the vicar in low tones. Anthony stood by the huge mound of flowers. He could not get used to the idea that Vincent was dead. Standing, chin in hand, he almost expected his brother-in-law to step from behind the winged seraph gracing the next grave to say, 'It's all a bad joke, old son.' A wreath caught his eye and he idly read the legend. It said, 'For a man who could not be bought or traduced – whose worth was beyond price.' There was no signature on the attached paper, only the royal coat of arms of Mysore.

But the day was not yet over. When Anthony arrived back Dr Majid was with Sam in the hall. 'I hope I did right, sir,' Sam said anxiously, before Anthony had even removed his coat. 'I tried to talk to Mr Rod but when he took the gun and shot the photograph of Mrs Porter with Mrs Jane in her arms I thought I had better call the

242

doctor. I put the gun in your drawer.' Anthony, who had come back before the others, stood irresolute in the hall. He wondered briefly, with a hint of hysteria, whether he should ask Majid to save his story until the entire audience was assembled. Outside there was the sound of cars and Sam said quickly, with spite, anxious to deliver himself of the information before the rest of the family arrived, 'He said it was a pity he wasn't shooting *her*. Then he said something about her being the architect of our misfortunes.' When the door opened and Arline came in with the vicar, Sam stepped back and became a servant again, taking the coats obsequiously and disappearing while Anthony wondered what to say.

Anthony strapped the case and did up the buckle, standing up with a sigh of relief. His packing was finished. He had survived a fraught interview at the hospital with Patricia and Majid that morning. 'Your husband is very ill,' Major Majid had said gravely, pressing his fingertips together, the pouches under his tired eyes bilberry purple with fatigue, 'but I think we may be able to cure him of this . . . ah,' he looked at the ceiling, 'addiction.' He looked at Patricia for a moment and then said, almost as an afterthought, 'He must see nobody at all for three months.' Escorting a weeping Patricia out of the hospital, Anthony said desperately, 'It'll soon pass. You'll be surprised.'

Arline had gone off with her daughters to the bazaar. He didn't know where Anne was now that she had finished with school. Since the ball, she had been secretive, slipping out of the house without excuses, and back in at all hours without explanations. Lately, bowed down by events, nobody had even asked. Mark was at school. Now Anthony felt the need for a sense of geometric security, a certain knowledge of where everybody in his family was. He looked at the papers Gur had sent down but his thoughts were elsewhere. When Sam knocked he felt pleased by the interruption. 'Come in,' he said jovially, and Sam opened the door tentatively, standing in the doorway with an uncertain look on his face. He seemed ill-at-ease and Anthony said, 'Well?' still smiling expectantly. Sam shifted from foot to foot, looking down. 'There's a man to see you.' Anthony beckoned Sam to bring the man in, thinking it would be the chaprassi or a messenger, and Sam opened the door and ushered a small bowed Indian into the study.

The man bobbed his head, washing his hands in agitation, and burst into a torrent of incomprehensible Tamil. Sam put up a hand, and the little man stopped speaking immediately, nervously shredding the end of his puggaree between his hands. Sam said, 'It's the man who was driving the bullock cart Mr Vincent hit,' he said apologetically, 'he wants to be paid for his cart and his bullock.'

Anthony looked at the man without speaking. The man ducked and bobbed, showing yellow teeth in an ingratiating smile. Something in Anthony's mind clicked and he began to laugh, putting his hands over his face. 'There's a hundred rupees in my wallet, Sam,' he managed to say, holding his stomach, 'do you think that's enough?' and Sam said in a shocked voice, 'I think fifty should be very adequate, sir.'

When the servant had ushered the man out, Anthony put his head in his hands and howled afresh. In the hall he heard Sam say reproachfully, 'You see how much you have upset my sahib. Because of your bullock and cart everything is oolta-poolta here. I am sure you didn't even have a light on the cart, did you? Jaow,' and the sound of the door slamming.

* * *

244

Mark sat in his bedroom looking at the mirror. His father had said to him at the station, 'Now you must look after mummy. You're the man of the family,' and Mark had resented the condescension. It consigned him to a child-like territory which he knew he no longer occupied. Apart from his secret business with Anne he felt that he had been the repository of wisdoms from both Vincent and Rod. He looked under the bed and found the gunny sack. It would do. It was big enough. The forked stick he had found on an illicit walk on the maidan stood behind the door. He went to his chest of drawers and took out a piece of sisal, expertly tying a slip knot with his thin brown hands and slipping the loop round the door handle to test the knot. He imagined how it would work, grunting quietly with satisfaction. He heard the mournful sound of the lunch gong in the hall and put everything under the bed.

Arline came in late, giving her sunhat and gloves to Sam. She looked accusingly at Anne, though, as always, her comments were general enough to have no particular edge. 'I've been in court,' she announced. 'Some of you may know that Jemadar Akbar has been on trial for assaulting Raju Bhose.' She paused theatrically. Anne looked down at her plate. 'Apparently he had been reliably informed that Mr Bhose had defaced,' here she gave an additional emphasis, 'our Hall. He had tried to discuss it with the boy and was told he was an English lackey for his pains.' Sam brought in her soup and she waited impatiently for him to put it down. 'Anyway,' she said, blowing on the soup in her spoon, 'I gave him a marvellous reference. William and I had known him for almost forty years. But,' her voice began to rise in still amazed indignation, 'he has been put in prison and young Bhose has gone free.'

Lunch was conducted in silence, only broken when the pudding came and Arline looked up at Sam under arched eyebrows and said, 'Semolina again, Sam?' disapprovingly, her spoon poised over her plate as she watched him shuffle out. By an effort of will she seemed to banish Vincent from her mind during the hours of daylight.

After lunch Mark went upstairs and lay on his bed. When he thought about his father leaving and Vincent's death and Rod going into hospital, he felt ill and strange. His limbs seemed to belong to someone else, and the small hand he held towards the ceiling, flexing the fingers, seemed far away and unnaturally well-defined, like a hand in a Botticelli painting. The house was silent and he could feel the lassitude of afternoon. Sam on his charpoy, everybody in the house asleep, and the house itself, sun-hugged and drowsy, settling down to sleep as the cicadas began to stridulate. He thought, The god will save us, dimly aware that his thoughts were irrational, yet unsure now of what was real and what had life only within his head. When he finally got up there was an inevitability to his actions like the inevitability of his dream.

He took the sack and put the sisal in it, taking the stick in his other hand. In the garden dragon-flies hummed over flowers, darting away on cellophane wings. The cicadas shrilled and the heat rose from the earth, burning the hard soles of his bare feet. The maidan was deserted. A dog yelped down the road and stopped abruptly. When the head came up in the thicket he was ready. The snake was still, the black eyes staring unwinkingly, and he slowly lowered the loop over its head, keeping the forked stick in his left hand. When he pulled the sisal up suddenly the snake hung unresisting. He kept his eyes on it, putting the stick down carefully and opening the neck of the sack, propped among the bamboo canes, with his left hand. It seemed to him that the snake acquiesced in what he was doing, understanding in some mystic sense beyond words the new relationship which was about to commence. He lifted the sack with the string threaded through around the neck, holding it away from his body. There was no movement from the sack as he carefully backed out of the bamboo grove.

The heat burned his shoulders through the thin cotton shirt as he backed out of the leafy cover. When he walked round the house he could hear Sam snoring through the open door of the godown. William sat on the back wall, his eyes barely open, swaying a little as he attempted to keep his balance. In the pantry Mark felt safe. It was dark, and the flaking, stone-flagged floor was cool. By the shelves in the corner there was a terracotta pitcher full of water, behind which the plasterwork was green with an accumulation of algae. Mark put the sack down and found a saucer on one of the shelves. On the top shelf there was a pitcher of milk and he filled the saucer, taking it across with exaggerated care to place in the corner. With infinite care he took the sack by the base and slowly eased the cobra out, coil by coil, on to the cold flagstones. It lay on the flat grey stones, quiescent, unmoving. He watched it for some time in the dusky light. It began to drink from the saucer, and he smiled to himself, rocking back on his heels to lean against the whitewashed wall. When he heard Sam cough and turn on the charpoy in the godown he slipped quietly out, and went back up to his room.

Rawalpindi, Punjab: 1947

Twenty-nine

Roger Henshaw sat on the edge of the desk, leaning forward on his forearms propped on one knee. Behind him Feroze Khan stood by the door, his face shadowed from the electric light by the green bakelite shade. Gur looked up quietly, sensing some quality of bullying menace in the man who sat over him, pushing a huge fist into the palm of the other hand with repeated, thrusting movements.

Henshaw half turned to address the silent figure behind him, using the hectoring, needling tone of the school bully. 'Look at how hard the zamindar's son works . . .' He looked at his watch. 'Nine o'clock and he is still at his desk when everybody else has gone home . . .'

Gur laid the pencil he had been using precisely along the side of the papers stacked neatly on the desk and sat back, putting the fingers of his two hands together. He looked straight at Henshaw and said quietly, 'Mr Henshaw, I am working late because I am sharing Mr Hodder's work with Mr Parsons. These,' he indicated the papers lying on the desk in front of him, 'refer to the Durbar tomorrow where we have three cases to hear. I have an hour's work to do yet, so I would appreciate it if you came to the point.'

Henshaw got up from the desk and went to the drinks cupboard. He poured himself a generous whisky, adding water from the lotah, and then poured another glass which he took over to Feroze Khan. When he spoke again, his voice was cold and menacing, and the stillness of his huge body suggested an enormous battle to keep himself under control.

He said, 'Information has been laid before us by a woodcutter that you were seen in the vicinity on the day that Parvati Singh met her death. Have you anything to say?'

There was no sound in the room except the ticking of the clock. Then far in the distance a door slammed, the echoes booming sullenly down the long corridor. A breath of air came through the door, raising the papers gently for an instant. By the door Feroze Khan scratched his crotch through the folds of his baggy trousers, and then was still.

Gur picked up the pencil and looked at it, then put it down again carefully. 'Let me understand you completely, Mr Henshaw,' he said. 'Are you suggesting that I had some complicity in the girl's death?' He lifted his gaze to Henshaw's face, watching the other man's eyes move away from his.

Henshaw moved to the bookcase, running his fingers along the spines of the books and taking a drink from his glass. He didn't look at Gur again, and his movements became more jerky, strangely at odds with the smooth, unhurried cadences of his voice. Almost apologetically he said, 'You know that your own paper on the subject is now official policy and circumstantial evidence is given much greater weight than would be permitted in the English courts.' He paused and closed his eyes. 'My department have spent a considerable amount of time sifting information and seeing likely suspects. Admittedly our assumption has been that these murders have sufficient in common to suggest one author. In the absence of fresh information the only person presently under consideration who has always been in the vicinity has been yourself . . .' He had reached the window now and stood with his hands in his pockets gazing out.

Gur began to laugh quietly, and Henshaw whirled round, the break in his voice showing the fragility of his control. 'Don't laugh at me, Mr Singh. I'll show you it's no laughing matter.'

Gur made a self-deprecating gesture with his hand. 'The irony is that I have been the one who has accepted the need for circumstantial evidence to be given weight in order to cope with the backlog. Now it seems I am hoist with my own petard.' After a moment he said reflectively, as if seeking the answer to a question of purely academic importance, 'And the motive? I take it you have already found something which will stand up to the most rigorous analysis?'

Henshaw had regained his control now. 'Your gardener saw you and Anne Hodder embracing in the forest one day when you were out riding. Such forbidden fruits can exercise a powerful influence over a young man of your age . . . And a schoolmate recollects an attack you made upon him . . . I think we have enough. Above all, you are a Hindu.'

Far away through the window came the sound of rifle fire, and then of distant shouting. A woman screamed, a long wolf-like cry of misery. Gur began to tidy the papers on his desk into the in-tray. 'My poor country,' he said.

When he had finished he stood by the desk while Henshaw charged him formally. When asked if he had anything to say he shook his head and ushered them out of the office before locking the door and walking down the long corridor ahead of them to the waiting jeep.

* * *

His cell in 'Pindi jail was very dark, and smelt of urine. By the light from the barred window, high at one corner, he could read the graffiti scrawled on the crumbling plasterwork 'Jafar Khan. Falsely imprisoned by the British. March 1934.' 'Mazuffar Zobeidi.' 'The food and services in this hotel could be improved.' In the corridor outside the guard was discussing his stomach ailments with his relief. 'Everything I eat goes straight through . . . whoosh,' he said with morbid satisfaction.

Gur lay on the bed and tried to sleep. He couldn't blame Henshaw. He and Anwar seemed to have grown desperate in their efforts, and there had been six murders now. He had been shocked when his father had come to see him. At first by his appearance; he looked ill, unkempt, but waved aside Gur's solicitous questioning as being of no consequence. But then he had said uncertainly, 'It wasn't you, was it . . .?' and Gur had realized, with a sick feeling of despair, that his father was not sure.

All things considered, Henshaw had been very fair. He had agreed that Gur could go down with a guard to keep his appointment in Amritsar with Anthony. He had looked at Gur very directly for a moment, as though he could lay bare the workings of the young man's mind. 'For the friendship I had with your father I will trust you,' he said. 'I suppose you will want Mr Hodder to undertake your defence.'

Gur had asked for details of the charges, the dates of the killings, so that he could discuss them with Anthony. (Poor Anthony who did not know what he was returning to.) Henshaw had called for the guard, saying over his shoulder from the door, 'We'll let Anthony have all details of the charges in due course.'

251

En route to Amritsar, India: 1947

Thirty

Anthony sat in the train with a mixed sense of guilt and relief. The flat fields outside the window hardly varied, monotonous green followed by monotonous brown. Sometimes a man in a hitched-up dhoti standing knee-deep in a brackish water behind a crude plough yoked to a buffalo waved as the train passed. The telegraph poles flicked past. Anthony looked out of the window for a while and then turned to his paper. A plot by the RSSS to assassinate Jinnah as he drove in triumphal procession through the streets of Karachi from Pakistan's Constituent Assembly to his official residence had been rumoured, but the police had not yet caught the alleged conspirators. One Tara Singh had led his band of men to destroy the first Pakistan Special in the Ferozepore District of the Punjab on 11 August. Anthony laughed briefly to himself, without humour, remembering that the Mysore Hindus would enter their temples at midnight on 14 August, the moment of Partition, to cast rose petals at the feet of their gods. What a country this is, he thought, skimming a paragraph which described the Holy Men of Madura near Madras who had been indulging in the outlawed practice of hook-swinging – impaling the flesh on their backs with iron claws suspended from a gibbet. His logical mind rebelled against the lack of a discernible, logical thread within the events taking place.

He had felt a strange pang looking at Jane and the

family gathered on the platform to bid him goodbye. He had looked at Jane longest, not directly, but hoping for some recognition from her. He felt that something irrevocable was happening to them in those moments, amidst the shunting of trains, the hissing of steam, with the station vendors crying, 'Hindu pani,' and selling their hot grammes and polly's dirt. Jane had stood with her arms folded across her stomach, her feet unforgivingly to attention. Grouped around her, Arline, Angela and Pat momentarily seemed like an old photograph of pioneer wives. Mark gave him an uncertain wave, and it was only Anne who dashed forward to kiss him as the whistle went. 'Oh, do take care, daddy,' she said, and he felt touched by her, not trusting himself to speak. The steam hid them from sight as the train began to labour forward, and then they were out in the open.

He was heading for Amritsar, thirty-five miles east of Lahore, where he would meet up with Gur in a few days. As the hours passed he began to feel like a child, returning home after a too-long stay away. There was a long time to go and many miles to travel, but his heart grew lighter with each hour, and he planned and replanned his meetings with Gur, and Sita and Joginder, and his friends at headquarters. For two days he lived in happy anticipation, leavened occasionally with a feeling of guilt at his own happiness to have left his family but to feel, yet, that he was returning home.

At Amritsar station he looked for a porter, reaching his own cases down from the train and placing them by a pillar. There was something unfamiliar and strange about the station, it took him a few moments to realize what he found so disconcerting. Then he realized why there were no porters. The station was full of Sikhs of the Akhali sect in their bright blue turbans, some of them standing

253

but most sitting cross-legged on the platform with their kukris across their knees. They sat in eerie silence, saying nothing to each other, only staring with impassive faces straight ahead.

Anthony took a case in either hand and walked up to the buffet. Over a cup of lukewarm tea he pondered his next move. The pakoras were stale, and the buffet dirty. He beckoned the attendant over and pointed to the bags. 'Look after these until I come back,' he said, putting some change into the man's hand.

He walked into the Station Manager's office. There was a map of India on the yellowing wall, and a few iron-framed canvas chairs around the walls. At a deal desk in the centre a man in a uniform sat with his feet on the chair, picking the nail of his right big toe. He looked up enquiringly, and Anthony said, 'I'm looking for the Station Master.'

The man smiled, showing gold teeth rimmed with black, and swung his feet on to the ground and into a pair of chuplees. He wiped his hands on his achkan and extended his right hand. 'I am Station Manager. Mr Rao,' he announced grandiosely, and Anthony shook the proffered hand with distaste. Mr Rao waved him to one of the rickety chairs. It was a deflating conversation. Mr Rao could offer no guarantees about trains over the new border that was now to divide India from Pakistan.

'There is rioting in Amritsar,' he said, beaming his all-purpose smile and swivelling his little finger into his ear and examining the detritus under his finger nail with minute attention. No, he couldn't recommend a hotel. They were all full of people in similar circumstances. No, it was impossible to ensure a taxi, even if one had a destination to give the driver. All the Sikh drivers were too busy with 'other things' (rolling his eyes to heaven and chuckling at Anthony) to be busy with such mundane matters. 'It is very hard to run a station under these conditions,' he said momentarily downcast, scratching his scalp ruminatively over the tea he had ordered for Anthony and himself. Anthony tried to sympathize. In the background there was a low boom followed by a sporadic crackling. 'That's why you are having no taxi driver,' said Rao, smiling again and scratching his armpit vigorously.

Anthony's earlier euphoria had worn off completely as he walked down the badly-lit corridor back to the buffet. At the sides of the corridor, refugees lay under piles of rags or newspapers. A woman lay with a child in her arms, swathed in a sari; by her side there was a hen with its wings tied behind its back, one mesmerized red eye staring unseeingly at something beyond human comprehension. He walked into the buffet, assailed immediately by the smells of food and the faintly carious odour of unwashed bodies.

A man walked towards him and Anthony stepped back to let him through, still wondering what he should do about accommodation. 'Hello, Hodder,' said a familiar voice, and he was shaking hands almost before he realized it was Andrew Prescott. He could have hugged the rangy figure in tired khaki. Andrew hefted the larger bag in his right hand and waited for Anthony. 'Your office called me,' he said. 'No chance of a hotel or even a taxi. You'd better billet with me for the moment.'

There was a jeep in the road outside, complete with a Sikh syce. Prescott put the bag in the back and motioned Anthony on to the hard seat, getting in by the driver himself. 'Don't be surprised at anything you see, old man,' he said as the vehicle started. 'Welcome to hell.'

Murree, Pakistan: 1947

Thirty-one

It was the beginning of August. Roger Henshaw was talking into the telephone in his office. The Murree traffic streamed past down the busy road. Henshaw said, 'Can you hold on a moment, sir?' putting his large hand over the mouthpiece and bellowing through the open door to the other office. 'Jaffer. Will you keep the noise down? I'm on the 'phone. And send the chaprassi over to the house to tell the memsahib I'll be . . .' he paused to consult the watch on his hairy wrist, 'half an hour late for tiffin.'

He took his hand from the mouthpiece. 'I'm sorry, sir.' The voice at the other end crackled on and he waited for a pause. 'Well,' he said, cogitating, 'I think he is trustworthy but we can't guarantee his safety if he chooses to make the journey. Not strictly necessary, is it?' He made mmmming noises while the voice carried on. 'It's anybody's guess. No, I'm afraid I can't spare two men to go down with him. I'm sorry, sir.' After a few pleasantries he put the 'phone down.

He sat for a moment, thinking. It was a relief that was over . . . He got up and walked into the outer office where the clerk sat with a room full of petitioners, perched on seats or on the floor, patiently awaiting their turn. The hum of voices stopped as he walked in. He dropped his voice and said to Jaffer, his clerk, 'I'll be a little late back from lunch, Jaffer. You're in charge now,' and walked out of the door whistling. Jaffer looked up from his papers, surprised. He had worked for the Commissioner for three months and never heard him whistle before.

Henshaw drove down the Mall, parking under the trees by the public drinking fountain. Two of the gracious Victorian houses bordering the road on the right had been burned down, their blackened walls protruding shakily from the ground. Someone with prodigious strength had wrested a length of metal railing from the fence surrounding the park, whose edge ran some five feet above the road on which the car stood. Henshaw looked at the damage for a moment, impressed as always by evidence of brute strength. He rubbed his fingers through his cropped hair and crossed the Mall walking up towards the entrance to the bazaar. A number of people greeted him, and he nodded pleasantly enough, maintaining his swift pace so that they would not feel tempted to stop and talk.

Halfway down the bazaar, he paused outside a shop selling brass lotahs, representations of the gods and goddesses, and ironwork. He picked up a representation of Kali in her aspect of Destroyer, enamelled so that her bare breasts were covered in blood and her red mouth gaped hideously, and turned it from side to side, giving the impression he was examining it thoroughly. But his eyes were watching the faces coming up and down the narrow alley. Satisfied, he put the figure down and moved swiftly into the interior of the shop, through a door covered with an old carpet. He stood in front of a wooden door beyond. 'Shawkat. Idre aow,' he said softly, and there was a grumbling of 'koi hai,' and the sound of shuffling feet. The old wooden door opened a fraction, and an eye peered through, rolling sightlessly, foiled by the sudden dark. The Commissioner said impatiently,

'Open up, Shawkat,' and the door was opened instantly. Henshaw walked into the room, hung with carpet upon carpet from Kashmir, Cooch Behar, Benares and the villages. He ignored the old man's concerned apologies.

There was a group of men sitting cross-legged, smoking hookahs in the middle of the room. The light filtered palely through the high, dirty window, muted by the deep colours of the carpets. Henshaw made a cursory namaste and sat down heavily at the edge of the group. Opposite him Feroze Khan pulled on his hookah deeply and looked at the Commissioner without apparent curiosity.

Though he had gone through the conversation already in his mind, Henshaw hesitated. He knew most of the others and had no fear of repercussions. If anything came out, it would only be their word against his. But the rape of an English schoolteacher in Hasooth Gali had unsettled him, chipping away at his absolute belief in the safety of being British. He cleared his throat.

'Feroze Khan. You have a big family. You will need even more to support them now.'

Khan looked at him impassively. The shop bell tinkled and the old man went out, closing the door behind him. Henshaw looked at the others and said, 'Perhaps it would be better if we talked alone as usual?'

The younger man glanced around him. 'We are of the same family. You may speak freely here.'

Henshaw began, aware that he was sweating profusely. 'I think that the new rules of land inheritance might provide that where a zemindar dies without a blood-heir his land would be divided by those dealing with such matters amongst members of the community . . .' He could see that he had their attention now.

Half an hour later he walked out into the blinding sunshine, and took a deep breath as he began to walk up towards the Mall. Initiative rewarded, he thought, remembering his sergeant saying those words to him when he did his National Service. Nothing had been said directly, as was the way with such things, but he was sure that each side had understood the other perfectly.

At the house he pushed open the door, calling, 'Margaret. Margaret.' Her voice came from the lounge faintly, and he walked through. She was standing with a glass of sherry in her hand, looking over the sloping garden towards the far hills. She was swaying slightly and he realized, with a tremor of disgust, that she was more than a little drunk again. He forced his face into a smile and kissed her on the cheek. What had happened to their passionate love-making? And how had her red hair faded so quickly, her white skin creased into lines of age, so that she now looked fifteen years older than she had when they met?

She said timorously, 'I went to Richard's grave today. There were fresh flowers in the urn again.' He took the glass from her hand and put it down on the table, leading her towards the dining-room with his arm around her waist. 'You must forget about Richard now, dear,' he said, and his voice was warm and comforting, like a man speaking to a small child. She put her head against his shoulder as they walked and the tears slipped down her cheeks.

Amritsar, North India: 1947

Thirty-two

It had seemed theatrical when Andrew said, 'Welcome to hell,' outside Amritsar's red-brick station. But, driving through the city under a monstrous pall of smoke, Anthony began to appreciate the comment. Andrew held on to the windscreen of the jeep with one hand as he turned in his seat to talk, while the Sikh driver accelerated and braked and swerved, avoiding youths who ran across the road, overturned vehicles blazing sulphurously on the melting tarmacadam, and once a barely moving pile of rags which lay sprawled across the carriageway. Prescott shouted, his voice sounding abnormally loud as the vehicle rocked to an abrupt halt again, 'The Army have no power any more. We cannot intervene.'

On the drive to headquarters, he told Anthony what had been happening. Some of it had been cursorily covered in the radio broadcast Anthony had half-listened to in the station buffet, and the papers he had read on the journey, but it was made more real, more poignant, in this mad ride through the streets of the city. He heard of the Sikhs ravaging the Muslim neighbourhood, slaughtering the male inhabitants and stripping and raping the women before marching them to the Golden Temple, where their throats were cut. Of the destruction of the entire Hindu quarter of Lahore while the Muslim police stood by and did nothing. Of the new sport in Simla where Sikhs waving kirpans rode down the Mall on bicycles beheading Muslims with shouts of, 'God is Great.' Anthony wanted to hold up his hand and say, 'Enough', to hear of warmer and more personal things which might dilute the horror, but he could not. He knew that Andrew needed to tell him and needed to see the horror in his face as part of some complex exorcism which he could only dimly understand.

Once outside the city Andrew became quieter. 'You can billet with me. I've cleared it with the Colonel,' he said with a self-deprecating laugh, and Anthony sensed his regret at letting go.

Inside the gates of the camp it was hard to believe what was happening in the town. Only a faint glow, like a late sunset, indicated that all was not well. But there was something reassuring about the orderliness of the parade ground with the barracks standing in neat lines at the edge with the stables beyond.

It was dining-in night. As the guest of honour Anthony sat at Colonel Sawyer's right. Sawyer was a small, balding drily humorous man with the liver spots of old age beginning to show on his face and hands. He presided over the dinner table, spread with crisp linen and laid with silver and crystal, like a genial headmaster. His watery blue eyes missed nothing, and Anthony noted that a deceptively mild glance was sufficient to quell the most unruly junior officers.

'Fairly bloody coming back, I'm sure,' he said, looking quizzically at Anthony and nodding a vigorous affirmative to his own comment. 'We've been betrayed by our compatriots in pursuit of an illusory ideal.' Anthony felt obliged to argue, drawing upon some half-forgotten reservoir of idealism. 'Surely, sir, we must appreciate that our colonies now have a right to self-determination? We can no longer usurp their lands and their administrations and rob them of their goods . . .' He fashioned an argument without passion, too tired now to feel really concerned, and Sawyer heard him out without interruption. When Anthony had finished he said gently, 'We have not exploited these people. Ours was a genuinely symbiotic relationship in which, on balance, good has accrued to both sides. As a result of what is happening now England will suffer in the future. Her pledges will be called in and she will find herself obligated in years to come to all who wish to live in the mythical land of milk and honey . . .'

Andrew, sitting two places further down the table, said seriously, 'It will be worse than that, sir. Singapore was the start and there will be others to follow when their refugees call in the promises made to them by the politicians. Oh, there will be plenty of attempts to evade the obligations, but in the end England will have to accept them. Then, in time, there will be a civil war between the inhabitants of those ghettoes beside which this will seem like a pale rehearsal.'

At the end of the meal the Colonel stood and raised his glass. The conversation slowly died away. He proposed the three toasts. The King Emperor. The Viceroy. The Regiment. He drained his glass and threw it over his left shoulder and behind him the Indian Mess Sergeant stepped forward and crushed the pieces of glass to powder under his heel.

The Colonel held up his hand and silence returned again. 'Gentlemen. There is one more thing which I must put to my native officers before I abandon you to your pursuits of the evening. You have been given the right to nominate whether you wish to join the Pakistan army or remain with the Hindustan one. You may collect forms from the table in the lobby, fill them in and put them in

262

my letter-box, and I shall put matters in hand. That is all, gentlemen.'

Anthony looked down the long tables. Indian captains and lieutenants and English officers alike all looked up at the Colonel. Anthony felt, for a moment, the vibrations of an enormous uncertainty, which reached into every man's heart and lodged there, accentuating their separation from each other and the loneliness of each man in taking the decision required of him.

In the morning Anthony got up at seven to find Andrew already sitting at the table in the main room, eating toast and eggs. He seemed to have recovered his languid, detached good humour. 'No hurry, old man. Bacon and eggs all right?' He called the bearer over. They ate in a civilized silence over the papers, occasionally regaling each other with items from the news, while the background noises from the parade ground sounded faintly through the open window. 'Byeeee the right, quick march.' The crud, crud, crud of boots on asphalt. After the second coffee Anthony said with surprise 'How can we just sit here? It's Partition today.'

'Not as if you'd missed a family birthday, is it?' said Andrew, stretching and yawning. 'Save your energy for getting to the station.'

Andrew had arranged for Gur to stay in quarters for a couple of nights, shrugging away Anthony's thanks. 'We need some diversion here. Gives us an excuse to put on a tamasha.' He helped himself to one of Anthony's cheroots, rolling it between his fingers before lighting it. 'Puts off the evil hour when we have to plan our own futures.'

On the way to the station Anthony thought about his family. He felt separated from them by some incommunicable experience. Vincent's death, Rod's hospitalization, the terrible domination of Arline – all seemed to be relegated to some less important, changeable, temporary dimension, diminished by the circumstances in which he found himself.

Mr Rao walked down the platform. Under his waistcoat his shirt hung over his trousers, and he held his hat in his right hand, scratching his head with his other hand. He greeted Anthony warmly, pumping his hand up and down. 'Have you been to the celebrations, sir? I am getting some of my workers to put up some decorations in honour of this great occasion,' he gestured grandiosely upwards where some ancient paper chains dangled listlessly from the metal cross bars. Anthony was lulled by the normality of the scene. Mr Rao consulted his watch. 'Perhaps after this train you gentlemen will join me for some tea?' Anthony declined for both of them gently, amused by Rao's enthusiasm, and the little man waved to them, walking up towards his office with a rolling gait. 'Tiar hai. Juldi. Juldi,' he shouted as he went to the porters who squatted in groups talking to each other, one of their number occasionally emitting an expert stream of paan over the railway track.

In the distance they heard the train rattle metallically through the points. Then the engine came into sight, with its enormous cow-catcher like a giant upper lip, seeming in perspective to gain upon the station inch by inch. Anthony felt a quickening excitement. There was so much to talk about with Gur, to catch up on. Andrew gave him a curious look and pulled him back from the edge of the platform by the arm as the crowd began to surge forward.

As the train came in, the talking and laughter died away slowly towards the part of the platform where Anthony stood with his friend. Always afterwards Anthony remembered the woman. She had rushed past him eagerly, in her red sari with a jewel in her nose. She had the air (to his romantic mind) of a woman about to be reunited with her lover after a long absence, and he had watched her with speculative pleasure. When the first two carriages had passed her she turned her face from the train and raised her hands in the air. She was too far away for Anthony to see if the gesture was one of joy or despair. There was now complete silence from the crowd, only the hissing of the steam and the slow clank of the wheels coming to a halt, the heavy grinding of iron on steel.

There was an arm hanging out of the window opposite Anthony, and from the limp fingers red rivulets meandered down the paintwork of the carriage. On the train there was no movement; there were no people at the windows.

A man opened a carriage door and jumped on, and Anthony pressed forward into the crowd to see what was happening. A few moments later the man's face appeared at the window. He took some time to open the catch and there was a uneasy titter from the crowd at his clumsiness. When the window was open the man said in a hoarse, unbelieving voice, 'Everybody is dead. They are all cut to pieces.'

Something caught Anthony's eye. On the last carriage there was a whitewashed message. It read: *'This train is our Independence Gift to Nehru and Patel.'*

Mysore, South India: 1947

Thirty-three

There had been a long pause in the conversation. Overhead the bats jinked and wheeled, squeaking shrilly as they pursued insects in the night air. At first Nathoo had felt uneasily that he must have said something which Indijeet might brood upon and distort, causing her to be irritable and bad-tempered for days. Through the bamboo grove he could see lights shining in the Porter household, but there was no noise. Since Vincent's death the family seemed to have drawn together into an alien remoteness. Arline would sit out on the verandah long after the violet sky had turned to black. Occasionally Sam would appear in response to the silver bell, and Indijeet would listen to the clink of the decanter and whisper to Nathoo, 'She's having another sherry,' with eyebrow upraised. Sometimes there would be the faint notes of the gramophone, whining thinly.

Giving every impression that Indijeet had his full attention, Nathoo began to think about Raju. The boy was out (in the woods with some girl, Nathoo thought enviously). There was no sign of his showing any interest in coming into the Bank. Nathoo had started work at thirteen and paid his wages over to his mother in return for his keep; but he did not want that for his sons. This was a new world in which it often seemed to him people were permitted the forbidden indulgence of looking for something satisfying to do. Though he disapproved in a heartily old-fashioned, moralistic way, he loved his sons and was determined that they should have the same benefits as everyone else.

After a long silence Indijeet only said, in a tone of uncharacteristic uncertainty, 'Do you think Raju was innocent?' and, without waiting for a reply, 'It is hard to know who was right. We have known Akbar for many years. He must have had a good reason to think it was Raju who painted the building.' Though neither of them had questioned Raju directly Nathoo was sure that it *was* his son who had painted the slogan. They had both agreed it was an outrage, neither questioning nor analysing their shock at the defacement, but it was more complex now, brought into the house in an unexpected way through Raju's involvement. Nathoo said, 'I don't know,' gently in the darkness, putting his hand out and patting her on the rump, amazed at his own temerity.

The gate clicked and footsteps crunched in the gravel. A few moments later the Porter's gate catch clicked, and Nathoo shifted uneasily on his cushion. Raju walked up the drive, a dark shadow against the moonlit foliage, and stumbled slightly as he sat down on the step. 'Hello, aged parents,' he said, and suddenly there was the report of the Porter's front door echoing briefly over the wall. Nathoo held his breath, aware of Indijeet's body stiffening under his hand. 'You're out late, my son,' he said, and Raju laughed wildly, lolling back against the verandah. 'Wild oats,' he said, 'that's what the British say. Sowing wild oats.' Nathoo felt some impropriety in the boy talking like that in front of his mother, but Indijeet leaned over and patted Raju's hand. 'Better than all that political nonsense,' she said, 'I'm sure you will be bringing a nice Hindu girl back to meet your father and myself soon.' There was a silence. Nathoo wondered if Indijeet shared his own suspicions. He had avoided talking to Indijeet about Raju recently, aware that she had unrealistic ideas of his ability to secure a good job for their son. And about other things.

Raju leaned over and helped himself to a pakora. He licked his fingers and with his mouth full said, 'Oh, Zia told me something strange a couple of days ago.' He waited, savouring their anticipation. 'Young Mark took him to the Hodders' godown. Zia said that he had trapped a cobra and is keeping it there as a kind of pet . . .' Children's fantasies, thought Nathoo idly, easier now that the conversation had turned towards slightly remoter matters. Indijeet moved abruptly, her voice rising in panic. 'I must tell Mrs Porter.' Raju laughed condescendingly, taking her by the arm, 'Don't worry, Mother. I told Anne. If there's any truth in it they'll sort it out.' He leaned back, grinning to himself. Nathoo's mind had returned to an old groove again. It was now impossible to avoid the conclusion he had reached. He could not see where it might lead, so he closed his mind to it.

Next door Sam drove the car into the garage and shut the metal door noisily.

Two nights later Raju waited in the gully under the trees bordering the maidan. He shifted on the blanket, peering over the shoulder of red earth, but there was no movement except the grass rustling in the wind, blurring across the lights from the row of distant houses the far side of the road. He turned on his back and put his arms behind his head. He had seen Nathuram and Veer Savarkar that morning. After the meeting, Nathuram had asked him if he could get a gun. He still felt the shock as Nathuram looked at him, waiting for a reply. He had felt a sense of purpose in the editor's stance, and had responded gravely,

'I'll see what I can do,' anxious to seem sophisticated, unconcerned. It was only later that he remembered his mother talking about Rodney firing a gun which belonged to Anthony. And Roger Henshaw had mentioned it. He'd ask Anne to get it for him. Under his back the loamy earth accepted his body comfortably. When he thought of Anne his heart began to race and he found it hard to breathe.

A twig snapped and he turned to see her standing on the ridge a few yards away. He only had time to get to his knees before she caught his face, holding it between her hands and covering it with small kisses. 'I couldn't get away for ages,' she said, and her breath stirred in his hair. 'Father had written to say he's arrived in Amritsar and the rioting was terrible, and everybody stayed up to talk . . . endlessly.'

He kissed her fiercely on the mouth and then on her throat where the pulse beat. He felt, as he always did at these moments, half-formed longings which evaded definition. He began to unbutton her blouse with clumsy fingers, kissing her in return until she protested, laughing. When she lay naked on the blanket he could just see her pale body. He swiftly removed his clothes. He wanted to preserve the moment as long as possible, already savouring in anticipation the curious flat contrasting sadness of afterwards when they lay, sweating slightly, in each other's arms. He began to kiss her again, first on the shoulder and then on her breast, feeling the nipple harden against his cheek. She put her fingers into his hair and pulled his head closer, and her complicity aroused him. He felt a sensation of drowning, and heard her say from far off, 'Raju, I must talk to you.' But there were no words for a long time.

Later, lying with his arm around her, in the melancholy

269

half-sleep of the aftermath, he said drowsily, 'What about the snake? Have you told them?' She moved against him, throwing a leg over his; her hair had a faint, elusive perfume in his nostrils. 'It's there,' she said, 'I'll have to tell them.' He caught some tremor of regret in her voice, and hugged her.

A little later he remembered. 'Do you know where the gun is?' he asked. She moved away, clasping her knees. 'Oh, that,' she said in a flat voice. 'Father must have taken it away with him.' She seemed far away, preoccupied.

They dressed in silence. Though Raju knew it wasn't Anne's fault about the gun he couldn't help feeling angry. If only he had been able to produce that nonchalantly from his pocket at the next meeting! All day he had imagined how it would be, and he was disappointed and thwarted. When they were dressed he felt guilty for his coldness. 'You wanted to tell me something?' he said putting the rug under his arm and taking her hand as they started to walk towards the houses. She shrugged her shoulders, pulling her hand away. 'Some other time,' she said. 'I'll tell you some other time.'

The call came late at night. Arline took it in her dressing-gown, a mug of tea in her hand. Angela said, 'It's all right, Mother. I'll go with Pat,' and her tone was so peremptory that Arline accepted without demur.

Sam drove slowly until Angela leaned forward from the back seat and tapped him on the shoulder. 'We're not in a funeral procession, Sam,' and the car gathered speed.

Pat was still too shocked when they arrived at the hospital to respond to Major Majid's warm greeting. In the porch Angela kissed him, saying urgently, 'Be careful. She's very shaken.' They walked down the corridor and

270

Majid whispered over Pat's head. 'He got hold of a bottle of whisky from someone.' He paused and then said, without emphasis, 'Mr Bulstrode-Henshaw dropped in to see him on the way to work.'

In the office he poured them a drink, and sat on the edge of his desk, swinging a leg. The white coat gave his skin a blue-black sheen. Patricia said, 'Do they have any idea where he is, Major Majid?' and he shook his head. 'Not yet,' with a reassuring gesture of his right hand. 'But,' he said with an attempt at humour, 'you should be proud of your husband's strength. He threw an armchair through the window to break it.' He ran his fingers through his hair in a worried gesture. 'The mali has made an official complaint. He told the Secretary it was difficult enough dealing with the ravages of nature but couldn't accept that an armchair followed by a thirteen-stone figure landing in his rose bed could be counted a natural hazard.' He smiled relieved when Angela laughed and even Patricia smiled hesitantly. 'Have another drink,' he said. 'Inspector Faroukh is leading the search party.'

It was almost four in the morning before there was a knock on the door. In the hours they had talked, Patricia had realized, even in her misery, that there was what her mother would term 'an illicit relationship' between Angela and Major Majid. Her gratitude towards him confused the issue, but there seemed something wrong in these exchanges of intimate glances, these hints and references to some covert, hidden life. She remembered her mother at the dinner when Angela had invited Majid as a surprise guest. And afterwards her mother again, saying, 'Never again. Do you hear me? Never again. Men are treacherous and deceitful at the best of times, even when we share a common heritage. How could you have anything in common with him?' Angela had just laughed and gone upstairs.

Patricia fell asleep finally under a blanket on the chair with the soft voices washing to and fro over her.

When Inspector Faroukh came in he seemed ill-at-ease, and Majid shot him a warning glance, gesturing the man to sit down and saying, 'You remember Mrs Peters, Mr Rod's wife?' Patricia, suddenly awake, asked, 'Did you find my husband, Inspector?'

'Yes, madam,' he said, grave-faced. 'My men are bringing him back now. He was on the waste ground below the bazaar. When we found him he kept saying, "I was looking for the widow to give her money." He seemed distressed.'

Rod woke briefly when they went into his room. When Patricia rushed forward and hugged him he looked over her shoulder with clear, innocent, expressionless eyes. 'All dead,' he said, 'all dead.' And fell asleep.

Amritsar, North India: 1947

Thirty-four

On the way to the hospital Anthony and Andrew didn't speak. Anthony hung on mechanically to the side of the jeep as it jolted after the ambulance, numbed by the remembered images of the train. He had jumped on in a blind panic. In the corridor he had brushed past a man leaning out of the window, putting out his hand to gesture his apology. As he turned the man began to slide to the floor, his arm flailing as it came through the window in a hideous antic gesture. Anthony, transfixed, saw that his throat had been cut from ear to ear and the blood had soaked into a coagulated mass on his grey shirt. Behind him, in a tone which had the forced oddness of mad gaiety, Andrew said, 'Never mind. Keep going,' and he stumbled on down the corridor. The raw smell of blood hung heavily in the air and in the carriages passengers sat like distorted dummies, teased into grotesque unnatural shapes.

Behind them, emboldened by their example, people followed. Women ululating their grief behind sari hems held in their teeth. The harsh whisper of names, 'Chaudry. Kithre hai?' 'Dirn, bhai, bhai.' When Anthony looked back pleadingly, he saw only Prescott's face, racked with grief or laughter, and his hand gesturing forward.

Gur was in the carriage near the front of the train.

At first Anthony didn't see him, bemused by the bodies

273

lying in the gangways, by the blood, by the flies which already buzzed thickly. By some merciful dispensation his mind refused to accept the evidence of his eyes. The scarlet and vermilion, the staring eyes, the half-severed limbs, took on the aspect of a child's nursery whose occupant had thrown the toys around. These battered bodies had never lived; the matter seeping from a child's head was transmuted to sawdust by some kindly chemistry. He knelt upon the chest of a man whose breath still bubbled and heaved, oblivious, and tugged a woman in a sari off Gur. 'Here,' he said, noting with a part of his mind that Gur was still alive. 'Careful,' Prescott said warningly. Gur's hands were folded tightly over his stomach, holding a mass which strained redly against his kameez. Dully, without comprehension, Anthony noted that he had a pair of manacles attached to one wrist. The other clasp was open.

The Station Master pushed through the crowd, clearing a path for them. 'This way, Sahib,' he beckoned, and they lurched crazily through the mass of people, carrying Gur. As Rao walked ahead of them with small mincing steps he foraged in the folds of his baggy trousers.

At the hospital a dishevelled doctor took charge. In the lobby he supervised a drip, explaining tersely, 'He's in shock,' and, in answer to Anthony's query replied brusquely, 'Far too early to say,' contriving to convey a sense of moral disapproval as he walked through the swing doors and into the public ward. Anthony went to follow the trolley on which Gur lay through the door to the operating theatre, but Andrew held him back. 'There's nothing we can do here, old man,' he said. 'We'll come back tomorrow.'

Mysore, South India: 1947

Thirty-five

'But you *can't* tell them,' Mark said desperately, and Anne looked at him unhappily for a long moment, and then turned to gaze out of the bedroom window. He stood up and walked over to her, clenching his fist by his side. 'I've done things for you . . .' he said, his voice threatening to break. A tear fell from her cheek on to the window ledge where she sat and she wiped it away with the back of her hand, regarding him steadily in silence. She got up and walked to the door, and he followed, stricken with fear at the prospect of retribution ahead. 'Oh, please. *Please*,' he entreated her as she walked slowly down the stairs. But already in his mind he had begun to formulate the means of his escape.

It was Saturday, and Sam had served coffee on the verandah. The guava tree, bowed with late fruit, dappled the gravel with violet shadows, and above the maidan kites swooped and hovered in multi-coloured dabs against the blue sky. As Mark followed Anne on to the verandah he heard his mother say, '. . . used to be so gentle. Something happened . . .' Jane shook her head disbelievingly, but Arline laughed, and said, 'Will you never learn?' stopping as Anne and Mark arrived. It was too late for words or warnings now. Anne stood in front of her mother and said in a flat voice, 'There's a snake in the godown.' Jane smiled up at her daughter uncertainly, shading her eyes against the bright sunlight with a hand.

There was silence. Then Arline said irritably, 'What are you talking about?' exasperated by the interruption, rapping her metal-tipped stick on the concrete in a staccato tattoo. 'In the godown,' Anne said again, gesturing, and Arline called the mali over imperiously and set off round the side of the house followed by the rest of the family.

'Go on, man,' she said impatiently at the dark door, and he ventured cautiously in, with the women crowding round, peering into the dusky interior. Mark stood at the back, praying that the mali would find nothing. It must have been Zia telling Raju, he thought bitterly, knowing that no one would ever understand.

The mali came to the door, his eyes wide, 'Cobra, mem,' he said, and tried to walk past her through the doorway. Arline barred his path and put her stick in his hands. 'Kill it, then,' she said, folding her arms, and moving in to stand by the wall.

Through a gap between the bodies of his mother and his aunts, Mark, his eyes now accustomed to the darkness, saw the mali advance warily towards the corner. His throat felt swollen and he couldn't speak. A small prayer addressed to the snake formed in his mind: You are a god; save yourself and protect me. He had not been able to think of any way in which this could be accomplished, and could only hope, in every part of his fear-ridden mind, that some undreamed-of miracle would return matters to the way they were before.

The casement in the Bhose house opened, and he could see Indijeet's face gazing curiously out of her bedroom window. From the godown he heard a thump, and then another, and his stomach tightened. The mali gave a cry of triumph, 'Dekko, Memsahib,' and there was a burst of applause from the watching women. Anne looked at Mark and he felt, in that moment her betrayal, her movement away from him and towards the distant world of adult compromises and womanly preoccupations.

The mali brought out the snake on the stick and threw it on the lawn beyond the patio. 'Well done, Shiva,' said Arline, taking the stick from him. The shaft was stained with blood. There was a flutter of wings and William flew down from the wall. He landed on the burnt grass, a few feet from the snake, and rearranged his wings with a self-satisfied air, striding round the limp coils like a plump businessman contemplating an expense account lunch. He walked up and down very rapidly for a few moments, and then put one claw over the head, pecking at the eyes with his black beak, tearing the head to bloody shreds. Sam had joined the party on the patio, and raised his hands to his mouth as if he were going to be sick.

Arline watched intently. 'There's my bonny boy,' she said to herself, so softly that only Mark heard. He looked at Anne and saw from her face that she half knew what he was about to do. He felt flushed, exultant, powerful. 'Do you know about Anne, grandmother?' he said, his voice sounding mocking and strangely adult. He could see his sister's pleading face, and his aunts ranged alongside his mother, all watching the spectacle on the lawn, and beyond, Indijeet, straining to see what was happening through the thinning edge of the bamboo clump. The feeling of power rose in him again. 'Grandmother,' he said again, but she was only half-listening, watching William with fascinated eyes. But when he began to speak they all listened. They all listened and nothing was ever the same again.

Murree, Pakistan: 1947

Thirty-six

Anwar Khan was playing tennis against Dr Mackenzie.
He was much the bulkier of the two but moved around
the court with deceptive speed. Roger Henshaw sat down
by Jean Mackenzie and the waiter brought him a lemonade. In the distance some of the boys from the college
were playing a game of water polo in the pool, taking
refuge from the fierce, oppressive heat. Their shouts came
faintly up the hill.

'Two sets all and three games each. They've been on
court for almost two hours,' Jean said behind her hand.
Watching, Roger hoped Anwar would win, remembering
Mac taking the Club competition by default the previous
year. He knew he could beat Anwar.

By the tenth game Mac had broken Anwar's serve twice
and Roger knew he must win. He placed his shots
delicately, with a sure touch, turning Anwar's savage
serves and volleys to one line and then another, or
dropping them just over the net. The bigger man's shots
began to drop just outside the court, and his first services
hit the net. They made a strange contrast, Anwar lunging
around the court with exaggerated energy, and Mac,
moving with a calm lack of effort, seeming to toy with his
opponent. But the two shots which won the match were
unleashed with a vicious sliced power which curved them
off the court without leaving Anwar a chance.

Mac had to leave immediately on his rounds, waving

hail and farewell to Roger as Jean went to collect him. Anwar sat heavily in the canvas chair by Roger's side and called for a drink. His shirt clung to him with perspiration, and his hair leaked moisture in great drops on to his shoulders. 'He was only fooling around. He could have finished me in straight sets. I can't think how he does it . . .' Anwar said, shaking his head in rueful admiration as they watched Mac and his wife drive away.

Roger said, 'I haven't got much time. I came down to make sure all the evidence is in place now that Hodder is returning.' He looked at Anwar, and the Superintendent avoided his eyes, laughing and shrugging his shoulders. 'Of course, of course,' he said soothingly. 'Feroze and I have taken care of everything, you'll see.'

Roger got up and looked down at the sprawled figure. 'I hope you're right,' he said shortly. 'Remember, this time it's our heads on the block.'

Amritsar, North India: 1947

Thirty-seven

As August wore on there were riots in Calcutta. The Punjab Boundary Force was overwhelmed in the face of violence and arson attacks in twelve districts. The rumour went round the mess that Auchinleck had informed the Government that Congress was against the establishment of Pakistan. Gandhi, moving as always in his own mysterious ways, gave the greeting of 'Id Mubarak' to the Muslim community and invited Muslims, Sikhs and Harijans to his prayer meetings. The 'trains of death' had become commonplace now and, apart from his decision to wait until Gur was well enough to travel, Anthony had realized that making the border crossing would be highly dangerous, and gratefully accepted the Colonel's invitation to stay until the riots died down. Through Gandhi's intervention, a fragile peace was restored in Calcutta until in September a rumour that a Hindu boy had been beaten to death by Muslims on a trolley car began the war of attrition again. Once again the Mahatma began a fast unto death to end the rioting and once again an uneasy peace returned.

In New Delhi Veer Savarkar's RSSS bands kidnapped a Muslim woman, soaked her burqua in petrol, and set her alight outside the gate of Jawaharlal Nehru's York Road residence in protest against the Indian Prime Minister's efforts to protect India's Muslims, and Gurkha troops were deployed to guard some twenty Muslim men who sought sanctuary in the house. Meanwhile the reconnaissance pilots monitored the progress of the refugees on the route from Amritsar to Lahore, from Lahore to Amritsar, and reported that the roadside was one long open graveyard. In the last few weeks before the monsoon the heat had grown stifling and the smell rising from the putrefying corpses was terrible. The roadside was littered with bodies, butchered, or dead of cholera or starvation. The observers reported vultures too bloated to fly, falling over as they attempted to rise from their meals, and Andrew said with disgust, 'Even the wild dogs have become connoisseurs now. They eat only human livers.' Sikh bands would wait for a Moslem column to pass and then swoop down on the weakest, the old men, the women and children, slashing at them with their kirpans. The others would look on apathetically, too fatigued and debilitated by hunger to offer any resistance. In Amritsar the sowars returned exhausted day after day, unable to keep pace with the rioting which flared up throughout the city, dying down only to relight elsewhere. Once Andrew came back after acting as an observer to report two columns several miles long shuffling past each other in total eerie silence.

The city was full of box-wallahs, eking out their savings in fifth-rate pensions, and losing no opportunity to complain of the looting of their stores or the burning of their factories whenever they saw a white face who might have represented an official with some power. At the Post Office, collecting the meagre overdue mail that had got through, Andrew brusquely turned on a teen pau businessman who was reciting a sing-song litany of his woes, 'Oh, for God's sake be quiet, man. You're alive at least.'

Dewali was celebrated, incongruously enough, in the ruined city, and Dashera. The fireworks, the dyed faces and hands, the frenzied celebrations merged seamlessly into the daily rituals of murder and looting. There was little for Anthony to do. He wrote to Jane and to Joginder and Sita, fretting because no replies came. He felt obscurely guilty about Mark and Anne, dismissing finally as fanciful his feelings of having abandoned them defenceless to a regime which would affect them profoundly. In the depleted military quarters, he combed through the heavily censored papers, occasionally made a four at bridge, and read. Sometimes he would watch the scratch polo matches held on the parade ground. Many of the seasoned players had left for new posts in Pakistan. Sometimes he would join Andrew for a trip into the city. Three times a week he would visit Gur, either on his own or with Andrew. He dreaded these meetings more and more, as his first optimistic hopes began to falter before the evidence that Gur would never completely recover. A letter from Roger Henshaw had got through finally, and he had replied formally. The charges were a nonsense, of course, but he could discuss nothing with Gur.

By November Gur was well enough to sit on the hospital verandah. The rain teemed remorselessly down and the gravel held pools of water which never dried up. In addition to his other injuries, he had suffered a stroke. His mouth and eye dragged down, and his left side had been completely paralysed. He could speak a few words, in a slurred, mumbling monotone, but his eyes seemed vacant and he showed no apparent curiosity about anything; about his parents, about Jane and the children, about his own condition. He was like a man severed from his past yet left with the rudimentary skills necessary to carry on a maimed half-life. Once Anthony had noticed his face when a child somewhere in the compound had screamed in mock terror. It had the expression of an old man's face, stricken with impotent fear and unable any longer to comprehend the world in which he existed. Dr Dutt, who had admitted Gur and fought for hours to save his life in the operating theatre, came by sometimes. He had a crumpled, lived-in face, creased by laughter and concern. One afternoon in late November he walked with Anthony to the jeep. Andrew had arrived to collect Anthony and stood involved in some grave exchange with a small boy with a bandaged arm.

Dutt said, 'You know there isn't very much more we can do for him here? I'll have to discharge him soon. We'll need the bed.' Anthony was immediately full of concern. 'But he'll get better, won't he?' They stepped aside to make way for a wheelchair and the nurse guided it past with a bright, impersonal smile. Dutt said doubtfully, 'Perhaps some speech might return. Not much else, I'm afraid.' At the jeep Andrew said, 'Bad news?' raising his eyebrows, and Anthony nodded, not trusting himself to speak. On the next visit Dutt sought him out and promised to keep Gur for another month, and to intensify the therapy.

As time passed Anthony had found Andrew an increasingly sympathetic companion. The offhand arrogance which disguised his shyness still returned when he was in the company of strangers, but had faded completely in the times they were on their own together. They were often companionably silent for hours in their shared quarters. Andrew wrote reports, frowning into the distance as he sucked the end of his pen, while Anthony read. Or they would listen with mutual enjoyment to Beethoven or Wagner. He was so like Vincent, Anthony thought, a brother after all under the skin; hard to know, complex, a mixture of irresponsibility and seriousness; completely and wholly his own man, finished, compassionate yet unbound and untrammelled by the demands of personal ties and commitments, moving slowly towards his own thought-out conclusions; witty, concerned, sad, funny, wise.

One night Andrew had taken him to a club in the red light district of Amritsar. Though it was officially off limits, there were three other officers there, very drunk and demanding more champagne, they greeted them raucously as they went through. There were a number of louche Indian businessmen, sprawling round a corner banquette under the red lights, and drinking illegally distilled cheap gin. At the table Andrew said, 'I've brought you here to see Bul-Bul,' and Anthony said stupidly, 'Who?' and his friend laughed, tapping his nose with his forefinger and saying, 'Wait and see.' Anthony remembered the rumours of an Indian mistress and was intrigued.

After three gins Anthony felt pleasantly hazy. Over the past few weeks his concern for Gur, the horror of the train, the daily broadcasts about atrocities and the lack of any news from Jane and from Joginder, and the frustrations of enforced idleness had made him irritated and melancholy. These concerns suddenly seemed to matter less in this cheap ambience, heavy with the fumes of patchouli, clamorous with the echoing rise and fall of conversations in Hindi, Tamil, Urdu, Telegu, which created a meaningless background susurrus of noise. At ten o'clock there was a burst of clapping from some late arrivals by the door and a woman came in. 'Bul-Bul,' said Andrew, gesturing, 'Now you'll hear something.'

The woman was small-boned and delicate, with the paleness of a Kashmiri and high cheekbones. She had brilliant blue eyes which contrasted with her black hair, and she wore a red sari trimmed with gold and goldthonged sandals on her small feet. Anthony noticed her hands immediately; they were beautiful, slender, expressive and delicate. Her voice was a disappointment as she started to sing, tinny and expressionless to Anthony's ear, but Prescott said, 'Isn't she marvellous?' after the first number, and Anthony was touched and surprised to see his friend transfigured, watching the small figure through the smoky atmosphere intently. The woman's act was so cheap and tawdry that Andrew's rapt concentration disturbed his picture all over again. It was hard to reconcile their shared times in quarters, listening to the *Eroica* or *Der Fliegende Holländer* with absorbed interest, with Andrew's animation at this performance.

When she came to sit at their table after an hour or so, the conversation was conducted in trivialities. She called for champagne and Andrew paid the extortionate price carelessly, leaning forward on his forearms and watching her talk. 'Do you like this?' she asked archly, putting out her hand to show him a ring. Andrew took the fingers, and examined the ring under her triumphant eyes. 'You bought me that. I used the money you gave me.' They looked at each other and Anthony felt an intruder, awkward and excluded by the intimacy between them. When she got up Andrew took her hand and said pleadingly, 'Do you have to go?' and she laughed coquettishly, looking down at him. 'I'll see you soon. I have to work, you know.' Behind her, the manager beamed at them, anxiously waiting for her to return to the podium.

The rain pelted down. Under the flimsy canvas hood the seats were wet. The engine fired first time and Prescott backed carefully out of the alleyway. 'One day,' he said, looking back over his shoulder, manoeuvring the wheel with his right hand, 'when all this is over, I'll settle down with Bul-Bul.' Unthinkingly, Anthony was about to venture a facetious comment, but the impulse died when he saw his friend's face. Andrew was serious.

On the drive to the camp his friend said reflectively, 'There are things I have never told you . . . ,' and Anthony felt tense immediately, reviewing in a moment all his worst fears. He thought he saw some pity in Andrew's brief sidelong glance but, as though reading his thoughts, the other man smiled crookedly and touched his shoulder with his free hand. He paused for a moment, preoccupied with swerving to avoid a pedestrian. 'I applied to Colonel Sawyer for permission to have Roger Henshaw arrested three weeks ago. He has been identified by our people as having close associations with the RSSS. Also, though it is technically outside our province, we have submitted a report to Police Superintendent Anwar Khan of Rawalpindi District regarding the murders of a number of young girls. It would appear from the, admittedly hearsay, evidence we have that Henshaw has been dilatory and unprofessional in pursuing enquiries . . .'

Anthony felt relief flood through him. In the same moment he found himself wishing that Roger would be exonerated.

Andrew's voice became brittle, clipped. 'Unfortunately Colonel Sawyer feels that arresting Henshaw would be bad form, would give the British a bad name. We were able to document recent meetings Henshaw had with Veer Savarkar in Mysore; his known association with Feroze Khan who is believed to be the inspiration behind the Trains of Death. I also pointed out that an innocent man was on trial for crimes he had not committed. Do you know what he said?' He mimicked Sawyer's voice, '"My boy, better that some misdemeanours go unpunished than the British record here is sullied." He wouldn't discuss it any more.'

It was the information that Roger had been in Mysore which arrested Anthony's attention. He remembered at the ball and before an excitement in Jane which he had not seen for years. As he tried to gather his courage to ask the question which grew in his mind, Andrew said, 'I am trying to get you information for the defence of your assistant. I mean, in a form which could be used in a trial.'

The moment had passed. Perhaps as well, Anthony thought bitterly, knowing that it would be hard to let anyone, even Andrew, so closely into his secret fears. They drove in silence for a while, and he struggled to assimilate this new information. Rules of evidence. Fair play. The artificial concepts which so often let truth and justice slip away. He felt vacant, dispossessed of his will. When the camp lights came in sight Andrew said flatly, 'Not a word of this to anyone, please. I'm sorry. I achieved nothing telling you without giving you tools to finish the job.' The sentry on duty at the gate saluted smartly and he slowed down.

Anthony said sadly, 'Nothing to forgive. The truth always recedes from one. One seems to have it and then it changes shape, like a Hydra . . .' Andrew shot him a puzzled glance as they came to a halt by the other vehicles, but Anthony felt too tired to explain, even if he had been able.

Christmas Day dawned cold and clear. Anthony bought Andrew a bottle of Glenlivet in memory of the Parsons incident (so long ago, it seemed now). Andrew looked blank at first, and then smiled comprehendingly. 'Eh, bah goom. That was a reet gradely do,' he said, and they both roared with laughter. 'You should have seen his face,' Anthony said. 'Bottom lip hanging down. He couldn't believe it.' He mimicked Parsons' voice. 'The Memsahib's telephoned to say that the booger's absconded with a bottle of my Glenlivet.'

Andrew had given him a collection of Tagore's poems. They sat in their dressing-gowns listening to the BBC long after breakfast had been cleared away. The parade ground had been silent since the notes of reveille had sounded, and for the first time Anthony heard the notes of bird-song. After they had drunk coffee, Andrew put on a record of *The Twelve Carols* sung by the King's College choir. He seemed, suddenly, uncharacteristically melancholy, but when Anthony said, 'Everything OK?' adopting the impersonal jokiness they had long since used as their means of private exchange by unspoken mutual consent, he looked up under heavy-lidded eyes, laughing in a self-mocking way as was his habit when touching upon something serious. 'Just brooding on my own mortality, old man.' Anthony knew that such brooding had nothing to do with self-absorbed hypochondria, or with any true presumption of approaching death on Andrew's part, but reflected rather Andrew's own periodic despair. Prescott would often say, 'Don't worry about me today, old man. Pondering the great unknowns again, I'm afraid,' or, with a smile, 'Wrestling with the demons again.' The very clipped banality of the phrases he used, in marked contradiction to his normal fluency, underlined to Anthony the depth of his despair. That Prescott could only talk at such times in the language of a schoolboy was a sign of how much he had to distance others from his private vision.

By lunchtime he seemed to have recovered his good humour. The Mess cook had managed to purchase guinea fowl in Amritsar market. Freshly killed that morning, the flesh was tough and leathery. 'My teeth ain't up to this,' said Colonel Sawyer, pushing his plate aside after battling gamely for several mouthfuls. 'After a Norfolk boyhood it's hard to take an Indian Christmas dinner.' When the coffee came he lit a cigar and looked down the half-empty table. A number of the officers had elected to go to Pakistan, and most had already left. Sawyer smiled to himself and said to Anthony, 'Planned a surprise for tonight. An evening like the ones we used to have when I was first out.' He had a smear of gravy down his chin and, for a moment, Anthony had the strange sensation that the old man was not entirely rational.

The Colonel had been genuinely sorry to hear that Anthony was planning to leave in early January. 'Can't really talk to the younger men,' he confided. 'Most of them second or third sons coming out for a couple of years experience before going back home. Full of talk of the wogs, ideas of their own superiority over the natives, contempt for everything Indian. To them these riots are a temporary irritation, and Partition a meaningless line drawn on a map.' He sighed heavily, his hand trembling as he raised his cup to his mouth.

When Anthony, irritated at his own childlike curiosity about the evening, asked what the Colonel planned, the old man shook his head, laughing at Anthony, 'You'll have to wait and see, my boy. I'll show you how things were done.'

After lunch Prescott and an Indian major joined them for coffee on the verandah. The hills to the north-east glittered with snow and the air had a stringent dampness. Sawyer said longingly, 'When it's all over I'm going back to the cottage in Norfolk. Belonged to my wife – God rest her soul – and it's been empty for the past few years since the boys stopped using it in their vacs. A bit of fishing, a shot at the garden, wine-making . . .' He trailed into silence and in a few moments, when Anthony looked, he saw that the old man had fallen asleep. Andrew took a rug from over the railing of the verandah and put it gently over his knees. He said softly, 'Poor old boy. This thing has finished him, you know. Everything he loved has gone, and he feels that we have disgraced ourselves.' The Indian major said heatedly, 'But that just isn't true. It is we who have disgraced ourselves. The English have behaved impeccably.' His military college voice shivered with passion. Andrew looked at him sadly and said, 'For every one Indian who thinks as you do, Aziz, there are a thousand out there who feel we have betrayed them. And we have.'

Mysore, South India: 1947

Thirty-eight

There was no letter from Anthony. Over Christmas lunch Jane sat and listened to the others in silence. There was a feverish gaiety at the table, helped by the unaccustomed sparkling wine which Arline dispensed as the turkey came in. There are so many forbidden topics now, she thought dismally: Vincent's death; Rod, who last time she had seen him seemed even more a denizen of another world set adrift in a frail craft upon inhospitable and alien seas; and now Anne. She felt an unreasoning hatred of Anthony. If he hadn't gone, none of this might have happened. Even as she had these thoughts she could see how unreasonable they were, how (as she could see now so clearly) people were only marginally affected by advice and guidance, moving according to the unfolding of some hidden purpose within themselves. She knew, too, that her mother had never accepted this truth, preferring to act as though she could control events by the putting forth of an iron will and ignoring anything which set aside her jurisdiction over their personal life. Patricia hid her grief for her brother and her concern for her husband, just as Angela conducted her liaison with Dr Majid, in secret. If Arline saw these things she gave no sign, only trying with all the power at her disposal to draw her daughters back into a world where hurt and tragedy could be dispossessed of their destroying power.

After Sam had taken the plates away he returned with

the Christmas pudding, decked with a sprig of holly and flaming uncertainly. The port was passed round the table, and Arline said, 'Absent friends,' draining the glass in a single gulp.

'For God's sake, Jane, it's Christmas,' she said, when Jane passed the decanter to Angela without pouring a glass for herself. From the other side of the table Mark said, 'Why don't you leave her alone? Can't you see she's worried about daddy?' Arline gave him a long, hard look and then laughed, pouring herself another glass of port and proffering the decanter to Mark, 'It seems to me that you are old enough to have some of this now,' she said mockingly. Mark looked at her without expression for a few moments and then said, 'I'm going to play with Zia.' He folded his napkin and pushed himself away from the table.

Zia was not in the garden, so Mark let himself out of the gate and walked across the road to sit at the edge of the maidan and watch the boys flying their kites. He felt separated from them and keenly sad that he could no longer really understand their excitement or put himself, in imagination, in their places as they ran to and fro, tugging to make their kites stunt or to pull them further up into the piercing white-blue vault of the sky. Since the day when the snake had been killed and he, full of power, had told the adults what he knew, he had felt alone. He had tried to play the old games with Zia, but they had lost their savour, and he felt that he had passed through some door which had closed behind him finally and irrevocably denying him any return to the feelings of childhood. He was only sustained by the memory of what Rod had said to him when he had visited him in his bedroom, and when he remembered Vincent's words before the picnic. He repeated what he remembered to himself like a charm until they grew stale and worn with usage and he felt afraid that their power might fade and their meaning would go.

There was nobody he could speak to any more. He had written to his father but there was no reply. Anne had gone and, anyway, he knew she would never again trust him with anything. Zia still wanted to play the old games, and Mark knew that his friend could not understand these new feelings. He put his head on his brown knees and sighed.

A kite came rushing down the wind, its torn paper flapping furiously, and hit the ground a few yards away in the shadow of the wall by which he sat. The bowed stick which maintained the tension of the paper had snapped, and it lay limply in the yellow grass. A small boy came over and looked down at it desolately. A tear trickled down his cheek, but when he saw Mark looking at him he stared back defiantly and picked up the kite carefully, cradling it to his chest as he walked away.

Amritsar, North India: 1947

Thirty-nine

As they dressed for Christmas dinner, Anthony in dinner jacket and Andrew resplendent in dress uniform, a bugle sounded on the floodlit parade ground. Anthony called Andrew over to the window, and they watched the energetic game outside for a few minutes. One of the junior officers ran ahead dragging a bolster behind him on a length of rope, zig-zagging, doubling back on himself, running back through the ranks of his brother officers who hunted in pairs, one acting the horse and the other the rider. The riders carried bamboo lances tipped with steel, and blue or red ribbons through their shoulder straps to denote their team. Each hit on the target was greeted with raucous cheers and drunken laughter, and the score-keeper ducked in and out of the mêlée, calling the rider's name and team score after each strike. 'Kill, kill, kill, kill . . . ,' screamed a lieutenant as his bulky steed, fresh-faced and fair-haired, thundered in pursuit of the bolster. Prescott said enviously, 'God, the energy . . .'

Over dinner the Colonel reminisced about Norfolk. Anthony sensed that it was the events of the past few months which had created this nostalgia, breaking some dream of Empire which the old man had held for almost half a century. He felt sorry for Sawyer, pulling himself together against the after-effects of some monstrous blow; the lined face had the waxy pallor of underlying illness. Sawyer talked of the school which the last three generations of his family had attended, a minor public school, distinguished for nothing more than its role as a testing ground for ambitious young headmasters aiming towards the higher reaches. 'No need for enormous academic ability,' Sawyer said gruffly, 'just a reasonable family and good manners. What are you doing about your son?' Anthony realized with sudden guilt that he had given no thought to Mark's education since leaving Mysore. 'Can't leave it too late,' the Colonel said. 'I'll put in a good word for you if you like. My brother's a governor.' Inside Anthony an instance of revolt against the assumption asserted itself.

After the toasts Colonel Sawyer held up his hand for silence. Down the long tables the conversation slowly died away, and faces turned towards the high table. The Colonel rested on his outspread fingers. In the silent hall his voice had a querulous, old womanish resonance. 'Tonight, gentlemen,' he paused theatrically, looking round the hall, 'we are going to have a ride.' By Anthony's side he heard Prescott's intake of breath, and his soft, 'Oh God. No.' There was a ripple of conversation round the hall and the Colonel held up his hand again. 'Regimental rules. Starting on my orders in the usual fashion at twenty-two hundred hours.' He sat down.

'What does it mean?' Anthony whispered, and Andrew grinned half-heartedly and said, 'You'll see soon enough.' Through the great windows the syces came in sight leading horses to the edge of the parade ground, the beasts snorting and pawing the ground. At five to ten the Colonel called the Head Bearer over and said, 'Charge the glasses, Parveez.'

When the bearers had filled the glasses the Colonel said, 'To the Honour of the Regiment,' throwing his glass over his shoulder as the reply rumbled back. There was an expectant silence as the Colonel called the Head Bearer over again and gave him a whispered instruction. As if by magic the servants reappeared with lighted candles which they placed on the tables. Then the lights dimmed, except for one bulb which blazed within a faceted crystal ball suspended midway over the high table.

Anthony watched, fascinated and appalled. The Colonel took his revolver from his holster and, as the grandfather clock in the lobby began to tell the hour, held it up in both trembling hands and shot out the light, the bullet whining away to embed itself in the ceiling in the far corner of the hall. Then pandemonium broke out. All around men were shouting, 'Bearer, koi hai?' and struggling to remove their trousers. The servants wandered impassively through, taking the trousers and hanging them over an arm, like tea-towels. By Anthony's side Andrew was galvanized into action. 'Are the umpires out, sir?' he panted, handing his trousers to Parveez. Anthony felt hysterical laughter rising in his throat. The Colonel nodded to Andrew, 'Usual route. Usual pack drill,' and then Prescott was gone, plunging through the door with shirt tails flapping round his bare thighs. Behind him a noisy mob of officers scrimmaged to get through the door. Anthony walked through after the Colonel on to the verandah, still barely able to control the spasms of mirth which racked his diaphragm.

There was total confusion on the parade ground. 'Koi hai, Piroo?' 'Idre, Sahib.' 'Moti, Moti, idre aow.' 'Atha ha, Sahib.' A trouserless subaltern tried to get on his saddleless mount and fell back on the tarmac, swearing vociferously. Anthony saw Prescott climb on to a tall grey and gallop off under the brilliant moon, crouching low over the horse's neck as he followed the leaders towards the gate. Beyond the perimeter fencing, three horses were moving slowly, picking their way to and fro over the broken terrain.

The Colonel sat with Anthony on the verandah, drawing deeply on his cigar. The night air was cool, with a hint of dampness. The shouting died away and the sound of hooves clattering over the tarmac slowly faded. They sipped their brandy, and Anthony said, 'What happens now?' still bemused by the strange scene he had just witnessed. Sawyer chuckled, 'First home has his mess bills paid for a month.' He took his cigar out of his mouth and looked sideways at Anthony. 'I can see you don't approve,' he said, ignoring Anthony's embarrassed gesture of polite dissent. He sighed. 'I realized long ago that for many people the army is an extension of the public school system. Hierarchical, governed by standards, operated by rewards and punishments, a simpler version of real life with limited aims and an imposed series of artificial absolutes. The system creates safety, and it also creates boredom, particularly during periods of inactivity. This,' he waved his hand towards the perimeter, 'burns off the excess energy. Gives them something to talk about for a few days.' He stretched yawning. 'We've got another hour or so before the leaders arrive. Time for another brandy . . .'

The first man home was Major Aziz. He reined up his sweating chestnut and handed the reins to the syce, slipping off in a graceful motion and running to the verandah. He was young for a major, his black hair tousled by the wind, and sweat pouring off his forehead. His voice was high and excited, like a child's. 'I am first, aren't I, sir?' he said, standing in the garden bed and grasping the balustrade, and Colonel Sawyer said gently, 'Well done, Major. I'd suggest you get your feet out of the flower bed before Parveez spots you, and join us for a brandy.'

Horses were coming through in bunches now. Lieutenant Greaves, Captain Ranjit Singh, Lieutenant Aukin, Second Lieutenant Jameson. The servants had laid out their trousers over the balustrade rail and with much good-natured chaffing and humorous exchange they wandered up and down struggling back into their trousers. A great tureen of mulled punch was set down on the verandah and they stood under the stars, laughing and joking with each other as they watched the late arrivals.

A young lieutenant reined in his horse and ran over to the Colonel. He was a boy of twenty-one or twenty-two, and Anthony, looking at him, was reminded of Reeves. He had the same pink and gold, fresh-minted look and his legs under his slapping shirt tails had the firm muscling of a schoolboy rugby player. It took a moment before he could speak. 'Sir,' he said, 'Captain Prescott has had an accident. Just outside the gate.' He looked at them. 'I didn't move him because he looked very bad.'

Before the boy had finished the Colonel had summoned Parveez. 'Tell the syce to bring the jeep round. Now,' he said, and Anthony followed him on to the parade ground. They drove down the lines of sweat-flecked horses, and behind them the young lieutenant shouted, 'Just by the compound gate, sir,' his voice just carrying over the roar of the engine.

As they got out Anthony could already see the horse, struggling to rise from the nullah which ran alongside the perimeter fence, and on the bank the figure of Prescott. 'Shit, fucking girth too loose,' said Prescott, managing a smile, his eyes tightly closed. Nearby the horse continued its struggle to rise, but its foreleg was broken. The Colonel nodded to the driver who had followed them, indicating

298

the animal. The man walked across unbuttoning his revolver. He pressed the muzzle to the beast's temple and pulled the trigger. The shot was muffled, the horse's head snapping back with the recoil. The whole body shuddered for an instant, and then began to spread and relax, sinking into the dew-damp grass.

Anthony knelt by Prescott's side. He had to bend close to hear his friend speak. 'Is it moral or venial to apply for entry without trousers?' Andrew said, and Anthony replied, 'Don't try to talk.' After a few moments Andrew said, 'Pity about the horse. Suppose none of you will do that for me.' He began to laugh and blood came out of his mouth. He coughed twice and then his head fell back and the rasping breath stopped. Anthony felt for his pulse but there was none. The Colonel said brusquely, 'Always had an odd sense of humour, Prescott.'

The driver had been joined by two other servants and the Colonel said, 'Cover him up, Abdul. Shabash. Now take him to the Mess and call the MO.' Anthony supported the Colonel as they stumbled back through the gates towards the lights of the Mess. Behind them the jeep came at walking pace, with Prescott's head over one side of the back, and his legs over the other.

Anthony was unable to mourn.

At the funeral he stood dry-eyed as the coffin was lowered into the ground, and in the Mess afterwards felt tongue-tied in the presence of Prescott's sister. He felt the loss incalculable, beyond tears. The finality of bereavement gave him a feeling of horror. The sense of an unaccustomed absolute precluded any further contact. He remembered the words from *The Lament for The Makaris*, 'Timor mortis conturbat me,' but he felt only a weariness, an idea that he could never accept the sense of loss. 'Had you known Andrew long?' the sister asked, and he said, 'A couple of years, on and off,' realizing that this gave her some calibration of their friendship. Anthony had arranged for Prescott's possessions to be packed up, a few books and records, and one or two ornaments, and they waited in the quarters for collection.

He had been shocked to recognize Bul-Bul at the grave side, expecting perhaps that she might make a scene, but she had behaved with quiet dignity. When she had thrown her earth on the coffin he saw her lips move and then she slipped quietly away, walking through the gravestones until she was lost from sight.

In the quarters Beryl Prescott looked at the small pile and said, 'Is that all?' and Anthony nodded. As the bearer started to get the pieces together he could see that she wanted to say something else. When the man had gone out she looked at him with a set expression and said, 'That woman. Was she . . . ?' and Anthony said quickly, not wanting to get involved, 'I don't know. He was very fond of her.' She said vehemently, 'Little gold digger. She won't get anything out of me.' It was only when she had left that Anthony felt angry.

When she had gone and all Prescott's possessions had been stripped from the rooms Anthony was alone. He sat for a while pretending to read the papers, but he felt such a sense of pain and loss that he couldn't settle, and finally went over to the Mess. Colonel Sawyer came in and joined him, sitting heavily in the leather armchair by the other side of the table. 'I've written to Andrew's mother,' he said. 'Always hard to know what to say.' In the muted light he looked shrunken, his neck stringy and corded. 'You don't blame me, do you, Hodder?' Anthony was struck, again, at the distancing use of his surname, recognizing the underlying codes by which propriety was preserved. 'No,' he said reflectively, 'there's no point in blaming yourself. You can't take responsibility for what happens to other people.' Sawyer looked at him strangely for a moment. He got up, looking down at Anthony with a crooked half-smile. 'There's less comfort in that point of view than you might think. If I accepted it I would make a nonsense of my life here. I cannot take the easy route to avoid my responsibilities.'

As he started to walk away Anthony said, 'Dick. I'll have to leave in the next few days. Can I go over the border as an observer?' Colonel Sawyer rubbed his nose, looking at the carpet. 'What about your friend?' he asked and Anthony said, 'I'll have to see if he's well enough to make the trip. I'll let you know.'

When he asked Dutt, the doctor shook his head emphatically. 'I didn't want to worry you before, but he seems to have had further haemorrhaging. I'm afraid he'll have to stay here for the foreseeable future.' Anthony felt guilty at his own relief. In the garden Gur was being wheeled round the flower beds by an Indian nurse. When he saw Anthony his face contorted and he tried to raise the hand which had become atrophied and wasted over the months of disuse. But when Anthony sat with him on the wooden bench with the sun beating down on them, and explained that he was going back on his own, he could not be sure that Gur had understood.

On his return there was a letter from Jane waiting for him. He savoured the pleasure of leaving it unopened while the tea was being made. When the servant had left he put *The Four Seasons* on the gramophone and sat down. He had read the letter three times before he could assimilate what had happened.

Mysore
September 10th 1947

My dearest Anthony
This is the hardest letter I have ever had to write in my life. I
keep thinking of you reading it in some barracks in Amritsar
with the riots going on round you and feel guilty, as if what has
happened is my fault in some way. It has been such an unrelieved
period of disaster with Vin's death and Rod in hospital – and
now this. I'm very, very sorry.

Anne has run away with Raju. Worse than that, she is four
months pregnant. When it all came out, she was quite defiant.
Mother suggested that Angela could arrange something through
Major Majid, but she refused even to discuss it. She said that
they loved each other and had decided to get married. That the
differences in colour, religion, upbringing didn't matter. Mother
called the Bhoses round and we had a discussion, if you can call
it that. He was very concerned but she seemed to treat it as a
social occasion, talking about the garden, and how we would be
seeing each other more in the future, and seemingly happy with
the turn affairs have taken. You may imagine Mother's subsequent comments about all *that*! Anne remained in her room
and the boy refused to come, and it became evident pretty soon
that there was no point in relying upon either of them to see
sense. Bhose obviously has no control whatsoever over the boy,
and *she* seems to think this is a feather in her cap. All this
happened three days ago and yesterday morning there was a
note from Anne for me on the breakfast table just to say that
she and Raju were going off together, that he had some money,
and please not to try and find them. Quite apart from the fact
they are both still children the disgrace is hard to bear. I dread
the Brigadier or Mr Bulstrode-Henshaw hearing of what has
happened. If only we'd been more careful. At first I thought
about the dance, but the thing had obviously been going on long
before that. An illegitimate child is bad enough, but this is
appalling.

I don't expect you to drop everything to come back. There
wouldn't be anything you could do, anyway. We have decided
to tell people that Anne has gone away to stay with friends. I
only hope this thing burns itself out in time for something to be
done.

It is a mad world we live in. The papers give some idea of what is happening in the North, but rumours suggest that matters are much worse than reported.

Take care of yourself and write when you have time. It may be hard for you to realize, but I do miss you.

Much love,

Jane

The light was falling over the compound, glancing through the evening clouds in shades of gold and red. Anthony poured himself a gin, and turned the record over. He felt sick at heart. He knew that his nature sought the paths of least resistance, and protected him from confrontations he was unable to deal with.

At midnight Colonel Sawyer was surprised to hear a knock on his door. He put down his copy of *The Possessed* with a sigh, folding his glasses and putting them on the table by his side, and donned his faded magenta dressing-gown before opening the door. He was shocked to see Anthony standing in the doorway holding on to the jamb for support, his tie askew and his shirt spilling out over his trousers. He said uncertainly, 'Come in for a minute, old man,' concerned at the vivid pallor of Anthony's face, but Anthony only said drunkenly, 'Very first patrol you can get me on, sir. A'right?' and stumbled away down the corridor. Sawyer watched him until he was out of sight but he never looked back.

Poona, India: 1948

Forty

Veer Savarkar had suggested that they move to Poona and live with one of Ghodse's aunts, but after almost four months Raju still felt a stranger. It was no longer a game which he could discontinue at the end of the day when he returned home, and the job he had cleaning at the headquarters of the *Hindu Rashtra*, assaulted by the constant noise of printing presses, was hard work and very badly paid. He had flared up when Anne criticized him for not looking for a position with prospects, and now her reproach was mute, a glance or a tightening of the lips he caught at some salient moment as she moved, with increasing clumsiness, round the small room preparing their meals or clearing up. He felt an obscure guilt at bringing her to this, and a disappointment that the idealism he had felt towards the cause in Mysore was being eroded by the drudgery of each day.

This Saturday at the beginning of January, he had come to visit Nathuram Ghodse. It was cold, and he rubbed his hands to warm them, as he waited for his employer to dress. The room in which Ghodse lived was sparsely furnished, almost ascetic in its unconcern with comfort, and there was a broken window through which the wind blew an unremitting cold blast. Ghodse stood in front of a crazed, dirty mirror, turning to look at himself critically from each side as he dressed. He put on a baggy white shirt over a raw cotton vest arranging his sarong-like dhoti in Mahratta style, hooking the left end under his leg and gathering the bulk of the folds on his right hip. Periodically he stopped and sipped the coffee he was addicted to, before turning back to admire himself in the mirror. Raju still couldn't believe what Apte had told him a few weeks before: that Ghodse and Veer Savarkar were lovers. It was a development he had never anticipated and didn't want to think about, the idea of this plump thirty-seven-year-old and Savarkar (who must be at least sixty, he thought with horror) locked in a carnal embrace; it seemed to diminish the importance of what they were doing.

Narayan Apte sprawled on a cushion in the corner of the room reading a magazine which depicted a Western film star on the cover. Occasionally he laughed unselfconsciously, scratching himself as he turned the pages. It never ceased to amaze Raju that they were partners, as Editor and Administrator of the *Hindu Rashtra*. In marked contrast to Ghodse's overt asceticism, Apte was a small, balding compulsive womanizer, a fleshpot with a talent for administration.

Since his arrival Raju had slowly become aware of the difference in the atmosphere, the political awareness of the people. Here, one hundred and nineteen miles inland from Bombay, there was a fierce Hindu nationalism which contrasted strongly with the more theoretical idealism he had been used to in Mysore. This was no place for defacing houses. He shifted uneasily, but both men ignored him, and he felt impotent, unworthy. If only he'd been able to supply a gun everything would be different. His southern softness made no impact here where Shivaji, Hinduism's greatest hero, had been born and had opened his guerila campaign against the Moghul Emperor Aurungzeb, and whose heirs, the peshwas, a tight clique

305

of Chitpawan 'purified by fire' Brahmins, had resisted India's British Rulers up to 1817.

Ghodse looked at himself in the mirror and stepped back, satisfied. He drained his coffee, and poured himself another cup from the copper vessel on the brazier. 'The Cobra managed to get us a gun from Digamber Bridge, the arms dealer,' he said casually, and Apte grunted, flicking over a few pages and settling back on the cushion, his hand under his head.

Ghodse walked over to the altar and stood before it. His back was towards Raju and when he spoke his voice sounded disembodied, the voice of the God. 'Gandhi said India would be divided over his dead body. India is divided but Gandhi lives.' The words hung in the air. Apte chuckled, still half-absorbed in his magazine, unmoved by any resonances in the atmosphere. 'It will sort itself out,' he said complacently. 'Now that Gandhi has decided to fast again to support Mountbatten in forcing Congress to pay the five hundred and fifty million rupees they say we owe Pakistan he'll die anyway. He's seventy-seven . . .' After a moment he said, 'If we don't pay, Pakistan will go to war with us.'

Ghodse turned abruptly from the altar. He slammed his fist into his palm trembling with passion. 'Don't you see, Narayan? Don't you see? It's not Jinnah who is the enemy but Gandhi. We will achieve nothing,' he picked a votive vase from the altar and smashed it on the floor, shards glinting in the light, '*nothing* if he dies by his own action.' Apte turned another page and said quietly, 'The information this morning is that his body has begun to devour its own proteins. If you wish to assist nature you'll have to move fast.'

He rose to leave, suddenly full of some secret purpose.

306

'By the way,' he said to Raju, 'how is your wife finding it here?'

There was a pause before Raju said loyally, 'Oh, she's enjoying it. She's settling down well,' trying to shut from his mind the picture of Anne, monstrously swollen with the child, turning her face towards the mud wall and weeping silently.

Murree, Pakistan: 1948

Forty-one

When Anthony reached the Murree Brewery, he stopped the car by the roadside. Already ivy had begun to swarm up the blackened ruins and the floors were tufted with couch grass and luscious deadly nightshade. The fire had swept up the hillside, defoliating the trees, and leaving a black swath of desolation amid the green. The vast open valley to his left, dominated by the crag on which Farmer Thorne's farm sat, lay peaceful and unchanged under the hazy mist. He reflected that it was strange that nothing in 'Pindi, the gaunt, gutted houses, the boarded-up buildings, the torn-up roads, had brought home to him the reality of what had happened as much as this act of destructive arson.

He felt momentarily sick, anticipating his meeting with Joginder and Sita. He hoped they wouldn't know too much about Gur's condition, remembering with a stab of fear his own journey through the border three days before. He had never envisaged it would be possible to become so indifferent to death. The fly-blown corpses besieged by scavenging vultures and dogs had shocked him at first. He and the three soldiers had driven down the road, mile after mile, wearing cologne soaked handkerchiefs round their faces to disguise the smell of putrefaction. But when the Sikh bands had ridden down from the copses, yelling and hacking at the stragglers in the long columns with their kirpans, Captain Foster had stopped the jeep and sat impassively while the slaughter continued round them. Anthony said, 'My God, man. We must *do* something,' but Foster had turned and said impassively, 'My orders are not to interfere at any cost unless we are personally in danger.' Three times they had stopped. Three times they had driven past the mutilated victims when the attackers had ridden off.

Parsons had been the only face he recognized at the Mess in Rawalpindi. He had been genuinely pleased to see Anthony, shocked into broad Yorkshire, as he pumped Anthony's hand up and down and hugged him round the shoulder. Over lunch in the Mess they had talked of other things, after Anthony had spoken haltingly of Andrew Prescott's death and Parsons had retailed his story of going in as an observer after the Pathan sacking of Bardmullah Convent and the rape of the nuns. 'Crazy boogers,' he said bitterly, 'but, anyway, the First Sikhs took the airport and Hari Singh finally signed the Act of Accession. I suppose it all achieved something.' His voice was disgusted. For want of anything better Anthony had accepted an invitation to dinner at his house, and was surprised to find himself enjoying his unsophisticated company. They played Lexicon after dinner. 'Never could get the hang of that bridge game,' Parsons had said, and his wife smiled at him fondly. Anthony had been sorry to leave and go back to the empty bungalow where he was being looked after by a villainous chokra temporarily seconded from the Mess.

His apprehension increased when he reached the gates at the head of Joginder's drive. He had not warned them of his arrival as the wires were down again and there was no means of making contact. When he got out of the car to open the gate he saw that the drive was grassy and mossed and the brambles stirring in the listless breeze overhung the verges. Past the bend in the drive the house itself came into sight and he saw that the flower beds bordering the verandah were rank with gross weeds, and that the wall by the stable block sprawled untidily over the gravel, as if struck down by a giant fist. The white stucco walls of the house itself were stained and cracked and the lattice screen at the side hung drunkenly adrift, secured carelessly with wire to the old rowan tree. When he had parked and walked over to the house, he saw that the sad neglect reached further still. The busts of Marcus Aurelius and Augustus in the embrasures by the door had been defaced, and the marble floors were fissured and cracked. He rang the bell, listening to its hollow echoes through the hall, followed by a silence so profound that he could hear the beating of his heart. He waited, and then rang again, and heard in the far interior the sound of shuffling steps, and a hoarse voice saying, 'Ucha. Atha ha. Atha ha.'

When the door opened Anthony could not restrain an exclamation of surprise. Though the figure which stood before him, searching his face with lacklustre eyes, was undoubtedly Joginder. He felt at once, as he had felt with Rod and lately with Gur, a sense of someone sunk within themselves and beyond any concern with the outside world. When Joginder smiled it was a reflex only, a painful rictus which bared yellowed teeth; the eyes remained dead, vacant, devoid of feeling. He wore mittens against the cold and (as Anthony had never seen him) a dirty shirt and baggy trousers. He was unshaven and his feet were bare. When he embraced Anthony his breath smelt of decay, and his voice, calling Sita, was a hoarse whisper, without resonance. 'Sita. Sita. Come and see who is here.' There was only silence.

They sat on the verandah despite the bitter wind, and

310

Joginder insisted on bringing Anthony a glass of sherry, drinking nothing himself. There seemed to be no servants, no malis tending the once immaculate lawns, no grooms attending to their charges in the stable block, no bearers carrying silver trays of drinks and sweetmeats. Joginder made no comment when Anthony talked about Gur, but stiffened in his chair as Anthony ploughed desperately on, wishing only that he could convey a note of comfort into the information he had to tell. Joginder said nothing when Anthony fell silent, just looked at his friend for some time with distant eyes, nodding in the manner of an old man only half-involved in the present. The door opened and Sita came out.

She too had aged, and when he embraced her he felt the frailness of an old woman. She held his face between her hands and looked at him, the tears running down her face. The skin under her eyes was pouchy and bluish, and there were tired brackets round her mouth. Anthony did not know what had happened, only that it was permanent, irrevocable, inexplicable. He blurted out, 'I was telling Jog about Gur,' and he saw her face fall and become guarded. From behind him Joginder said, 'A lot has happened since you left. I have no son now,' and Sita gave Anthony a quick apologetic glance. 'I'll make some lunch,' she said.

Joginder talked and Anthony listened. All the servants had left one night after Feroze Khan had raided the house with his followers. The Muslim thugs had been more intent on destruction than looting – breaking furniture and using pickaxes to destroy the marble floors. Joginder shrugged his shoulders uncomprehendingly. 'It seemed they were trying to drive us out,' he said. 'Took Henshaw two days to inspect the damage. And then he wouldn't take it further. He said that Feroze Khan and his men would create alibis for each other, and even questioning them might result in reprisals. Best to leave everything as it was. I got the impression he had never quite forgiven me for coming across him with Reeves' aunt.'

All he would say about Gur was, 'He has brought shame and disgrace to our family.' He was about to say something more but Sita came out with the food and Anthony felt unable to bring the subject up again.

After lunch they walked in the garden. Sita took the secateurs, stopping from time to time to prune the dead wood from a rose bush or to pick a dead brown head and put it in the trug she carried, and Joginder held a reaping hook, swinging half-heartedly at the brambles which had proliferated through the flower beds. There was a certain graveyard humour, a desperate gaiety in Joginder that afternoon. 'D'you know what that bugger Feroze Khan said?' he growled, slashing a bramble and ignoring Sita's remonstrations as he hacked through a rose with his follow-through. 'There were Sita and I, up against the wall with two villainous sods with kukris at our throats and he was ferreting through the drinks cupboard. "No Remy Martin. What kind of zemindar are you?" The little sod ignored the Fabergé boxes, and the Lalique. Whenever I hear the Ingresi being piously condescending about India's ancient culture, I remember that comment.' And later, 'I gave up collecting the rents after the fifth house was burnt down. I can't even contact the insurance company to see what clauses they will avoid liability for loss under.'

At four o'clock Anthony said, 'I must go,' and they walked back towards the house for tea. Joginder said, 'The Silver Saddhu was right, you know.' He paused, looking towards where the beggars had stood. 'He came again last week. This time by himself. He only said, "I grieve for you and your friend," and then he went away.'

Anthony's throat felt dry.

He said, 'That's impossible. The Saddhu was killed a year ago in a bazaar brawl in 'Pindi. You must have been mistaken.' From the house the late sun glinted from a window, hurting his eyes.

Joginder said, 'This is India. What is death, my friend?'

Poona, India: 1948

Forty-two

On Saturday, January 17 1948, Raju went round to Ghodse's office to meet Veer Savarkar and Apte. It was a brilliant, cold day, and he shivered, breaking into a little run from time to time to keep warm. The roadside barrows spilled their wares over the pavements, and the Mall was crowded with bicycles, gharries and tongas seeming scarcely to move as they came down the long incline towards him.

When he arrived he could hear Apte's heated voice through the thin partition which separated the office from the presses. 'No, no. We must book today,' he was saying excitedly. He paused a moment, looking back as Raju came in and then carried on, 'They'll give in on the money issue anyway. But it may be too late. The medical report is that Gandhi's urine is showing traces of acetone and acetic acid. The man is old and frail. This may be our only chance.' Raju wished again, as he had before, that Roger Henshaw was with them but the Englishman had refused to take part in the plot. He'd said, with passionate disgust, 'This killing will achieve nothing . . .' When he had gone Savarkar had said sneeringly, 'How could we expect an Igresi to understand? We must do things ourselves now, brothers.'

There was a knock on the door and a slimmer version of Nathuram Ghodse came in and was introduced as his brother, Gopal. He listened for a while in silence while they discussed possible plans, his dark intelligent eyes looking from one face to another. When he spoke his voice was very soft, which had the effect of making the others stop to listen. 'Why don't Karkare and I register in one hotel and Madanlal Padwe Pahwa in another? He has a bomb and is prepared to make the first attempt.' Nathuram said, doubtfully, 'But can he be trusted?' and Savarkar, taking off his glasses said, 'I can vouch for his commitment.' He breathed on his glasses and polished them, 'If not for his intelligence. He is expendable.' And so it was agreed.

Walking back Raju no longer felt cold. He had a sense of awesome destiny stretching before him, a certain sense that he would be a part of some great historic event which would set right the wrongs done to the Hindu people. He thought of his parents and his brother with sadness and a sense of shame until he remembered Savarkar's words at the first meeting in Mysore in the back room of a shop in the bazaar. 'You must give up the ties of family and friends. You must live with no thought for yourself. You must only remember that our cause is great and, because it is so, will demand great sacrifices from you even to everything you have. And you must give all that is required willingly, without resentment, and without holding back.'

Anne was cooking when he returned. She straightened up, holding her hands to her back with a grimace of discomfort. The bloom had gone from her face, and she seemed sullen and withdrawn, and older than her years. But it was some indefinable distancing, a turn of the head away when he spoke to her, the lack of expression in her eyes when she looked at him, that Raju noticed most. He knew that he was in part to blame. It had been hard for him to tolerate the changes that pregnancy had made in her, the bloating of her body and the slowing up of her movements. Her enquiring glance seemed to contain some hint of contempt of him, and her words suggested a weariness with him which she no longer bothered to hide. 'Well, what was it all about?'

He mimicked her cruelly, walking ponderously round the small room with his hands clasped round an imaginary swollen belly.

'Well, what was it all about?' he jeered, imitating her direction, angry with her for robbing him of any importance. When he saw that she was crying he felt instantly contrite, but she waved him away listlessly. He felt baffled, unable to communicate to her the importance of what they were doing.

'This meeting will change our lives. If we are successful in carrying out our plan we will become part of history.' As he spoke he saw himself returning to his parents house with garlands round his neck, being embraced by Nathoo and Indijeet while a crowd waited outside the gate. Anne said passionately, 'I'm not interested in history. We're living in a hovel. I've left my family so that we can make a life together, plan things, raise our child – and all you can talk about is your secret meetings and how they will change the world.'

She was crying openly now, her distorted body shaken with sobs, and he felt ashamed and guilty that he couldn't comfort her, did not wish to comfort her. As she talked he looked out of the window down the red mud track, thronged with shoppers returning from the market. He felt her words closing around him like a net, pleading for a cosy domesticity which only spoke to him of the death of passion, of idealism, and a long littleness of preoccupation with small and unimportant things. He got up and walked to the door. Anything must be better than listening to her voice diminishing him, relegating him to a future of domestic responsibility, cut off from the great causes he saw dimly before him.

When she paused he said, 'I can't do it, Anne. I can't give up everything for you and the baby.' As he closed the door behind him he heard her say, 'Please come back, Ra. No good can come of it.' But he walked out into the blinding sunshine of the road, feeling a sense of relief steal over him.

Rawalpindi, Pakistan: 1948

Forty-three

After the day with Joginder and Sita, Anthony felt a bizarre irresponsibility. Something about the afternoon, the dilapidation of the house, and the changes in his friends, had pushed his mind beyond some limit. Despite himself he could not take matters seriously, as though his mind had decided to act independently of his will. He reflected, in the days following his visit, amazed and slightly afraid of his own irresponsibility, that it was a natural and understandable attitude since there appeared to be nothing he could do to alter matters.

In the days after receiving Jane's letter he had sat down several times to respond, throwing sheet after sheet into the waste paper basket. The words had seemed stilted and irrelevant, and his severance from his old life made more complete by the journey over the frontier. When he tried to think of Jane and Mark, and to speculate about what they might be doing, and above all when he thought of Anne, he felt a strange sense of unreality, as though all that had happened to him prior to his return had been merely a dream. Sometimes he dreamed of Jane in the early days of their life together, waking tumescent and disturbed, but such dreams in themselves only served further to increase his detachment. He felt almost happy, albeit with the happiness of a man who knows that the dim future already contains some terrible, final, unavoidable circumstance which is inescapable.

Much to his surprise he found Parsons and his wife sympathetic and understanding. They had driven by the house one night and joined him for a stengah on the verandah. They had invited him to dinner the following night and soon it became an accepted understanding that he would dine with them. They had the slightly selfish immaturity of the childless couple, still enthusiastic about their games of Lexicon and canasta, their thoughts unburdened by agonizing over children's schooling or upbringing. Two nondescript cats roamed the small bungalow, clawing the furniture and demanding food and affection with small, cracked miaows. There was a refreshing affection between Parsons and his wife, a capacity to shut away the world outside and reduce it to some more manageable perspective. Once, when they sat in the garden with *La Paloma* playing on the gramophone and his wife supervising supper, Parsons said sadly, 'We wanted bairns, but it just never happened. When we were younger people used to say, "Who's fault is it you can't have children?" They didn't mean any harm. But before it passes you sometimes feel that the Almighty is punishing you for something you may have done.' When his wife came out he patted her haunch affectionately and she put her hand over his. He had said, 'Sorry about young Singh,' in a way which showed his embarrassment and Anthony had nodded and left it at that.

Work at the office piled up in Anthony's absence, and added to the backlog was the problem of having to train new staff to replace those still absent, and to assist with the official Indianization policy. Some of the inter-office memoranda were almost incomprehensible, couched in a verbosely orotund style, full of mis-usages and glaring malapropisms. One headed *Beverage shortages* read, 'We are in the moment anticipating the remitting dispatch of transhipments of fundamental raw materials for these matters which are in process of being delayed pending reopening of shipping ports and resuming passages of goods and chattels across novelty demarcation lines.' 'Yes,' said Abdul heavily, without a smile when he had looked at the memorandum and handed it back to Anthony, 'it is only meaning the last consignment of coffee beans haven't got through.' When Anthony, exasperated, said, 'Why can't they use plain English?' Abdul said, in the manner of one humouring a child, 'Sir. Just be thinking of some of the memos those boys had passing through their hands when they were humble clerks,' and Anthony was forced to agree, remembering the purple prose used by the young trainees fresh out of England.

Towards the end of the third week in January Parsons came in to join Anthony for coffee. He seemed melancholy and abstracted and, after they had chatted desultorily for a few minutes, Anthony said, 'What's up, John?' Parsons said, 'Look at this,' taking out a memorandum headed *Confidential priority 1. Security M.G.* The report was prepared by a Mr Mehra and detailed the account of a bomb explosion and the subsequent arrest of a man named Madanlal Padwe Peshwa who had confessed that this was part of an RSSS plot to kill the Mahatma. Mehra went on to complain about the difficulties attendant upon trying to protect 'a saint who is unconcerned about the prospect of martyrdom', and Anthony permitted himself a wry smile, recognizing a bureaucrat protecting his back against any future disaster. He said reassuringly, 'Nothing new there, surely? There have been attempts on everybody, so far as our information goes. Nobody has actually been killed yet.' Parsons only looked at him mournfully and said, 'I hope you're right. I have a bad feeling about this . . .'

* * *

It was a chance comment by Parsons, when they were taking an evening walk in the grounds of his bungalow before dinner, which began all over again the processes of thought from which Anthony had temporarily withdrawn. At first he fought against the knowledge it conferred, but as he had been powerless to force himself to think of Jane and the children and Prescott and Gur and his other friends for so long, he was now powerless to prevent the insights which grew into certainties, leaving him finally with the realization that only he could act, since only he had observed the pattern of events and had drawn the correct conclusions.

Parsons had been talking about Prescott. 'I had a lot of respect for Andrew's judgements. Despite all that business with the Glenlivet,' and he laughed wholeheartedly at the memory. An Army lorry burped and spluttered down the road past them, swirling dust in its wake. 'Andrew always felt there was something wrong about Roger Henshaw. I remember going into the Murree bazaar with Andrew and spotting him sitting with a villain called Feroze Khan. They were drinking tea and slapping each other's backs and generally being pretty pally. That attractive young Indian schoolteacher, Premla Purveys, was there too. I know one shouldn't condemn a man before he's tried, but the word we have is that Khan has got away with several robberies. Quite brazenly boasts of his friendship with Henshaw.'

Anthony said, 'You say you saw Roger with the Indian schoolteacher?'

Parsons looked at him, surprised. 'It was common knowledge that he was concerned about Reeves's infatuation with that girl.' He laughed, remembering something. 'You may think Henshaw odd but you probably never heard him talk about his parents. According to him they were real dyed-in-the-wool reactionaries. Their ideas about racial purity and the superiority of Anglo-Saxons would have made Goebbels look like a liberal.' The dinner bell sounded faintly and he touched Anthony's elbow. 'She'll never forgive me if the Yorkshire pudding goes past the peak of perfection. Come on.'

Driving back through the dark streets, Anthony could not shake free from the thoughts that assailed him. Henshaw's association with Feroze Khan; Feroze Khan's alleged involvement in the Trains of Death and his open attack on Joginder's house. He remembered, too, Henshaw giving him the gun with which Richard Reeves had killed himself. Nothing made sense, beyond the fact that at every turn he was confronted with the figure of Henshaw. When he tried to remember Roger he could not, recalling only the smell of sweat, the pressure of a hand on his shoulder as he walked down a featureless corridor. The day of the tiger, the impromptu horse race, had no connection with Roger now. That Roger he had loved. Admired.

Preoccupied with his thoughts, he drove automatically. The roads were deserted. Occasionally a pi-dog slunk from the approaching headlights or a cat scurried across the road. The gin had given him a feeling of insulation, taking the edge off his anxieties. He put away his feverish thoughts with an effort. Soon he would be home, and he accelerated, savouring in anticipation a hot drink and some music, an end to the day alone, free from the pressures of being with people.

A movement caught his eye and he braked, stalling the car as he pulled it to a shuddering halt. He could not be sure later of what he had actually seen, but it seemed to him in that moment that a tall man with a stick, his skin silver in the headlights, walked across the road. The lights dimmed as he restarted the engine and when he looked again the man was gone.

Forty-four

A few evenings later he heard a knock on the door and found Dr Mac on the doorstep. Anthony stood so long without speaking, swaying with the shock of seeing the familiar face, that Mac said drily, 'Don't overwhelm me with the warmth of your welcome.' In the drawing-room Anthony felt ashamed of the untidy neglect. 'Servants' day off,' he said, affecting nonchalance. 'Let's go out for a meal.' But he had seen Mac's eyes run appraisingly over him, and round the room. At least he chose to keep his observations to himself.

Over dinner Mac was oddly reserved. He knew about Vincent from Sita who had heard via some mutual acquaintance. 'The only honest man I ever knew,' he said in a rare unguarded moment. He looked at his whisky reflectively for a moment, adding, 'The only man whom nothing could buy,' and Anthony remembered the dedication on the wreath. He knew about Andrew Prescott, too, shocking Anthony and the waiter with a burst of immoderate laughter. 'Sorry,' he said, wiping his eyes. 'It's a defence against tears. Somehow the idea of Andrew presenting himself to St Peter without his trousers has an irreverent appositeness.' More seriously he added, 'It was the best thing, you know. He had some idealistic, untenable dream of settling down with that little prostitute.' He laughed harshly, clearing his throat. ''Tis pity she's a whore. It would have been like somebody trying to make

323

an honest woman of Gunevati in the old days. Perhaps he was happy in his blindness.'

'You know that Gur has been charged with the murder of Gunevati – and the other girls?' Anthony said. As he started to speak he saw Mac shrink back from the table so that his face was in darkness, beyond the circle of light cast by the low shade. The flies buzzed sleepily over the remains of their meal.

The waiter came forward and cleared the table. When they were alone again Mac sat forward so that his face was in the light. He looked serious.

'No,' he said. 'Not Gunevati . . .' He held up his glass and the waiter hurried forward to pour another stengah. 'But I believe that Richard Reeves was murdered. And I think there is sufficient circumstantial evidence to suggest why the other girls died, if not who did it . . .'

There was something in Anthony's mind which screamed, *Enough*. He felt sick of the sudden cheapness of death, the subject of conversation over a drink, or – here – an interpolation in a meal. He looked at Mac, observing him narrowly, and thought: It's all right for you; to you it is just entropy, an inevitable stage in the processes of decay. You've seen too much of it. You rob it of meaning . . .

Aloud he said, 'If you must then,' stiffly, wishing that the other man would stop, would talk of something else, would not involve him. But Mac only said softly, 'I've spared you the worst. But now that you have returned why should you be exempt?'

Anthony sat back, closing his eyes, and Mac sipped his drink quietly. The restaurant was empty. Occasionally a car moved past. Once a police siren sounded faintly in the distance. The waiter brought both of them another whisky in response to Mac's gesture. Dully, Anthony remem-

324

bered a long-forgotten day of childhood. A Samuel Palmer day by a river. Sedge grass and rushes shivered in a light wind. His father asleep on the bank, his mother reading. The ceremony of innocence is drowned.

Finally, he said flatly, 'You'd better tell me everything.'

When it was over he felt sick. In a grotesque way all that Mac had said contained a logic which eschewed morality as irrelevant. Only Gunevati remained, but Mac had said, 'Within the scheme of things she was unimportant.' When they had paid and were out in the open Anthony breathed in deeply. The streets were shadowy, lit inadequately by the few street lamps left unbroken. Mac put a hand on his arm. 'We cannot go back any more. We can remember the good times, but that is all. And, thinking of those, we cannot escape the knowledge that these things were germinating, even then.'

Mac was surprised when Anthony asked him to come to the office with him. Copies of the transcripts would have to be lodged in 'Pindi. They had probably been dealt with by Parsons, who had decided to say nothing, in hopes that it would slowly fade away. He couldn't blame him for that. Because of the people involved, Mac had been powerless. As he drove through the deserted streets the appalling realization came to him again. There was no one else who could deal with what had happened. 'Corruption breeds corruption,' Mac had said, and Anthony had replied, bitterly, 'Were we really so blind then?'

The file was in Parsons' office. Anthony read it, sitting at Parsons' desk, passing the pages to Mac who sat the other side. They had given up any attempt at furtiveness and Mac had poured them some of Parsons' Glenlivet into coffee cups. 'Not again,' Anthony said, half-amused despite everything, ignoring Mac's questioning look.

The file was headed: *GURUCHUNDER SINGH/Confidential/Commissioners Only*.

Anthony began to read:

The suspect, Guruchunder Singh, son of Zemindar Joginder Singh of Murree, had carried out legal duties for the Commissioner's Office, 'Pindi, for a period of fifteen months, reporting first to Mr A. Hodder and subsequently to Mr J.C. Parsons.

During this period the standard of Mr Singh's work was exemplary. You will see from Dr Narayan's report that he appears to possess a precision and punctiliousness which borders on the obsessional . . .

'Dr Narayan?' said Anthony, raising his head.

'Police psychiatrist. Very much in the other camp.'

His appearance was meticulous, and (see chowkidar's statement) he often worked until past midnight. At the request of his department head he had prepared a paper entitled PROPOSALS CONCERNING THE ADMISSIBILITY OF CIRCUMSTANTIAL EVIDENCE whose conclusions have now been put into practice by our area officers.

As the annexed reports and affidavits will demonstrate, Mr Singh was regarded as reclusive, almost solitary. His social contacts were few, but included a young lady schoolteacher, Premla Purveys, for whom evidence suggests he had a romantic regard, and to whom he appears to have introduced the first victim on the attached charge sheet, Mr Richard Reeves . . .

'The bastards,' Anthony said softly, under his breath.

During this period immediately before and after the first murder, certain salient behaviour was observed. Several officers in the Mess witnessed an incident between Singh and Mr R. Henshaw (affidavit annexed) in which Mr Singh became abusive towards Mr Henshaw. Mr Singh's behaviour while out riding

326

with Miss Anne Hodder, 16-year-old daughter of the aforesaid Mr A. Hodder, was observed (see annexed statement). Dr Narayan characterizes Mr Singh as quiet, but potentially extremely volatile, with strong sexual drives which could have been exacerbated by frequent contact with the aforesaid Misses Premla Purveys and Anne Hodder. It is reasonable to suppose that Singh was angered by the intimate relationship which developed between Miss Premla Purveys and the first deceased victim, Richard Reeves, and, perhaps, upon hearing that Miss Purveys was pregnant by the deceased, could no longer contain his anger. Reference is made here to Dr Narayan's conclusions which state categorically that, in his opinion, Mr Singh would be capable of murder under pressure.

Anthony rubbed his eyes and took a drink of his whisky. Tiredly he thought, Was it really like that? Were those things really happening? His mind felt numb, incapable of absorbing fresh information. Mac looked up. He said, quietly, 'I know. You start to distrust your own perceptions after a while.'

Regarding the other deceased females. First, the annexed schedule will demonstrate that Mr Singh was in the vicinity on each occasion, and on two occasions he was witnessed in close proximity to the deceased within minutes of the times of death (see reports by Dr Aziz, Coroner – annexed). Dr Narayan's report hypothesizes that Premla Purveys' rejection, and subsequent pregnancy by Reeves, may have unhinged the suspect. Further, that it would be easier to commit future murders after the first, particularly if the motivation was disgust, anger, and, in small part, still unslaked sexual needs.

As the annexed minutes will show it was agreed by the Commissioner in conference with Superintendent Anwar Khan and District Commissioner Roger Henshaw that the defendant should be permitted to proceed under guard to Amritsar to acquaint the defending officer of his choice, Mr Anthony Hodder, of the charges laid against him. In retrospect the aforesaid regretted the decision, but it must be pointed out that a state of Civil War existed, the cells were overcrowded with

327

rioters, and very strong representations requiring us to free the prisoner on bail, pending the court hearing, had been made. In the opinion of all concerned the prisoner was unlikely to attempt an escape, given that his parents were living within the local jurisdiction.

Regrettably the train was attacked by extremist factions and the prisoner's escort was killed. He himself received injuries which subsequently led to his hospitalization. The attending doctor, Dr Dutt of Holy Sister Hospital, Amritsar, had filed a report which indicated that it was unlikely the defendant would long survive.

In all the circumstances the undersigned propose that the cases on the annexed sheet be considered closed.

It was signed by the Commissioner, Roger Henshaw, and Superintendent Anwar Khan. Under a heading *Approved for Action* further down the page there were six signatures. Parsons' was one of them.

Anthony read Henshaw's account of the incident in the Mess. It bore no relation to his memory of what had happened. Through the window the first grey light of dawn washed the sky. He started to put the papers back into the file, and Mac handed him back the sheets he had been reading.

'Have Joginder and Sita seen these?'

'Yes,' said Mac. 'Worse, Joginder seems to have accepted them.'

When they had locked up in silence, and were walking back to the car Mac said hesitantly, 'There is something else. Premla Purveys brought the baby to me with a cut a couple of weeks ago. The child appears to be a mongol, you know. Dr Aziz was away, and she was in a bit of a panic. Well. I had to put in a couple of stitches and he was as good as new then. Afterwards I had an idea. I analysed the child's blood.'

They drove slowly down the road. Ragged workers

328

carrying loads dragged wearily along the verges leading buffalo.

'I did the autopsy report on Richard,' Mac said softly. 'He couldn't possibly have been the baby's father.'

New Delhi, India: 1948

Forty-five

With the stubbornness of the weak man Raju said, 'I can't tell you. I have to go.' He put a shirt in the battered case, a pair of flannel trousers, some socks, a towel and, as an afterthought, some neem sticks. Anne sat on the rickety chair loaned from Nathuram's sister, Sharmila. The sink was full of plates surmounted by a battered mountain of used saucepans. Her back had hurt too much for her to stand and scour them. She said, 'Where can I get hold of you if anything happens?' and he said, defensively, 'I'll only be gone a couple of days. Sharmila will look after you.' He stopped himself in time from suggesting that she should spend more time with Sharmila. The two evenings they had spent with Sharmila and her bania husband had not been a success, occupied mainly with Sharmila showing off her possessions. He checked the lock on the case, hefting it to make sure it wouldn't open of its own accord. She sat quietly watching him, and he felt an irritated tenderness in the face of her resigned acceptance. 'I'll bring you something back from New Delhi,' he said, and she looked sharply up, startled. 'New Delhi? Why are you going to New Delhi?' Fear lent her voice a tremulous edge. He walked over and stood in front of her, leaning forward to take her by the shoulders, talking to her as to a child. 'That's the secret,' he said, putting a finger to his lips. He smiled, willing her to cheerfulness. 'I'll be back soon. Everything will be all right, you'll see,' and she

330

recognized with a sinking heart the unfounded optimism of some obscure desperation.

On the 'plane he felt stricken by remorse. I'll make it up to her, he thought, the reality of the last few months fading before a sudden memory of how they had been before the day when everything had changed. The stewardess tapped him on the shoulder and pointed to the no smoking sign, and he smiled apologetically, stubbing it out in the ashtray. He thought of the day: Anne, in tears, telling him that she was pregnant and that both families knew. 'I tried to tell you,' she cried, and after a moment's hesitation he had taken her in his arms, making soothing noises, stroking her hair. There had been one moment when he had the initiative and could have changed the future. He was still tormented when he thought of it and wondered if his capitulation had been for better or worse. He was glad when the 'plane touched down, and he was more involved in things to be done.

At the ramshackle hotel in New Delhi he saw Karkare and Ghopal in the lobby. Karkare sat at a round table, by a dying fern, reading the *Hindustan Standard*. Ghopal sprawled on the faded red leatherette settee at his side, sipping Vimto, and observing the other occupants through dark glasses in imitation of some Western film star. Raju felt a momentary unease, as if they were amateur players wildly overacting their lines in a drama they were unable to comprehend. There was fruit on the table and a bowli-glass surrounded by apricot stones and pomegranate seeds. Neither looked at him and he followed the chokra up the stairs to a small room on the second floor. There was a charpoy in the corner, and a threadbare dhurri on the floor. A chipped ewer stood under a table whose leg was propped with cardboard in the corner opposite the charpoy. The boy waited by the door, expressionless as he closed his hand over the two anna tip before slipping from the room.

Left to himself Raju sat on the bed, taking a deep breath. It didn't feel as he had expected it would. There was no exaltation, none of the feelings he had anticipated. He wanted to go to the lavatory. There was a knock on the door and Ghopal and Karkare came in. Raju groaned inwardly, feeling that his urgent need for the toilet was inappropriate at such a time. He hoped they would not stay long, even as he motioned them to sit down with a welcoming smile.

Ghopal spoke in a hoarse whisper, like a stage conspirator, 'It has to be today. Madanlal made a confession a week ago, on the 23rd. They will have broken him by now. So Nathuram is going to do it this afternoon at the prayer meeting at Birla House.' He walked round, hugging himself, and punched Raju on the shoulder as he passed. 'We will be the back-up if he fails.' He opened his waistcoat with a theatrical gesture and Raju saw that two grenades sat in a false pocket in the lining. Ghopal laughed, watching his face. He said, mockingly, 'I can see it's no good giving you one of these. Perhaps you'd better just stick with Nathuram and help him get away, if possible!' Raju felt afraid, aware for the first time of what he was involved in. If only Roger Henshaw were here, he thought again, remembering Henshaw teaching him and Ghodse to shoot on the Maharajah's estate.

Ghopal gave him the time and simple directions to the Birla Temple where they were to meet to take darshan, repeating the instructions twice. When they had gone Raju felt a warmth on his thigh and realized with disgust that he had wet himself.

* * *

332

When he got to the temple they were already there with Nathuram and Lakshimi. The trees hid the sun, and the marble floor struck cold. Raju went in with the others to take darshan in front of the statue of Kali in her manifestation as Destroyer and then walked out to where Ghopal stood by the statue of Shivaji. He felt sick with apprehension. Brown leaves scattered across the marble terraces in the wind, whispering in dry eccentric flurries before lodging under the parapet. Nathuram exuded a noumenal, other-worldly peace, and Raju felt, momentarily, a cessation of the nagging feeling of uncertainty which had remained with him since he had met the others in the hotel that morning.

Nathuram was dressed in a khaki bush jacket and blue trousers, his hair neatly combed. He had an air of rigid detachment and Raju sensed that he saw nothing save some intense inner vision, even as the brown eyes flicked impersonally over him and a faint smile acknowledged his good wishes. At four-thirty Ghopal came out of the temple, followed by the others. From the grounds of Birla House the noise of the crowds had grown, a low humming punctuated by an occasional burst of laughter or a high pitched shout. Nathuram said, 'It is finished then,' vaguely patting the pocket in which the Beretta was concealed. When his brother embraced him he looked impassively ahead, unfeeling, in some life in which the others no longer had a part.

When they were in the grounds of Birla House, amongst the huge crowd, Nathuram put a hand on Ghopal's arm and made an almost imperceptible movement of his head. There was no need for any conversation. This was part of the plan worked out again and again over the past few weeks, and words were superfluous. Raju, shivering slightly, watched Nathuram move to the edge of the path. He felt within himself a feeble wish to avoid what lay ahead, even as he knew it was too late. The man next to him smiled toothlessly and said, 'Peace, brother, he will soon be here,' and Raju smiled indicating that he was being pushed by the crowd behind. There was a swelling of sound in the crowd nearer the house, and he craned his neck to see over the massed backs of followers.

In the late sunlight a frail man, his arms resting on the shoulders of two young girls, shuffled forward on rickety legs. Apart from a swathe of cloth over his shoulder, his chest and legs were bare, showing skeletal and emaciated. As he walked forward he smiled, his round glasses glinting, and the sparse tonsure of white hair fanning round his head like a halo. For a moment Raju remembered his grandfather visiting when he was a child, and the sense of warmth and continuity his presence had conveyed. He was dislocated from the present, moving forward with the disciples for his darshan.

He saw Nathuram move forward and make the gesture of namaste. Knowing already what would come the next few seconds seemed to move very slowly. Nathuram took the pistol from his pocket and fired three times in quick succession, the pistol moving downwards as a Royal Indian Army sergeant moved to grapple with him. The Mahatma raised his hands above his head and said, 'Oh God,' and began to fall. There was another shot and Raju fought to push away from the scene. All round him the crowd surged forward and he almost lost his footing. He felt terrified, convinced that his connection with the deed must be apparent. Someone in the crowd shouted, 'It was a Muslim,' and there was a deep baying roar from the crowd. He managed to fight across to where the press of bodies was thinner. He could not see Apte or Karkare. All round there were inquiring voices. A man caught him

334

by the arm saying, 'What happened, bhai?' but Raju shook his head and broke free, plunging towards the main gate.

By the gate he felt a pain in his chest, and sat down on the grassed verge. People passed, glancing briefly at the crying youth, their momentary curiosity instantly forgotten as they joined the huge crowd from which the sound of keening came. With his head on his arms Raju wept, oblivious of the mucus spilling from his nostrils on to the sleeve of his shirt. He said, 'Forgive me,' again and again, like a charm, but could feel no relief. In his mind he saw Gandhi's hands rise up in the greeting and then begin to fall. There was no one to whom he could turn for comfort.

He remembered that he was to meet Ghopal and the others at the hotel at seven. Nobody at the gate paid any attention as he staggered out to the edge of the road and stood between the oleanders, waiting for a gap in the traffic. The cars and lorries moved past, nose to tail, in an unbroken stream, and he began to feel a sense of panic again. Then two cars raced by very fast, and he balanced on the balls of his feet. There was a big enough gap to reach the centre island if he ran fast. He had almost reached the island when the car hit him. When the fender hit his knees he felt his body being thrown high into the air, and then he fell heavily on to the windscreen which broke under the impact. The car veered crazily over the road for a few seconds and then crashed into a telegraph pole. Raju only felt, from very far away, the sensation of falling as he slipped off the bonnet on to the road. There was no pain, only the sound of a great wind in his ears. He could see nothing.

The driver was copiously sick over the side of the car. A policeman had appeared and knelt over Raju with his hand on his heart. Raju sighed and said, 'I didn't get Anne's present,' in a regretful tone. After a moment the policeman stood up and said, 'He's dead,' moving into the road to redirect the roaring traffic.

Rawalpindi, Pakistan: 1948

Forty-six

Two evenings after Mac's visit Anthony came home early, having turned down Parsons' invitation to dinner. Ahmed had met him at the door, saying with an insolent leer, 'Young lady to see you, sir.' It was Bul-Bul, reclining on the sofa with a gin and tonic in her hand, leafing through a photograph album with the casual attitude of an old friend of the family. She jumped up and kissed him and he felt hot with embarrassment, hearing Ahmed's snicker as he shut the door. She had come to collect some money which Prescott had left for her at his bank. 'After we had been going together for some months he left me a letter in case anything happened to him,' she said, holding her cigarette affectedly in carmine-tipped fingers and blowing the smoke across the room in little puffs. The border had been no problem – 'except the smell on the road,' she said, wrinkling her nose at the memory. Later, after much more gin, she became maudlin. 'There were other men, but I only really loved him,' she said, and the tears in her eyes were genuine. She didn't want dinner, and chattered on while he had his sandwich, flitting from her career to memories of her time with Prescott.

'He wanted to marry me and take me to England, you know,' she said, daring him to laugh, but Anthony remembered the evening at the Club, and felt sure that it was true. He looked at the unread papers on the table with an inward sigh, wondering how he was going to get rid of her.

When Ahmed had cleared away and said goodnight the atmosphere changed. 'Don't you like me a little bit?' she wheedled, plumping the cushion at her side with suggestive hands, and he felt, despite himself, a desperate longing. Her lips were suffused with blood, and through the thin material of her bodice he could see her nipples clearly. Ahmed would talk anyway, he thought, imagining her body lying in the bed upstairs. She got up and walked unsteadily across the room, and knelt down beside him, resting her breast against his knee and putting a hand on his crotch. He held her hand firmly, moving it away, and she said, 'Why? Why?' in a soft cajoling voice. He cleared his throat. 'Because he was my friend,' and she said, unbelievingly, 'But he is dead.'

He could feel her silent incomprehension as he drove her back to her hotel. Towards the end of the drive she said, 'I've ordered some nautch costumes with the money. There's a very good durzee who's making them up for me.'

When he opened the door to let her out at the hotel entrance she asked him up for coffee, laughing at his refusal. He watched her walk into the lighted foyer, swinging her hips, and link arms with a man who greeted her. He turned away and drove back home.

Mysore, South India: 1948

Forty-seven

Anne had returned in the summer, waiting at the station for hours with her son until Arline dispatched Sam to fetch her under cover of darkness.

There was a new hardness about her, and her face had the sallow, strained look of a much older woman. She had known what would happen when she telephoned her grandmother. She sat with her child in the waiting-room, working through her memories with an occasional grim smile, as she waited for the car. There would be some price to pay for what she had done and, upon certain terms and conditions, she had steeled herself to pay it. From time to time she looked into the carrying cradle, abstractedly offering the child her finger to grasp. The baby was fair-skinned with a light crop of soft rufous hair and chapped apple-red cheeks. He watched the world through wondering, vacant china-blue eyes, never crying, solemn. She loved him with passionate intensity, frightened of her desire to hug him fiercely, and sometimes of her thoughts. Oh, I could eat him, she would think, and feel a momentary fear of the perversity of the idea. When the news had come she had already known that something had happened to Raju and had also, with unsentimental logic, seen it as the best that could happen. The fire had begun to burn to ash on the day that she had told him she was pregnant and had seen the momentary glance of a wild animal seeking escape. Nothing could cover over, hide, excuse, or subvert that insight. It had eaten away the present and the memories of the past, even while they were together, and, ameliorated by the sense of shock at his death, still persisted. She faced the future unflinchingly with the grim certainty of day after unvarying day, and the narrowed horizons of a woman twice her age.

When she had installed Anne and the baby in the upstairs room, Jane had come down into the lounge and wept.

Arline had snapped the light on, looking for her reading glasses, and had shut the door, sitting across the room until the crying stopped. 'What is there to cry about?' she asked and Jane said hesitantly, 'She has become so hard,' trying to find some words to express the feral withdrawal, the sense of alien completeness which held out nothing to grasp. It was not the baby, nor Raju's death, she said, still grasping for words, and Arline had said with grim certainty, 'But that is precisely what it is. It is those two things which have set her aside, which we must find some means of living with.' For a brief instant Jane saw the shape of their dependence upon her mother: the harsh, decisive certainty, the sense of direction, the absolute authority which created a geometric pattern to the uncertain present. When her mother put a hand on her arm and said, 'Don't worry. We'll sort this out,' she was not certain whether relief or fear predominated. Vincent once said to her in this very room, 'With Mother you are the sacrifice seeking the sacrificial knife,' and she had felt angry with him, the inchoate phrase returning to worry her unexpectedly over the following months. She felt both devoured and safe, and saw, in that brief instant, for the last time, the irreconcilable paradox upon which her equilibrium rested.

* * *

It took Indijeet Bhose four days from the moment she glimpsed Anne in the back garden, briefly, to screw up her courage to pay a visit.

When the news of Raju's death had first come in a message brought by a police constable she had seemed preternaturally calm. Nathoo had stayed at home for a couple of days, taking her to the shops in an effort to divert her attention. On the second day he had held out a brilliant green sari trimmed with gold, inviting her to feel the material, and she had stepped forward and hit him. 'I'm not a child, to be bought with clothes and trinkets when my son has died,' she screamed as he attempted to restrain her. In the tonga on the way home she had wept, turning her face from him into the pleated leather seating. Even that had been better than the following week when she had lain in the bedroom mute, dry-eyed, staring vacantly at the ceiling. He had invited her sister Lillee to come over from Bangalore, afraid to leave her on her own during the days. In the evenings they would hold whispered councils on the verandah. Several times Lillee said, 'She wants to see the child. That's all she talks about,' and he felt helpless. Anne's letter, arriving a few days after the police messenger, had told them she was almost due, but there was no address, nor any indication she would write again. 'I know, I know,' Lillee said soothingly, looking at his anguished expression. Privately she felt that Indijeet was being over-dramatic. She remembered the childhood games when Indijeet would always marry the Maharajah and she always played the younger sister for whom a suitable, but less grand, consort would be found.

One night Indijeet had returned to the verandah and started speaking in English, settling down upon a cushion, and dipping her fingers into the sweetmeats. Two days

341

afterwards she had a furious row with her sister, who refused to tell Nathoo on the way to the station what had happened. Normality returned. A normality which Nathoo perceived, for the first time, as an unequal equilibrium in which his role was secondary and supportive: provider, conciliator, comforter. I have no life of my own, he thought, in panic one evening sitting by himself on the verandah when Indijeet had gone to bed. He resented the insight, wishing it gone and the old happy servitude of running to fulfil her every wish returned. But it was not be be.

Indijeet had said nothing to Nathoo about Anne's return or about her intended visit. She had met with Arline and her family a few times since the elopement. After the first meeting she had been forced to accept that nothing intrinsic had changed; that there would be no interfamilial dinners, no picnics in the Mysore forests together, no bridge evenings, no gradual rapprochement. Angela had been sympathetic, filling the awkward silences with a laugh or a bridging comment in open defiance of her mother. But Nathoo, recognizing at last the discontent in Indijeet which nothing could ever appease, had responded when she later asked him his opinion, 'You will never accept the way things are, my love.' But she had not been listening.

At her insistence Sam reluctantly showed her into the drawing-room. She could hear his footfalls dying away down the tiles, and then a door close. Through the open window she could hear the mali humming to himself as he scraped in the dry earth and, beyond, the occasional roar of a passing car. She looked at the Copeland bust of Gladstone standing on the mantelshelf, and then at the silver-framed photograph of Arline and William by its side. The ormolu clock slurred its slow tick. She felt oppressed by the weight of these unfamiliar objects, springing from some past whose cadences and rhythms were foreign to her. The pictures, reproductions of Crome, Cotman, Holman Hunt, seemed cold and impenetrable, and when she sat down the hard skeleton of the chair began to impress itself uncomfortably upon her well-upholstered bottom. She remembered her fixed intention, closing her eyes to shut out the dense, serried ranks of alien shapes and textures which seemed to stand against her in mute reproach.

The door opened and Arline came in.

'Good morning, Mrs Bhose,' she said and Indijeet nodded, overawed as always by the overpowering impression of complete certainty which Arline possessed. Arline walked to the window and closed it, drawing the curtains slightly across, so that the sun only slanted over a small patch of carpet. She turned to Indijeet saying in tones of confiding exasperation, 'These servants never learn. I keep telling Sam not to let the sun in. It fades the patterns. But it does no good,' and she lowered herself into the chair by the window with her face in shadow and her hands folded in her lap.

Indijeet twisted her hands together nervously, sitting on the edge of her chair. She started to speak, and her voice squeaked so that she had to clear her throat and begin again. She said, pleadingly, 'I . . . I wonder if I may be allowed to see my grandson?' Emboldened by the silence following her comment she went on, 'I know you didn't approve, Mrs Porter. Can't we let bygones be bygones? My son is dead and this is all I have left . . .' The words brought an overflow of emotion, and she began to cry, seeing a picture of herself as a bereaved mother with ashes in her hair. Through her tears she looked at the still figure by the window.

When Arline spoke her voice was low and quiet and she emphasized her points with a raised forefinger. 'It seems I must make the position absolutely clear, Mrs Bhose. First, I never wish to see you in this house again upon any pretext. Second, I intend that the child's parentage shall remain a secret. Third, I must ask you to stop your son Zia playing with my grandson,' she paused, touching the jet beads round her throat for a moment, and then held her hand up as Indijeet half rose to protest. 'I haven't finished yet. Though it is not known generally, or even to the police, my granddaughter has left us in no doubt that your son was heavily involved with the group of political agitators who assassinated the Mahatma. While you comply with my demands your secret will be safe, and your husband can continue with his job, and you can tell your friends whatever you wish. If, however, you should ever feel tempted to break any of these prohibitions, I will inform the Inspector of what I know, and ensure that the newspapers and your husband's employers are told also. I am sure I do not have to underline the likely consequences.'

Indijeet sat, stunned. The room which had seemed oppressively hot now seemed cold, and she felt faint. She closed her eyes, gripping the arm of the chair. The blood pulsed in her head and she dimly heard Arline walk across the room and come over to the chair. Then she smelt the acrid fumes of sal volatile, choking as they irritated the back of her throat. Arline said, 'Sit back for a moment. When you feel better I will get Sam to take you home.' Her voice seemed kindly now, even concerned, and the menace of a few moments past had disappeared. Arline took the silver-framed photograph from the mantelshelf in her beringed hands. 'Since William died I have had to uphold our standards and our customs. It has not been easy.' Her tone carried a faint hint of apology and regret.

When Arline walked to ring the bell to summon Sam, Indijeet heaved herself out of the chair with difficulty. 'Please do not bother, Mrs Porter. I can see myself out,' she said with precarious dignity, and Arline inclined her head in acknowledgement.

But in the afternoon, shrilling with minatory cicadas, Indijeet daydreamed again of the Maharajah, and his passion and fervour were undimmed. Perhaps things were not so bad, after all.

Rawalpindi, Pakistan: 1948

Forty-eight

Three days after Bul-Bul's visit a note arrived from Mac together with a yellowed, faded newspaper clipping. Over breakfast Anthony read the clipping, an account of the death of one James Bulstrode-Henshaw at the hands of Indian women during the Mutiny in 1857. The note was brief.

Since circumstantial evidence seems de rigueur how about this for a hypothesis? [Mac had written.] Perhaps we can find our own Dr Narayan to clothe it in some semblance of pseudo respectability with some appropriate gibberish. I recollected Henshaw referring to an account of the Mutiny which dealt with some distant relative. The archivist at 'Pindi Library was most helpful in turning this up. Taking the fact that Henshaw hated his mother, and the girls were sexually molested, we could construct a case at least as valid as the one they have constructed against Gur. Can't you see the headlines in the *Murree Times*? DISTRICT COMMISSIONER DRIVEN TO REVENGE RAPES BY CENTURY OLD ACCOUNT OF MUTINY. They'll love it.

Sorry to be facetious. You're the only one who can act, and all this delay is frustrating.

All right, all right. In my own time, Anthony thought irritably, putting the clipping away in a drawer. He was convinced that Mac had not told him the entire truth the night they had dined together. If this was a joke it was unfunny and in bad taste. And it touches on something, he thought, angry with his friend for this reminder of tardiness.

As the weeks passed Anthony had felt a strange lassitude. He dined and played scrabble with the Parsons, went to Mess dinners, and even accepted an invitation or two for mixed doubles. 'Ey up,' said Parsons, digging him with a nudging elbow in the shower room as he towelled his hair dry, 'that Fairfax girl hardly got a ball over the net for watching you,' and Anthony said, 'Nonsense. It's your imagination,' aware of her interest and secretly pleased. As with everything, these activities, and the social round of cocktail parties and official receptions, all began to take on the features associated with some secondary means of passing the time. He dealt with his work efficiently, but without enthusiasm, laughing with Parsons at the anomalous, contradictory memoranda which flooded into the office daily.

When the second letter arrived from Jane he left it lying on the table unopened for several days, unwilling to start anything which might detract from or alter his progress towards the hidden destination where he knew his steps were tending. The evenings, when the light filtered in soft mauves and golds through the haze, and the distant hills began to fade into the darkening sky, were events to be savoured. Daily he felt more and more a sense of the finiteness of life. It was not a morbid apprehension, though he occasionally felt a mild regret at his own passivity, a sense that he had always accepted the easiest course, and in doing so had denied himself achievements granted to men of lesser abilities. But the goals themselves had become unimportant; money, position, and even the memories of his family, the events of the past year, all were subdued, relegated to a perspective of things long past and unchangeable.

Two memories recurred to him, inexplicable yet comforting in some promise of continuity, standing proud from the flat, featureless plain of his life since his return to Rawalpindi. First Joginder's conviction that he had seen the Silver Saddhu, and had spoken to him; and then his own brief glimpse of a figure in the failing lights as he drove back from Parsons. Though he scoffed at his own gullibility from time to time, surrounded by the prosaic machinery of the office, there was growing within him the conviction that there was a purpose to his existence, operating beyond the level of mere fallible will and blind faith. Sometimes, sitting under the cold light of the stars and aware of the sleeping city, he felt a sense of being part of some order which had pre-existed him from time immemorial and would continue far into the future. At such moments he would feel that there was, after all, some purpose immanent in existence transcending the rotting down, the lowly place in the eternal onward movement of the nitrogen cycle. Immortality.

All he felt when he finally read the letter was a sense of mild curiosity and relief. It changed nothing. The distance remained. He knew that his daughter would survive and live out her span, and that his presence would change nothing; he imagined his worried concern and her irritation growing into indifference over the passing years. Indian summers passing with their picnics and parties, and the child, loved and yet not loved, infecting their lives with its innocent presence. From Jane he felt further estranged still; the letter was a recital, without reproach or anger, of events. It evoked memories of her in those last months, tight-lipped and disapproving. It was only when he thought of Mark that he felt an impotent sadness, hoping without belief that he had passed on some secret endurance, some talisman against the savage and uncertain future. Afterwards there might be time for them again. Not now. There was a valediction in his thoughts that night, and it was well past midnight when he stumbled upstairs, to lie fully-dressed upon his bed until the chokra brought his chota hasri at seven.

As though summoned by a malign deus ex machina the telephone call came through to the office in the morning. The line crackled with static and the dry chirping of innumerable distant conversations. He waved the clerk into the outer office, concentrating on the faint voice.

It was Dr Dutt. 'I tried to get you but the lines were down,' he said apologetically, and Anthony knew instantly that Gur was dead.

Gur had been alternately agitated and depressed for a few days, trying vainly to speak to Dutt, and then subsiding into melancholia. Two nights earlier the nurse had called Dutt urgently, and he had realized the end was near. Finally Gur had sat up, the veins at his temples bulging with the effort. He had said, quite clearly, (and here Anthony heard the rustling of paper), 'Tell Anthony that I did none of those things.' He had stayed sitting while Dutt wrote the message down, and then smiled, sinking down upon the pillow. A few minutes later he had lapsed into a coma, and died at seven o'clock this morning. Dutt sounded like a man relieved to have discharged his duty, and Anthony thanked him. 'I'm sorry,' Dutt said, 'his will seemed to have gone. It sometimes happens like that.'

The long waiting was over. He was aware of a certainty which he had not felt since he was a schoolboy, when his life had been governed by bells and the inalterable demands of a curriculum.

He instructed his clerk to bring the jeep round, and dealt with his mail and the contents of his in-tray. There was a round robin, couched in execrable English, and full of hyperbolic gravitas, which deplored the fact that there were still separate toilet facilities for the British and the Indians in the Mess. 'Can we indure (sic) this insulting of the flower of our manhood by the suggesting (sic) that they may not employ the same facilities for the basic functions of voiding their bowels and their bladders? Our equality is now a fact and should be shown to the entire world at large.' The clerk had been astonished to hear Anthony laugh aloud, before gravely dictating his reply. 'I agree with the sentiments expressed but would counsel against toilet facilities in use being thrown open to the view of the public at large. Speaking for the colonial community, I do not believe they are ready for this at the moment.' The clerk looked at him out of the corner of his eye, but Anthony was gravely unsmiling.

Later the clerk was unable to recollect anything out of the ordinary in Anthony's behaviour. No, he had noticed nothing unusual about the sahib. Yes, he had seemed quite cheerful when he left the office. The mali remembered him driving himself out in the jeep and waving in salutation. Even Imam Deen, the harijan mathre bearing away the euphemistically termed 'night soil' in a wicker basket on his head, remembered that 'Sahib was smiling.' It was all very odd, said the Chairman of the Commission of Enquiry, removing his spectacles and rubbing his eyes before marking the file 'open' and moving on.

The chokra had heard noises in the house and come in from the godown where he was having his afternoon siesta to find Anthony buckling up a small leather attaché case. The sahib had seemed in good humour, too hurried for tea and a trifle preoccupied, but that was usual. He omitted, restrained by some peasant cunning, to tell the Commission that Anthony had given him the equivalent of three months' wages without explanation, but his simple mind, unused to the tortuous considerations of such enquiries, could not see that this might be material evidence. All that he felt, instinctively, was that the Commission might accuse him of theft and take the money away. No, the sahib had said nothing about returning for dinner, but it was not unusual for him to be unspecific.

In the end it all came down to a problem of filing. Nothing could be entirely dispensed with unless it was typed up in a statement which offered a premise and a conclusion, and the members of the Commission, to a man, felt uneasy about unsolved mysteries which could not be neatly tabulated. But even their most specious deliberations failed to provide a firm answer: over stengahs they ranged over a variety of possible conclusions (interspersed with commentaries on the general unreliability of native witnesses and other such portentous matters) but the Chairman was finally forced to observe that the available evidence offered no possibility of a firm verdict. So, consequent upon an apathetic but unanimous show of hands, the file of papers marked *Hodder, Anthony* was dispatched with the filing clerk to the open cases cabinet, which was hidden in a small office occupied by three very junior native office clerks.

Murree, Pakistan: 1948

Forty-nine

Anthony drove steadily up the road. He was in no hurry, planning to arrive after dark. He stopped on the bend of road overlooking the farm, bathed in sunlight, with the vast, bruised sweep of the valley beneath. A flock of pigeons wheeled and turned in perfect flight over the dovecots. The cows grazed along the swollen contours of the green slope, and in the field beyond a fire breathed acrid yellow smoke into the cloudless sky. Above him he heard the woodcutters' axes thump and echo, and the cautionary cry and tearing sound as another pine crashed slowly down with a massive rending of branches. He sat against a wheel of the jeep, facing the valley, and read through the letters he had received from Jane, trying for one last time to experience some connection with what was past. But their resonance had gone, with the finality of a love ended, and he put them back into the briefcase with a sigh, and lay looking out towards the far horizon. He ignored the passing woodcutters who led their loaded donkeys, eyeing him curiously as they made their way to the village below the farm. The dust raised by the passing vehicles swirled past him, but he paid no heed. Only the distant muezzin sounding finally returned him to the present. He got stiffly to his feet and climbed back behind the wheel.

It was almost midnight when he arrived. The moon sucked colour from the vegetation, and gave the trees a ghostly incandescence. He cut the engine and rolled the jeep gently down the slope to the clearing above the house. Nearby a feowl screamed mournfully, and a heavy body crashed through the thicket to the left of his path. The house bulked dark before him and he walked carefully on the grass verge, avoiding the gravel, round to the front. The dining-room lights blazed through the french windows, slanting across the verandah to fade on the gravel outside. He paused for a moment in the shadow of the oak and looked in. The table was covered with the remains of a dinner party. The candles still guttered in their holders over the five place settings, and bottles stood on the white linen cloth amid the plates and half-eaten trifles. He could see movement on the verandah outside the dining-room. Once again he began to move cautiously around.

There was a lantern on the verandah table by whose dim light he could make out three figures. He heard a few words in Roger Henshaw's voice – '. . . the stomach for it, I suppose,' and then a burst of laughter. Pipe smoke drifted in the still air. He stopped by the weeping willow. In the darkness behind him the guinea fowls carried on their domestic quarrelling.

A match flared briefly and he could see Roger's face, the pipe glowing red as he pulled on it until the tobacco was alight. Roger poured himself a whisky and then said gently into the darkness, 'Gentlemen. My oldest friend is here to join us. We've been expecting you. Come up and have a drink.'

Anthony felt sheepish walking up the steps to the vacant chair at the back of the verandah, past the two men who he could still not make out. He sat down, putting the heavy briefcase carefully down beside the chair. Henshaw picked up a glass from the table and held it up to the light. 'You don't mind using Margaret's glass, do you? Whisky?' Anthony took the proffered glass in silence, putting it carefully down on the table. 'How did you know I was coming?' he said.

'Parsons rang my office this afternoon. A few moments earlier and you could have had the pleasure of Dr Mackenzie's company. I believe you know my other guests, Superintendent Anwar Khan and Feroze Khan.' Henshaw's voice was almost amused.

One of the figures stood up and stepped forward and Anthony saw, with a shock of recognition, that it was indeed Anwar Khan. He seemed to have aged, or perhaps it was a trick of the light. There was a livid scar from the corner of one eye to his mouth. Anthony sat without moving and after a moment the policeman sat down again.

'I can't reacquaint you with Margaret for the moment,' Henshaw said, gesturing towards the whisky bottle. 'I'm afraid that nothing would wake her until the morning. That's the way things are these days.' He leaned back in the chair, putting his hands behind his head. The small sounds of night filled the silence; a rafter creaked, and the gravel at the front of the house crackled under the feet of a prowling cat.

The certainty which had grown over the past few weeks in Anthony strengthened and he put his hand down to touch the briefcase with an involuntary gesture. With the certainty came a terrible sadness. For these few moments it almost seemed that they were still at college together, and Joginder and Mac might even now be coming round the corner to join them for a drink. He fought against the warmth, but it was insidious, bringing with it the memory of a happiness he had not felt since they were students together so many years ago. When Roger said, 'I've

354

missed *you* above all,' the mad gaiety had gone from his voice. For a wild moment Anthony thought, We can do it. Everything that has happened doesn't matter. We can make things as they were again. Except, of course, for Richard Reeves, for Gur, for Gunevati. No, there was no way back.

Roger stood up, stretching. 'Anwar, Feroze. Forgive me for bringing the evening to an end. I have a friend who was lost and is found, and we have a lot to discuss.' Anwar muttered a few words of conventional politeness to Anthony, and Feroze walked down into the darkness without a word. A few moments later there was the sound of the jeep starting behind the house, and then the engine note changing and dying away as the vehicle moved up the road. 'So relaxing to spend the evening with friends,' Roger said. There was a febrile antic gaiety in his voice again. He sat down, pouring himself another glass of whisky.

'I wasn't aware that Mac was one of your friends,' Anthony said, and Roger laughed.

'I remember you always used that sanctimonious tone of voice to defend him when we were students. Well, I suppose friends would be too strong a collective noun to describe our dinner party tonight. Let's say we have a mutuality of interests.'

Anthony picked up the briefcase and placed it on the table. He slipped the buckles and lifted out the revolver, put it on the table and replaced the empty case by his feet. He watched Henshaw, but there was no gesture or movement in the dim light to suggest the other man was at all concerned.

'It was Dr Mac who led me to the report in Parsons' office. He also talked to me about the other murders . . .'

'But not about Gunevati, I suppose?' Henshaw said,

and Anthony was silent. 'I didn't think so. Since you and Prescott . . . oh yes, I know about the surveillance . . . ,' he said, responding to Anthony's involuntary movement in the chair, '. . . seem to have been playing private detectives, I suppose I had better give you the correct version.' He could have been offering to tell a risqué after-dinner story.

'When Anwar called me out to Gunevati's body I didn't want to get involved, at first. But he had his suspicions that the killing had been committed by a European – though he didn't say so in as many words. Well, my father was a butcher – ' here he looked briefly at Anthony ' – so I wasn't afraid of seeing a corpse. The first thing that struck me was the efficiency of the murder. And when Aziz examined the body, the first thing he said was, "Whoever did this knew what they were doing."'

He took a sip of his whisky, and proffered the bottle to Anthony who shook his head. From the road far below the chowkidar's call came faintly, to be answered by a still fainter cry from the principal's estate to the north east.

Roger gestured towards the revolver on the table. 'Whatever else I may be, I'm not a murderer. Richard was an accident. He learned that I was having an affair with Premla Purveys. I had gone round to tell her that it was over, that I was serious about Richard's aunt, Margaret Preston. He followed me in and started to attack me. Told me I couldn't treat people like this. We had a struggle and he got hold of my revolver which went off. I took his body down to the forest clearing and you know the rest.'

Anthony said, 'You know that Mac has confirmed that Richard couldn't have been the father. So it was you, was it?'

Henshaw stood up abruptly and went to the verandah

356

rail. 'Premla would have told me,' he said, but his voice sounded shaken, without conviction.

After a while he sat down again. When he spoke he sounded tired, no longer attempting to disguise his voice with false gaiety. 'A few weeks later Mac came to see me. He accused me point blank of murdering Reeves. After a little while I began to get the feeling he had some idea of talking to the authorities. As he was leaving I said, "I've got a deal to propose," and he stopped by the door. *Mine* was an accident, I said, and the balance of probabilities was that I'd get off. But *his* killing of Gunevati was nothing but cold-blooded murder . . .'

Anthony was shocked.

'*Why*?' he said, and Henshaw laughed grimly. 'It always hurts when you find your idols have feet of clay, doesn't it? About the reasons, I can only speculate. There is a report on file from Dr Mac two weeks before the murder pointing out that Gunevati was infected but had refused to stop plying her trade. He is a fastidious man, as you know, and that might have been enough.' He shrugged his shoulders. 'My own view is that following the death of the lady Mac had been having an affair with he visited Gunevati himself. He was very strange about that time and if she had infected him . . .' He left the sentence unfinished.

'And the others . . . ?' Anthony said, and Henshaw held up a large hand.

'All in good time. As you know, at first I had left Anwar to make a mess of the investigation. Quite by chance I happened to be in the village and found that Feroze Khan had "inherited" Gunevati's land and another parcel of land from the first murdered girl. I didn't say anything to Anwar at once . . .'

From inside the house a woman's voice screamed, 'Oh,

no, no, no,' followed by a brief sobbing. Anthony turned, but Roger said sadly, 'It's all right. She cries in her sleep all the time. Sometimes she talks about Richard. That one tragedy has destroyed us . . .'

He seemed eager to continue now, like an actor engaged in performing the illuminating soliloquy at the end of a play. Hear me, he seemed to be saying. There are reasons for all this. I know that terrible things have happened, but I must make you understand. The brashness had gone, and Anthony was reminded, from time to time, of the curious lost innocence he had observed in Roger so long ago when they were friends. It lent a strange unreality to the narrative, as though, despite the story being told, that old friendship had resumed upon the same terms, with Roger as the leader, and Anthony the compelled follower.

'I had other business with Feroze myself. It was probably that which gave him a feeling of security. Yes, he said. The murdered girl was worthless in herself. And hadn't I killed Reeves Sahib and hadn't Dr Mac killed Gunevati? Where was the difference? When he put it like that I could suddenly see his point of view. It seemed as if we were saying that it was all right for us, but not for him. Anyway, I told him he must stop immediately, and I decided to do nothing further about it. After all, the damage was done. But when three more had died I went straight to Anwar. That was when I got the biggest shock of all . . .'

He leaned forward and tapped his pipe on the verandah rail. A shower of sparks fell into the nasturtium bed. He began the ritual of filling it again.

'Anwar knew about it and was in on the deal. His version was that, now the British had let them down, it was up to every man to do the best by his family, in the

358

matter of land, I mean. In any case, nobody would inform against Feroze and he had already made it clear that he would not make a formal confession. So, there was a logic to making the best of what had been done . . .'

This time it was Anthony who broke the silence. His voice was harsh, unforgiving, and he felt a passionate anger. He put his hand openly on the revolver on the table as he spoke.

'Despite the coolness between us I had always admired two things about you. Your courage and your honesty. I see that they have deserted you now.' The lantern had burned low, and he couldn't see Henshaw's face. 'You omit to mention your "arrangement" with Feroze Khan that he should take over Joginder's land. You pass over the false evidence laid against Gur, and your complicity in his death. After all, you were party to the arrangement whereby he was allowed to go to Amritsar and you knew the dangers of sending him on the train.' He said bitterly, as an afterthought, 'The plot on Gandhi's life? Was that you, too? What else were you doing in Mysore?'

Henshaw jumped to his feet, sending the table flying. 'All right,' he said. 'All right,' and Anthony could hear the tears in his voice.

Roger walked over to the edge and sat on the step so that his back was against the pillar. His shoulders and his whole body shook, and he buried his face in his hands. Anthony, watching him, felt a cold pity mixed with disgust. This was the moment that had been maturing in him, unconscious and unknown, for the past months, but he felt no triumph. The thin, sour taste of bile flooded his mouth. I could do it now, he thought, but the impulse had no reality. The strangest thing of all was that somewhere, beyond thought, he still clutched some inviolable hope that the years between could be blotted out, that it could be as it had been when they were young together, united in the machan, waiting for the tiger.

Roger shifted so that the slanting moonlight showed his face. Behind him the oak leaves bobbed silver in a light breeze. Every trace of bravado had deserted him now. When he began to speak Anthony knew that now, this moment, some meaning might emerge if that were ever possible. He had to strain to catch the dry whisper.

'I had always had a vision of India as a society where class would be irrelevant. When my father told me stories as a boy it was all Kipling, and deeds of heroism along the Frontier. I hated my mother for giving in, for not seeing that it was possible for me to rise above those narrow Yorkshire taboos. Well, she was right and he was wrong.' He paused, looking around as though the words he needed would come to him from the darkness outside. 'Even with you, whom I loved, I knew I could not expose myself utterly for fear of losing your friendship. Don't think I was unaware of what people said about me. The upstart grammar school boy trying to crash the hallowed bastions of British India tradition. Trying too hard. Going over the top. Too pushy. What would they have said if they had known I was a butcher's boy, eh?' He laughed shortly at his own rhetorical question.

'I found that even being better than everybody else made no difference. First in examinations, a better shot than anyone else, a first class polo player. You have no idea what those things cost me to achieve, or what hopes I invested in their achievement. But it made no difference. For the stain I carried was ineradicable in the eyes of your society. Birth, breeding, education. Those are the only things that matter. Your sort have made a virtue of their ignorance of the people whose land they have plundered and despoiled, and cheap bar room jokes about people

360

whose cultural heritage is immeasurably richer than their own.'

Anthony's leg felt dead and he shifted in the chair, scuffing his foot on a flaw in the concrete floor. The blood flooded back into his leg, pricking and tingling. He half turned to look through the french windows into the long room. Behind the windows covered with a mosaic of moths the candles were guttering to their ends. Across the verandah Roger said bitterly, 'Excuse the apologia pro vita sua. But even the condemned man has a right to a defence.'

'What about Gur?' Anthony said.

'Touché. I associated Joginder's family with the British, I'm afraid. Like everybody the British touched, they too had been spoiled, robbed of their certainty . . .'

'You really believe that?' asked Anthony incredulously.

Henshaw didn't answer at once. Then he said, 'My ideals foundered upon a woman, inevitably. Premla. That led to Richard's death, and the rest of the compromises. That vision I had of a true partnership between some of us and the Indians disintegrated into mercenary arrangements with that brigand Feroze, and with Anwar and Mac. But still, I thought, even when I met with Savarkar in Mysore, if Jinnah was disposed of then Partition would be averted and we could try again.' A thought seemed to strike him, and he looked up at Anthony. 'It was only later when I realized that Vincent had kept his word, had not told you that I was in Mysore, that I found my honest man in a place that I had not looked. But it was too late. He had been killed colliding with an ox-cart dragging a load of provisions I had arranged for delivery to Savarkar. It was then, really, that I felt defeated finally.'

Behind Anthony the candles had gone out. He felt drained, exhausted, but through everything he felt the pressure of what had to be done. There was no future, no past. Only in the darkness some mysterious balance was being struck, out of time and divorced from these surreal surroundings, the moon-bled landscape, the dark vacant house, the sleeping woman who had cried out in her despairing sleep. The pity that he still felt, looking across at the slumped figure, blurred the sharp judgements with which he had started, the black and white, right and wrong perceptions of a child. There was some misogynistic sympathy in him, smiling crookedly at a picture of Arline as he remembered her, and saying, almost, 'I understand about the women,' but he knew that was unfair. That his own antipathy towards Arline alone could not equate with Henshaw's mad perception that women had been his downfall. In his mind the sensation of an equal balance remained, but there was yet one subject which had not been touched upon.

'And Jane,' he said. 'That carried on even after we were married, didn't it?' Already his mind shrank from the answer, and he felt an urge to run and hide, blocking his ears like a child against the response he dreaded.

Henshaw looked up at him and then at the gun, as though it was the first time he had seen it. The moonlight refused to give definition to the face, but Anthony fancied that Henshaw was smiling then with some secret knowledge. 'Oh yes,' he said. 'But even most of that was to get somehow closer to you, to feel some sense of sharing something with you. Her mother, her sisters knew . . . ?' he said then, an interrogative afterthought.

Roger stood up. Something appeared to have restored his vitality and he seemed, again, to possess the huge presence which Anthony had remembered. Anthony picked up the gun and Henshaw laughed, stretching out his hand to show that he had not intended to threaten.

'Now that all is lost, let me help you towards accomplishing what you came for. After all, it's twenty years since I took confession and they turned the candles upside down for me years ago.'

Anthony stood up and said, 'Stop. I don't want to hear anything more,' pointing the revolver at Henshaw's chest with both hands.

He willed himself to fire, but his finger refused to obey.

Henshaw spoke with massive indifference. 'Do you think that worries me? The number of times I have sat out here and heard Margaret mourning Richard's death and known that she suspected and could not forgive me. The number of times I have sat with Anwar and Feroze and felt my dream die, little by little, before the greed in their faces. The number of false reports I have compiled in the belief that the ends justified the means – even when I knew that the ends no longer were attainable. There is nothing left for me, now.' He sat down again on the chair, turning it so that the back was towards Anthony.

'The last thing, then,' he said. 'Circumstantial evidence again, so we deal only with the balance of probabilities. You will recall that you took a long leave and went to Delhi to try to appeal to be released so that you could volunteer for war service?' He looked across at Anthony a moment, before resuming. 'You will recollect that your daughter had gone to stay with her grandparents briefly, and Jane had said she would pay a visit to some friends in Peshawar. Instead, she came to me . . .' He leaned forward in the chair, looking out beyond the verandah. 'I have no reason to doubt what Jane has told me. That Mark is my son.'

Anthony screamed, 'No! No!' and fired. The figure in the chair jerked spasmodically, and he fired again. This time the shot ricocheted off the far wall, and sang into the trees. He put the gun down blindly, suddenly unable to see clearly. His chest hurt and he gulped at the air feverishly. He heard Henshaw's guttural, pain-ridden voice say, 'Do it properly, old man,' but he lurched on unsteady legs to the verandah edge and leaned against a pillar. As he vomited on the gravel he heard the voice say, 'Oh, please, please,' but he stumbled down the steps and round the front of the house, moving by instinct. One step in front of another. He dared not think.

He was almost at the jeep when he heard the shot and looking back he saw a light come on, illuminating the tracery of black branches.

There was no returning, ever. He drove for hours, using the old roads. When the dawn had begun to strip the darkness away from the sky he had crossed the great open valley, and the peaks towered above, like crinkled paper in the early light. The path became steeper, the mud rutted with iron-hard ox-cart tracks. Driving upwards his head began to ache, and the engine started to misfire. It was becoming harder to breathe in the rarified air.

He stopped by a stream under a great escarpment of rock in which small shrubs clung tenaciously, and washed his face. Hundreds of feet above, a cataract spouted from the sheer black rocks, and the muted roar came faintly to his ears. The jeep would not start. The starter motor whined plaintively, slower and slower and then stopped. He got out and began to walk, picking his way over the rocks. Below him the abandoned jeep slowly assumed the proportions of a toy. He looked back once before the massive contour of the hill hid it from sight. It took him an hour to traverse the shaled rock and reach the snow-line. Here light cloud shrouded the view, eddying and drifting in response to the wind. He felt dizzy and his chest hurt. Unbidden, a memory of his father reciting Macaulay came to him, and he spoke the words to himself, suiting his steps to the beat.

> 'But hark! the cry is Astur.
> And lo! The ranks divide.
> And the great Lord of Luna
> Comes with his stately stride.
> Around his ample shoulders
> Clangs loud the fourfold shield,
> And in his hand he shakes the brand
> Which none but he can wield.'

A pause. He thought he could remember one more verse. He began walking again.

> 'He smiled on those proud Romans,
> A smile serene and high.
> He eyed the flinching Tuscans,
> And scorn was in his eye.
> Quoth he: "The She-Wolf's litter
> Stands savagely at bay,
> But will ye dare to follow
> If Astur clears the way?"'

He remembered no more. He could see his father reading from the book, with an upraised forefinger to emphasize the metre. The memory faded. His mind wandered as he kept steadily on. Everything that had happened possessed the distance of a dream. Yes, he loved his family. Mac, too. And the dead: Vincent, Andrew. Everything was circumstantial, after all. He walked on. The snow was thicker now, powdery on the surface and crisp below. After a while it seemed that someone had joined him. When he turned to look, it seemed that the figure by his side had no face, and when he looked down there were no other footmarks but his

365

own in the snow. But he was not concerned. They walked on together into the white snow. Into the white snow.

Like all unsolved mysteries, it was, at first, the subject of gossip and rumour on the cocktail circuit, running the entire spectrum of comment. 'It's rumoured he had a married lady in Peshawar and her husband found out,' Jillie Morgan told a distraught Diana Fairfax. At the other end of the scale Dr Mac, owlishly drunk over post-dinner brandies one night, confided to an equally drunk Parsons, 'He had taken three major tragedies in one year – Vincent, Andrew, Gur – all dead before their time – and God knows what else. He was a man who gave the impression of coping at whatever cost to himself.' He poured some more brandy with exaggerated care, dripping it down his safari suit. 'Oh, fuck!' he said, dabbing ineffectively with a handkerchief at the stain before resuming sententiously, 'Sometimes the string breaks and the next crisis – whoosh!' He made a violent gesture with his hands, and Parsons nodded. Mac could always be relied upon to come up with the right explanation.

In time it became the stuff of legend. Sightings were reported in the hills of two lepers who, miraculously clad only in loincloths despite the killing cold, begged for their living in the string of villages and hamlets straggling upon the lower slopes of the Himalayas, imparting folk wisdom and prophecy in return. They had always left for some unknown destination just a few hours before, whenever a European traveller enquired, and the evidence of their stay was slight. A few charcoal twigs in the dead ash of a fire on waste ground where they had squatted with the village elders. A few footprints still crisp in the snow. Nothing of import.

Mysore, South India: 1949

Fifty

It was 1949. The Great Soul of India was dead, cut down by a Hindu fanatic's bullet. The Quaid-e-Azam, his body wasted by the ravages of disease, his huge intake of whisky, and chain-smoking, was also dead. In Hindustan a new process of 'Indianization' had begun. In long-established East India companies, this often meant the effective demotion of long-serving British personnel, now technically 'supporting' the decisions of their inexperienced new replacements. Many of the new politicians in both Hindustan and Pakistan were discovering that their new positions gave them access to substantial extra funds; for endorsing contracts, for agreeing to commend a relative in the Lok Sabha, for turning a blind eye. The feudal symbiosis of the great estates of the Nizams and the Maharajahs had fallen into decline. The fierce new spirit of independent nationalism would have no truck with the slaveries of the past. The land disputes resulting from Partition, many of which would drag on for decades, had begun their progress through the courts. The estimates of the Civil War dead varied according to the political persuasion of the source of the statistics. Everywhere the British were reviled; in Mysore and Bangalore shopkeepers in European dress talked to each other in singsong English, whilst their shops displayed the stern notice, *British Quit India*. In Rawalpindi mobs of goondas systematically raided the hallowed bastions of Colonial

India, the racecourse, the Polo Club, and drove home the same message with stones and lathis. In the outlying regions of the Punjab the new government was offering armed guards to those colonial administrators reckoned to be vital to the establishment of the new heaven upon earth.

In Mysore, Mark had done his entrance examination to his father's old school in Somerset. The Freemasons were paying his fees. When the papers came in he had looked at them with total incomprehension: calculus, Latin, Greek. But, as it happened, Rod's attempts to explain calculus and the complexities of Latin syntax bore such a close example to the set papers that he was able to answer the questions with a degree of accuracy.

He felt his stomach contract with fear whenever he tried to imagine going to school in England. The very idea of England itself, apostrophized sentimentally as 'Home' by so many acquaintances with that certain faraway look in their eyes, had no stable reality for him. He had amassed a vague assemblage of clichés from adult conversations, from magazines, which suggested it would be green, grey-skied and wet, and possessed of a culture and heritage which were undeniably superior to any other.

The confirmation of Anthony's disappearance had come just after Rod had returned from hospital. The protracted separation had muted the effect of the news on Jane, as though this were merely an official confirmation of a state of affairs which had commenced long before, when Anthony had made the choice to leave his family behind (she always thought of it thus) and return to the North. To friends it was given out that his duties demanded he remain in the North for the foreseeable future, and was reluctant for his family to join him until it was safer. Bulstrode-Henshaw, with rare tact (and much admonishing of Daisy to curb her instinct for gossip) never referred to the small article he had found in the *Rawalpindi Times* left by a visitor, detailing the mysterious death of Roger Henshaw and, in a paragraph juxtaposed in such a way as to suggest some connection, the disappearance of Anthony Hodder. In response to his letter as a 'concerned relative', written at Daisy's relentless prompting, a Mr Parsons had sent him a copy of a report compiled by a High Commissioner of Police, Anwar Khan, which said that there had been no eye witnesses to the tragedy, but circumstantial evidence suggested that Roger Henshaw had given his life while heroically protecting his property against some unknown assailant.

Sometimes Mark saw his mother's face assume the vacant and distracted air which he associated with her thinking about his father, or heard his mother's rhetorical questions, superficially addressed to one of her sisters, but part of some continuing angry dialogue with Anthony. 'Why did he do it, why, why?' There was no explanation, no body, no end. Only vague conjecture, unsupported rumour, and the torment of uncertainty.

Anne rarely went out, spending whole days behind the lace curtains of her bedroom. The soft bloom which had caught Vincent's breath on the night of the dance had gone. She had the listlessness, the sallow, seamed skin of a careless woman twice her age. Young William was swamped by a flock of great aunts, grandmother, great grandmother, all eager to colonize him into some acceptable image. He was dressed in pink, and his pale brown hair was allowed to grow into ringlets. Arline would take him out in his pram with Angela or Jane, wheeling him down to the shops under a flowered parasol. Sometimes Patricia would take him out, play acting the part of his mother with a strange, hungry possessiveness, or would come downstairs red-eyed and sniffing when she had spent some time with him in the bedroom. The story, retailed with varying degrees of disbelief, was that Anne had met and married a young Cornish officer who had been decorated in the Chindit campaign, only to be posted to the Khyber and killed in some border incident.

Once Nathoo had walked to their gate to watch the baby go by, and had then returned to sit by Indijeet on the verandah, his usually cheerful face uncharacteristically solemn and depressed. 'It is absurd. He is our grandson too. I must try to talk to Mrs Porter.' But Indijeet had said, 'Hush, my rajah,' laying her hand upon him with such a lascivious look that he forgot everything. Later, lying in bed by her side, he reflected upon the vagaries of women. 'I will never, never understand how they work,' he said to himself, lying naked on the coverlet with his hands behind his head. But, though he sometimes stood at the gate when William was taken past, he never greeted Arline or her family, nor ever attempted to approach them in any way.

With three weeks to go before he left for England Mark already felt the loss of impending separation from the house and his family. He sat with Rod that hot afternoon on the patio. Rod had been told that he had cirrhosis, and that another drink would kill him. Most of the time he was quite lucid with an occasional strange dark humour which would twist his normally gentle mouth. Sometimes he would seem seized by a mad gaiety, and his laughter would be loud and tinged with hysteria and his gestures exaggerated. Today was one of the better days. Sam had brought out glasses of chilled barley water, and they sat all three together on the step of the patio behind the house, idly talking. The house was empty. Arline had gone to the market with Jane and Patricia, and Angela had taken Anne and William to the hospital en route to her by now well-known tryst in Major Majid's bed.

When the crow jumped expectantly down from the wall, stretching first one wing and then the other over alternate legs with luxuriant gestures, Mark bent down and picked up a stone without thinking, throwing it in the air and catching it. He was suddenly aware that both his uncle and Sam were looking at him with an unusual intensity, willing him to do something, and he looked back at Sam with a puzzled enquiring smile. When Sam looked at the bird and then back at him, Mark suddenly remembered the death of the snake, and then Arline saying to his mother, 'You're better off without him, dear. They're of no use beyond the getting of children.' He stood up and poised himself on the balls of his feet, taking careful aim. The stone hit William and the bird thrashed around on the ground moving in broken circles. He took the neck between his hands and twisted sharply, throwing the limp body into the dust by the wall. He felt as he had when he told them about Anne. Powerful, exultant, but somehow sad. When he looked back Sam had his hand over his mouth, and Rod looked shrunken, afraid.

He felt old and alone, and again the sense of having done something important whose reverberations would continue far into the future. 'Don't you remember, uncle? Be Thou like th'Imperial Basilisk, killing Thy foe with unapparent wounds . . . Don't you remember?' But they sat and looked at him without comprehension, and he said to himself, 'And now the cycle begins anew,' without having any precise idea of what he meant.

Susan: 1985

Fifty-one

Susan began to pack for the holiday. She remembered that Miranda Carew had telephoned to cancel dinner: something, according to Mark's vague message, about Andrew reaching the climacteric. She mused over the items on the bed. Two books by Yukio Mishima. A guidebook open at a page showing Nagasaki after the bomb had fallen. She made a mental note to cross *that* off the itinerary. There were clothes on hangers, neat piles of ties, socks rolled one into the other, shirts, silk slips, dresses, pyjamas.

Outside, the engine of the motor mower fired and she walked to the window to watch Mark climb on to the seat and begin the long, sloping traverse of the lawns down to the lake. He was wearing a white canvas hat and his grey gardening flannels, stained with oil and creosote. The willows, the laburnum sporting its long, yellow ringlets, stood in brilliant sunlight against a slate-grey sky. She loved this view of the garden. There had been no order when they first bought the house: couch grass, sedge, the rambling fruit trees which had long outgrown their strength, the golden rod choked with white convolvulus, taking the eye down to the lake where rusted iron poked brown shapes above the surface. And now: the lawns striped neatly down to the lake's edge, bordered by the brilliantly coloured marigolds, poppies, and geraniums sat in deep beds at the sides. The small walled kitchen garden was neatly packed with beans, tomatoes, courgettes, onions, and an asparagus bed. Mark began his traverse back from the lake towards the patio and she waved at him. He couldn't see her through the glass, and drove steadily on, carefully keeping the edge of the mower against the previous cut. She smiled to herself, thinking that he looked like a figure in a Manet painting.

She set the ironing board up and began to iron abstractedly, thinking about the holiday. She wondered, briefly, if she had been wise to insist they went, based purely on Mollie's and John's enthusiasm. They had brought back some beautiful things: splendid lacquered bowls, two exquisite kimonos. A depressing thought suddenly visited her – that these holidays, represented some empty hint of desperation. That, in part, they reflected some search for status, some indication of advancing age and increasing earnings, some competition with their contemporaries which became less satisfying and more irrelevant as time passed. In another, and no less sinister, aspect they seemed to represent some hungry desire to see as much as possible before night came. Night, that friendly euphemism, had begun to loom large in her thoughts of late. She remembered (without pleasure at the contrast) the times when it was always Alicante or the Balearics. Dreadful food and a crying child who hated the sun. She had forgotten, until she looked through the album, two days before, that she had had at least two swimsuits per holiday – and the figure to wear them.

In the garden the mower engine misfired and stopped, and she heard the faint sound of Mark's curse. The direction of her thoughts changed as she carried on ironing mechanically. She worried about Mark, still unable, after all these years, to reach a clear, comfortable definition of him. She no longer suspected another woman, though she had had her suspicions a year before. Ironing the collar of one of his shirts with sudden venom, she remembered how she used to turn up unexpectedly at his Chambers, half curious, half terrified. Looking, as unobtrusively as possible, for a smudge of lipstick or a hair on his lapel. He was so other-worldly that he didn't notice a thing. For herself, she had felt guiltily glad when he had stopped being quite so amorous, if one could use such a word for his fumbling advances. All that panting and heaving didn't seem an appropriate activity at their age. No, it must be something else. In the garden the engine fired again, checked, and then ran on. She turned the iron down and left it to cool before she started to iron the silk blouses.

Arms folded, she stood at the window. The iron clicked tinnily as it cooled. A 'plane rumbled above the house and the windows rattled briefly. She remembered the dinner party they had given for Andrew and Miranda Carew a couple of weeks previously to celebrate his appointment as a Judge. Mark had been in a poisonous mood as he moved around the bedroom dressing for dinner. Acid, quite unlike himself. When she had reminded him of his long friendship with Andrew he had hinted darkly that friendship, like all relationships, was a variable state that had to be constantly monitored and adjusted, and that Andrew had done them both some disservice in the past. She didn't know to what he was referring, and she had the uneasy feeling that his comments were a veiled reference to their own marriage.

She picked up a silk blouse, and began to iron again. She remembered her own shock when Miranda had leant across the table and said, with no effort at concealment, 'I've trained him well, haven't I?' Miranda's open contempt for Andrew was both fascinating and horrifying.

The mower's engine coughed and then stopped again. Susan watched Mark go into the shed and emerge looking grimly purposeful with a spanner in his hand. The surface of the lake was roughened by wind, and the ducklings bobbed like small boats behind their mother. The silk under her hand had puckered where the iron had caught it, and she held it up to the light. It was acceptably hidden. She sucked her finger and dabbed it against the iron to test the heat.

It was the visit to Pakistan which had started this process of dissolution. Afterwards she had blamed herself, knowing that her opposition to the trip would have been enough to prevent it. It was only when Mark arrived back at the hotel in Murree, after going off on his own, that she had realized that something was wrong. He had suddenly become even more withdrawn, uncommunicative, impenetrable. She smiled to herself, recalling that she was packing then, too, mechanically sorting their clothing for the tour while she thought of ways to frame her questions. With surprise she realized that she hadn't really wanted to know the answers; only to restore equilibrium.

After that there had been his mother's death and that terrible funeral, with the sister clad in black who had looked over Susan's shoulder with wintry eyes while they were introduced, and whose hand had been as cold as death. That strange half-caste pouf who hadn't been introduced to anyone. She remembered that Anne had called him William. It was the first time she had really realized how little she knew about Mark and his family. She had come to terms with that, realizing that she would never know: it was idle to speculate about what had happened between Mark and Anne, or what had happened to their father. She had always felt oppressed by the mysteries of Mark's past, and had put it out of her thoughts as much as possible.

Behind the window, yellow smoke billowed into the air. Susan clicked her tongue against her teeth, half-angry, half-amused. In a minute, she knew, he would go into the shed for some paraffin, afraid of what she would say about the smoke. Mark looked over his shoulder at the window before going into the shed and returning with the paraffin container, and Susan laughed to herself, without humour, turning back to iron another garment from the decreasing pile of clothes.

The snake and mynah bird were from that period, she remembered. Her hands smoothed the garments expertly, without thought. Facetiously she thought, Thank God common sense had prevailed before they became a wild-life park. Mark wasn't a man with whom one could joke about such things. He had accepted that she wouldn't have anything to do with the snake or the mynah. He and Mrs H. shared the feeding and cleaning out. Susan could have understood a doberman or a labrador. At least it would have served some useful function.

She stopped ironing for a moment and held her hands to the small of her back, swaying from the waist to ease her stiffness. She remembered her mother's hands, distorted by arthritis, and held her own hands out for a cursory inspection, as she had done hundreds of times before. But her thoughts were really elsewhere. She glanced out of the window to see that Mark was moving down the lawn on the mower again. From the pocket of her black suit hanging behind the door she took out the letter and began to reread it, trying to piece together the contents. It had arrived several days before, postmarked Rawalpindi, and addressed to Mark. It had lain on the salver in the hall awaiting his return for almost the entire day, before her memories of the trip to Pakistan persuaded her to open it. The address at the top was The Department of Geriatric Psychiatry, Hospital of Mary and Joseph, Rawalpindi, and the writing was very shaky, almost impossible to read. Susan had hidden it in her handbag.

It was from a Mr Parsons, and it had been forwarded on from Mark's old public school. (Again Susan made a mental note to renew his subscription. He never remembered.) It was hard to give much credence to the rambling contents. Mr Parsons had deliberated for ten years before writing. He must be even less decisive than Mark, she thought! Anyway, Mr Parsons had, it appeared, fulfilled a life-long wish in taking his wife for a holiday in Tibet. The letter began very emotionally. His wife had fallen ill during the holiday, and had died soon after their return.

It was a strange feeling to read the letter, like a partially sighted person attempting a complicated jigsaw puzzle. As she reread it, one part of her mind was recalling names Mark had mentioned. Her conviction that she must not let Mark see the letter strengthened. Despite his legal training and his innate scepticism, she felt sure that he would not give sufficient weight to the fact that Parsons was undeniably suffering from delusions. To her mind, at least. She read on.

The narrative told how Parsons had left his wife on her own one morning and had decided to walk, without a guide, up to a monastery on the crag dominating a Tibetan village. He found it a relief to get away from the village, full of long-haired bearded young Americans and girls in vulgarized ethnic dresses.

Once on the mountainside he felt an enormous sense of peace to be on his own, and it was some time before he realized that his goal was much further than he had thought. The steep path was in a terrible state, overgrown with briars and half washed away by the rains. He was sitting by the verge with his shoes off, massaging his swollen feet, when a Holy Man appeared, clad only in a loin cloth, and carrying a staff and a begging bowl. He had advanced leprosy and the scales gave him a silver, ghostly appearance. His eyes, Parsons had written, seemed 'ferociously, demonically alive'. Though his hair and beard were white he carried himself like a young man. To Parsons' surprise this apparition offered in faultless English to guide him to the monastery, and they proceeded on their way in silence.

From time to time the Saddhu stood patiently and waited for Parsons to catch up. He was an old man and in the rarefied air his lungs felt raw. He found he was having difficulty with his vision. When they arrived at the monastery, some time before noon, he found he was famished.

Three monks came out to greet them across the great, tessellated Outer Courtyard, shaven-headed and saffron-robed, bearing figs and honey as though they expected the visit. Parsons had sat on a wall overlooking the valley, with a sheer drop of one thousand feet below, to eat to the tinkling chime of prayer bells from the Inner Courtyard. A young novice of fifteen or sixteen brought him a bowl of icy, pure water to wash his hands.

Mark shouted something from the garden and Susan put the letter on the bed and went to the window. He waved the shears in his hand and pointed to the willow. Susan raised the window and leant out, calling, 'Yes, but not too drastically,' concealing her irritation that he was starting to clip the willow before he had finished mowing the lawn. She ducked back into the room, pulling the window shut, and picked up the letter again.

378

After Parsons had eaten, the most incredible thing had happened. The Saddhu had been sitting with his legs crossed and his forearms resting on his knees, palms open to the sky. (Parsons had felt ashamed to be eating with such a good appetite in the face of the other man's abstinence.) The Saddhu had got to his feet and beckoned Parsons to follow him. By this time (he pointed out with some diffidence), the thin air had affected him and he felt a little unreal. He followed his guide across the huge courtyard and through a long cloister and into a sunlight-bathed courtyard open to the mountains on two sides. Several monks walked past, going about their duties as if the two of them were not there, and this reinforced Parsons' feeling of unreality. 'Truly, I was in the frame of mind to see visions,' he said in the letter.

At the far end of the courtyard was a stone enclosure like an open bandbox, built into the wall so that it overhung the valley. A monk sat there, with a roll of parchment between two sticks on the table before him. As they approached Parsons could see that he, too, had been ravaged by leprosy. His features had dissolved so that their definition was lost, and the fingers of both hands had 'rotted away'. To Parsons' surprise (since he had vouchsafed no information about himself), his guide introduced him to the silent figure as a visitor from Rawalpindi.

He felt too shy to question the monk. ('The odour of sanctity is the best deterrent against would-be detectives.') The leprosy, too, conferred some mystical, noumenal quality which reinforced his sensation of being a pupil before a master. But Parsons was amazed by the questions the monk asked. His voice was sibilant through the ragged tear of mouth, and the questions had the dispassionate flavour of a merely intellectual curiosity. He nodded from time to time as Parsons gave him news of the outside world.

The monk vouchsafed no information about himself, and Parsons eventually stole a glance at his watch, a little worried about the long trek back down to the village. Immediately his guide stood up and said something like, 'Are you now released from the Great Wheel?' But the monk said nothing, merely lifting his hand in a gesture of farewell.

Parsons wrote that the question had been on his mind from the moment the monk had started to talk, but he hadn't dared to ask. On the way down, emboldened by the proximity of the village thronged with tourists and bazaars, he asked, 'Was that Anthony Hodder?' But the Saddhu gave no indication of having heard. At the Yogi's Grave, above the village, he had stopped and indicated the path down. All he said, before turning to leave, was, 'He is at peace now, having attained that estate where the demands of this world trouble him no longer.'

Susan folded the letter and put it back in the pocket of her suit. She looked out of the window. Well, she thought, the willow will probably recover in time if it is left alone. She took the letter out and read the last few paragraphs again. Parsons had felt guilty about the delay but he, too, had hesitated to reopen the past. In any case, she was now convinced that this was the senile fantasy of an old, grief-stricken man. It was probably her conscience pricking but she had thought Mark oddly sharp when he had asked if there were any post for him the previous evening. But she knew Mark. If he read the letter, it would only bring about another long period of introspection, without any resolution. Thank goodness their son, Andrew, seemed to have developed a much more active view of things. 'You only go through once, Mother,' he had said seriously when she had made a moue of mock-amazement at his busy schedule. He would be at Tennis School while they were in Japan. He certainly was no genius, she reflected ruefully. But, with the way things were going these days, if he concentrated on his sport he could keep them in their old age.

She thought, Is it wrong that I try to protect Mark from what I feel may harm him? Surely that is the duty in care we all owe each other? She turned off the iron and folded the ironing board. She rechecked the ironed garments against her list, ticking the items off, one by one. She remembered that there were two coffee mornings before they left. One for the lepers of India, by curious coincidence. And one of Mollie's terrible bring-and-buy sales for a local hospice. And so we shore up the ruin, she thought, with a sudden, sharp hunger for something more. She remembered the things she had found in the attic which were just saleable. Some old furniture which had been in store for years, a teddy bear, some dolls. There was an old tin full of Mark's schoolboy treasures: letters, a few feathers, some used cartridges. She hadn't thrown it out before, knowing how he hoarded the most unlikely things.

Later she went down to the bonfire. The smell of paraffin hung heavily in the air. Mark had finished the lawn, and was putting the mower away. She stood between the incinerator and the shed and dropped the letter into the glowing centre of the fire, watching it burn.

Mark: 1985

Fifty-two

My forties have been full of altered perceptions. It is surprising that a few twists of focus have changed, made uncertain, my entire life. I thought I had built firmly and the shaky foundation stones no longer mattered. That certainly seemed so in my thirties. Perhaps these new feelings are the inevitable companions to growing older, the hidden concomitants of dimming eyes and arthritic joints, the true partners of this long new life we now enjoy. Perhaps, too, returning to Pakistan was a catalyst, insidiously bleaching the vivid colours of these earlier years to these sere shades of grey and white – introducing a seemingly unending cycle of uncertainty and self-doubt.

At first, while I was there, I thought that facts were important, could provide some approximations to the truth. From the villagers I had learned that Feroze Khan was now the biggest landowner for miles around having acquired the major part of Joginder Singh's estates. He was now a much respected member of society, though many of the older people remembered him as having been a wild youth. Anwar was now Commissioner of Police. He was having to take things quietly following a stroke suffered while fishing for mahseer with Feroze Khan. Mr Malik's wife, I had later discovered, was Premla Purveys, and together they had brought up the mongol son to whom she had given birth after Richard Reeves' death. Joginder and Sita had lost all their money and retired to live with a cousin of hers in Lahore. Dr Mac had been killed in a riding accident. And there were other facts, too.

But by then I had realized that the facts held nothing. I lacked the experiences, the perspectives, the first-hand knowledge of relationships which could fashion these into a cohesive whole. And there, so far as I can place it, began my dissatisfaction with the bare, mechanical data upon which so much of the trade of my life has rested. That visit to Pakistan began the process of questioning, the search for meaning which appears to preoccupy so many of us in these middle years. A few years ago the important questions were what car we should buy; where should we go on holiday; what did we think of the siting of Cruise Missiles on British soil? I thought I had laid aside, even escaped, the great philosophical unknowns which now gnaw at me, standing like the Eumenides at the bottom of our bed, coming between me and sleep each night. What is the meaning of existence? Why are we here? Is there a God? These absurd questions have unfairly returned me to a realm of unappeasable hunger. Even as our material wants were finally solved or, at least, ameliorated (the holiday home in the Lake District, the second car, the steady rise through my profession, the exotic holiday in Japan) those twists of focus have rendered all these material comforts unimportant. And I am reminded, persistently and constantly, that we are only temporary occupants of these tenements of clay.

I sense a kind of bewildered despair in Susan sometimes. We cannot speak of it, but I surmise she feels, as I do, a dismay that the achievements of the goals we set ourselves when we first married has not brought fulfilment. That this baffling hunger is never satisfied but, rather, grows sharper. That the new goals are more nebulous and as distant as ever before. In part it is to do with the devaluing of oneself, one's own achievements.

I used to think, in my thirties, that she was the true inheritor of my grandmother, in the fashionably accept-able guise of modern liberation. That she was seeking to exact payment from me for some general perception of the wrong that men are purported to have done women over the years. Now I see that she and I, both, have castrated each other in the way specific to some couples whose relationship, based on a fear of loneliness and an inability to find the words to part, has ossified into a rigid structure. The areas about which conversation is imposs-ible have spread ever wider with the passage of time. Inevitably, as they are those vulnerable areas in which each of us exists most profoundly, our exchanges about trivia have a threadbare apathy about them. Silently we blame each other for the small, everyday disappoint-ments, as well as for the greater disasters. And we are prone to belittle each other (in the acceptable guise of good humoured badinage) and to triumph secretly over each other in adversity, while showing an outwardly compassionate concern. And there are other things: I cut the willow knowing that Susan will not approve; I light the bonfires to dare her displeasure. Yet, though these reflections might suggest a sense of bitterness, that is not the case. I recognize my part in these silences, in this desert of level sand we now inhabit, which stretches to the horizon under a pitiless sky.

Obviously Susan thought I hadn't read the letter. I saw her burn it, too, interposing her body between me and the fire. Was she trying to protect me? Or again attempt-ing to submit my life to *her* control, *her* order?

Alerted to the existence of *something* by an indefinable

384

nuance of her manner, I did an uncharacteristic act of which I am still ashamed: I looked through her handbag and, like a guilty schoolboy, took Parsons' letter to the bathroom to read. At first I had no difficulty in dismissing the narrative as the disjointed ramblings of an old man. Running the bath taps to add local colour and pulling the lavatory chain once, I sat on the edge of the bath to read. Curiously enough it was the news of the Saddhu – the most unlikely and ephemeral constituent of the whole scenario – that nagged at my mind with some sort of truth.

Two weeks before we left for Japan, Miranda Carew called to cancel a dinner party to which she had invited us. 'Andrew's a bit under the weather. We'll make another date when you get back,' she said with that absolute assurance I found so formidable at close quarters. It was nothing specific. She'd arranged for him to have a complete check-up. 'It's the climacteric – your version of the menopause. That's all,' she volunteered before ringing off. I felt reprieved. It had seemed to me that Andrew was taking the importance of his new appointment over-seriously.

Four days after our return she telephoned again. In the midst of my shock I felt the strange sensation of pitying someone I disliked very much. Andrew had suffered a heart attack after lunch, and was not expected to live. As his closest friend would I accompany her to the hospital? I was touched by the sound of tears in her voice.

Nevertheless, Susan had good cause to reproach me for my levity when I told her: the fact was that I couldn't, at first, take the news seriously. The mind's defence, I suppose. Divorces, affairs, even paternity suits were acceptable in one's forties – instantly provoking both belief and an appropriate response. I told myself, as I settled behind the wheel, that the Grim Reaper was far too busy culling the starving heartlands of Africa, or the teeming crop of geriatric homes which had been spawned round the Home Counties, to step aside for a squash-playing Circuit Judge. But the look on Miranda's face when she opened the door to let me in from the pelting rain was enough. Anything that could turn her into this tremulous and weepy woman must be serious.

It was Miranda's anger that struck me most as we sat in a traffic jam on our way to the hospital. It was as though Andrew had deliberately done something against the rules: as though, in fact, he had deliberately engineered this heart attack solely to expose her inability to control every aspect of their lives. But, in the clinical bustle of the emergency admissions ward, I was, once again, visited by pity for her. She sat with her hands folded on her lap, and I noticed, where her stocking had laddered, a distended blue vein marbled her calf. There was a smudge of powder on her collar, too.

At Andrew's bedside I was suddenly confronted with a different order of experience. By the side of many of the beds in the ward stood the paraphernalia of sickness: drips, television screens upon which a dancing dot endlessly repeated its journey from right to left of the screen, catheter bags hung from the iron-framed bedsides. And, looking round the ward as I walked in, I was struck by the anonymity conferred by impending death. The trappings of office, the medals of achievement, had all been taken away. A wrinkled, bald, brown-faced man smiled at me with a ghastly, ferocious hunger. On his bedside, a set of false teeth in a pink solution grinned through a glass. He held up his plastic bottle towards a young trainee nurse. 'Nurse. Nurse. It's full . . .' There was something obscene in the childlike satisfaction in the cultured voice. 'All right, then,' she said, as if to humour him.

I remembered reading Gray's *Elegy* and *The Rubaiyat* at school. I remembered, too, reading Donne's sermon, and the poem in which he sees his body as a map of the world, and reflects upon his death – 'per fretum febris, by these streights to die'. And now I saw that they had ennobled death, had robbed it of one great reality. Miranda and I faced each other on either side of Andrew's bed for the best part of three days and nights. And what struck me then, and remains with me still, is the threadbare banality of the experience. That, viewed as an event, it is nothing at all.

At the beginning Andrew had occasional moments of consciousness. I, who had only ever shaken him formally by the hand, and had kept my affection at the acceptable distance prescribed by social conventions, now sat with his hand in mine as he smiled at me and said, 'My friend, I'm glad you're here,' before he fell asleep instantly, a child once more.

When he tossed restlessly, and his forehead felt hot under my hand, I ran a flannel under the tap, and bathed his head and face. When he cried out once, looking past my shoulder with unseeing eyes, I comforted him as I had comforted our son as a baby. Over the days I saw the volume of the urine in the catheter bag decrease, changing from a clear golden to a muddy brown. On the first evening, a young houseman came and looked at the notes, saying nothing. Miranda leaned forward in her chair, looking at him intensely, with her mouth slightly parted, but he avoided her eyes and went away. Each time Andrew's eyes opened I saw her lean forward expectantly. Sometimes she would whisper to me about how she would make him cut down on his work. 'After all, we've got enough money to buy a little place in the sun and live simply . . . ?' It was a question, really, and my courage would fail so I could not say the words in my mind.

Often she would say, 'Shall we sit him up?' and we would take him under the arms and drag him up the bed. It was a comfort to be so close to him, to feel that we could do something. But by the second day I saw how hard he breathed after we had lifted him, and watched the colour of his lips change from a clear pink to a cyanosed purple, and I said to Miranda, 'He's more comfortable as he is. Let him be.'

Like a ragged chorus, preparing us for the future, there were twelve deaths in the ward over that period. Some to the accompaniment of the muffled sobbing of attendant relatives; some alone and unattended in the dark hours of the night, paged out only by the high pitched scream of the redundant heart monitor. It may have been tiredness, or the ever-present reminders of mortality, but I felt closer to Miranda over those days and nights. There had even been the bizarre intimacy of snatching a few hours sleep on the floor of the tobacco-fugged nurses' rest room while she slept on the sofa. But now she began to talk of getting Andrew moved to a private ward. 'There is no dignity here,' she said by way of explanation, and I was struck by the incongruity of it. There is no dignity when you face the Absolute (for that is now, after all, a tenet of my wavering belief), only some absorbing struggle at some level far beyond the reach of medical skills. She was thinking of herself, the Judge's wife, I suspected, though I could not altogether blame her for climbing back towards the light and to familiar preoccupations from the dark and vicious places we had now shared, so far as we were able, with Andrew. I only said reprovingly, 'The cost of purchasing dignity will be the shortening of his life,' and felt ashamed, watching her face fall.

On the first day, despite the medical prognosis, I had willed him to live. Now, on the third day, I found myself wishing that he would die. Before my eyes all that made him familiar – the shifting musculature of his face, the expression in his eyes as he formed a response, the careless gesture of a hand to emphasize a point, everything that had been the outward show of my friend over the years I had known him – had disappeared. It was like watching the removal men dispossessing a loved house of the furnishings and objects which had created its familiarity, its warmth, its security.

On the third evening the Staff Nurse told me that he could remain in this state for weeks, and I persuaded Miranda that we should take a few hours off. Andrew's eyes were open when I leaned down to tell him we'd be back. He held my hand quite strongly for a few moments and said, 'I'm not frightened, Mark. I love you.' Still, even then, I could not say it. I concentrated hard on the faces passing us as I took Miranda by the arm and walked her down the long corridor out to the car park. He had come back after all, if only for a moment.

Miranda telephoned me at my Chambers at ten o'clock the following morning. She sounded curiously unlike herself when she said, 'He is at rest now with his Maker.' The cliché phrase, so often used to distance the terrible intimacy of death, sounded oddly vulnerable coming from her. The mouthpiece of the 'phone seemed grimy. I said, 'I'll take you in to collect his things, and perhaps we can see him together for the last time?'

Winter's hand had stripped the chestnuts of their plumage. The wind plucked fiercely at our clothes as we walked to the entrance. The Staff Nurse who had told us that Andrew might survive for weeks met us. 'I'm sorry,' she said, and Miranda stopped her from saying anything further. Formally she said, 'I'd like to thank you for all you've done for my husband.' There was an awkward pause, and the girl flushed and dropped her consoling hand without touching Miranda. I collected Andrew's case, and we walked stiffly down the long corridors to the Chapel of Rest. There is the gap where the dead return.

I was unprepared for this. The room was small and, surprisingly, overheated. The shaded lighting glanced from the tarnished brass cross standing on the lace-covered altar. Andrew lay on a raised bier under a white sheet, with a single red rose on his breast. Round his neck, and under his fair head, a blue frill sprayed like a wilting halo. His eyes were open, seeming to stare at some spot on the ceiling with manic intensity, and I noticed that the blood which had drained from his face had begun to settle blackly in the lobe of his ear, where the ruff had flattened out. There was a mordant theatricality about the scene. It was, nevertheless, strangely moving. If Miranda cared about dignity, I thought, I wonder what she feels about this? But I felt the tears burn my eyes when she stood by the bier and cradled his head. I tried to shut my ears, but I heard the small, broken intimacies. 'So cold,' I heard her say, and stifled an irrational desire to giggle. There was no comfort I could give her, or she me.

We were there for a few minutes. In that time, confronted by my own mortality, I knew beyond doubt that the figure on the bier was merely an empty vessel, an abandoned house, the clay which held the presence of the god who had only gone into another room. It was, above all, the sense of unfinished business which stood accusingly before me; the small jealousies I had not yet had time to expiate, the things I had not told him. It was that lack of completeness which has, above all, convinced me that there is more than I can see. And, convinced of that, I *know* that my father had loved me, had survived, might still be alive. And also, that this belief, engendered by a letter from a senile old man, was too fragile to put to the test: that I would not make another pilgrimage to seek him out.

And now?

Salus populi suprema est lex. Though that wasn't one of the main strands in my eventual decision to read for the Bar, I came to believe it, for a while. *No man is above the law* was another. For a time, at least, they sat in my mind alongside the blindfolded figure of Justice holding the scales and the sword. *Natural justice* was another catchphrase. It was a slow accretion of incidents which made me realize that persuasive argument had more force and importance than seeking the truth. The circumstances in which Duffy killed himself nibbled at my certainties. A party the night before the trial verdict on a well-known financier – when I heard Blackstock say, 'We can't have the great unwashed putting him down; he's one of us,' – eroded them further. There were other examples, too, which gradually made me realize that the truth I had looked for in the law could never be found there. Truth, in the sense I wanted and needed it when I began to be a man, had never resided there. I see that now. But I am grateful for the years of illusion.

I am becoming a victim of my own sophistry. I joined the law for safety. It would afford me the mechanical structures, the facts, to make life comfortable and secure. A frame of reference in the chaos. I could see, in the distant future, that, bolstered by its tradition and safety, even death's narrow and divided sea might seem safely navigable. It was my return to Pakistan which set aside forever any notion that factual data possessed anything beyond a temporal and transient importance.

I began as a child – formless, without opinions: the flowers smelt as sweet to me without their names, the sky blue, the sun warm on my skin without the need for further thought. I perceived Reality directly, then. It was the middle years which dealt solely in illusion: the belief that we occupied some ghostly paradigm of things, poised between Heaven and Hell; that Good and Evil existed, and must remain a prime consideration in each decision. That judgement must be passed to enable me to move on.

Now I see that entropy is part of the natural order, returning us towards the state of childhood as we grow older. In my prime (to use one of Susan's convenient phrases) the material world of possessions, facts, useful acquaintances, invitations to gatherings of famous people, all possessed a potency that is as hard to recollect as sexual passion. I cannot say, 'The best is yet to come,' for that is to subscribe to some hierarchical, combative view of the human condition. But I have seen myself naked now. And, in Andrew's death, I have found the one thing which gives life meaning to me. It is a small thing, after all, beside the wealth and excitement and pageantry of the world. The facts are relatively unimportant. That in the end I will recognize and take part in the communality of that human condition. It was the Judge, dying anonymously and alone in the company of strangers, which brought me back to that. I use those words because now I recall I felt involved in humanity as a child. I am going back, and I am happy to do so.

I cannot give this comfort to anyone else, nor live their lives for them. Another illusion of the middle years was the sense of responsibility for others: the belief that I could increase their store of happiness. I know now that things do not work like that. We are responsible for ourselves only. That is enough.

Standing by Miranda's side in the crematorium chapel after the brief service, I watched the coffin move forward on its rollers through the doors and into the furnace. It is not the end. It is not the end. And, knowing that, I could at last look into the heart of the fire where Reality lies.

Historical Note

This is a novel, though I have tried to ensure that history is never subverted but is rather amplified through the experience of the characters.

The main events of the novel take place during the dying years of the British Raj in India and in 1947, which was the year in which Partition finally arrived. The movement towards Independence and Home Rule for India, led among others by Mahatma Gandhi, had been afoot since before the Mutiny of 1857, and had gathered momentum by the Second World War; after the War, with the election in Britain of a Labour Government, the decision was taken to grant Independence. It can be argued that the roots of dissension between Indian and Indian had been exacerbated by British attempts in the eighteenth and nineteenth centuries to impose institutions for government, law and enfranchizement, though there has been a tendency to simplify the divisions along purely religious lines. Under the direction of Earl Mountbatten, the last Viceroy, it was hastily decided to partition the country. The territories which subsequently became East and West Pakistan were apportioned to Muslims under the leadership of Jinnah, the remainder of the sub-continent went to the Hindus under Nehru. This involved the uprooting and resettlement of large numbers of people. The rule of the Raj ended in August 1947, but the immediate legacy of Partition was a hideous toll of casualties: refugees were butchered, riots flared up at the slightest provocation, and sectarian killings on both sides reached uncontrollable proportions. The Punjab, where much of *Household Gods* is set, was itself divided by Partition, and its mixed population of Hindus, Sikhs and Muslims fought savagely, sustaining heavy losses on both sides of the new border.

For purists I would add the following comments. I have taken the liberty of making the Training College which existed in Ghora Gali in the Punjab, prior to Partition, a cramming school for Indian Civil Service examinations as well as what we would now call a Technical College. Old India hands might object to the intrusion of my character, Roger Henshaw, into the ranks of 'The Heaven-Born' (or the Indian Civil Service, to use its more prosaic title) whose numbers had been reduced to around a thousand by Partition. It is true that until the end of the Great War of 1914-1918 the ICS recruited almost exclusively from the great English public schools, but the ravages of that war, and the growing realization that the Raj was coming to an end, opened the ranks of the ICS to admit those from less privileged backgrounds. Until Partition this corps and the Indian Political Service, the Viceroy's staff, effectively governed India. In this they were aided by the British Army of around 60,000 regular soldiers backed up by 200,000 native troops of the Indian Army.

I have taken advantage of the confusion that existed over the whole period of Partition – particularly in the outlying regions which were at some distance from the administrative centres – to allow certain anomalies. Roger Henshaw continues in office after Partition; there are postal delays, particularly across the new frontier; there remain some Sikhs in Pakistan and some Urdu-speaking Muslims in Hindustan. Historical happenings, particularly the confused after-effects of wars, are never as clear-cut in their workings as historians might have us believe, and the old order prevails for a period, simply because specific instructions have not been given nor received.

I have used Anglo-Indian terms liberally to avoid anglicizing the novel. I think they are appropriate and I hope that their meaning will be clear from the context.

I was born in Murree in the Punjab and, as a child, was one of the colonial refugees who made their way to safety in the south of India, only to find themselves travelling on one of the infamous 'Trains of Death'. Ironically enough, our family had left to avoid the riots and murders which had accompanied Partition, in which many of our acquaintances were butchered. If my book conveys a sense of dismay at the part played by Radcliffe and others in the division of India, I can only offer the appalling statistics of the dead and wounded to temper any tendency to satisfaction. Though I am sure the mistakes were not wilful or malicious, but rather the product of an arrogant inability to understand the true nature of the problems, I must confess that history's bemedalled heroes are not my own.

JON THURLEY
LONDON
1987

The world's greatest novelists now available in paperback from Grafton Books

Simon Raven
'Alms for Oblivion' Series

Fielding Gray	£1.95	☐
Sound the Retreat	£1.95	☐
The Sabre Squadron	£1.95	☐
The Rich Pay Late	£1.95	☐
Friends in Low Places	£1.95	☐
The Judas Boy	£1.95	☐
Places Where They Sing	£1.95	☐
Come Like Shadows	£1.95	☐
Bring Forth the Body	£1.95	☐
The Survivors	£1.95	☐

'First Born of Egypt' Series

Morning Star	£2.50	☐
The Face of the Waters	£3.50	☐

Paul Scott
The Raj Quartet

The Jewel in the Crown	£2.95	☐
The Day of the Scorpion	£2.95	☐
The Towers of Silence	£2.95	☐
A Division of the Spoils	£2.95	☐

Other Titles

The Bender	£2.50	☐
The Corrida at San Feliu	£2.50	☐
A Male Child	£2.50	☐
The Alien Sky	£2.50	☐
The Chinese Love Pavilion	£2.95	☐
The Mark of the Warrior	£2.50	☐
Johnnie Sahib	£2.50	☐
The Birds of Paradise	£2.50	☐
Staying On	£2.95	☐

To order direct from the publisher just tick the titles you want and fill in the order form.

GF381

Outstanding fiction in paperback from Grafton Books

Barbara Pym

Quartet in Autumn	£2.50	☐
The Sweet Dove Died	£2.50	☐
Less Than Angels	£1.95	☐
Some Tame Gazelle	£1.95	☐
A Few Green Leaves	£1.95	☐
No Fond Return of Love	£1.95	☐
Jane and Prudence	£2.50	☐
An Unsuitable Attachment	£2.50	☐
Crampton Hodnet	£2.50	☐
A Very Private Eye (non-fiction)	£2.95	☐

Elizabeth Smart

By Grand Central Station I Sat Down and Wept	£2.50	☐

Maggie Gee

Dying, in Other Words	£1.50	☐

Ruth Prawer-Jhabvala

A Stronger Climate	£2.50	☐
A New Dominion	£1.95	☐
Like Birds, Like Fishes	£2.50	☐

Clare Nonhebel

Cold Showers	£2.50	☐

To order direct from the publisher just tick the titles you want
and fill in the order form.

All these books are available at your local bookshop or newsagent, or can be ordered direct from the publisher.

To order direct from the publishers just tick the titles you want and fill in the form below.

Name _____

Address _____

_____